THE PARK OF
Sunset Dreams

AVA MILES

ISBN-13: 9781940565095
www.avamiles.com
Ava Miles

To my sister, Janell. I knew this book was going to be yours when I had to ask for your help on Jane's designer clothes and shoes. No one knows that topic better than you. Here's to the inner quest for your bliss, more trips to Paris and Provence, and lots of laughter and good food. I love you.

And continued thanks to my divine entourage, who continues to redefine my beliefs about abundance.

Acknowledgements

So many people continue to support my efforts as a writer. To all of the members of Team Ava. Special thanks to Gregory Stewart for the incredible cover and a million other things.

To Mayor Sue Fuchtman for giving me the scoop on running for mayor in a small town in Nebraska about the size of Dare Valley.

To Mark King for continuing to teach me about poker and scripting the incredible scenes in my books.

T.F. For showing me love is without form and not bound by time.

And all of my amazing readers, whose support for me living my dreams is one of the greatest blessings in my life.

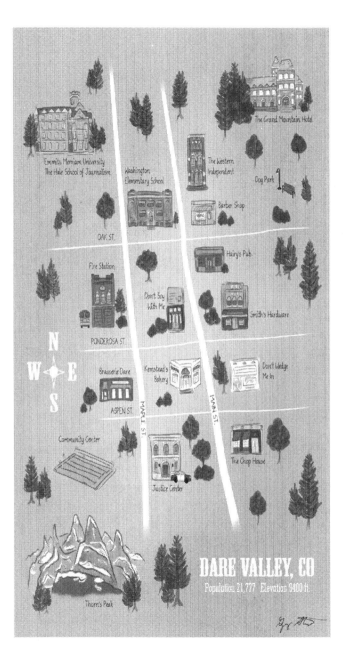

PROLOGUE

It wasn't every day a woman said goodbye to her entire wardrobe, especially one worth more than half a million dollars. Most people swapped out a piece of clothing here and there, perhaps donating some to charity, but not Jane Wilcox. Now that her alter ego Raven, the luscious poker babe, had gone into retirement, it was time to say goodbye to the goddess stash.

Fortunately, packing up the hordes of shoes from the finest designers—Christian Louboutin, Miu Miu, Alexander McQueen, Jimmy Choo, Manolo Blahnik— didn't make her tear up. Those four- to six-inch heels had given her arches fits, requiring way too many visits to her physical therapist. Jane had long ago learned the old adage was true: *beauty hurts*.

It was comforting to hear her darling four-year-old rescue chocolate Labrador, Rufus, and Annie, the cutest Chinese Crested puppy alive, scratching at the door as she packed up her old life, but she wasn't about to let them into the guest room that had been converted into her poker babe closet. Both were good dogs, but she had zero desire to see her beauties nosing through all the double-D bras and breast enhancers lying on the floor. She didn't know if something like that could scar a dog for life, but she wasn't about to take the chance.

Her hand stroked one of her finest raven-colored human hair wigs, the shade symbolic of her persona, Raven. Each of the nearly twenty wigs in different hairstyles she owned had cost a thousand dollars. When she'd worn this particular one, the thick curls had cascaded down her back, making the women who saw her pea-green with envy. It was a total contrast to the pixie cut of her God-given brown hair. She was anonymously donating all her human hair wigs to a cancer society in another state. Her synthetic wigs were long gone since they'd made her break out into hives, defeating her attempts to look like a femme fatale.

Jane surveyed the racks of sequined dresses in every shade imaginable—the brazen red Versace and gunmetal gray Armani were her favorites—and heaved a sigh as she started to box them.

Oscar Wilde was right. *A woman's face is her work of fiction.* As herself, she was no more a femme fatale than she was an astronaut. And now she was retiring at the mere age of thirty. Were her best days behind her? Had she been more impressive as Raven than she was as herself?

Well, it didn't matter. Not really. She couldn't stay a fake forever.

She started stuffing as many breast, hip, and butt pads as she could find into another box. They'd given her a curvy, luscious body that had made men salivate when she'd accompanied her boss, World Series of Poker champion Rhett Butler Blaylock, on the poker circuit. Of course, she couldn't take her clothes off in front of any of those men. She was like a leftover box of holiday chocolates, wrapped up in tantalizing silver paper and a shiny red bow, promising nothing but delight...and empty on the inside.

Of course, taking off her clothes for men she barely knew was much too brazen for the real Jane anyway.

Which was why play-acting as Raven had been so fun. And that wasn't the only reason. No one besides the three of them knew the real reason why she and Vixen, her best friend and fellow poker babe, always accompanied Rhett to the playing tables and tournaments, treating him like the mighty pasha in their harem.

In truth, she and Vixen were Rhett's poker scouts. They both had MBAs from Harvard University, where they'd become besties for life. Oh, how many times had she wanted to shove *that* in some leering, scotch-swilling poker player's face?

Now, she was back to being Jane, the real Jane. She didn't have to pretend to be vapid or hang over Rhett with her gigantic fake cleavage hanging out to distract an unseasoned poker player.

She could be smart again. Be herself.

As she looked in the full-length mirror across the room, she wondered what that would entail. For years, she'd been living a double life. It hadn't always been comfortable, but it had given her the one thing she'd craved most while growing up: freedom from her overbearing family.

Her hands slid over her petite figure. She turned sideways to examine her nearly flat behind in the mirror. No lust-inspiring butt there. Her breasts...well, they were the size of those hot stones used in day spas. Okay, not stones, she thought, putting her hands under them. More like small apples. Oh God, she was back to being an A-cup again. *An A-cup!*

As she gazed in the mirror, she realized the fairy tale she'd been living had just gone in reverse. After Harvard, she'd gone from being a smart ugly duckling to a smoking hot swan.

Now she was the ugly duckling again.

She leaned closer to the mirror, staring into her big brown eyes, her best feature.

Hello! Is there another swan in there?

Unlike in her favorite Disney movie, *Snow White,* no booming voice assured her she was still the fairest of them all.

It would have been a lie anyway.

She turned away and decided to keep her favorite wig and the red sequins dress with its matching shoes. God only knew what she'd do with the thousands of dollars of Chanel makeup. Too bad she couldn't hold a garage sale and put up a sign saying, Babes 'R Us. Of course, that would make the townspeople's mouths flop open like codfishes in the conservative small town of Dare Valley, Colorado. This was her home now, and it wouldn't do to make a bad impression. She no longer had another person to hide behind, after all. Even though she was still Rhett's secret poker scout, she had a new cover story. Officially, she was only his dog caretaker. Annie might belong to Rhett, but she lived with Jane and Rufus because Rhett didn't want to deprive the dogs of each other's company.

As she wrapped up her old life, bidding goodbye to Raven, she was shocked to feel herself brought to tears over those *stupid* shoes that had pinched her toes and made her insteps weep.

CHAPTER 1

Sunset was upon Dare Valley, its fiery orange, primal reds, and soft pinks touching the towering mountains around her. This time of day was Jane Wilcox's favorite, and if she could manage it, she always spent it in the nameless park that overlooked the valley. A snowy gravel path made for a pleasant stroll with Annie and Rufus.

The cold January wind made the pines on the ridge above her sway like a crowd doing the wave at the Super Bowl. But it was the view at the edge of the park that always captured her attention and made her feel small in the best way possible. Dare Valley stretched below her. Snow still covered the town and the surrounding land, and when the sunset light touched the white ground, it looked like swirled sherbet in lemon, orange, and raspberry, her favorite flavors. During every walk since arriving here over six months ago, she took a moment to think about her dreams, the ones that hadn't come true yet, the ones she wasn't sure ever would. And when the first star rose in the sky, bold and bright, she always made a wish they *would* come true. Some day.

Okay, so that wasn't the only reason she only came to this park. She enjoyed seeing Matthew Hale walk his two-year-old golden Labrador, Henry. *Henry*. Who named their dog Henry? A practical, down-to-earth lawyer, that's who. One she'd secretly had the hots for since his return to his hometown a few months ago. They saw each other almost every day, but they'd never spoken. All he did was *nod* to her. Henry was poorly behaved and beyond rambunctious, so Matthew had his hands full when he took him for walks.

She eyed her watch. It was about time for them to show up. It was sad she knew that, but since he kept a pretty regular schedule, his arrival at the park was like clockwork. And sure enough, a few moments later his black SUV crunched snow as he pulled in alongside her forest green Range Rover.

Jane was from a small town. She'd never wanted to live in one again, but she loved her job as a poker scout more than she hated her roots. So when her boss had made the decision to relocate from Las Vegas, she'd followed him. The first time she had felt happy about making that decision was when she saw Matthew Hale walk into his cousin's local coffee shop, Don't Soy with Me, a few months ago. Dark thick hair, arresting blue eyes, and a smile that was more like a quirk had set her heart to racing. She'd decided to overlook the fact that he was a lawyer, just like her politician dad and all his sleaze-bag friends, and smiled at him hesitantly across a mountain of delectable pastries. His brows had risen, and he'd returned her smile.

There'd been nothing since.

Zip. Nada. Bupkis.

Annie looked over her shoulder at Jane, her pointy muzzle bobbing up and down in agreement as if to say, *yeah, girlfriend, that totally blows*. Gosh, wasn't she the cutest thing ever? Since she had a dark brown hairless body dotted with white spots and streaks, Jane had bought her a pink doggie coat with matching legwarmers to keep her warm while also protecting her delicate skin from the sun.

Since Jane wasn't a poker babe anymore, the budget for Raven's clothes had been transferred to Annie. She dressed the dog in zany outfits when Rhett played poker to attract media attention and keep his flamboyant reputation alive. This new setup didn't generate the kind of attention that had been garnered by the lovely Raven and Vixen, but he was newly married now—hastily, as his wife, Abbie, would say. The two of them had been in love for so long neither had wanted a long engagement. It had lasted all of ten days.

It was good that Annie was the one who was playing dress-up now instead of Jane. The little dog certainly enjoyed it more, but still…

Raven would have attracted Matthew Hale's attention, even if he'd never date a woman like that.

Without her longtime alter ego, she was just plain Jane.

Again.

She angled the dogs back to the main path as Matthew and Henry wove across the park. God, even while wearing a black stocking cap and a matching North Face fleece, he was arrestingly handsome. The broad forehead, the granite jaw, and the slash of cheekbones. Yum. And a nose her people back in blue-blood Connecticut would call aquiline. She'd always wondered what in the world that meant until she saw Matthew. It meant breeding and handsomeness in an old school way. He rather looked like John Hamm, she realized, and who didn't think he was a dreamboat?

Walking behind Matt every day was her routine. So sue her. It meant she could watch his spectacular butt without being noticed. His coat ended at his waist, giving her a tempting view of muscular glutes and strong thighs.

Sigh.

That she was objectifying him as she'd been objectified for so long only bothered her a smidgen. Of course, she'd prefer to talk to him and get to know him than admire him from afar. It just hadn't happened yet.

She smiled as she watched Rufus and Annie walk together in tandem. A true gentleman, Rufus walked more slowly so Annie, who was much smaller, could keep up. Training them to work together had been easy. All she'd needed to do was what she did with poker. Read books. Studied tape. Observed other players.

A man who was walking toward them stopped so his German shepherd could sniff a bush, and a huge wind gust suddenly crested across the park. Jane braced herself by planting her feet wider and watched in horror as the man's hair blew off as though the wind had scalped him.

What the... *Oh my God!*

His hair trailed over the snow like sagebrush as the wind continued to gust. He cursed and dropped the leash, running for that brown nest.

And then the man's dog gave chase.

Jane had to bite her lip to keep herself from laughing out loud. Should she help...catch his hair?

The dog beat the bald man to the toupee and clamped it between his molars. The man tugged on it. Jane almost cried out, "Don't!" because the dog did exactly as she'd expected. It thought the hair tugging was a game. And since he wasn't leashed, the dog had extra freedom. He ran toward the parking lot with the man's hair, the owner yelling and giving chase.

Her shoulders started to shake, and she could feel laughter bubbling up. Desperate to hold it in until the owner was out of hearing range, she put one hand to her stomach and watched him. He'd made it all the way to the cars, swearing a blue streak.

Far enough.

She let out a bellowing laugh, which slowly trickled into some serious giggling.

Matthew Hale craned his neck to look at her from where he'd frozen on the path, watching the same thing. Henry was barking, and it almost sounded as if he were laughing too. There was a half smile on Matthew's face, like he was fighting his own mirth. Their eyes met, and then Henry raced around him with the leash.

"Dammit, Henry!" he called, trying to untangle the red leash in his hand. The dog raced around him again, and the leash went taut around Matthew's legs.

"Shit."

And just like that, he fell like a tree struck by lightning. Right in front of her. Henry licked his face, and Matthew shoved him away.

"Get away, you cretin."

Henry couldn't go anywhere with the leash so taut, so he started to crawl over his owner.

"Need some help?" Jane asked, still laughing as she and the dogs approached them, secretly delighted she finally had a chance to talk to him. "You look like a damsel in distress."

"A damsel, huh?" He grabbed the dog's collar. "No, I'm an idiot for ever thinking I could handle a dog. Stop biting me, Henry."

She transferred both leashes into her left hand. Rufus was prancing, and Annie was doing her little Lipizzaner walk in place. "Sit." They did.

"How did you do that?" he asked, still pushing Henry away as the dog tried to lick his face.

"Training. Authority."

His mouth curled. "Yeah, we failed doggie school. Twice. Any ideas?"

Oh, he was too cute, trussed up and humble. A full smile stretched across her lips. "Henry!" she shouted as loud as she could, the sound echoing in the grand expanse of the park.

The dog froze, his brown eyes seeking hers in question. Like *how could you talk to me like that?*

"Holy shit," Matthew muttered.

"Now, sit," Jane commanded and reached for his collar. The dog didn't move a muscle as she stared him down. Then he plopped on his butt without so much as a whimper. "Unclip the leash and untangle yourself. I have him. Rufus. Annie. Friend."

Her dogs wagged their heads at him in acknowledgement but didn't engage, exactly like she'd taught them.

Matthew's arctic blue eyes sought hers. "Are you sure? You're pretty...tiny, and he really likes to jump."

As though she didn't know she was tiny. She'd spent her whole life being underestimated for it. "Don't worry. He won't, will you, Henry?"

Matthew unclipped the leash, and she moved Henry off him, staring into the dog's eyes all the while. "Stay," she called when his muscles bunched.

Matthew rolled over in the snow, unwinding the red leash with the movement. When he stood and brushed the snow off his clothes, he clipped Henry's leash back on. She let the dog go, and he immediately jumped on his owner.

"Sit," she ordered, and the dog instantly obeyed.

"Amazing," Matt said. "I want to worship at your feet, oh great dog whisperer."

So he had a sense of humor? Man, that was such a turn-on.

"It's just a matter of finding the right balance between discipline and love," she told him.

His mouth quirked to the side in a half smile that made her hands break out in a sweat inside her gloves.

"I'm Matt, by the way. Matt Hale. And you're Jane, right? Rhett's dog walker."

Matt. Not Matthew like the sign on his law practice read. And he knew her name. *Yeah.* She didn't want to think about all the people they knew in common or the fact that Dare was such a small town.

"Yes, that's right. Jane Wilcox."

"You must be a hell of a dog walker to be hired professionally."

She only hummed in response. If he only knew what her real skills were.

"I see you almost every day here," he continued, "Henry's a handful, but I should have introduced myself earlier. This is Dare Valley, after all. My cousins, Meredith and Jill, have said great things about you."

Right, and people here introduced themselves to outsiders all the time. So unlike Las Vegas.

"I saw you laughing at that man before I got all tied up," he said.

"Yes," she said, not bothering to fight the grin. "I know it probably wasn't nice, but I couldn't help myself."

"I know! I wasn't sure whether to laugh or help him, but I didn't dare give chase with Henry. If he'd gotten to the toupee first, he would have destroyed it."

"That poor man. Looks like he's finally leaving." And sure enough, he was shoving his dog into his SUV and slamming the door. "That had to be embarrassing."

"Hopefully he'll remember to use more glue...or whatever it is that holds that sucker down."

It wasn't glue...or at least it shouldn't be. Jane could have given the bald man a tutorial in how to properly secure a wig to his head. She'd become a master at it. "I wonder if he'll be washing it out in the sink."

"Now there's an image," Matt said and snickered.

And then they just stood there smiling at each other.

"Well, seems like the sun is about to go down, so we should probably finish our walk," Matt said. Henry jerked at the leash again.

"No," Jane called out, and the dog instantly stilled.

Matt's eyebrows shot up until they practically met

his hairline. "Seriously. I worship at your feet. Do you take on other clients? You seem to have made a dent in this numbskull's head, so I'd love to have your help. Whatever the price."

Money? Ugh. That was so not what she wanted from him. "I don't take on other clients per se, but since we come to the park at the same time, why don't I work with you both here?"

His brows knitted together. "Still, I'd like to compensate you somehow."

"How about you buy me a beer at Hairy's sometime?" she suggested and was instantly proud of herself. That was her best friend's influence rubbing off. Elizabeth always met men casually for beer. Granted, Jane didn't like beer or bars, but who cared? It would give her a night out with Matt—not Matthew—Hale.

"That works, although as bad as this guy is, it might be a lot of beers."

"Dinner then," she said, "if he's *really* uncooperative."

His eyes scanned her face, and she knew what he was seeing. No makeup. Nothing but cherry-scented organic lip balm. And then she remembered the way he'd called her *tiny*, and she felt redness spread across her chest.

"Deal. If you get Henry in shape, you'll be a miracle worker."

Truth be told, if she could get Matt Hale to fall for her, she'd be a *real* miracle worker.

But miracles had never run in her family.

CHAPTER 2

Matt Hale took the measure of the woman in front of him. She was skinny as a bean and barely came to his shoulder, but her chocolate brown eyes were enormous in her flawless, makeup-free face. Her cheekbones were a slash above her jaw, and the slender line of her neck made him want to trace it with his fingertips. He'd seen Jane in town without a stocking hat on, so he knew her brown hair was cut short to her skull, rather like a young Audrey Hepburn. And her voice...well, Jane spoke like a member of the upper class from back east, rounding out her vowels and drawing out her words. It was a brilliant voice, strong and powerful, a remarkable contrast to her slight frame.

No wonder Henry had responded to it.

Her suggestion of dinner made him wonder if she was flirting, which surprised him since she'd always seemed so reserved, as though she wanted to keep to herself. Perhaps he had misread her. When her eyes flickered down as if she were nervous, he had his confirmation. *Well, well.* She was adorable and friendly, and if she could make Henry come to heel, he'd paint the town red with her.

Not that there was much to paint in Dare. He was still getting used to all the differences between his hometown and Denver, where he had spent the last seven years.

"I'd better head out. The Hales are all getting together. You got any plans tonight?"

"Ah, not sure yet," she replied, still studying the ground "My best friend and I have a standing date for Saturday night, so I'll probably do something with her."

Right, the gorgeous blond everyone was talking about. Rhett's personal assistant or publicist or something. He'd seen her, and she was undeniably a bombshell. But not his type. He liked his women somewhat more conservative.

"Okay, I'll see you next time." He gave Henry more leash, and wouldn't it figure? His numbskull dog jumped on him. Again.

"Want some help?"

Her dogs didn't even sniff at Henry or bark at him like other dogs did. They simply stood there like high school kids would, shaking their heads over the little kids' antics.

"Please."

He approved of her chocolate lab. But the girly dog dressed up like Barbie's pooch made him think of that movie an old girlfriend made him watch. *How to Lose a Guy in 10 Days*. It was the same dog that had made Matthew McConaughey wince with pain.

"Tell Henry to sit and stare at him. You're a lawyer, right? Stare at him like he's a defendant who's guilty as hell and is lying to you under oath."

"Henry," he said, using his courtroom voice. "Sit."

The dog danced, deliberately mocking him.

"Sit, dammit!"

"There's no need to swear at him. If you do it enough, he might start to think his name is Dammit,

Henry."

"That's actually how he got his name."

There was no way he was telling her that he'd renamed this dog from Otis to Henry. Or why. Not when they'd only just met.

"Really."

"Yep. Growing up, when you'd ask one of my great uncles, 'What do you say, Henry?' his response was always, 'I say, dammit.' As kids we used to laugh ourselves silly asking him that. It was awesome."

Henry's name was a reminder of a good and funny memory...something he'd needed when he'd agreed to raise the dog after the death of his client.

"I guess you had to be there," he said.

"You're not a very intimidating lawyer," she commented, cocking her head to the side as though she were studying him.

"I can be." He just didn't want to be that way anymore. When the time had come at his firm to choose between having a soul and losing it, he had chosen the former. Another reason he'd returned to Dare to be closer to his mom and brother.

"If he doesn't obey your vocal commands, you might have to use another tactic until he understands you mean business."

"Yeah, he seems to know I'm a pushover." But he wasn't usually. He just couldn't be stern with Henry. Not after the poor dog had lost his original owner in such a horrible way. Most days he felt like Henry's behavior was his penance.

"Let me show you something. Let's trade dogs for a sec." She extended her leashes.

He hesitated. Almost looked around to see if anyone was watching. God, to be seen holding the leash to that girly dog. His brother, Andy, would have a field day. Probably put up flyers around town with him and the dog with a caption like: *Have you seen my brother? He was last seen with a girlie dog wearing a pink parka.*

How in the world did Rhett keep his head up at the poker table with this dog? Word around town was that he'd given up his smoking hot poker babes as a compromise with his new wife, Abbie. But this dog? Seriously?

"Afraid your manhood might be affected?" she asked, a smirk on her face.

He cleared his throat. "No, it's fine." The dogs didn't move so much as a muscle when he took their leashes, and part of him wished, just this once, they'd misbehave so he wouldn't feel like such an idiot. Or a failure.

Jane grabbed Henry's leash from him. "Let's walk back to the car and see what Henry pulls."

He followed Jane, the little dog prancing like a queen while her lab walked sedately beside her. "What are your dogs' names?"

"Annie is the Chinese Crested, and she's technically Rhett's, but we agreed they're happier together so she stays with me and Rufus full-time."

Henry kept to the path, not jerking once on his leash, pausing only to mark his territory when Rufus did. It was as if he knew who was in charge. The little pixie girl. And didn't that make him feel like a doofus?

Matt took a moment to gaze across the park. The sun had completely sunk behind the mountain now. Twilight was rolling in, smothering the rosy streaks of sunset with the deeper tones of violet and jet. God, he'd loved this nameless park while growing up. There had been picnics here with his family, and, of course, some parking with girls and drinking with friends. Now he was back in Dare as a man, forging a new road. His private practice had just opened, and he already had a few clients. Some of his Denver clients had come with him, which was one of the reasons he'd been able to make the move. Now he lived in the town of his birth in a big new house on the north bench of Dare. And he always left the office in time to watch the sunset, something that had never happened in Denver. It had been the least significant of his many reasons for making the move, but he still appreciated it.

When they arrived in the parking lot, Jane was still fighting to hide her smirk. Yeah, she knew she was good. And she had to be, right? How else could a woman make a living as a dog walker for one client, no matter how rich that client was? His gut told him there was more to the situation than met the eye, but he had no idea what.

"Well, it seems like Henry can walk sedately for a few minutes. That's a good sign." Then she leaned down and kissed the dog's forehead and rubbed him all over his shiny coat. "Yeah, you're redeemable. What a good boy."

Henry barked and fell to the ground, instantly rolling onto his back so Jane could rub him there too. Rufus gave a bark, and she turned toward her dog. Her mega-watt smile was filled with so much love and playfulness it hit him right in the solar plexus.

She held out the leash to him, and Henry immediately jumped him. Her dogs scurried out of the way, and Matt pushed the lab down with a hand.

"No," Jane called out in that booming voice. "Sit, Henry." Her voice made his belly quiver. God, the power of it was such a contrast to her small frame.

His dog instantly sat.

"We're going to need lots of help, aren't we?" he asked with a sigh.

"Oh, I think you'll be all right. We just need to get you in touch with your Inner Alpha."

His mouth parted as he fidgeted with the end of the leash. "Excuse me?" She was questioning his alphaness? Well, dammit.

"You just need to show him who's boss," she quipped, trying not to laugh.

"There's nothing wrong with my Alpha," he felt compelled to add.

"I'm sure you're right," she said, unable to keep a straight face now.

"Fine. Laugh. Just because I can't control this lamebrain doesn't mean anything's wrong with me."

And yet their dog instructors had said a million times that a dog's behavior is a reflection of the owner's. Didn't they say the same thing about parents and kids?

"You're going to be fine," she assured him. "You're just a nice guy who's had a high-pressured job and doesn't want to use excessive will on anyone anymore."

What the hell? Was she a shrink too? "That's a pretty big leap."

"Well, I've known a lot of lawyers." There was a cynical thread in her voice that spoke volumes.

"Oh yeah? Boyfriends?"

Her mouth flattened. "No, my father. Well, I'd better get going. Have fun tonight. And if Henry jumps, put your hand on him and hold him down. Keep giving him the same command until he stays there. Be patient with him and yourself. You've got this."

And with that, she gathered her dogs up and hustled them into her Rover. How in the world could a dog walker or whatever she was afford a Rover?

Yes, something about her definitely didn't add up.

As he waved goodbye, he realized he was more than intrigued. Well, since she'd agreed to help him with his dog, he'd have plenty of time to figure her out.

He opened the door to his own car. "Ready to go home?" he asked Henry, praying the dog would just jump in nicely. It grated on him when he had to drag him by the collar and shove him inside.

It was like Henry had read his mind. He stood where he was, refusing to budge an inch.

If only Jane were still around.

CHAPTER 3

Meredith's house was about a mile from Matt's, on another section of the bench. Both he and his cousin lived in the newer part of Dare Valley. Custom-built houses with acres of land butting up against forest and rock. It felt like a different town than the section where his elderly relatives had lived while he was growing up with their older homes and sweeping porches. Of course, his Grandpa George and Grandma Eve had passed away, but his great uncle, the journalistic legend, Arthur Hale, still lived in the house he'd bought over fifty years ago. The house where Matt had grown up was now owned by a young professor's family. He drove by occasionally while making his way through town, and it was always jarring to realize the house was no longer *his* house.

Matt hadn't made the move to Dare Valley alone, thank God. Though his three sisters were still in Denver, he, his brother, and his mom had all returned to their hometown. His mom had separated from their dad and was renting a house not far from Main Street, while his widower brother had bought an A-frame house with a big yard close to his son's school. A change in environment had brought them all peace.

When he arrived at Meredith's craftsman house, the mountain wedging in Dare to the west towered above him like a giant. He stepped into the cold night and leashed Henry, who bounded out of the back seat and started barking for his pal Hugo, Meredith and Tanner's dog. When the knucklehead jumped on him and tried to lick his face, making him laugh, he gave him a good rubdown and tried out his new commands. He could ignore the wet marks on his fleece, since he liked it when Henry was affectionate.

"Sit," he said. The dog just stood there, giving him a strange look.

"Still struggling with that?" Tanner McBride asked, coming down the porch steps.

Meredith's husband was a former war correspondent in places like freaking Iraq and Afghanistan. Now he taught journalism at Emmits Merriam and worked at the Hale family newspaper, *The Western Independent*. Matt liked him a lot.

"Hey, man. Yeah, the whole obedience thing hasn't been working for me."

Henry made a dash toward Tanner as though he were going to jump on him too. The guy just put his hands on his hips and stared the dog down. "Sit," he said, without even raising his voice.

The doofus dog immediately obeyed.

Jane's earlier statement about getting in touch with his Inner Alpha replayed in his mind. What did she think he was? A eunuch?

"Come on in. It's a mad house. And just a warning. Jill's trying to scare Meredith about labor. Some seriously disgusting things have been said in the presence of Arthur, who slammed his cane down and put a stop to it. But Jill's still mumbling."

"Part of her charm," Matt said, already smiling. Ah,

family.

Tanner snorted, a habit he'd picked up from spending time with the Hales, and they went inside. Tanner took Henry off to a playroom with Hugo, thank God. It would be nice to have a short respite.

And his friend was right. It *was* a madhouse inside. Jill's baby twins were resting on a pink blanket with lime-green polka dots, so his cousin's style. His nephew, Danny, was running around while making airplane noises, obviously trying to play with the girls or entertain them. But Mia and Violet just drooled and squirmed in place like beetles stuck on their backs.

Brian was chasing Jill around the couch with a wooden spoon—God, he wasn't even sure he wanted to know why. Married couples.

"Well, here he is," his brother Andy called out, beer in hand. "About time you got here."

"Uncle Matt!" Danny called out and rushed him.

Matt lifted him off the ground and threw him in the air, making the five-year-old squeal. Once he finished with his duties as an uncle, he headed over to his mother. April Hale might be over sixty, but she was still glowing and beautiful.

"Hey, Mom," he said and kissed her cheek.

"Hey, kiddo. Henry still giving you fits?"

"Yeah."

Leaning back, he studied her, making sure she looked...well, not depressed. When his mother had announced she was leaving their father three months ago because he didn't really want to be married anymore, he and his four siblings had been worried. All she would say about it was that life was too short to spend with someone who no longer appreciated you, who thought marriage to you was just *comfortable*.

"Hi, Uncle Arthur," he said. Looking just as sharp as always, his white-haired great uncle was sitting in a corner armchair, surveying the insanity through his wire-rimmed glasses.

"'Bout time you got here. Someone needs to calm Jill down. If that girl gets her gums a-flappin' again to scare Meredith, she's going to feel my cane on her backside. I don't care how old she is."

Just then the troublemaker herself wrapped her arms around Matt from behind, squeezing with all her might. "Dammit, Jill, will you ease up a bit?" he said.

"She doesn't know how," Brian noted. He held up the spoon. "I figured it might help if I shoved this in her mouth, but she's being even more contrary than usual."

Jill jumped around so she was in front of him. "That's because I had three hours of sleep last night. Breastfeeding sucks, Matt. Men are the lucky ones."

"Not another word, Jillian Marie Hale," Uncle Arthur said. "Or I'll tell everyone you're buying generic coffee in that shop you own and serving it up as the real stuff."

Jill sucked in a breath. "You wouldn't?"

"Try me," his uncle responded.

And interestingly enough, Jill stood down, almost like Henry had in Jane's presence at the park. He laughed.

"What?" she asked.

"You remind me of a Labrador puppy."

Brian shook his head and snagged him around the neck. "Babe, I'll go beat him up somewhere." As they angled away, Brian whispered, "You'd better thank me for saving your ass. No woman likes to be referred to as a dog, even if that particular comparison is spot on."

Andy met them at the door to the kitchen and handed Matt a beer. "How was small-town law today?"

He grinned. This was the game they played with each other. Both of them had worked back-breaking hours in Denver, him as a lawyer, his brother as a doctor. The slower pace of life in Dare Valley was definitely a perk of their move.

"Incredible," he commented. No clarification needed. "And how about the hospital?"

"No one died." And his deadpan expression made them all laugh.

Matt chugged on the beer and then bent to kiss Meredith's cheek when she appeared by his side. "And where were you, my beauty?" he asked.

"I'm afraid to admit Jill made me hide in the bathroom. I couldn't listen to another word about her experience with the twins." She caressed the small mound under her green sweater.

"I'll defend you," Matt said easily, earning himself a half hug from his cousin.

"All in good fun, sis," Jill said, popping across the room. "Plus now you have Champion Matt in your corner, so I'd better toe the line."

"Yeah! Uncle Matt is the best champion ever," Danny shouted as he dove over like an airplane.

"Why aren't you playing with Mia and Violet?" Jill asked his nephew.

"Because they don't *move*. All they do is stare and slobber. They're not very fun." The last part was said in a whisper.

"They're still little," Andy said, hoisting him up. "Why don't you go wash up? I think we can eat now that your uncle's here."

"What's for dinner?" he asked, looking pointedly at Brian.

"Since I spend all day making French food at Brasserie Dare, I went with Greek tonight. We're having pastitsio. And Meredith made garlic bread and Caesar salad and some sides."

Matt's stomach growled. "Oh, man. If you weren't a guy and already taken, I'd marry you just for your food."

Brian snorted. Okay, so he'd definitely picked that habit up from the Hales. "What I wouldn't say if the kid wasn't here."

The big raucous group clustered around the giant dining room table, which probably had three extra leaves in it to accommodate the number of people. Violet and Mia stayed on a blanket in the den, and since the floor plan was open, the adults could keep an eye on them from the dining room. Danny was right. They didn't do more than blink and drool and toot in their pants, which made his nephew squeal with laughter.

Ah, to be a little boy again.

The dinner was ridiculous. Meredith had roasted garlic and spread it over Brian's handmade baguettes with some butter and tossed them on the grill, making the best open-faced garlic bread he'd ever had. The pastitsio was a mix of hand-ground lamb sausage Brian had whipped up—who whipped up sausage?—and al dente ziti, also homemade, covered in béchamel sauce and parmesan, topped with allspice and cinnamon. A little weird, but oh so good. The sides of pan-seared zucchini with lemon and stuffed mushrooms had him groaning. He ignored the salad. And then Meredith brought out dessert, a ricotta cheesecake with currants and pine nuts, and he grabbed another beer. He could work out extra tomorrow. It was worth it.

"Glad you married into the family, Bri," he announced and lifted his beer in acknowledgement.

His cousin-by-marriage nodded and plucked a fussy Mia off the floor.

"Can we eat here every night, Dad?" Danny asked, scraping his plate with his fork. "This is *so much* better than macaroni and cheese."

His brother didn't respond immediately, and Matt's gut clenched. He knew Andy was thinking about how Kim, his wife, had been the cook in the family. They had all been devastated when she died of breast cancer. His brother had tried to continue his work at the University of Colorado hospital, but the job was too strenuous for a single father.

"Maybe we can eat at Brian's restaurant more, Danny," his brother finally said. "How about that?"

Danny just nodded. He'd been three when his mom died, and he didn't remember her much except for the stories they told him. Matt stood up from the table—everyone was just talking now, having polished off the rest of the food—and grabbed the boy's hand.

"Let's go take the dogs outside," he said. Danny's eyes lit up and he raced over to grab his coat.

Andy got up and patted him on the back. "Thanks."

He bumped him. "Please. Don't thank me yet. Henry will probably try and jump on him, but I'd never let him knock Danny down."

"I know you wouldn't let anything happen to him," his brother said.

Matt huffed out a breath. Goddammit. Sometimes life just sucked, and the fact that his brother was a widower at the prime age of thirty-six just wasn't fair. *Life* wasn't fair, as the world had seemed bent on revealing to him over the past couple of years.

"Go play with Danny," his mother said suddenly, pushing back from the table and rubbing his back.

There were tears in her eyes, and he had to bite his cheek. Dammit, he hated when his mom cried. Losing Kim was an unhealed wound for all of them—one of many.

He and Danny went out and played and, fortunately, Henry behaved for once. Tanner and Brian joined them, and the four of them played catch with a football that had seen better days.

When it was time to go, and he made his rounds for goodbyes, he volunteered to take Uncle Arthur home. He had an idea to run by him, and this was just the time to do it.

When they were driving back to his house on the far side of town, his uncle glanced over at him. "So, you going to keep me in suspense or will you spit it out?"

Sharp old man. "Why would you say that?" he said, just to have a little fun with his uncle.

"You live the farthest away from me, and yet here you are, driving me home. You might have been a Boy Scout, but I know when someone's up to something."

Henry bounded back and forth between the windows in the back seat, as though he were fascinated with the scenery. His drool marks were all over the panes, making them look like frosted glass. He needed to get his car detailed practically every week now that Henry was around.

"Do you remember what I told you about my last client? The way the system failed her has been burning a hole in me, challenging me to do my part in the community. I've decided to run for mayor. I wanted to be the one to tell you." Family news had a way of getting around.

Uncle Arthur harrumphed. "Well, darn it. I thought coming back here to open a law firm might not be enough for you, but politics? You know we Hales try and keep out of that."

There was a strict rule about the Hales being politically neutral since Arthur ran *The Western Independent,* which featured a comprehensive local section. He had expected his uncle wouldn't be overjoyed to hear his news. "Your direct line, yes, but not me. It will have no impact on the newspaper, I can promise you that."

"And how would you be knowing that, all thirty-four years of you? The Hales *report* the news, and now you're going to *be* the news. The mayor, should you be elected, for cripes' sake! I'll have to report on your decisions, young man. Oh, this is going to be a mess."

None of his comments were unexpected. "I think I'll be good at it."

Another "hmm" sounded in the SUV. "Well, you're smart enough and good enough with people. Other than those assholes you used to work with."

Yeah, the lawyers at his firm had mostly been assholes, all right. And he'd been one of them until he saw the light of day. "Thanks. I'm hoping it might lead to higher offices."

Another harrumph. "Well, you're pretty enough to be a senator or a congressman. Or were you thinking governor?"

He lifted his shoulder. "I'd like to be governor. After being at the firm, I'm not sure I want to live in DC. I've heard it has more lawyers per capita than ants in an ant colony."

Uncle Arthur snorted. "It does at that. Your mother is pleased, I expect."

"Yes."

"What about your father?"

He hadn't spoken to his father since he'd let his mom walk out of the house without a word. His dad had always been a workaholic with an intense career, but still... How could the man he'd idolized not have stopped his wife from leaving him? Not tell her that he loved her and valued her and wasn't just *comfortable* with her? But he hadn't, and Matt's rage bloomed again, just thinking about it all. Not to mention how he'd railed at Andy and him for leaving behind successful careers to settle for *less* in Dare.

"No. If he wants to find out how I'm doing, he can pick up the phone."

This time, there was no harrumph. "Henry, enough of that bounding about. Sit."

And from the rear view mirror, Matt could see the evidence of yet another person other than himself who could make his dog obey.

He and his uncle traveled the rest of the way to Arthur's house in silence. When they arrived, Matt insisted on seeing him to the door.

"What am I, some girl you plan to kiss after a hot

date?" he scoffed. Uncle Arthur had his pride, but he was close to eighty and had a cane, and there were patches of snow and ice on his sidewalk.

"Just doing what any good nephew would do."

"Coddling me. My body might not be prime, but my mind surely is."

"Fine. It's icy out tonight, and I don't want you to fall. Sue me."

"That's your business." Uncle Arthur's mouth tipped up.

Still, he took Matt's arm, and they walked to the door at the older man's pace.

Once they reached it, Uncle Arthur turned to look him in the eye. "Let me give you some advice. My best friend and mentor, Emmits Merriam, ran for the Oklahoma senate seat and had the pants beat off him. It didn't make him any less of a man, and if you don't win, the same is true of you."

Matt spontaneously leaned in and hugged his uncle, soaking in the comfortingly familiar smell of Old Spice. "Good night, Uncle Arthur."

"Goodnight, Young Matthew."

He walked back to his car with a smile on his lips. It had been a while since his uncle had called him that and, like always, it made him feel important.

At moments like this, he was one hundred percent sure moving back to Dare had been the right thing for him to do.

CHAPTER 4

Elizabeth Saunders rapped on the door of Jane's house the next morning. When her friend opened it, the dogs at her feet, she held up a white pastry bag.

"Provisions for the courageous," she said. "You deserve a gold medal for telling Matt Hale he could take you out for a beer in exchange for helping him with his dog."

For Jane, this was as big as landing on the moon.

"And let's not forget that I told him he could buy me dinner if his dog was *really* bad," Jane said with a grin.

Elizabeth shucked off her boots at the door, giving Annie and Rufus the expected rub down. "Then let's pray he is *really* bad."

"Which one?" Jane asked with a smirk, planting her hands on her slim hips.

"You know who. Weren't you the one who got all hot and bothered when you saw him trussed up on the ground in a red leash?"

Elizabeth made herself at home, flouncing onto the caramel-colored leather couch, while Jane disappeared into the kitchen. Unlike her own preference for cool tones and clean lines, her friend's decorating leaned toward warm colors and accents. The walls were butternut squash yellow, which contrasted beautifully with the cherry wood floors and wainscoting running through her rustic, lodge-style home. The oversized windows provided a breathtaking view of the valley, cushioned between the snow-capped peaks of the mountains. The artwork on the walls was a mix of European café scenes and expansive landscapes of sea or forest. Everything about her friend was cozy and sweet.

Jane might not like it, but she was still a small-town girl at heart.

And Elizabeth loved that about her even if she couldn't relate.

"I didn't even know if I could get hot over something like that," Jane said, emerging from the kitchen with a tray holding a silver coffee service and two place settings. The cups rattled when she set it on the coffee table in front of the couch.

"It does take a lot to make you hot," Elizabeth said, coming over to sit beside her. She had known Jane for long enough to pick up on any number of personal details. After all, they'd started out as roommates in Harvard at eighteen and lived together until they graduated with their MBAs. They'd been friends for almost twelve years and were closer than sisters.

"Yeah, the polar opposite of you." Jane's mouth twisted as she arranged the sage green plates, silverware, and napkins. "How was your date last night?"

The chocolate croissants Elizabeth had brought from Brasserie Dare were both spongy and crisp when she drew them out and put them on the plates. Her mouth watered. She hadn't expected to find a bona fide French restaurant in such a small town, but she was grateful for it. It was the next best thing to eating in a

Parisian café.

"Yeah, sorry about that. It came together last minute at the grocery store."

"Of course it did."

Her friend's sarcasm was so normal she didn't even respond to it. "I've seen Jeremy at Hairy's before, so when we ran across each other in the produce section—"

"He commented on your melons, and you offered to let him feel them."

"You don't need to get on my case just because you're missing your Wonder Woman bra."

They might be a world apart in cup sizes, but their IQs were about the same. Both genius level and proud of it.

"It's just that I don't think Matt's going to want...this." She gestured to her body.

Elizabeth took her hand. They'd had this conversation a million times. "Listen, you're nuts. You're beautiful in a petite way. And now you don't have to worry about men liking you for your fake body. Don't you remember *that* conundrum?"

Her friend grabbed the croissant and bit into it, moaning a little. "Yes. The same guys who liked Raven's big hair and fake curves wouldn't look at me twice after I took off my costume. Something you never had to worry about."

It was true that Elizabeth resembled her alter ego more, but she hadn't let any of the men she'd dated on the road see her without the wigs and other disguises that had transformed her into Vixen. She guarded her personal identity as though it were Fort Knox, and since she never went out with someone more than a few times or stayed over after sex, unmasking herself hadn't been a huge issue. Well, except for her padded bras, which had taken her natural C-cup size to double Ds. Even when she wasn't wearing a wig, her hair color changed every few months, and right now it was caramel brown.

While life without her alter ego of Vixen was an adjustment, she didn't miss the color contacts, stage makeup, or fake beauty marks. The makeup had clogged her pores and given her chronic acne. Now her skin glowed, and all she had to use was a tinted moisturizer. Her own parents wouldn't recognize her—as Vixen or Elizabeth—and that was better for everyone, since they were leeches and drug addicts. If they knew who she was now and where she was, they'd try to suck the life out of her. Just like they'd done after finding out about her friendship with Jane, a connection they'd hoped would open new doors of money and opportunity for them.

"So you're getting used to being the real you all the time," she said, shaking off the past. "Me too. We were every man's fantasies in those outfits. Now it's time to channel the true fantasy. You. Me."

Jane polished off her croissant. "I can't see the real me being any man's fantasy."

Being a man's fantasy was easier than Jane made it out to be, but that was just Jane. She wanted hearth and home.

"The one who loves you will, trust me. He won't see anyone but you."

"I can't even imagine what that feels like."

Her self-esteem had been in the crapper since the day she'd been born a girl. The esteemed Phillip Wilcox and his perfect political wife, Helen, had wanted a boy more than anything, and Jane always joked that their intention had gotten crosswise with the Universe. She had a boy's body, just not a boy's parts.

Without a male heir, they'd pushed Jane to be the most accomplished child a couple could boast about. She'd had a resume at age two to get into the elite local preschool, knew how to count to ten in five different languages. By five, she played two musical instruments. By ten, she'd composed her first symphony. By fifteen, she'd won a national mathematics competition. And by twenty, she'd accumulated a million dollars managing her own stock portfolio, something she'd built from her math competition award of ten grand.

While their parents came from radically different social spheres, they had one thing in common: they were accomplished manipulators. It was one of many reasons why neither Jane nor Elizabeth had any contact with their families.

"It *will* happen, Jane," Elizabeth said. "Give it time."

"So back to your date." Jane dug out two slices of quiche next and arranged them on their plates.

"Right. We went out to a movie. The new Ben Affleck flick. Not bad. And then he drove me home. We made out for a while and then I said goodnight." She shrugged and dug into her own croissant.

"So he wasn't worth bringing inside."

"No. I just wasn't that into him." And that had been a recurring theme since moving to Dare Valley. She was used to high rollers, and while she still met some at the casino at The Grand Mountain Hotel, no one had grabbed her attention and held it.

Which was pretty much her whole dating experience, besides...

Well, the only man she'd ever loved had been drastically inappropriate. And by the time she realized it was love, she'd already headed for the hills.

"It's ironic, don't you think?" Jane asked. "I want to find Mr. Right, and you can't run fast enough in the other direction. Maybe we're both out of balance."

"Too bad they don't have a remedy for that. But I have to tell you again how proud I am of you for going after what you want. And I'm glad you didn't let the fact that he's a lawyer make you cross him off your list."

She bounced in her seat. "It's not as though he's running for political office. *That* I couldn't handle. How many times did Dr. Utley say the safest way to have a successful marriage was not to marry your father?"

Their psychology teacher at Harvard had been a trip, lecturing in houndstooth jackets while spouting common sense. "Of course, I don't have to worry about marrying my father," Elizabeth said with a bitter taste in her mouth. "No drugged-up mobile home managers in Dare."

When a knock sounded at the door, Elizabeth turned on the couch and watched as Jane headed to answer it. "Maybe it's Matt, here for his first lesson."

Jane shot her a dirty look and opened the door. "Ha ha. It's only Rhett."

"Only Rhett," he said, snatching her up in a huge hug.

Given that Rhett was six feet six without his usual boots on, he pretty much lifted Jane a couple of feet off the floor.

"What's got you in such a good mood?" Elizabeth said as he set Jane aside and scooped up Annie. "Or do we even need to ask?"

"Ladies, there's just no words for wedded bliss," he said, stroking the tiny dog, who was decked out in a purple sweater and matching legwarmers "Now, who did you think might be at the door?"

"Elizabeth," Jane warned, reaching down to pet Rufus so he wouldn't feel left out.

She threw caution to the wind. "Matt Hale. Jane finally managed to have a conversation with him at the park yesterday. She's going to help him with his dog. Apparently he's flunked training twice."

"Well, well, I'm happy to hear it. He's a pretty down-to-earth guy from what I can tell. I like him for you, Jane, I really do."

"She's all, 'But I'm not Raven anymore. No man will look at me,'" Elizabeth said with dramatic flair and touched the back of her hand to her brow like a Victorian lady in distress.

Rhett barked out a laugh and set Annie aside. "Honey, I hate to tell you this, but a real man—the kind you want to settle down with—isn't going to want someone like Raven. That's for show." He took Jane's shoulders in his hands. "He's gonna want someone like you because you're darn near perfect."

Jane ducked her head. "Oh, Rhett."

"Now," he said. "I have good news, ladies. Abbie's given me a pass to head out to Cabo San Lucas for that celebrity poker tournament in a couple weeks. I've heard from Rye that Kenny Chesney and a few other country singers might be attending."

Rye Crenshaw, one of Rhett's best friends, was one of the hottest tickets out there.

"Always good to see Rye," Jane commented. "Is he going to sing?"

"Not sure, but it'll be nice to have some guy time. Of course, he thinks I've become boring since marrying Abbie."

Elizabeth vaulted over the couch, a spontaneous act that was too fun to pass up. Rufus barked in surprise. "No, you're as sweet as ever."

"Be nice to my furniture, Elizabeth. This isn't an Olympic training facility."

She waggled her brows. "Not yet, but now that you and Matt are getting friendly, you never know."

"Okay, ladies, enough hullaballoo. I brought a list of people who might be attending the tourney. It's time to get to work. I have a hankering to win."

"When don't you?" Elizabeth mused. "Is Mac going?" Mac Maven was Rhett's oldest friend and now brother-in-law, another successful poker player who had opened a booming poker hotel in Dare Valley.

"Not sure yet. He and Peggy and Keith are still getting settled in her house. He likes his luxuries, so we keep telling him he's slumming it, but he's happy as a clam. And I can't say I mind living in the house Abbie and Mac bought together when they first moved to town. My wife sure has a knack for making a house into a home."

"I'm so glad how everything has worked out for you both. You deserve it."

"He's struck the jackpot with Dare's deputy sheriff and her sweet son," Rhett commented.

"Of course, you haven't done too badly for yourself with Abbie and Dustin."

"Yeah, who would of thought I'd end up adopting a sixteen-year-old boy? That kid about brought me to my knees when he told me he wanted to take my name and be my boy. Heck, Abbie bawled like a baby, but I stayed tough."

Jane punched his shoulder. "Yeah, you're such a tough guy."

Well, he had been when they'd met him in a casino in Atlantic City while celebrating their new MBAs. Rhett had hit on her, but that was before Jane started messing with him by revealing how much they knew about poker. Soon Rhett's eyes had stopped roving up and down Elizabeth's body. His charming smile had faded, and he'd started volleying questions at them about who had which cards and other tells. By the end of the evening, he'd offered them jobs as his poker scouts.

"Convinced you both to wear poker babe outfits, didn't I?" he mused.

Of course, it hadn't taken much convincing. Both of them had realized that new alter egos would be a welcome escape from their lives and their parents. And she...well, she had needed to hide for another reason as well.

"Now, I have this sweet but insane-looking dog that has a clothes budget," Rhett said. "It's a good thing I'm confident because another man might feel emasculated by this new act I've created to keep Abbie happy."

"She's a lucky lady, Rhett," Jane said. "Elizabeth can

make all the travel arrangements for Cabo, and I'll be sure to buy some celebrity dog outfits for our little Annie here. How do you feel about jewelry?"

He groaned and leaned down to tap Annie's brown nose. "If you weren't so cute, you'd embarrass me to death. Well, marriage is all about compromises, and this one's mine. Plus, I'm happy y'all don't have to use false identities anymore."

Rather than replying, Jane looked down at her shoes.

"You need any advice about men, Janey," Rhett said, using his rare nickname for her, "you just ask. I won't interfere or say anything, but I'm here for you."

"I know it, Rhett," she said.

Neither she nor Jane had a natural brother, but they had Rhett, and neither could imagine a better one.

"Someday pretty soon, Jane, I'm going to be walking you down the aisle," he said, winking at her before opening the door.

The cold wind rushed inside, but it didn't take away from the warmth in Elizabeth's heart.

"Thanks, Rhett," Jane said in a soft voice.

"Bye, Rhett. I'll start tweeting up a storm about you hanging with the celebs, especially Rye. His fans adore you."

He winked. "That's 'cause we're cut from the same cloth. Enjoy the day, ladies. I know I will."

And with that, the door swung shut behind him.

"That Rhett," Jane mused, dropping to her haunches so she could rub the dogs.

"Yeah, he's the best. Have you ever wondered what might have happened if we hadn't met him?"

Her brow knitted with tension. "Yes, I'd be a robot, working for my father, shuffling political favors around and campaigning every couple years like I did for most of my life before becoming Raven."

Elizabeth rubbed her hand over the hard ball that

had formed in her stomach. "Yeah." And she didn't even dare think where she'd be. For all she knew, she'd be dead if she hadn't taken Rhett's offer.

"Come on," Jane said, rising. She gave Elizabeth a brief hug. Yeah, Jane knew where her mind had gone. She knew how scary that time had been for Elizabeth...heck, for them both.

"Let's sit down and go through the list, and then we can pull some files and see what info we already have on the players. Time to get to work."

When Jane released her and left to go to her office for the files, Elizabeth sank to her knees and laid her head against Rufus, who leaned in to give her kisses.

You're safe now, you're safe, she reminded herself. There was no sense in dredging up the past.

But the old fear had never completely gone away, and deep down, she feared it never would.

CHAPTER 5

It was a brisk eighteen degrees outside, and snow swirled around Jane as she gazed out across the valley. The sun was an orange ball hovering above the far mountain, and the sky was layered in colors of turquoise and peach. Feeling the urge to run today, she had arrived a little earlier than usual and jogged about a mile along the mountain path that extended beyond the park. Running at this altitude had put her in the best shape of her life, and she freaking loved that. She'd left Annie, dressed in a warm yellow fleece, in the SUV.

Jane was heading back to her vehicle, Rufus running beside her, when Matt drove up.

Her heart started pumping double-time, and her whole body felt flushed and alive.

"Hey!" he called as he got out of the car, shoving an overzealous Henry back to keep him from bounding out of the backseat and through the driver's side door. "Where's Annie?"

Nice of him to notice. "I went for a run, so left her in the car."

"Oh, are you leaving?" he asked, gazing at his SUV

door as though he were afraid to let the dog out. *Woot.*
Woot. Woot. Woot.

Okay, so she didn't need that song running through
her mind right now.

"No, just coming back to get her. She's too little to
run with me."

"Right," he said and smiled at her.

Just smiled.

And she grinned back at him like a lunatic. Man, she
had it bad.

At Elizabeth's suggestion, she was wearing navy
thermal tights, her turquoise running shoes, and a hot
pink fleece with an insulated shirt underneath. A
matching pink hat covered her head and ears, and her
navy gloves had hand warmers in them. She looked
sporty cute, her friend had said. And then she'd told her
they were immediately going to buy more "park" outfits.

"Wasn't sure you'd be here," Matt commented, still
not opening the SUV. "Storm's supposed to be blowing
in."

"Not yet, and I love this kind of weather. I missed
winter, so it's good to have it again."

"Where did you live before Dare?" he asked, finally
opening the car door, leash in hand.

Henry shoved the door open the rest of the way and
raced off before Matt could catch him. Jane had seen it
happen before, so she knew what would happen next.
He would swear a blue streak at the dog and then chase
him around the park for ten minutes until the dog tired
of the game.

"Dammit, Henry!" Matt called out.

She thrust Rufus' leash at him. "Here, take him and
get Annie out. Her leash is on the seat. I'll get Henry."
When he took it, she headed after the errant dog.
"Henry," she called.

Fortunately, no one else was in the park due to the
brisk wind and falling temperatures because technically

all dogs were supposed to be leashed. Not that everyone followed that rule. Owners could be just as disobedient as their dogs.

"Come, Henry. Right now!" She yelled across the park and watched him chase his tail and then kick up some snow. As she walked toward the dog, she drew up to her full height and stared him down. "Sit!"

He stopped nuzzling the snow and looked up, as if to say, *are you talking to me?*

"Yes, I'm talking to you, Henry. Now sit. *Sit*. And if you're good, I'll give you a treat."

His ears perked up at that.

"Yeah, he knows that one, all right," Matt said when he appeared beside her, leading her dogs. "He gained five pounds before I started cutting back on that carrot."

"Well, we're going to use it as an incentive today so we don't run ourselves ragged chasing him. He has zero obedience skills."

"Don't I know it? If Annie weren't so girly, I'd gladly trade Henry for her. She just stood there smiling as I clipped her leash. I almost teared up."

She glanced over and laughed. "Been bad, huh?"

"He turned over the water bowl three times this morning. The kitchen floor hasn't been cleaner. He's trying to break me. Of course, then he lays his head in my lap and acts all sweet, making me forget the other stuff for a little while."

"He just doesn't like rules. Who does? Henry. Treat. Now. Come."

Henry regarded her warily. "You don't always give him a treat when you use that word, do you?"

Matt sighed. "I've been desperate."

"Right. But now he doesn't trust the offer. We'll work on that too." She grabbed a bone from her pocket and held it up so the dog would know she wasn't faking it.

Finally, he pranced forward warily, eyes dancing.

Yeah, you little devil. You know you're running him a merry race.

"Step back a bit. I want him to come the full way and not..."

"Take off because of me. Got it."

He stepped back, and she waited. Sure enough, the dog came forward. "Now sit," she said.

Henry sat and inclined his head toward the treat. "Only when your leash is attached, my man." She clipped it on and then gave him the treat. He chomped it up in one bite. "See, that wasn't so hard."

"It's like ice skating in the Olympics. You make it look easy, but if pretty much anyone else tried it they'd face-plant."

And then Rufus barked and nuzzled her pocket. "Yes, I know, he got your treat." She rubbed him behind the ears before pulling out the extra she always kept on hand. "See, I have one for you."

Annie gave a small yip, as if asking for a treat of her own.

"You haven't done anything yet to deserve one."

"She should get one for standing so still while I attached her leash." Matt leaned down and rubbed her. "I've been wondering. How many outfits does she have? I've lost count."

He'd been counting? "Well, as Rhett's ah...*special* dog, she has a clothes allowance, so she has a lot of them." Today, Jane had dressed her all in yellow since the day was so gray. Her fleece zipped on the sides, her little knit cap had butterflies on it, and her leg warmers made Jane think of beams of sunshine.

"It's incredible," he commented neutrally.

But she could tell he thought Annie's outfits were absurd. "Well, people really love dogs, and Rhett is known for his flamboyance."

"But she's not a poker babe, and man, were they hot. No offense."

Her mouth tightened. "None taken," she almost said, since he was talking about her without knowing it.

"Has Annie really brought the same kind of publicity?" Matt asked.

"Well, Elizabeth has been tweeting about her a lot, so his fans are getting to know her. They love the regular tweets about what she's wearing. So far a few of the dog-focused magazines have run spreads on her. We haven't taken her to a big tournament yet since Rhett has been staying here with his new family, but that's about to change." And then they'd all see how well it worked. It would, she knew. No one could ham up a situation bigger and better than Rhett.

"Do you like poker?" he asked.

She had to bite her lip to keep from barking out a laugh. If he only knew. "Yes," she said. "Very much. It helps...since I'm around it a lot." Jane had been to hundreds of tournaments. She'd even been pinched by some pretty big stars, not that she was naming any names.

"Yeah, but the action at The Grand Mountain Hotel isn't the same as a big tournament. You must be excited to see what it's all about." Fortunately, he didn't ask about her job there. All the town knew was that she and Elizabeth had moved to town for employment in Mac's new hotel. It wasn't publicly known that they were long-time friends or that they'd known Mac and Rhett for the better part of a decade.

"I'm sure it will be great," she commented. She hated not disclosing the full truth, but her secrets weren't hers to tell. Other people were involved. "Let's try a few more commands."

For the next twenty minutes, she worked with Henry and Matt. The dog seemed almost deaf when it came to his owner, but the man was relentless in trying to learn how to make the dog obey him. A wrinkle appeared between his brows after five minutes of being ignored.

Yeah, who liked that? She'd felt that way growing up.

Soon the wind was gusting so hard it was blowing loose snow in their faces. When she checked her smart phone, the temperature said eight degrees. The dogs didn't need any more winter exposure, and the night sky was smothering the last orange and blue rays of the sunset—it was time to go home.

"I think we'd better call it a day."

Matt looked over, and his jaw tightened. "We were just starting to gel, I could feel it. Are you sure?" Then he shook his head. "I'm sorry. I was so far in the zone I didn't even notice your lips are blue."

They were? She touched them with her gloves and then dropped her hand.

"And the dogs must be cold too. Sorry, guys. Let's get them back to the cars."

His reluctance to end his lesson warmed her heart. "No need to cut things short when you're starting to gel."

He was right. When he delivered commands, Henry was starting to look at him and consider obeying. It wasn't an automatic response, but it was an improvement.

"I live about a half mile from here. If you'd like to continue, we can do it indoors." Her heart sputtered a little, hoping he would agree. It would be fun to keep spending time with him.

"I don't want to put you out."

"You're not. Really. I love helping. Come on. Who knows? He might actually shake your hand by the end of the night."

His mouth turned up at the side. "I doubt it, but you're right. I'm desperate. I can't take another water bowl incident. See, his ears turned up. He's plotting again. He's going to turn on me as soon as we're out of sight."

She laughed. "Well, he's one smart dog. Why don't

you just follow me, and we can pick this up where it's warmer? My feet are freezing." Her running shoes didn't have any insulation, not like her snow boots.

"Right. Let's go. And thanks, Jane. You're a life saver."

"What color?" she quipped as she led Annie and Rufus to the car.

"Green was always my favorite," he volleyed right back. Henry jerked on the leash when he saw they were heading for the car, capturing Matt's full attention.

"Tell him to sit," she suggested. And then ran him through the commands again.

It took another four minutes to get Henry into the SUV. Matt sank against the side of the vehicle when he shut the door. "He hates going home."

"Follow me. We'll have him ship-shape in no time."

When she reached her own car and opened the door, Annie and Rufus scrambled into their respective spots in the backseat without any prodding, and she buckled herself into the driver's seat. She took off, keeping an eye on the vehicle in her rearview mirror.

Her belly warmed as she thought of him being in her house. Should she suggest he have one of the beers she kept around for Rhett and Elizabeth? Too casual? What about ordering pizza? She tapped her head back against the seat.

"Oh, I suck at this."

She used her Bluetooth to dial Elizabeth. When her friend answered, she immediately said, "Matt is following me home to continue dog lessons. Do I offer him a beer? Dinner? What do you think?"

"First, take a deep breath. Second, bravo. I'm so proud of you. We'll hope the weather continues to suck so you can do all your obedience training inside. Now, as for a beer, tell him he deserves one after everything his dog has put him through. Plus, it will help him relax."

"Should I change or would that be too weird?" she asked as she turned down the lane to her house. Her mind was buzzing with ideas.

"Tell him you're going to pull on something warmer because you're freezing."

"What about a fire? Too obvious?"

"It's five degrees outside with wind gusting at twenty. Of course you should start a fire."

"Right." It didn't have to be about romance. It could be about survival. She almost laughed at herself. "Okay, we're here."

"Call me later."

Her smile was soft. No one could talk her down from a massive freak out like Elizabeth.

Matt was coming around to get Henry when she emerged from her SUV. "Why don't you let me get him this time? Neither of us wants to chase him down. Can you get my dogs?"

"Sure. At least we know they won't ignore me."

When she opened the door, Henry hung his head. "Yeah, you know I mean business. Let's go."

They brought the dogs inside, and in the foyer, she knelt in front of Henry. "Now, you're a guest here, so you're going to be good, right?"

"Oh, shit," Matt commented. "I hadn't thought of that. And you have a really nice house."

The thought had crossed her mind, but they would manage. "Sit," she said to Henry, and she unclipped his leash as soon as he did. "Now stay."

When he did, she smiled. "Good dog." Her hand gave him a good rubdown as his tail whipped madly through the air.

Matt knelt beside her and unclipped the leashes on her dogs. Annie pranced over to Jane, and she unzipped her fleece and removed her hat.

Standing, she rubbed Rufus behind the ears. "I really am freezing, so I'm going to change. Make yourself at home. I'll be right back."

She'd made it to her bedroom when her phone buzzed in her fleece. Elizabeth's text made her smile.

Brown cashmere sweater. Skinny jeans. Brown Uggs. A little scarlet lip gloss we bought in Atlantic City. You're rocking this.

After texting back her thanks, she changed clothes, her toes almost weeping in relief when she shoved her feet into the insulated boots. Looking in the mirror, she winced at her cap hair. It was soothing to run a brush through it, and the lip gloss she applied felt like magic on her chapped lips. She studied herself in the mirror again and tried out a few smiles.

Her phone buzzed again.

Stop analyzing. Just be yourself. You look great.

Laughing to herself, she headed out of her bedroom and into the den.

Matt was still standing by the door as though he were uncomfortable. His coat was in his hands, and he'd removed his cap and gloves. It was incredible to see him without his winter gear, standing there in just his jeans and a thermal cotton navy long-sleeved shirt. His broad shoulders made her mouth water, and without his cap on, all she wanted to do was run her hands through his thick dark hair. He had cap hair too, and somehow it made him more approachable. Breathtaking but approachable.

And he was keeping an eagle eye on Henry, who was sniffing the floor. Rufus was lying by the fire she had yet to start, as if to say, *aren't you going to light this thing?*

"Here, let me take your coat, and relax. Henry's doing fine. Aren't you?"

The dog barked.

"Rufus wants a fire, so let me get that started."

"Ah, sure." He handed her his coat and then shoved his hands in the pockets of his jeans. "I meant what I said before. You have an incredible house."

She heard the question in his voice and decided to address it straight out. "You're wondering how a dog walker could afford a place like this on the bench."

He glanced over. "It's none of my business."

"But you're wondering. I'm great with investments." That was true.

"Really," he said, but she could tell he didn't fully believe her.

"I had a trust from my grandparents that I came into when I was twenty-five, and I've managed to do very well from it. I love playing the stock market." She wasn't going to mention how she'd turned her academic prize money into a fortune. Or the foundation she'd created to fund women's educational scholarships.

"I do too," he said, and slowly he walked forward to join her. "I can take care of starting the fire. It's the least I can do after all your help. Rufus here seems to be waiting on us. Thank God he and Henry get along."

"Rufus is easy going. He makes friends with everybody. Annie's a little more selective, but she's always nice about it."

"She likes me," he said, taking the wood and arranging it in the fireplace with ease.

"Yes, she does. She's a good judge of character."

He looked over his shoulder, his blue eyes punching a hole of pure lust in her belly. "Good to know."

In fact, if Annie didn't like someone, Jane probably wouldn't like him or her either. Dogs just knew.

"Where's your gas key?" he asked.

She pointed to the right, and moments later, the whoosh of air and oxygen coming together to make fire filled the silence. Rufus yawned and padded closer before settling down in front of the warm hearth. Annie joined him. Henry, of course, got his nose as close to the fire as he could before Matt had to push him back.

"No," he ordered. Henry looked like he simply rolled his eyes. He plopped on his butt and licked his leg.

Watching their interactions, Jane wondered again what made Matt keep Henry when they seemed so ill-suited. Was Matt one of those can't-fail types, or was it a matter of loyalty?

"Sorry about that," Jane said. "Since it's such a large hearth, I didn't want to spoil the effect with a grate."

"Who can blame you? It's stunning."

"Thanks for making the fire. How about we let everyone warm up, and then we can start again? Would you like a beer?"

Be casual, she told herself. *Act like you offer beer to men all the time.*

Matt glanced over, and warmth shot through her body. "Are you having one?"

This she could be honest about. "I'm going to have a glass of wine."

"Then I'll have that too."

Oh, a man who appreciated wine. "Red okay?"

"Preferable."

"Come on into the kitchen then." She led the way, his footsteps echoing behind her in tune with the percussive beat of her heart.

Her wine chiller was embedded in the counter next to a cabinet, and she opened it to take out one of her favorite bottles.

Matt's brows slammed together. "Wait. Please don't open a Châteuaneuf-du-Pape for me. That's like—"

"Don't make a fuss. I love wine. I don't drink anything crappy." Wine was another passion of hers—one on which she was happy to splurge.

"But that's like a hundred-dollar bottle at least."

It was two, but she didn't correct him. She took out two wine glasses. "Like I said, I like good wine. And it's a pleasure to share it with someone who appreciates it. Rhett and Elizabeth could care less."

"I'll take a beer. Really."

She took out her waiter's corkscrew—she hated

modern corkscrews with a passion. "Do you always protest this much?"

His mouth twisted at that. "Not usually, no. It's just a really pricy bottle."

"Want to see my collection?" She pointed to her wine cooler. "I've loved wine since I studied in France for the summer in college. This is one of my indulgences."

He edged closer. "Okay, I'll peek." When he knelt down in front of the glass, she was aware of his head being near her hip.

"My God, you have a Château Margaux. I've never seen a bottle of this in real life."

"When you get Henry to follow all your commands, we'll open it to celebrate."

His mouth dropped. "But that's like a grand."

That vintage was over two thousand actually. "Isn't getting your rambunctious dog to obey you worth a celebration?"

He shut the door to the cooler and stood. His gaze scanned her face, as though he were seeing her in a new light. "I don't know what to make of you."

Well, at least she'd gone from being plain Jane to a little bit mysterious. "What?"

"You live about an eighth of a mile from me in a house built by the same contractor, so I know what these go for. You have a love for wine that extends back to a semester abroad in France, and your cooler is filled with some of the priciest bottles out there. You also tell me you're a wiz at the stock market. Where did you go to school?"

Another thing she could share. "Harvard."

He blinked. "Harvard."

"Where did you go to school?" she asked, even though she already knew. She'd looked him up on the Internet.

"I went to Columbia for undergrad and law school.

It's kinda family tradition. Uncle Arthur, Meredith, and a few other Hales went there."

Her family had a tradition of attending Harvard. They were going on with their fifth generation. It stopped with her. "It's one of the top ten law schools in the country, but it's a few spots below Harvard if I recall." And she gave him a teasing smile.

"A couple, yes. You don't strike me as one of those stuffy Harvard types, though."

She had been without even knowing it before meeting Elizabeth. She hadn't realized she could act any other way. Thank God, her friend had shown her the light.

"Not everyone is stuffy, but there are many. It's just a place where I got my education and met my best friend." She had a moment in which she wondered if she should have added that last part. After all, it was up to Elizabeth how much she wanted to reveal about herself.

"You don't mean Elizabeth?"

Her smile was over-bright. "Yes." She finally poured the wine and handed him a glass.

"But I thought you both worked at The Grand Mountain Hotel before Rhett hired you?"

Rather than answering, she swirled the ruby nectar, pretending to stare at the wine through the crystal. Then she put her nose deep into the goblet and sniffed. "Blackberry and cherry, licorice, and a touch of oak. This is going to be good."

Setting the glass to her lips, she let the wine touch her tongue. Her eyes closed. The bold fruit blended beautifully as it rolled through her mouth. The licorice and oak at the finish made it all the more exotic and rich. She could see the workers in the field, picking succulent purple grapes in the glorious golden French sun. It would warm their backs as they leaned down to pick the grapes. A few of the laborers would pop grapes in their mouths, unable to avoid the temptation. The juice would run down their lips, and they'd swipe at it with their sleeves. She sighed. Took another sip. And then opened her eyes.

Matt was staring at her, his blue eyes darker now, almost like the violets at the deepest part of sunset. "Where were you just now?" he asked in a voice that had gone soft.

Awareness went shooting through her in response to his intense gaze. "In the Rhône Valley when they pick the grapes." She described her thoughts to him.

He was still holding his glass, though his eyes were glued to hers.

"Try it and see."

Not breaking her gaze, he raised the glass to his lips and drank. His eyes fluttered as well, but he didn't look away. "It's incredible."

"Yes," she whispered, not wanting anything more than to keep gazing into his eyes, the taste of the delicious wine on her tongue.

Henry barked suddenly, and the moment shattered like broken glass. Matt set his wine aside and jogged into the living room. She grabbed his glass and followed. When she arrived, Matt was pulling on Henry's collar.

"No. You don't get on people's furniture."

"Henry. Down." She set Matt's glass on the coffee table and pointed to the floor. "Sit."

He immediately leaped off the couch.

"Good dog."

"I almost forgot why we were here," Matt mused, and Jane felt a small thrill of victory.

"Okay," she said, putting her wine down as well. "Then let's resume."

Twenty minutes later, Henry was more biddable, even yawning as though they were boring the crap out of him.

"Why doesn't he like me?" Matt finally asked, sounding aggrieved, as the dog joined Rufus and Annie by the fire.

"He does. He just doesn't like to work."

Matt laughed out loud, and the sound sent tingles down her spine. "I get it. This is the Universe's practical joke on me for all my years as an over-achiever."

Aha! So she might be right about his motives for sticking with Henry.

"And you're finished with all that?" she found herself asking.

His laughter faded, and he looked down at his feet a moment before meeting her gaze. "I didn't find the partner track to be...my cup of tea, as my mother would say."

"I heard around town that she's moved back to Dare, and that's why you and your brother came home." She hadn't met his immediate family though.

He shrugged. "Andy and I both wanted to have a life outside our careers. He has a young son, and I...well...I was starting to become someone I didn't like."

Well, this honesty and sharing were encouraging. She liked this side of him, and the way the contours of his face looked when they were illuminated by the fire only made her heart beat faster. "What were you becoming?"

"A drone," he said with a slash of his hand through the air. "Someone who was paid to be mean to widows and kick puppies. And then the system destroyed a client I deeply cared about, and...I lost faith."

"I know I don't know you well, but as the daughter of a lawyer who's mean to widows and dogs, let me tell you how proud I am that you chose not to go to the dark side."

He made a Darth Vader noise with his breath, which to her sounded like "*Kahhh, chiii.*"

"You're a fan?" she asked.

"Going back to my first Jedi light saber. Of course, I wanted to be Han Solo. He got the girl. Andy liked Luke, since he saved the universe. The guy has the doctor complex down to a T. We used to beg our sister, Caroline, to put her hair up like Princess Leia and dress in a white bed sheet. She only consented when we paid her two dollars from our tooth fairy money."

"That sounds like a happy childhood." Stories like this one made her wish she'd had a sibling, but then she thought of how much her parents had messed her up, and she was glad it had stopped with her.

"Mostly. What about you? Do you have any siblings?"

"No," she said. "Just little old me."

They were both quiet for a long moment, just staring into each other's eyes again, and then Matt looked away. "Well, Henry and I should be going," he said. "The blizzard's starting to come in."

She glanced out the windows. He was right—the snow was coming down in big, fat flakes. "Are you sure you're okay to go home?"

Stay, she wanted to say, but didn't. Even she knew it was too early.

"I grew up here. I'll be fine. As I said, I live close by."

"Okay then."

Annie must have understood because she hopped up and pranced over to Matt and rested her head against his leg. He glanced down and smiled softly.

"She really does like you," Jane said, glowing at the sweet sight. Rufus barked, but didn't rise from his place by the fire. "And that's his way of saying goodbye."

Matt held his arms out to Henry. "You ready to go home, buddy?"

"Did you have a dog as a kid?" she asked.

"No, Mom said she had enough animals to watch with all five of us. We begged, but she's as tough as they come."

"Sounds like she put your needs first."

"She's the best," Matt agreed and then snagged

Henry's collar.

"Why don't you tell him to go to the door and see what he does?" she suggested. "Say door and point to it."

When he did as she suggested, Henry dropped onto his stomach and put his paws over his eyes. Jane couldn't help it. She laughed with gusto. Matt seemed less amused.

"He doesn't respect me."

"No," she said with total honestly, "but sometimes you have to laugh about it."

"Well, your Inner Alpha isn't taking a beating."

"I'm sure we can do something about that," she said, and even to her ears, it sounded sensual.

He must have noticed too since he looked over at her with a new spark in his eyes. His gaze slid down her body.

"This was fun, Jane. Despite the whipping to my ego. I'm just sorry I didn't have a chance to enjoy my wine."

Her mouth tipped up into an easy smile. "Another time."

"Yes," he said with a little pause. "Another time."

"Henry. Door. Now," she said, and the dog lazily got to his feet and went to the door.

Matt walked over and grabbed the red leash. Henry jumped on him, but he'd braced himself for it, so he quickly grabbed the dog's collar in one hand and snapped the leash in place with the other. "Got ya."

Annie pranced by Jane's side as she sauntered over to the door to bid him goodbye. "I think it's a good idea for us to keep working together indoors when it's this cold outside."

"Thank you, Jane. Really. Henry and...I would be lost without you."

That heart she wasn't so sure of simply throbbed at those words. His gaze slid over her face and settled on

her lips. She desperately wished he would kiss her—
ending the perfect evening in the perfect way—but
Henry jumped on the leash and destroyed the moment.

"He has a thing for timing," Matt mused. "You have
to give him that."

"Yes," she said. "Drive home safe. Slow."

"Yes, Mom." He shrugged into his coat one-handed.

"Here," she said, taking Henry's leash. She stared
the dog down while Matt put on his gloves and hat. "Be
good for Matt, Henry, or you'll have to answer to me."

The dog actually whined, making them both burst
into laughter.

"Maybe I need to record you saying that and play it
to him every time he thinks of being bad."

"I'll be seeing you, Matt," she said.

That long, slow stare again, as though he were
seeing her for the first time. "I'll be seeing you, Jane," he
repeated.

As he opened the door, the wind gusted in, and snow
flurries swirled around them. He was humming as he
shut the door.

She started humming the same tune before realizing
what the song was. "I'll Be Seeing You" by Frank
Sinatra.

No one sang it like Frank.

CHAPTER 6

In his new job, Matt had plenty of down time, which had been a foreign concept at his old law firm. Standing at the window in his corner office, Matt was throwing basketballs into the hoop on the back of his office door when his phone rang. A quick glance told him it was his younger sister, Moira, so he immediately picked up.

"Hey, Mo, what's shaking?" he asked, knowing she'd frown at the nickname she'd never completely shaken.

"I don't know, Matty Ice. What about you?" He wasn't Matt Ryan, quarterback for the Atlanta Falcons, by any stretch, but it was a nickname he'd inherited as a lawyer after an incident with a hostile witness. A woman he'd been cross-examining had jumped off the witness seat, flung herself at him, and clawed his face. Instead of freaking out, Matt had remained calm, restraining her as best he could until the officers had swarmed around them and dragged her away.

"Okay, nickname truce. So, how are you? We miss you."

"Yeah, I know. I was talking to Mom on my way to work this morning, and she said the same thing. Danny almost broke my heart over Facetime last night, saying he missed sledding with me at the park. Why did you all have to up and leave Denver? Caroline, Natalie, and I were moaning about it at our regular Thursday Sisters' Night."

She darn well knew their reasons. "Because Andy and I both needed to get a life, and Mom...well, she needed to get away from Dad."

"Jill's been trying to talk us all into moving back to Dare. I swear that girl is a—"

"Fart on a skillet," he finished. "I don't even know what that means, but it sure as heck was fun hearing Uncle Arthur call her that growing up. I took him home the other night and told him I wanted to run for mayor." He'd already scheduled a conference call with an old friend and colleague he wanted to hire as his political consultant. And his computer was filled with notes about his plans for his campaign and what he wanted to do as mayor.

"And? Did he bean you with his cane?"

"No, but he glowered and did that whole harrumph thing."

"God, I love that old man. And now I get to see more of him since I'll be coming up to visit a lot. Caroline, Nat, and I all agreed we'd do a road trip soon."

"Good. I miss you." He loved all his sisters, but he and Moira had been Irish twins, less than a year apart in age, so they were incredibly close.

"Miss you too. You really should think about moving back to Dare, Mo. Leave the big city behind. I can't tell you how great it feels to leave the office at 4:30 so I can get a walk in with Henry before the sun goes down. It's incredible."

"4:30, huh? That makes me want to cry."

"And there's no traffic..."

"Stop it. I'm tearing up. Seriously."

Yeah, Mo's commute was a good forty-five minutes

each way, just like Matt's had been when he lived in Denver. He'd listened to a lot of books on tape while sitting on the heated butt warmers in his car. He didn't miss it.

"How's business?" she asked.

"Well, it's early days, but since I'm from here, there's like a built-in trust system. Meredith told me Uncle Arthur even mentioned me at Bingo night. I had ten people show up the next day to arrange DNRs and wills."

"That's...sweet, I guess."

Andy appeared in the doorway.

"Guess who just showed up," Matt said, putting Moira on speaker. "Mo's on the phone."

"Hey, Mo," Andy said as he strolled in and shut the door behind him. "How's human resources in the big city? Fire anyone today?"

"Hey, Andy Cakes!"

"How did you get a pass from the hospital?" Matt asked, throwing one of the small basketballs on his desk at his brother. "You cancelled our lunch run this morning for an operation."

Andy easily deflected it. "The patient miraculously healed at the last minute and didn't need his scheduled surgery. Living here is like heaven, Mo. When would I ever have had the chance to leave the hospital during the day in Denver? On a Tuesday at that."

"Okay, I'm going to get back to the grind. You guys totally suck."

"We know," Matt said, "but we *happily* suck."

"Aren't you funny? Love you both. Have a good run."

They all said goodbye, and Matt disconnected the call.

"You ready for me to kick your ass running?" he asked his brother.

"Like that could happen, but maybe you have a shot today. That blizzard sucked. After not running for two days, I feel like my arteries are clogging."

"Right. This from a man who eats like a vegan." And one he never beat in a race.

"I'm not a vegan," his brother said, nailing him in the head with the mini-basketball he'd picked up off the floor. He'd played high school varsity while Matt had only been a sub and had a much better aim. "I just like to keep healthy things in my body."

After Kim's diagnosis, she and Andy had done everything they could to make their lifestyle healthy. It hadn't been enough to allay her breast cancer, but Andy still ate mostly organic food. Sometimes he got on his soapbox about preservatives, which could be annoying, but Matt never took offense. And since he realized kids wanted to eat mac and cheese and hot dogs just like their friends did, Andy didn't impose his diet on Danny. Still, the kid ate much more healthy stuff than they had while growing up. His nephew even liked kale. Crazy.

"Moira said Danny almost broke her heart when he talked about missing their sledding matches."

"Yeah," Andy said. "I heard. He really misses his aunts, but he's made some new friends already. I knew he'd be fine with switching to a new kindergarten halfway through the year. Especially with you and Mom as anchors. Plus, he's totally fallen in love with Jill."

"She's something."

"So, get your butt up and let's get going."

"Okay, but we need to stop at my place so I can get changed. I left my stuff at home when I got your text this morning. But I'm not going to bring Henry. It'll be nice not to have him on a run for once."

"Still not obeying you?" he asked as they left his office.

Matt paused to tell his secretary, Alice, that he'd be back in about an hour.

"No," he answered as they left his office. The sun was shining and there wasn't a breath of wind, a perfect winter day. Main Street was buzzing with shoppers enjoying the nice weather.

"But someone's helping me with his training," he continued, "and it seems to be making all the difference."

"Really," his brother drawled. "Someone of the female variety, I take it."

"Yes. Go get your gym bag."

As his brother jogged to his SUV, Matt thought about his new dog trainer, as he'd been doing a lot lately. He couldn't stop thinking about how things had changed between them in her kitchen last night. Watching her savor her wine, eyes closed in apparent ecstasy, he'd felt a definite shift between them. Then she'd told him about her enchanting vision of the vineyards, which had made him notice her even more as a woman, a woman he'd badly wanted to touch. Without her scarf and hat, the exposed line of her neck had made him want to run a finger along it. Her short hair made her big brown eyes pop in a face that was becoming more arresting each time he saw her.

"Who is she?" Andy asked when he returned with his black canvas duffle.

"Jane Wilcox," he responded as he unlocked his SUV.

Andy threw his bag in the back seat, and they both buckled their seatbelts.

"Rhett Butler Blaylock's dog walker and dog sitter," he continued. While Matt liked Rhett, he didn't know what to make of the situation. Why would a Harvard grad who was obviously incredibly smart choose to be a dog walker for a champion poker player?

"I've seen her around town. Petite, right? Short hair. She's cute."

Yeah, he'd thought so all along, but she wasn't his typical type. Usually he liked forthright women with endless legs, and being a lawyer at one of the most cutthroat law firms in Denver, he'd had no trouble meeting women who met the bill. Those relationships had never become serious, but who had the time for that sort of thing anyway? He hadn't—not while he was in Denver.

"That's her. She goes to the same park on the far side of the bench, and she came to my rescue when Henry pulled one of his stunts." He could still see her smiling at him as she joked about him being a damsel in distress.

"You ask her out yet?" Andy had always been able to read him, so it didn't surprise him that his brother was picking up on his interest.

"No, but it was so cold the day the blizzard rolled in that we continued Henry's dog training at her house."

And what a place it was. She was a nester. His sisters Moira and Caroline were nesters too—like Jane, they chose warm colors for their walls, decorating their homes with carefully selected artwork and scattered accessories.

"Where does she live?" Andy asked as Matt pulled into his driveway.

"Not too far from here," he said, leading his brother down the sidewalk he'd shoveled at least six times during the blizzard. They'd gotten eighteen inches in total, and he'd had to clear a path for Henry to go outside and do his business. And, of course, Henry hadn't wanted to come back inside, so Matt had chased him in the freaking blizzard, muscling through the snow drifts. He'd almost called Jane to ask for advice, but he didn't have her number. Yet.

"She lives on the bench?" Andy asked as Matt unlocked the door and opened it carefully so his dog wouldn't bolt.

Henry was dancing around excitedly, and Matt slipped inside to grab his leash so he could take him out to do his business. Andy followed him into the front yard.

"Yeah, she does," he continued. "Surprised me too. And get this...she went to Harvard."

"You're kidding me! And she's a dog walker? No offense, Henry."

His dog simply lifted his leg.

"I know!" His brother's response mirrored his own, which made him even more curious.

They headed back inside, Henry tugging on the leash now. "We'll go for a walk later, numbskull," Matt said. "This is bro time."

After changing, they took off again, choosing the Bear Creek trail, since it was an asphalt path that the city always cleared and salted after a snowfall. Matt smiled as they jogged in tandem—the wind was ruffling through the pines and aspens, and the sun felt warm on his head and shoulders. The cardinal he spotted in the nearby bushes looked blood red against the blinding fresh snow. This moment felt good, peaceful.

"So, let's get back to the dog walker," Andy said once they'd settled into a good pace. "Run me through what you know about her because I can tell you like her."

He gave his brother a slight shove, but then he shared what he knew. He'd been spending so much time thinking about Jane that the words just spilled out.

"So a stock portfolio, huh?" Andy commented, his breath creating sparkling white clouds in the cold air. "She sounds great, but there are a lot of things that don't add up. Did you Google her?"

"I thought about it," he admitted, but he'd stopped himself. That would make it a big deal—it would mean that he *really* liked her—and he wasn't ready for that yet.

His brother punched him in the arm, salt crunching under his feet where it hadn't melted. "So this is why you left your soul-sucking job. You have too much of a conscience. I'll have to tell Mom. She'll be so proud."

He snorted. "Suck it."

"You first." Andy picked up his pace. "Think you can keep up with me?"

"I dared you earlier. You're the old man here, not me," he said, as if thirty-six could be considered old.

Matt lengthened his stride and soon they were neck and neck.

"You're going to eat my dust. Race you to the post by the picnic bench."

"You got it," he said, spotting it ahead.

Their casual jog accelerated to a flat-out sprint. Ah, sibling rivalry. Gotta love it.

Matt was pushing so hard his lungs started to burn from the cold, but just like always, Andy was a foot ahead of him. This was what thirty years of defeat felt like. It totally sucked. When they were growing up, he'd blamed it on Andy being older, his body more developed. Now, he'd have to resort to blaming it on Andy being an inch taller that he was, at six-two.

But that didn't mean he could play dirty. "Hey!" he gasped. "I think I see someone lying over there by the creek. They look like they need help."

His brother's doctor instincts kicked in, and he slowed just a fraction, scanning the snow around the creek. "Where?"

Matt ran past him as hard as he could. "Sucker!" he yelled.

"Shit," he heard Andy mutter behind him.

Apparently his brother had a Pavlovian response to the Hippocratic oath. He'd have to use that one against him more often.

Matt made it to the pole before his brother did, and even though he'd only won by cheating, he did a victory dance.

His brother glared at him. "And here I thought you were an ethical person. You should know better than to call medical wolf."

"I know," he admitted, but he couldn't stop smiling. He'd finally passed the finish line ahead of Andy after decades of losing. "I'm a terrible person."

His brother leaned down and palmed some snow in his glove. Uh-oh. His brother had a mean fast ball. He tried to duck out of the way, but Andy adjusted his aim and the little missile smacked him right in the chest. The sting of it meant he'd probably have a bruise. He held out his hands.

"Now who's the sore loser? Is that what you want to teach Danny?"

Another snowball smacked him in the chest. He winced. Okay, so that hadn't been the smartest comment ever.

"You got the second one for impugning my fatherly abilities," Andy said, grinning like the mischievous boy he'd been. "Now, do we have that all out of our system, or should I keep pelting your cheating ass? We should probably turn around and head back."

"You're still a bad loser."

"Butthead cheater."

Yeah. Brother time had never felt so good.

They jogged back at an easy pace, no more races or banter. Once they reached the SUV, they stretched and climbed inside. Andy immediately dug out his phone, and Matt drove in silence, letting him check his emails. His brother's job was to help people get healthy, and sometimes that couldn't wait. His own emails were usually far less urgent, and the bonus of having his own practice was that his inbox had experienced a major slim down. At his old firm, he'd never been able to keep up with his emails, but now he cleaned out his inbox every day.

"Wow," Andy finally commented a few minutes later. "Even if Jane wasn't good at the stock market, she'd still be pretty well off. Her family's loaded."

"What?" His hands tightened on the steering wheel,

and when he glanced over at his brother, Andy was scrolling on his smart phone. "Dammit! You looked her up, didn't you? Is that what you've been doing? I thought you were doing work stuff. Saving lives."

"You like her, so yes, I totally did. Big brother's privilege. Her family is from old manufacturing money. Currently lives in Greenwich, Connecticut." Then he whistled. "And guess what? Her father is a long-standing state senator who's running for U.S. Congress in the next election."

Well, maybe that was a good thing. He was running for mayor, and this woman knew the score. God, what was wrong with him? They'd only just met.

"Her mom is a career politician's wife. Very polished. And I found a picture of Jane with them when she was in college. She looks nothing like she does now. She looks as polished as the mother in this photo. Hair shoulder length too. The mom is wearing a red suit, and hers is blue. Really toeing the line between subtlety and heavy handedness."

Interesting. He had never seen her in anything so polished. That kind of radical departure had to mean something. He had three sisters, so he knew how the female mind worked. Well mostly. They always made major changes to their hairstyles and wardrobes when something *significant* happened. Heck, who could forget the way Natalie's hair had developed a greenish tint when Caroline and Moira poured hydrogen peroxide over it in an ill-advised attempt to dye it blonde after her break-up with her high-school boyfriend? He'd laughed at the sight and gotten socked by all three of them. Good times. He wondered what Jane's life-changing event had been.

"She's a major brainiac. Graduated summa cum laude from Harvard both undergrad and M.B.A. Big-time honors. The only recent mention of her is on a website called The Woman's Freedom Scholarship

Foundation. She's the founder, and they grant college scholarships to women from low-income families who are trying to change their lives. Cool! I like her already."

Matt smiled in spite of himself. Jane liked giving back. It was another thing they had in common.

"Other than that, there's no other sign of her...at least not on the Internet. No work history or resume. She's not on LinkedIn or any other social media websites."

Yeah, something had gone down. His gut twitched. He hoped it hadn't been traumatic. Being a lawyer, he'd heard endless stories about people's lives being blasted apart.

"What about her job with Rhett?" he asked. "Is there anything about that?" Might as well wade in since his brother was going to look anyway.

"Nothing. Just hundreds of pictures of that dog on Twitter and Facebook. God, that is one girlie animal. Her outfits are going to give me nightmares."

He'd felt the same way at first, but she was just the sweetest dog. "She's a heck of a lot better behaved than Henry."

"Yeah, there's definitely some power struggle between you and that dog. He's always going to be rambunctious, but he mostly listens to other people."

"Don't I know it?" It was frustrating, and sometimes it made him worry that Henry just didn't like him. But then the dog would give him a big lick in the face, and he'd realize it wasn't anything so simple. His mind turned back to Jane. "Something happened to Jane, didn't it?"

His brother tossed his phone into his gym bag. "That would be my guess. You should ask her when you two get closer."

Matt gave him the fisheye. "What makes you think we're going to get closer?"

"Like I said, I can tell that you like her. It's more

than that, though... Before she was cute and a little mysterious. Now, she's looking like a damsel in distress, and the whole reason you went into law in the first place was to help people. You won't be able to stop yourself from caring about her now."

Funny how Jane had told him that *he* was the damsel when they'd first talked. He sighed. "I guess we both got the need-to-help-people gene. Must be from Mom. Dad's too big of a dick for us to have gotten it from him." Even if he was a doctor. But unlike Andy, who engaged with all of his patients, their dad was a surgeon. He didn't need to get involved in people's lives to fix what was wrong with their bodies. Most of them were drugged when he worked on them anyway.

Andy sighed. "He wasn't always a dick. I don't understand what happened between Mom and Dad, but it's best if you don't let it eat you up."

"He hurt Mom."

"I know, and that pisses me off too. But having been married, I know it takes two. I love Mom, but when things fall apart, it's never just one person's fault."

His brain didn't want to hear that, and he felt like punching the steering wheel. "Does he call you?"

"A few times. Mostly to talk to Danny. He knows he's in the dog house with all of us."

They arrived at Matt's house, and Andy pulled out his gym bag. "Can I wash off here? Your shower is a hell of a lot nicer than the one at the hospital."

"Sure," he said, slamming the door. Banishing the swirling thoughts from his head, he took a moment to appreciate the beauty of the day. The sun was warming him, the snow shone like diamonds, and the fir trees swayed in the wind. "Can you believe how lucky we are to be here, taking a break like this mid-day?"

Andy glanced at him as they walked to his house. "Moving back here is going to be one of the best decisions you and I have ever made."

For some reason, Matt found his mind traveling again to the mystery that was Jane Wilcox, to the park where they walked their dogs each day at sunset.

He had a hunch that his brother was right.

CHAPTER 7

When Matt arrived at the park at sunset, his mind was spinning with all the revelations his brother had discovered about Jane. She and the dogs were standing at the edge of the park, and he found himself eager to see her bright smile.

Fortunately Henry didn't pull any antics when he opened the back door to leash him. When Jane turned and waved at them, Henry jerked on the leash in his eagerness, his tail flapping in excitement. Even from this distance, Matt could swear Annie was smiling at him. She was wearing a red fleece jacket with a hoodie and something that looked like boots for dogs. My God, he couldn't imagine the product design that went into something like that.

"Hi," Jane called when they reached them, and she immediately reached down to give Henry a nice rub behind the ears, which made him dance and bark.

"Hi," he easily responded, running his gaze over her face. Knowing what he did about her, it was like looking at a new person. *Jane Wilcox, who are you?*

"Do I have a smudge on my face?" she asked him,

tilting her head to the side. "Rufus was giving me kisses after nosing around in the trees at our place."

He shook his head, embarrassed to have been caught studying her. Although it was hard to look away... Her cheeks were rosy from the winter wind, and her big brown eyes sparkled.

"No. I don't think he marked you. So, how was your day?" he asked. He'd start out there. See what she did during the day. Surely two dogs couldn't take up all her time.

"Great. How about yours?"

Okay, that wasn't useful. They started to walk along the path, and just then a few deer bounded across the park about a hundred yards away from them. Their hindquarters were covered in snow, and while Matt marveled at their graceful leaps, he had to control a wildly barking Henry, who immediately lurched in their direction.

"No. Stop. Sit. Dammit, Henry!"

Of course, Rufus and Annie just watched the deer without moving an inch.

"Okay," Jane said by his side. "I think it's time to get out the big guns. Well, perhaps not big. Henry, I was hoping we weren't going to have to do this, but I think it's time."

Matt was so busy trying to hold Henry back that he didn't see what Jane was talking about until a stream of water hit Henry in the back of the head. The dog stopped dancing. When Matt swiveled around, he saw a pink water gun in Jane's hand. Henry finally looked over his shoulder.

"Stop," she demanded. "I know it's cold out, and I don't plan to do this more than once."

His lip trembled like *you just shot me*.

"I know deer get you all flustered, but *seriously*." She extended the water gun to Matt, and then reached down to pet Henry. "I still love you, but when we say stop, you stop."

"Thanks," Matt said, fitting the water gun in his hand, wishing it was any color but pink. Still, if it worked... "I'll give it back to you when we leave."

"No need," she replied. "It's yours."

Great. Just what he needed. A pink gun. Might as well emasculate him on the spot.

Her mouth twitched. "Oh, you should see your face. I brought it as a joke. Your real present—a navy one—is in my car. I knew you'd want a manly color."

He laughed. "What a relief! I don't think my Inner Alpha could have handled a pink water gun." Especially since she'd joked about him being deficient in the Alpha territory, which he so was not. And now that he knew he liked her...well, he was planning on showing her his Alpha as soon as the time was right.

"So tell me about your day," he suggested again as they resumed their stroll. "What did you do?"

Her eyes flickered over to him. "Nothing special. Just hung out with my besties here," she said, and Annie barked in agreement.

He hoped his lawyer training would serve him well in persuading her to talk. Getting people to break and say things they didn't want to say had been his trademark while he was at the firm. He'd excelled in court, looking like a nice guy until...well, he pulled out cold and calculating Matty Ice. Not that he was going to pull those tactics with Jane. They were in his past. "No big stock trades today?"

"Ah, nothing special. Just a little dabbling here and there."

"Got any hot tips for me?"

This time she laughed, the gusto of it scattering the robins in the nearby trees. "Are you really pumping me for stock tips? Isn't helping you with your dog enough?"

He gave her a winning smile. "Just trying to learn more about you. My stock portfolio is in pretty solid shape, honestly." Which was true.

Before he knew it, they were talking stocks—anything from blue chip to small and large cap. He didn't meet many people who understood more than the basics of the stock market, but Jane had a command of it that he'd never come across in a layman. Then she blew his mind when she shared her thoughts on hedge funds. Their pace was leisurely as the sunset colors changed to deeper hues of blues and gold, and they only stopped when the dogs marked their territory or did their business. Fortunately, Henry was behaving other than giving an occasional bark at a singing bird or a mischievous squirrel. A few runners passed them in a blur, eager to eat up the path before the valley succumbed to night. By the time Jane changed topics, veering into investments in overseas gas and oil pipelines like those in Azerbaijan on the Caspian Sea, her eyes were twinkling, and she was gesturing with her free hand.

"You really love this stuff," he finally commented. This side of her fascinated him—her eyes gleamed with passion and intelligence as she spoke.

As if suddenly self-conscious, Jane lifted her shoulder and looked away for a second. "I like playing the odds. That's really what the market is all about."

"When I first met you, I didn't think you had an appetite for risk."

Leaning down, she stroked Rufus and Annie and then had to pet Henry too when he nosed in. "Some people are full of surprises, I guess."

Yes, she definitely was, at that. If you could weigh the sheer information in a person's brain, hers would probably weigh more than her tight, petite body.

Which looked sleek and sexy tonight in skinny jeans, brown suede snow boots, and a red winter coat with a matching hat. He let his gaze linger on her backside for a moment before pulling it back to the path.

"Why aren't you off working for a big investment firm in New York City?" he asked. "I mean, it must have seemed like a reasonable track after you graduated from Harvard."

The way she rose was too stiff, and some of the sparkle in her eyes faded. "That wasn't what I wanted."

"What did you want?" he asked in a serious tone.

"At that time, I wasn't sure." Then she looked away and gestured to the sky. "It's almost dark. We should head back."

For a moment, Matt grew frustrated that the sunset was dictating how long he could spend with this woman. Then he realized their time didn't have to end just because their walk was over. "Since you treated me to wine last night, why don't you and the dogs come over to our house tonight? We can order pizza and see if the water gun works as well as you think it will. Henry always tries to eat my pizza."

Her mouth parted, the only indication that his invitation had surprised her. "Ah...we'd love that. Shall we follow you this time?"

"Usually I would say, 'ladies first,' but that won't help you find my house."

"That's okay. I don't expect a man to be a gentleman all the time."

His muscles tightened at the thought, and he looked over to see if she'd meant anything sexual.

Her cheeks went red instantly. "Oh...I mean...just that I can open my own door sometimes if it's...more convenient."

He had to bite the inside of his lip to keep from smiling. "My sisters say the same thing, but they'd still kick our butts if we didn't at least try to be gentlemanly. Natalie especially. She always says having three sisters was good training for me and Andy."

"You're lucky to have them." Something like wistfulness crossed her face.

Henry barked at a squirrel running to the nearby metal garbage can, interrupting the moment. And Jane shivered.

"Come on," he said. "You're cold, and I expect the dogs are thirsty."

They walked back to the SUVs, and out of the corner of his eye, he could see her stealing glances at him too.

Andy was right. He did like her. And she liked him.

The only question was, what was he going to do about it?

CHAPTER 8

Jane couldn't believe her luck. As she followed Matt to his house, she dialed up Elizabeth over the Bluetooth in her car.

"You aren't going to believe this," she said as soon as her friend answered.

"You bought more dog coats online today."

Okay, so she'd gone a little overboard last week. Twelve coats in an array of animal prints and polka dots, not that she was admitting that. "No, I'm following Matt back to his house for pizza. That's two nights in a row. That's gotta be statistically significant, right?"

"Get a hold of yourself, Einstein. If you start talking about probability, the man might head for the hills. Kidding! Of course it's significant. Did he invite you?"

"Yes," she all but sang out.

"What are you wearing?" And she said it with just enough salaciousness to make Jane laugh.

"Wouldn't you love to know?"

The dogs barked as if to back her up.

"Okay, my little pixie, just relax. This is a big step for you, but have fun. Let him steer the conversation. What were you talking about at the park?"

"Stocks," she said. Pure joy had shot through her when he'd brought up the subject. It had felt so good to be herself with a man.

"Dear God. Call 911. Stat."

"Hah! No, seriously. I think he's a closet market geek like I am."

"Well, that makes me want to upchuck. If you get married, your kids will both have trust funds and education funds before they're out of diapers."

That had been the case for Jane, but it hadn't made her feel any more loved, any safer financially. Her parents hadn't created those funds for her. They'd done it for themselves. To show off to their friends. It was expected, and it was what people of their class did. Cripes, how that whole world exhausted her.

"I'm sorry, Jane," Elizabeth said softly when she didn't banter back.

"It's okay. So, can I safely put on some lipstick before I go in without having him think I'm making a big deal out of this? I can only use lip gloss when I'm outside, or my lips get chapped."

"Definitely wear lipstick. You're better off with a matte color in case he kisses you. Funny, his name is Matt. Don't make a pun inside. Promise me."

Kiss her? Her hands jerked on the steering wheel, and her belly tightened. God, it had been a while. That would be...awesome. "You know me too well. Okay. What shade?"

"Why do you think I asked what you're wearing?"

Right. Jeez. She was acting like a novice beauty queen contestant. "I wore skinny jeans with a red scoop-neck cashmere sweater under a red pea coat. Just about froze my ass off."

"You wanted to look good for him, so it's worth it. Let's go with La Caline. The rosy tone brings out the pink in your cheeks and makes your eyes pop without being too obvious."

"I'm glad you made me keep some of the makeup."

"Like I was going to let you toss thousands of dollars of Chanel in the trash."

"You're such a Chanel whore." Growing up, Elizabeth hadn't been able to afford it, which was why she loved it so much now.

"Damn proud of it too."

They'd gone through their makeup together, and Elizabeth had picked the colors that suited Jane—not Raven—best. They'd donated the rest to a fledgling beauty school in the inner city.

When Matt turned off the street onto a private drive, she blew out a breath. "Okay, we're here."

"Stay calm. This is a walk in the park."

"Nice pun"

"Sorry, I couldn't help myself. Look. You've got this. Have him pour you a glass of wine and then just chill. Talk about the dogs. Talk about him."

"Yeah, because I can't talk a lot about me."

"Don't go there. You're doing the best you can. And he can learn a lot about you without knowing what you really do for a living. Just don't play strip poker."

"As if." Just the thought of it made her mouth water. But it *would* be one way to see him without clothes 'cause she'd beat him hands down. Even Rhett had a hard time beating her. He said her poker face was one of the best he'd ever seen, a whopping compliment coming from him.

"Let things evolve naturally. Now, slow down and put your lipstick on before you stop. No need to be obvious."

"Right. I'll call you later."

"Better. Have fun," Elizabeth said and ended the connection.

Jane slowed down so she could dig in her purse for her Louis Vitton makeup bag. She pulled out the lip liner she wanted and then sorted through the lipsticks until she found the right shade. Rising in her seat to look into the rearview mirror, she quickly applied the makeup. Elizabeth was right—it did make her eyes light up. Her friend always knew the right shade to use. It was something Jane had come to Harvard knowing very little about. Her father's image consultants had always done her makeup for public appearances or political photos. She'd hated makeup until she met Elizabeth. With her friend, it was pure fun, all about enhancing attributes and playing dress up.

When she reached the front of his house, Matt and Henry were already standing on his porch. The driveway was clear, so he'd presumably had enough time to stow the SUV in the garage. After snagging his *manly* water gun and her purse from the passenger seat, she left the vehicle and went around to let Rufus and Annie out. They were so well behaved that she didn't bother with the leashes.

"Thought I'd lost you back there," he said.

"Nope. All here. Ah, this is your manly water gun." She held the navy toy out to him.

The smile he gave her made her melt into a puddle, like snow around a campfire. Of course, Henry gave her an accusing look.

"Sorry, kiddo," she told him, rubbing behind his ears. "If you obey, your master here won't have to use it."

"Let's hope," Matt agreed. "Thank you."

"No problem."

She glanced around then, taking in the sight of his house. Like hers, it was a two-story, craftsman-style mountain lodge with three triangles in natural wood siding piercing the roof. The center one arched above the porch, showcasing an impressive window that would soak in the waning Western light and sunset. The main difference between their homes was the extra stone that ran along the foundation and then up his porch. Her own porch wrapped around the right side, allowing for a breathtaking view of the surrounding forest and mountains. His second story also had a few more windows than hers did, and the main body of the house was painted a rugged tan while hers was a deep sage.

"I like it," she said.

"You should. Same style mostly. Let's head indoors and get the dogs some water. You're probably thirsty too."

When the door closed behind her, she shrugged off her coat. His hands stilled for just a second while he was taking off his stocking cap, and the heart that was already jogging in her chest raced forward in a full sprint. She'd suffer a thousand moments of frozen legs if he looked at her like that again. With appreciation. Like he was seeing what he liked.

Her Inner Woman roared.

"Make yourself at home," he said, unclipping Henry's leash as she unzipped Annie's coat.

Henry danced away before Matt could wipe his paws and immediately bounded over to the sofa and jumped on it. "Dammit, Henry!"

"Use your water gun," she gently suggested.

"Right. This is going to be fun. He's going to be a moving target, so my aim will have to be solid." He palmed the gun and advanced. "No. Off the couch. Please."

The earnest way he gave the dog a second chance made her heart beat faster. Of course, Henry blew it. So Matt squirted him. "I said, 'no.'"

Henry stared at him for three seconds before jumping down.

"Great! It's a minor victory, sure, but I'll take it. Believe it or not, I used to have nice furniture."

As soon as he said that, she saw the chew marks on a nearby antique chair and the claw marks on the back of his leather sofa. She wouldn't have tolerated that one bit.

"I've been wondering," she asked. "What made you get a dog?" And keep it, she almost asked?

"Let's go into the kitchen and get some drinks while I tell you the story."

He filled two extra bowls for Annie and Rufus and set them down. Annie pranced over and rubbed her head against Matt's shin.

"That's her way of saying thank you," Jane informed him.

Leaning down, he stroked the hair sticking up wildly from the top of her head. "You really are the sweetest dog ever."

"So, Henry..." she reminded him.

"Let me order pizza. What's your preference for toppings?"

"Fully loaded."

"Oh, a woman after my own heart."

Jane could practically feel herself floating off the ground. He ordered their pizza and then gestured to his wine cooler. The machine was a good brand, but it only held twenty-four bottles.

"Mine is bigger," she commented and then snapped her mouth shut. Great. She'd unintentionally insulted his manhood again.

He smirked. "Oh, how I'd respond if I hadn't been raised to be a nice guy."

"I didn't mean..." she felt compelled to say.

"I know. But you do seem to have a preoccupation with my Inner Alpha, so let's address that right now. I'm going to have to kiss you."

Her hand flew to her throat as his words sent a shockwave through her body. "What?"

"I'm going to have to kiss you," he said, a new gleam in his eyes.

Determined sensuality had never looked so hot.

"Oh, well, if it's to prove a point..." Heck, he could prove that point whenever he wanted.

"And there's also the fact that I want to."

She could work with that.

The line of his shoulders seemed broader as he crossed the kitchen toward her, making her pulse beat harder, faster. God, he really was ridiculously handsome, she thought as those arctic blue eyes scanned her face. And that half-cocked smile he wore, as though he were going to enjoy putting her in her place, made her want to swoon.

She stood there, waiting for him. When he was mere inches away, he cupped her cheek and then let his fingers trace her neckline. Her breath huffed out, and she was moments away from throwing herself at him. But he wasn't going to lurch in and give her a smacker like so many of her first—and last kisses—had been with other men. That was clear from his deliberation. No, Matthew Hale was intent on making sure she never questioned his Inner Alpha again.

He lowered his head, his eyes never leaving hers until the moment his warm, soft lips grazed hers. Her lids fluttered shut, and she was standing there, waiting for more pressure, when Matt suddenly plowed into her. A quick look revealed it all. Henry had jumped on him from behind and was barking in loud bursts.

"Dammit, Henry."

Great. A hot kiss interrupted by a misbehaving dog. Wasn't that just her luck?

"I'm sorry I ran into you." Matt cupped her cheek. "Are you okay?"

She only nodded.

"He's earned himself a Big Squirt." And with that, her would-be kisser grabbed the blue water gun.

Henry instantly raced off, Matt chasing him out of the kitchen.

Annie pawed her ankle, and when she looked down,

she could swear the sweetheart was saying, *girl, I feel ya.*

A door slammed in another part of the house and then Matt stormed back into the kitchen.

"Let's try that again," he said, tossing the water gun on the counter as he strode toward her.

Determined. Intense. Hot.

He yanked her to him and pressed his mouth firmly to hers. The heat of his body, the urgency of his kiss had her eyes closing immediately. Awash in her senses, she heard his rasping breath as he changed the angle of their kiss and nibbled at the corners of her mouth. She smelled spice and pine from his cologne. But most of all, she felt his hands as they slid across her hips to nestle her more tightly against his rock-hard body, his warm lips still claiming her mouth.

Her hands slid up those strong, muscular arms, and she rose on tiptoes to tunnel her hands into his thick hair. He hummed against her mouth as she kneaded the back of his neck with them, wanting him to take their connection further, deeper, darker. When his tongue slid across her lips, she opened her mouth to tangle with him.

The kiss turned into pure fire, its heat spreading the more they fed it with their dance. A delicate pass here. An urgent twirl there.

Dear God, did he know how to kiss, and she never wanted it to end.

She moaned before she could hold back, and his thumb grazed the side of her mouth where they were fitted together. Stroking. Stroking. Stroking.

His teeth nipped her bottom lip and then his mouth left hers, grazing down her cheek. "You have the most incredible cheekbones."

She'd always thought they were too arched for her face, so the compliment made her glow. "Glad you like them."

"And then there's your eyes..." His mouth continued its sensual trek across her face, igniting fires on her skin now.

"They're big," she whispered lamely and pressed closer, realizing all this talk was making her self-conscious.

"They were the first thing I noticed about you," he murmured, nipping her jawline.

Okay, no one had ever done that, and she rather liked it. She angled her head back to give him better access.

"That's probably because all I had on was a hat." What were they talking about?

His chuckle sent her nerve endings aflame. "That's not all you had on."

Oh, so he was funny. "True. Streaking through the park would be a terrible idea. Plus, it's winter."

"It won't always be," he said, his voice husky.

She rose even higher on her tiptoes and ran her nails down his neck, applying gentle pressure. Elizabeth always said it was a move that drove men wild.

His groan confirmed her bestie was always right about these things.

"Oh, I like that," he whispered. "Do it again."

She used a little more pressure this time, and he groaned as he took her mouth in a rough, hot kiss. This time there was no dance. It was a hot press of tongues, which made her feel bold and brave. Desired.

When he finally released her mouth and leaned back, his wicked smile and the knowing glint in his eyes made a grin break out on her face.

"Hi," he simply said, his voice all husky.

"Hi," she answered, and to her, her voice sounded hoarse. Like it wasn't sure what to say.

"You just keep surprising me, Jane," he said in that same sexy voice.

Her grin might have grown wider at that. She liked

surprising people in ways they didn't expect. Growing up, she'd always been chasing her parents' perfect persona for her. It wasn't until college that she'd started to become her own person.

"I'm glad."

He rubbed a finger over her cheek and then stepped away from her. "So, how about some wine?"

When he turned around, she rubbed her throat. Okay, time to act normal again. But her head seemed to have fallen off her body, and she was suddenly grasping for conversation.

Fortunately, he didn't think it was odd that she didn't reply. When he bent over in front of the wine cooler, she had a fantastic view of his firm butt, which she'd loved watching at the park even before they met. Most men had flat butts, Jane knew, but not Matt. His muscular curves flat-out made her salivate.

"You're staring at my butt, aren't you?" he asked, and she could hear the smile in his voice. "I know you used to check me out at the park before me met."

"Well, it is a nice butt," she said, and then thought, *Oh God, did I just say that?*

He laughed and withdrew a bottle. She was so busy staring at him that he had to waggle the bottle to grab her attention.

"Earth to Jane. I know you have pretty fine taste when it comes to wine, but this is the best I can do. It's not Châteuaneuf-du-Pape."

"Don't be silly. I love Freemark Abbey," she told him. "It is a beautiful winery too. Have you ever been?"

"Yes," he replied. "I love going to wine country. San Francisco is my favorite city in the U.S."

"Mine too," she said, and wanted to rub her hands together in delight at this additional evidence of their suitability.

He brought out some lovely red wine glasses and then uncorked the bottle with quick efficiency.

"You use a waiter's corkscrew," she commented, crossing over to him. Now she could stand close to him without feeling awkward. Kissing had changed the whole personal space ratio between them.

"Yeah, all those other ones on the market are way too complicated."

Her Inner Wine Diva danced at that. "Yeah, sometimes simpler is better."

He poured her an ounce of wine as if they were at a tasting. *"Madam."*

She laughed at his impression of a stuffy French waiter and picked up the glass, twirling the red liquid briskly, eying the fingers trailing down the glass. Then she breathed in the scent and closed her eyes. "Blackberry. Cherry. Leather. Spice. Oh, this is a good bottle."

When the wine flowed into her mouth, it seemed to soak into her the way rain soaked into the earth. Yes. This. Galileo was famous for saying "wine was sunlight, held together by water." And he was right, for with every taste of wine, it felt as though good things were going to happen. Like the first rays of sunlight always promised.

"Wonderful," she finally pronounced, the purr in her voice there for a different reason now.

"I could watch you drink wine all day," he murmured, and the hushed tone in his voice, one she now recognized as desire, made her eyes pop open wider.

"That might get boring," she said and rested the wine on the counter. "It's only wine."

"I doubt it. I'd love to go to a wine tasting with you, but I don't think I could handle it."

It took her a moment to understand what he meant. The joy rising in her made her feel more alive than she had in years.

"Oh, that *would* be terrible."

"You're what we call in my family an imp. But a

lovely one." He reached for his wine and performed his own ritual, swirling it, breathing into the glass, and then taking a sip. "It is really good wine, but it's not a Châteuaneuf-du-Pape."

"Few are. And you can come over and have some anytime you want." Well, that was bold, even for her.

His eyes turned slumberous. "I'll keep that in mind."

The doorbell rang. "Pizza time."

"Do you want me to let Henry out while you get it?" she asked.

"He's in the garage," he said. "Down the hall."

She retrieved Henry and leaned down and talked to him about being a good dog until he stopped dancing around and finally sat. When she emerged with him, the dog immediately lunged for Matt. He had to hold the pizza box over his head while Jane grabbed Henry's collar.

"No. Down."

Matt shook his head. "Cripes, I thought doggie time-out would work, but it seems like we still have a problem. He's out of control."

"He's still just a puppy, but you're right. He needs more discipline."

"I really am trying."

She stroked his arm when he set the pizza on the counter. "I know you are. Be patient. We'll have him in ship-shape." Best not to add, *in no time,* because that seemed farfetched.

"Inside or outside for him, oh mighty dog whisperer?" Matt asked. "I don't want him causing trouble while we eat."

"Does he have a crate?"

"Yeah, in the mudroom, but it's almost impossible to get him in there, and I hate caging him up."

"People have different views on that, but honestly, I think it makes them feel safe. So let's get him in there and quiet him down. He's just overexcited. Sometimes having new company over does that to a dog."

"Or being a numbskull." But he patted the dog's head gently. "Henry, you do try my patience."

"We'll get Annie and Rufus to help him into the crate."

She called her dogs, and together, they led Henry into the mudroom. His muscles bunched when he saw the crate, so she kneeled down and stroked him, murmuring to him softly. Matt leaned against the doorjamb, his shoulders slumped. It wasn't hard to feel his frustration.

It took her a solid five minutes, but Henry finally went into the crate. She locked the door and then looked at Rufus and Annie.

"Stay."

They both plopped down beside Henry's crate, heads on their paws.

"I know I've said it before," Matt said, "but you amaze me."

She rose and followed him into the kitchen. He pulled out some plates, silverware, and water glasses, and she helped him set a cozy corner of the enormous farm table in his mocha-colored dining room.

"That's a pretty big table," she commented.

"I have a big family, so when I bought this house, I wanted to be prepared for guests and family dinners. My mom doesn't need to do all the hosting."

"Must be nice to be from such a big family."

He set their wine by their plates. "It is."

When he brought the pizza box to the table, she sat to his left and dropped a napkin in her lap. Waiting to see if he was going to use silverware to eat the pizza, something her family would have done if they'd ever lowered themselves to order pizza, she grabbed her wine.

"Something wrong?" he asked.

His perception was a bit unnerving. "Ah...I was

waiting to see how you were going to eat your pizza."

His brow furrowed, so she added, "you know, with your hands or a fork."

"Hands work for me if that's okay with you."

"Perfect."

"I forgot to ask if you'd like a salad."

"No, this is fine. I'm not much into salads." And she took a bite of the loaded pizza.

"Another reason to like you," he said. "My sister, Caroline, would be horrified. I think she subsisted on salad all throughout high school."

"That's sad," Jane said as she plucked a piece of sausage off her pizza and popped it into her mouth. Her mother had made her do the same. It was a polite meal, she'd say, and it would ensure they didn't gain any extra pounds for the cameras.

"You really appreciate food," he commented. "And wine."

She raised her glass in a toast. "They go together. To new friends."

"To new friends," he repeated, his eyes meeting hers when their glasses tapped together, the crystal chiming.

It hadn't always been that way between her and food. Growing up, they'd employed a chef. As part of her father's business and political interests, she'd eaten several five-star meals in her own home, paired with the right wine for each course. Just not too much of anything. Her mother had instructed her on the proper portions, which wouldn't have sustained a small bird, and made sure she was never given a large portion of anything. Not even her own birthday cake.

And then Rhett had taken her and Elizabeth to a hole-in-the-wall BBQ place outside Memphis when they'd played a poker tournament at Tunica. The dry rub ribs had been smoked to perfection with pecan wood, something she'd never heard of. The meat had literally fallen off the bones. The rest of the meal had been fried too: okra, mushrooms, French fries, and then fried blackberry pies. But it had finally awakened her taste buds.

The same had happened with champagne. When Rhett won the World Series of Poker, he'd bought the priciest bottle on the hotel's wine list because that's what he thought a man who'd just won seven million dollars should do. She'd hated champagne growing up since it had been associated with memories of her father's pricy political fundraisers.

But drinking it with Rhett and Elizabeth as they laughed over the monumental win…well, that first hit of champagne on her tongue had been like fireworks. From then on, she'd made her peace with the past and ordered whatever bottle suited her fancy. Of course, the finer bottles suited her fancy the most, but since she was a millionaire herself, she could afford it.

"Okay, now that we're safe from interruptions," she said, "why don't you tell me about how you came to own Henry?"

When he didn't say anything for a long moment, she set aside her pizza and waited.

"He was the dog of my final client at the firm in Denver," he finally said, but his reluctance to share more was clear.

When she gazed at him, his face had fallen, and he seemed lost in thought. She trusted her instincts and put her hand on his arm. "Tell me."

He let out a massive sigh. "Well, I suppose I might as well tell you, since…" Those words hung between them for a moment, and then he continued. "I was representing a woman who was dying of pancreatic cancer. A nurse had blown the whistle on my client's doctor. He was giving patients half a dose of their chemo at his cancer clinic and selling the other half on the side. The nurse ended up being discredited in court because her nursing license had been revoked when some drugs were stolen in a clinic where she'd worked ten years ago. There wasn't enough additional evidence of the doctor's malpractice, so we lost the case."

Even she knew there was a heck of a lot more to it than that. Seeing this side of him, a door in her heart simply opened. This was a good man. One she could fall for. She left her hand on his arm.

"My client didn't receive the full dosage of chemo soon enough to help her," he said, looking down at his plate. "Before she passed away, she asked me to take care of her dog...to give him a good life. He was the only family she had. I couldn't refuse her."

"I'm so sorry," she said quietly, remembering how he'd told her earlier that he'd lost faith in the system. God, she couldn't imagine the emotional toll that case must have taken on him. No wonder he'd left Denver afterwards. "It broke your heart. This case."

He pushed his pizza around, not bothering to pick it up. "It's been broken before, but this time...well, it broke my faith in the system. I...just didn't want to be part of cases like that anymore. Not if the wrong people were going to win."

"What was her name?" she asked.

In response to her question, he finally turned his head and met her gaze. "Patricia."

"We'll take care of Henry for Patricia, Matt. I promise." Now Henry's behavior made sense. The dog was grieving.

"People keep saying I should just give him to another family, but I can't. I can't fail her in this too..."

The guilt clearly weighed on him like a stone. She didn't question it, just rose and wrapped her arms around him from behind, resting her chin on his back.

He coughed. "Not exactly light dinner table conversation."

"I grew up with that," she told him. "I hate that. You told me earlier that you'd given him the name Henry."

His hands covered hers. "I...decided to change it. I felt like we both needed a clean break...when I took him on."

Another missing piece of the puzzle.

"Did I do the wrong thing, changing it?" he asked, sighing. "I've tried so hard to do the right thing."

She pressed a kiss to the back of his neck. "I know you have. You've both been through a lot." Henry wasn't the only one who was grieving. "They didn't know Rufus' name when I chose him at the pound. And we've done fine."

"Thank God," he murmured. "Some days I feel like he's punishing me for failing Patricia."

Oh, you poor man. She squeezed him tight. "I expect he's hurting, is all. There's always an adjustment period. Have faith."

He nodded and then edged his chair back so he could pull her onto his lap. His finger stroked her cheek. "Thank you, Jane."

"Thanks for sharing with me."

His hand cupped her face. "Jane," he said. Just once.

And she flowed into him, the kiss as much a comfort as confirmation of this new, fragile connection between them. When they broke apart, his eyes bored deeply into hers, as dark as twilight now.

"You'll have to tell me about yourself now. The good, the bad, the ugly."

"Another time." She made herself smile and slid off his lap.

That was shaky ground, and while his revelation showed what a good man he was, she couldn't tell him all her secrets. Her silence protected the two people she loved most in the world: Elizabeth and Rhett. There were too many good reasons for keeping quiet. This connection with Matt was too new for her to know if it was sturdy enough to entrust him with her dear ones' lives. Or her own.

"You're a good man, Matt Hale," she said.

His mouth quirked up, and some of the sadness weighing down his shoulders seemed to lift. "I'm trying."

They resumed eating, but there was a new quiet between them, as though neither needed to fill the silence. They kept sneaking glances at each other, which made her chest feel tight. For once, it wasn't easy to chow down on pizza. When they finished eating, she insisted on carrying her own plate to the kitchen, but he wouldn't let her load the dishwasher.

Wrapping his arms around her waist, he pulled her close. That spicy aftershave he wore smelled heavenly as she rested her head against his chest. He just held her and then leaned back to caress her cheek.

There were banked fires in his eyes, as though he were giving her the chance to decide if she wanted to stay. But it was too soon for her, and because this new bond with him was special, she didn't want to rush it. Since he wasn't insistent, she figured he was feeling the same way.

She rose on her tiptoes and kissed him on the side of the mouth, not yet bold enough to claim a full kiss. "We should probably go," she said when she was fully back on the ground again.

"Let's get the dogs."

When they entered the mudroom, the dogs were all dozing, but they perked up when she and Matt entered the room. Annie trotted over to them, her tail wagging madly. Rufus only yawned. Jane was extra sweet with Henry now that she knew what he'd been through.

"If you can, leave him in the crate tonight. Let's see if this structure will help. If he puts up a fit when we leave and doesn't settle down, go ahead and take him outside. Where does he usually sleep?"

"With me."

Her face started to flush as she asked, "In his own

bed or yours?"

He took a beat longer to answer, and the awareness crackled between them. "My bed. He wouldn't stop barking when I tried to..."

"Okay," she said quickly, trying to keep her cool, but her mind pumped out horrible visions of her and Matt trying to make love with Henry rudely interrupting them.

As if reading her mind, he murmured, "I'll try the crate tonight," in that same husky voice he'd used before kissing her.

"Good idea. Discipline. Structure." She was so full of shit.

After she dressed for the elements, he insisted on walking her to the car.

"But your coat," she protested.

"I'm a native. Thick blood."

The indigo sky was dotted with stars, and she made out the Big Dipper as she put the dogs in the back.

"Hey," Matt said, placing a hand on her arm when she opened her door. "How about an evening without the dogs? No crazy interruptions from Henry. Just you and me. Dinner? Maybe a movie?"

If her heart could glow, it would have chosen hot pink.

"I'd love that."

"Are you free Saturday night?" he asked.

Elizabeth would cheer the fact that she was finally the one to break up their regular plans with a date. "Great."

"I'll pick you up at seven. Brasserie Dare, okay?"

"I love that place."

"Good," he grinned. "I like to support the family."

"Of course." Suddenly it fully dawned on her. He was related to one of the most powerful and respected families in Dare. He was truly a native here, while she was...not.

"You'll have to tell me about growing up here," she said.

"There are tall tales, but it was great. And Denver was awesome in its own way when we moved there. Different. Bigger. Lots of people. No one cared you were a Hale or expected you to act a certain way because of it."

Yes, she knew how that had felt. Being a Wilcox had been a heavy weight to carry. She'd only broken free of it by becoming Raven.

"Thanks for tonight, Matt. It was...I had a great time."

"Me too."

Was he going to kiss her? He stood there in the cold night with the stars twinkling above them. Then his mouth quirked up, as though he were enjoying something, and he leaned down to brush his lips over hers. It was a slow, gentle kiss—the perfect goodnight kiss, she decided.

"I'll see you soon, Jane. Drive safe."

As she drove off, she touched her fingers to her still tingly lips.

Dialing Elizabeth on the way home, she started to tell her friend about their whole evening. When she finally finished forty-five minutes later, she and the dogs were sitting in front of the fire in her house.

"I'm falling for him, Elizabeth, and it's only been a few days." Even saying it out loud sounded strange, but her body felt that way. It was like she was floating on the clouds she'd seen earlier.

"I know you are," her friend simply replied.

Jane fell back onto the rug and stared up at the ceiling, letting the fire warm her. That was why Elizabeth was her best friend ever. She knew Jane well enough to know she was serious even if some people might think it was crazy to fall this fast, this hard. But it had happened all the same. Matt Hale had stolen her heart over pizza and wine as he told her about defending a cancer patient and then taking in her dog. He was one of the good guys. And he liked her. Part of her still couldn't take that in. He liked the *real* her. The one with the scrawny body. The one with the smart brain.

"I've never felt this way."

"I know."

CHAPTER 9

Zumba, the hot Latin dance class, had arrived in small town Dare Valley, and Elizabeth couldn't have been more delighted. If there was one thing she missed about being Vixen and living in Vegas, it was dancing in the nightclubs.

Granted, a dance class like this didn't boast any men in it save one retired man in his seventies who came with his wife.

Most of the women were married with kids. So far they'd been friendly. Of course, the really uncoordinated ones who stumbled through the steps and couldn't shake their hips if someone was pointing a gun to their head eyed her with envy. But she was used to other women being jealous of her.

Then there were the ones whose mouths dropped open when she did a few of her favorite moves, like bending over and shaking her backside. And when that happened, Elizabeth had to bite her lip to keep from laughing.

Exercising this way wasn't a bad way to burn the calories she had to watch more carefully than Jane. Not that she still had any insecurities when it came to her body. Of course, when she'd met Jane at Harvard, she'd stuck out like a sore thumb at the preppie school. Her long curly blond hair with bangs had been too untamed, her clothing too provocative. When someone had called her trailer park trash, she'd been spurned into action. She and Jane had cut her hair to a one length *boring* bob and dyed it a *serious* dark brown. Then they'd bought her a swathe of dull, curve-concealing clothes. Finally she was taken seriously, but she never felt comfortable in her own skin in those days.

As the spicy Latin beat started, she followed the teacher like the rest of the class into a salsa routine, one that involved shaking her bosom like there was no tomorrow. An hour later, she wiped sweat from her brow and chugged water from her green bottle labeled *Have Fun*. She smiled at the other women as they were leaving. The teacher snagged her by the arm before she could follow them.

"Hey," she said, her sleek body clad in a hot pink workout top and short black leggings. "We haven't officially met. I'm Carol."

"Elizabeth."

"You're really good, which I expect you know already. I was wondering if you'd be interested in teaching a class. We have more interest in Zumba than I expected, and since I'm capping the class at twenty, I need help. I'm teaching two classes on Thursday and Friday already. What do you think?"

Elizabeth scanned the room in the community center. It didn't have any mirrors like her posh gym in Vegas, but the platform in front helped people see the teacher better, especially from the back. This might be fun.

"Maybe. Tell me more."

Twenty minutes later, she had Carol's cell number and a few papers outlining the steps she'd need to take to become certified. Her car was parked on Main Street, so she walked the two blocks over. With her winter gear on, the cold was doable even though her hair was a little damp from her workout. When she reached Main Street, she heard someone call her name. Turning, she made out Ryan James, a guy she'd gone out with a few times.

"Hey," he said when he caught up to her. "You didn't return my calls. I expect you've been busy."

She hadn't been. There wasn't any spark between them, and since she hadn't agreed to make plans for another outing on their last date, she'd hoped he would get the message. "Hi, Ryan. No, everything's been pretty normal on my end."

The words hovered between them, and he frowned. She prayed he wouldn't force her to be blunter. "Look, it's cold, and I need to get home," she finally said. "Have a good night."

As she turned to walk away, he grabbed her arm, and she instantly went on alert. "Hey!"

"Sorry, but...Elizabeth, I'd really like to go out with you again. I thought you and I had a real connection."

Struggling to stay calm, she removed her arm. He didn't fight her, which made her want to heave a sigh of relief. "Ryan, listen, I'm sorry, but I didn't feel that way. I'm sure you'll find someone special, but I'm not the one, okay?"

He stepped closer, making her want to edge back. "But I thought—"

"Ryan, I'm heading to my car now. Goodbye." Any further conversation with this guy wasn't going to do much good for either of them.

Fortunately, he didn't follow her, and when she reached her car, she immediately locked her doors. Suffocating fear threatened to pull her under, and her hands shook as she tried to start the engine.

She might feel mostly safe in Dare, but old habits

died hard. Being un-costumed only made her feel more vulnerable, as though there were nothing to hide behind. On the way home she checked her rearview mirror constantly to make sure he wasn't following her, totally paranoid now.

The freedom and joy she'd felt while dancing was a distant memory.

CHAPTER 10

A couple of mornings later, Matt headed over to The Grand Mountain Hotel to see his cousin, Jill. Between owning Don't Soy with Me, serving as the hotel's creative director, and taking care of her baby twins, she barely had a spare minute, so Matt thought it was best to grab her during the work day. Jill was extremely well connected in the community and would have some useful advice for him on his run for mayor.

He and Andy had come to the hotel for a boys' night out after they first arrived in Dare. They'd both lost at poker to some pros staying at the hotel, but it had been a fun time anyway.

When he wasn't out in the elements running or skiing, Matt used the hotel's state-of-the-art health club to work out, like he planned to do today. He loved the weight room and had become pampered enough at his Denver gym to still want to hit the steam room or sauna occasionally, especially when it was freezing outside.

As he drove down the driveway, the majesty of the restored hotel rose up before him. A few people were skiing on the slopes of the mountain, and they looked like small ants sliding down an enormous hill. The stone work of the two-story structure held the gravitas of another age while the windows sparkled in the sunlight. Unlike most of the casinos Matt had visited for bachelor parties, this one was full of light. There were no dank, dark gambling rooms here. The hotel was warm and inviting. He and Andy needed another night out, he decided as he parked in the underground garage, grabbed his gym bag, and went to find his cousin.

Jill's office was on the second floor in an alcove housing hotel management. He nodded to Casey, Mac's receptionist, whom he knew from his visits to the hotel to meet Jill for an occasional lunch.

"Hi, Matt," she said, her sleek brown ponytail accentuating rose-tinted cheekbones that made him think of Jane. Jane had her beat in the cheekbones department.

And then he realized he was actually comparing women's cheekbones. Dear God.

"Hey, Casey," he greeted in return.

When he entered Jill's office, he braced himself against the glare. His cousin had a major Salvador Dali obsession. The wall behind her desk was painted bright turquoise with a streak of red across the middle. The side walls were the same fiery red. Then there was the ceiling. It was a violet purple with a white metal mini-chandelier showcasing ten small cranes.

"You know," he said as he crossed to her desk, "I'm always amazed Mac let you decorate your office like this."

She jumped out of her seat and rushed over to him with her trademark enthusiasm. Her hug might have cracked a few ribs, but he bit back his groan. Otherwise she'd rib him about being a wimp. It was what cousins did.

"Mac adores me. He knows I work better in surroundings that suit my creative pallet."

"Plus, there's no way Brian would let you do something like this at your house."

Their new home had streaks of bold color throughout and enough brightly colored pillows to arm a hundred people in a pillow fight. But nothing *this* out there.

"His vision is limited when it comes to color. We had to do some compromising." She led him over to a purple leather couch—another monstrosity, especially since it was Italian—and bounced on the cushions. "So, you'd better be here to tell me what I think you're going to tell me."

He hummed. So Uncle Arthur had spilled the beans. "And what's that?" he asked, just to be contrary.

She shoved him in the chest back against the cushions. "That you're going to run for mayor."

His conversation with Jane the other night had only strengthened his resolve. The system was broken, and he had to start somewhere if he wanted to fix things. He loved Dare, and it would be a good place to begin. There was no way he could run for an elected office in the big city. Perhaps in time, but he needed to establish a new resume, one that went beyond being a lawyer. Those were a dime a dozen. Dare had a good education system, an expanding health care system, a prized local university, and a thriving community. He could be a part in making the town he loved even stronger.

"I am. Running, that is."

Her squeal pretty much punctured his eardrum, and he would have rubbed it if she hadn't launched herself at him to deliver another python-style hug.

"God, you really do remind me of Henry."

She punched him in the shoulder. "Better watch it. Aren't you here to ask for my help?"

"Yes, especially with the business community. Now, I know you have lots going on—"

"Are you kidding? You'll be the first Hale to give it a

go. I'm almost put out about that. I plan to run someday too, but this isn't the right time." Her face formed a pout before she bounced on the cushions again in excitement, her red curls dancing.

"Well, I can thank Emmits Merriam for that," he said. "The man was smart enough to petition the town council to change the residency requirements in the 1940s when he was thinking about running for mayor. Since I lived here before for at least three years consecutively for six months each year, I meet the requirements."

"Emmits was always creating a political loophole to help promote his personal interests. Oh, I wish I could have met him. Grandpa's stories about him are legendary."

"So, a friend of mine who's a political consultant in Denver is coming down to help out here and there, but his suggestion was that I get the list of every organization that's registered with the Chamber of Commerce. Our plan is to send out letters to them, announcing my intention to run for mayor and my desire to meet with them and their members. The first hurdle will be the primary in May."

"Well, you'll likely run unopposed in the primary once you announce. Everyone's wanted a Hale to run for mayor since our family first put down roots here. The current mayor, Jim Kewars, is from the other party, and while he's okay, he hasn't been a vibrant leader. He's part of the old school Dare Valley political machine. But no one would challenge him. We need new blood. New ideas. You!"

Her enthusiasm was everything he could hope for. "Jill, seriously, I have lots to catch up on with Dare. I've been gone for a long time, and family visits don't exactly count. Tell me the truth. Do you think I have a chance? Or should I take another year to settle in and become more established in the community?"

"Like it's in your nature to wait," she scoffed. "When you told me you were moving home, I worried about you. You can't go from driving eighty miles an hour on the interstate to thirty on a county road."

"Point taken. Okay, let me tell you what I'm thinking campaign-wise. I...ah...already have a platform in mind."

"Of course, you do, being Mr. Lawyer Superhero. Give it to me."

Her brow wrinkled as he talked, and she rose to grab a florescent green legal pad—dear God, when had they started making them in that color?—and a purple pen with sparkles. She didn't interrupt once. A rare thing for his cousin. She just took notes.

When he finished, she unloaded on him, throwing question after question at him for the next thirty minutes. Some he could answer. Others he flat out flubbed, causing her to cry out, "Aha and gotcha." They brainstormed. Refined his ideas. He grabbed a clean legal pad from his gym bag and one of the hotel pens, scribbling down some of her ingenious suggestions.

Top of the list. Accompanying Uncle Arthur to Bingo Night.

"Why?" he asked stupidly.

"Because it's the hotbed of the old guard, one of the biggest grist mills in town, and because being seen there with Grandpa will help win people over. The Hale name is nice, but you need to shake hands with the old ladies and fist bump the old guys."

"Seriously, Jill? Fist bump them? These guys are veterans."

"Okay, maybe not fist bumps. You might break their arthritic wrists. But you know what I mean."

"I'm waiting for you to suggest kissing babies next."

"Oh, I can do better than that. You can come with me to my La Leche Group."

He gulped. "Isn't that a breastfeeding group?"

"We don't only talk about our boobies. In fact, some of the girls are downright funny. You should hear the new names they've come up with for Don't Soy with Me now that I'm pumping like a maniac for Mia and Violet. My favorite is—"

"No. Please. God. Don't tell me!" Okay, so his Inner Alpha drew the line at breastfeeding talk.

She shoved off the couch and pointed to a machine that looked like...

Oh no. She had her pumping...machine in full view. If only he could go blind at will.

"You men think you're so big and tough. If you had to stick your boob in that contraption four hours a day—"

"Jill. Please. I beg you. Do you want to hear that women are superior? That you beat the male sex hands down?"

Her shoulder lifted. "Yeah."

He had three sisters. He knew how to keep the peace. "Well, you do. I bow to your superiority."

"Good. Now, just one more thing. The reason you've come back to Dare... It's not enough to talk about the evils of the big city."

"I wasn't saying—"

"It's implied. You need to talk about your last case. How the system failed your client."

His chest grew tight. Talking to Jane about it the other night had been challenging enough, but telling the townspeople of Dare? "But I failed her, Jill. Why would I want to focus on that?"

Her eyes softened. "First, you didn't fail her. The system did. Second, because it humanizes you and makes people see your lion's heart. It shows why you want to be a community leader. Why you want to make things better for people."

He'd never been comfortable talking about himself and his motives. "I don't know."

"Matt, growing up, I always admired you and Andy for your total save-the-world complexes. If you don't share this, you'll come off as nothing but a burned-out lawyer who's returned home from the big city with his tail between his legs. It might be enough to win you the primary, but it's not enough to beat Jim. Plus, it's time to show people there's more to you than the lawyer."

He knew she was right, but he'd always been private—something that was about to change big time now that he was running for mayor. Deep down, he'd pretty much thought his profession defined him. Now he was searching for a more meaningful existence, but the price would be his privacy. "Okay, what do you suggest?"

"Let Tanner do an interview. Man to man. He's not a Hale, and while he's married to one, people know he has his own mind. They respect that. Plus, he has the same save-the-world complex you do, although it's more balanced these days now that he's married to Meredith."

"She got lucky with him. He's a good guy."

"Yes, Tanner is the best. I've never had a brother, so I'm feeling pretty lucky these days. Even if he's as big of a wimp about breastfeeding as you are."

"We men grovel at your feet, Jill."

She snorted. "So, I've also heard through the grapevine, aka your brother, that you and Jane Wilcox have been spending some time together. Do tell."

Shit, she was going to be as bad as his sisters. Andy was probably delighting in the prospect of him being ribbed and tortured by their family.

"We're just starting to get to know each other." Although he still didn't feel like he knew much.

"I like her," Jill said. "Anyone Mac and Rhett are over the moon about... Well. I hear she's helping with Henry."

That was practically an understatement at this point. Jane was even more helpful now that she knew about Patricia. She had researched grieving dogs and refined their training sessions to target Henry's problems. The dog seemed to be responding better, even if he was still rambunctious and totally disobedient with Matt. It was like he couldn't forgive Matt for failing his former owner.

"Since you brought Jane up, how much did you interact with her when she worked at the hotel?" he asked. Might as well see what other information he could uncover. Jane wasn't saying much, using the dogs to slip through the conversation volleys he'd thrown at her since their first kiss.

"Hardly any. She and Elizabeth worked exclusively for Mac on special projects. Hush, hush. Strange hours too. Sometimes they worked from home. I was pregnant when they got here and had baby brain, meaning I don't remember many details about that time. Then I went on maternity leave. Mac has a lot going on around here all the time, so it didn't seem too strange."

Interesting. But still as clear as mud. "Mac wasn't upset with Rhett for stealing them away?"

"Nah. They're old pals. They'd never let business come between them. Rhett probably asked for Mac's blessing before hiring them." Then she narrowed her eyes. "Lots of questions, Mr. Lawyer. What's up with that?"

He held up his hands. "You brought her up. I was just making conversation."

"You were making something, all right."

"I'm going to hit the gym and let you get back to work. Thanks for helping me think things through, and for supporting my plan to run for mayor. And please don't say anything to anyone. It's early days yet." Jill had been the biggest blabber mouth growing up, but he'd needed her advice badly enough to risk it.

"So long as you promise you won't make a lifelong career out of being mayor. I want the office in the courthouse to be all mine one day. Mwuh-ha-ha-ha."

He pulled her in for another hug. "You're terrifying."

"Tell Brian that. I need to keep him on his toes a little more. Getting me all barefoot and pregnant so soon has made him lax."

An eye roll seemed appropriate. "He adores you, and before you hit me, I'm leaving. Bye, cuz."

"Bye, Matty Ice."

"Shit," he said, closing the door. He'd hoped that nickname was going to die in Denver. Of course his sisters had told her. It was probably their idea of torture by proxy.

Time in the gym helped him mentally focus. He mulled over Jill's ideas as he lifted, laughing out loud as he thought about attending Bingo night with Uncle Arthur. Well, no one had said politics was easy.

He was bench pressing about three hundred pounds when Rhett appeared by his side. "Need a spotter?"

"Sure," he replied even though he could lift this much safely without any assistance.

They completed the weight circuit, the two of them trading off to spot each other. And then Rhett had to up the ante and started betting him twenty dollars who could lift more. Matt's muscles were shaking by the time they finished, and he'd only lost twenty bucks. Considering that he was up against a professional gambler, he felt pretty good about that.

"So, I hear you've been spending some time with my girl," Rhett said casually in his signature Southern drawl as he wiped sweat off his face.

The Dare grapevine seemed to be doing overtime. Probably Jill was to blame for this one. "Your girl?" he asked, since it seemed like a pretty sexist thing to call his employee.

"Jane," he said. "She'd probably kick me for calling her my girl, but she works for me, so it's how I see it. I look after my own."

His protective stance was puzzling since Jane could only have worked for him for a few months tops. "Okay."

"Just telling you to be good to her, or you'll answer to me."

Matt wasn't short by any means, but at six feet six inches, Rhett towered over him—an abnormal situation for Matt. But he didn't intimidate easily.

"Since I plan to be good to her, I doubt we'll have a problem."

The man studied him for a long moment and then slapped him on the back. It took effort not to jog a few steps forward from the force.

"Good. Glad that's clear. Y'all have a good day."

Rhett sauntered off, leaving him even more puzzled.

Jane was utterly sweet and had a big heart, but Rhett certainly hadn't known her long enough to be this defensive. She'd hooked him pretty fast too—they'd gone from barely acknowledging each other in the park to pretty much seeing each other every day—but that was different...

Yes, there was something wrong here. Jill knew squat about Jane's position at the hotel, which was odd, and now her boss had put him on notice about hurting her.

It was time to do more digging.

CHAPTER 11

It was Saturday, the night of Jane's big date night with Matt, and Elizabeth was helping dress her to the nines and do her makeup. Tonight Jane didn't have to try to look cute in what she now called "park gear." Brasserie Dare's patrons went from casual to classy, and she planned on being in the latter category. Somehow she imagined Matt would do the same.

"How do I look?" she asked Elizabeth.

"For the hundredth time, you look beautiful."

Jane gazed at herself in the mirror. They'd chosen a Chanel aubergine dress that draped over her breasts, adding a little extra volume to that area. With the bias cut of the neckline, her creamy skin glowed against the fabric. The skirt was loose since she essentially had no hips, but she was wearing killer silver heels to give her a little height and accentuate her toned legs. Her feet protested even these piddly heels, only three inches high, after having been freed from Raven's "stilts" over a month ago.

"Are you sure about the heels?" she asked again. "What if I fall and break something? It's winter."

"That's what a man's arm is for. This way you get to touch him under the pretense of needing support."

"Or he'll think I'm an idiot for wearing them."

"I doubt it. He'll be looking at your legs, which really look fantastic, by the way. If I was a man, I'd totally do you."

"As you've said constantly since our first party together at Harvard," Jane said with a laugh. "I really like this necklace, but you don't think it's too big?"

Designed with Cleopatra in mind, the four large silver strands flowed over the aubergine material, creating a dramatic effect.

Elizabeth's caramel hair swayed as she shook her head. "It's fine. And before you ask me one more time, no, we did not make your eyes too smoky for that dress. It's perfect with the pale pink lipstick and liner. And just look at your lashes. I wish mine could be that thick and long without falsies."

The only thing that could possibly be deemed wanting about Elizabeth's appearance was her eyelashes. They were thin and pale blond. Jane pitied her. Not.

Checking her slender silver wristwatch, she realized it was close to seven. "Okay, let's head to the living room. It's almost time for Matt to arrive. But promise me you're going to—"

"Hide," Elizabeth finished. "Of course. I'll hang with the dogs for a bit and then take off. Looks like I'm going to be the one watching the movie alone tonight."

"You could have gone out with...with *him* again," she said as they walked to the front of the house. She winced when she couldn't remember the guy's name.

"Yes, but then I'd risk stabbing myself in the eye or stabbing him out of boredom, so it's for the best. He's way too nice for me."

"You always say that. You deserve a nice guy, Liz."

"The problem is that I'm just not attracted to them. And even nice guys aren't always what they appear to be."

Jane's mind leaped to the story Elizabeth had told her about the guy who'd cornered her near her car. It made Jane's heart bleed to see her friend so scared. "I wish I could find you someone who's nice *and* attractive."

"Honey, let's concentrate on you right now," she said as they walked into the living room. "From what you've said, Matt's got it all. Winner, winner, chicken dinner."

Since she was being totally neurotic—and she knew it—Jane shook out the black velvet coat they'd selected for her to wear. Rearranged her silver cashmere scarf. Straightened her black velvet gloves.

"Jane. Your OCD is showing."

"I know. I just want everything to be perfect."

Her friend wrapped her arms around her and lifted her off the ground in a bone-cracking hug, making her laugh.

"Perfect is overrated. Have fun! That's the key to a great date. Sit back. Enjoy flirting with him. Hell, enjoy being without the canine clan."

Rufus whined at that comment. "I know, honey," Jane said, walking over to him and rubbing his shiny coat. "She just doesn't get it."

"I do. I just think it will be nice for neither of you to have to worry about cleaning up doggie business during your time together."

She shrugged. "You're right. Poop isn't romantic."

The sound of Matt's SUV crunching on the snow in her driveway had Rufus and Annie trotting over to the front door in anticipation. Jane was reaching for her coat when her friend stopped her with a hand.

"No, let him see you like this first. Then he can help you with your coat."

"Okay," she said when she heard a car door slam. "Thanks. Now hide."

"The things you do for a sister," Elizabeth said with a wink as she high-tailed it out of the room.

There was a cute rap on the door—who knew a sound like that could be cute?—so she smoothed her hands down the front of her dress, took a deep breath, and went to answer it.

Matt had on a red scarf and a long cashmere double-breasted coat in navy blue. It was the most formal attire she'd ever seen him wear, and she had to admit that she really liked it.

His mouth dropped open when he caught sight of her. "Wow! I mean...you look incredible."

When he simply stood there, his eyes sweeping from her face all the way down to her shoes, she strove to remain calm.

"Are you sure we shouldn't be heading to one of the finest restaurants in Denver tonight? Dare might not know what to do with you, Jane."

Heat suffused her cheeks. "Oh, stop."

He came inside and stomped his shoes on the rug and then followed her to the couch, where she'd laid out her coat. "Seriously, Jane. You look beautiful."

And as she met his eyes, his gaze smoldering, she knew he meant it. She wanted to run and kiss her best friend on the cheek for helping, but of course she couldn't. "You look handsome too."

"Had to dig out some of the big city clothes for tonight," he commented and reached for her coat and held it out for her.

She threaded her arms into the sleeves, and when his hands settled on her shoulders, she felt his face near her neck. "You smell good too," he murmured, making her wonder if he was going to kiss her now, before they even left.

Annie barked once, and he stepped away. "Sorry, was I ignoring you? Hey, Annie." He gave her a good scratch behind the ears and then did the same with Rufus when he padded over. "Ah, you guys spoil me. Makes me think someday Henry might be as nice as you."

Elizabeth was right. It *was* going to be nice to be away from the dogs for a night. No interruptions.

"Did something new happen with him?" she asked as she adjusted her scarf and tugged on her gloves. Her head was going to freeze, but Elizabeth had argued adamantly against a hat.

"He peed on my bed, the stinker. Wasn't happy when I got home and saw that."

Uh-oh. That wasn't good. "Anything unusual happen today?"

"Since I saw you yesterday at the park? No. He's like a general. He always concocts a new strategy for breaking me."

She smiled and held out her hands to him. "You won't break."

He hesitated and then took them. "You sound pretty sure about that."

"I have a sixth sense about people. You're not going to fold." Grabbing her silver clutch, she walked to the door.

"Rhett's poker talk must be rubbing off on you," he commented as he came up behind her.

If only he knew. Poker had taught her a lot about people and a lot about life. She had a knack for seeing who would break and what it would take—at the table and in life. Matt might crack around the edges, but he wouldn't break. He had too much internal strength and integrity for that.

God, she was really into him.

"Shall we?" she asked, giving Annie and Rufus a last rubdown before walking through the door. "Bye guys. You behave."

After she locked the door, she cocked her head. "Ah, do you mind giving me your arm down the stairs? The heels..."

"Of course," he replied and held it out.

As she edged closer to him, his body heat wrapped around her, and his scent—all spicy and fresh—had her awareness of him growing. He opened her door and saw her inside before heading around to the driver's side. She'd known he was a gentleman to the core, but it was nice to be treated with such care. She settled back into the seat.

"How about a hot seat?" he asked.

It took her a second to figure out what he meant, and she finally laughed when she did. "Oh, a butt warmer. Sure."

Within minutes, her seat was toasty. As Matt maneuvered the snowy roads on the bench to downtown Dare, he asked her about her day, which had mostly been filled with preparation for their date. Not that she told him that.

He cruised down Maple Street and found a space on Aspen, the cross street. "Let me come around," he said when she unbuckled her seatbelt. "Don't want you to slip."

Music to her ears. It was lovely to stroll with her arm threaded through his down the short stretch to Brasserie Dare, which was one street over from Main Street. Downtown Dare was brightly lit with street lights from another era mixed in with modern lampposts designed to blend in. The brick storefronts always reminded her of the small town she was from, right outside of Greenwich. Oh, how she'd hated it.

Jane had arrived in Dare with a chip on her shoulder, certain that the townspeople were going to be as cliquey and nosy as they'd been in Greenwich. But everyone in Dare had been nothing but welcoming. Sure there was an old guard, and she was a newcomer, but that didn't seem to matter. Yes, people asked about her business in a way they hadn't in Vegas, but so far, a few pleasantries had managed to sidetrack even the most curious of interrogators.

Of course, no one really knew who she was or what she'd done with her life. She planned to keep it that way. Having strutted by a few locals in her six-inch hooker heels as Raven at The Grand Mountain Hotel when Rhett had played poker there, she'd seen the disapproval and flat-out judgment in their gazes.

No, Jane Wilcox blended in much better, and she planned on keeping her past and present distinctly separate.

The stores around Brasserie Dare were closed, but through the lights in the front windows, she made out some Impressionistic art in one gallery and a collection of lovely hand-blown vases, arranged in a rainbow of color, in the craft shop next door.

When they stepped into Brasserie Dare, Jane inhaled deeply, loving the smell of freshly baked French bread, which was cooked in the brick oven in the middle of the restaurant, right in front of the guests. Bread was her weakness, she had to admit, and if she wasn't careful, she could inhale a whole baguette by herself.

"Matt," the hostess at the welcome stand said. "It's good to see you. Can we check your coats?"

Once again, Matt helped Jane with her coat. Then he helped her with her scarf too, his fingers lightly brushing against her neck and chin, lighting fires along her nerve endings.

"I can—"

"Allow me," he murmured, causing her hands to fall to her sides.

Having a man remove her scarf with the slowness Matt was employing felt as decadent and sensual as could be, and judging from the twinkle in his blue eyes, he darn well knew what he was doing.

"Are you planning to help me with my gloves too?" she quipped.

"That might be a little too much for this place. It's a family establishment, you know."

She had to fight a smile. The hostess returned after dealing with their coats. "We have your table ready," she said. "Please follow me."

Once they reached the table, Matt pulled out her chair and seated her before taking his own. No date had done that for her since her Harvard days, and even then, they'd done it more out of propriety than anything else. Deep down, she knew Matt was acting like a gentleman because he *was* a gentleman, so she didn't mind the extra attention.

"I'll just let Brian know you've arrived. He wanted to come out and say hello." The hostess hurried into the kitchen.

Jane smiled when the server appeared—an eager college student if she was to lay a bet—and disappeared after bringing them menus and waters.

Brian strode through the dining hall wearing a chef hat that resembled a limp mushroom. The name of his restaurant was stitched on his chef's jacket in red thread, and his pants were a black and white houndstooth she'd seen chefs wear on TV.

"Hey, Matt. Hi, Jane. Welcome to Brasserie Dare."

Matt and Brian shook hands easily, while Jane only nodded.

"So," Brian said, turning to her. "Matt tells me you have quite the affinity for wine."

She met Matt's eyes and quirked her brow. What was he up to? "Yes," she said. "Having been trained at the Culinary Institute of America, I'm sure you have one as well."

"I do," he said and shared another glance with Matt. "That's why we have a special treat for you tonight. I'm going to uncork this baby myself."

When he left their table, she looked over at Matt, who was sitting back in his chair, all casual elegance.

"What did you do?"

"You'll see," he said.

Soon Brian was back with a bottle and a waiter's corkscrew. Their server followed him and set two red wine glasses on the table. Brian strategically turned the bottle away so she couldn't see the label.

"How about a blind test?" he said, a challenge in his eyes. "I want to see if your palate is as good as Matt claims."

"Okay. Do you have a blindfold lying around somewhere?" she boldly asked.

"You could use Matt's tie and go all *Fifty Shades* on us, but I do try to run a family-friendly establishment."

Matt chuckled. "Please tell me you didn't read that book."

Brian waggled his brows. "Jill did. She only shared the interesting parts."

Good God. Were two attractive men really discussing *Fifty Shades* right in front of her? She felt a blush breaking out across her face. Okay, Elizabeth had read her the dirty parts too. She'd been horrified. And she'd needed to ask what some things meant, which had only made Elizabeth guffaw and fall off the couch.

"I assume you mean that wine? You're covering the label, so I think we're safe." She gestured to the bottle.

He poured her an ounce and extended the glass to her, which she picked up with excitement. Her eyes fluttered shut as the mingled aromas of black cherries, oak, spice, and a hint of plum hit her nose. Bold mature fruit. Just the way she liked it.

"Clos de Vougeot. Grand Cru." she said after all of ten seconds.

Like Chanel No. 5, a Clos de Vougeot had a signature scent. One she could never forget.

"Holy crap," she heard Brian say.

"Told ya," Matt responded, but she was so eager to taste the incredible wine that she ignored them and took a sip. The richness of the Vougeot valley flowed into her mouth, and in her mind, she could see the vineyards under the hot French sun and the warm stone of the mansion where the wine was made. She'd visited France many times, and with each trip, she always dove into another part of the wine country. She had been to this particular vineyard many times. Had sipped from its barrels. The pleasure of that magical time swirled through her as she swallowed the wine. The richness of the flavor tantalized her taste buds before nestling back into the deepest corners of her mouth, fading like the kiss of a lover after a heartfelt goodbye.

She opened her eyes, and her gaze locked with Matt's. Those blue flames were so intense she set the glass aside to look at him.

"Care to guess the year?" Brian asked.

That was always a little tricky, but she took another sip, letting the fruit slide over her tongue, tasting the minerals and the early spring of the wine. "Well, I'd say 1997."

"You're kidding me," Brian said. "If I didn't have twins to support, I'd give you the bottle on the house. There aren't too many people who can do what you just did."

Now she was really blushing. "Well...I've taken a lot of courses at the Rudd Center for Professional Wine Studies."

"Hey, that's part of the Culinary Institute of America!" Brian exclaimed.

"Yes," she answered, "but in Napa, as you know."

"I take it that you didn't know that, Matt," Brian said, brow cocked.

"No," he said, never taking his eyes off her. "But I've learned that Jane is full of surprises."

The soft smile she gave him was irrepressible.

"Well, then. I'm going to let you enjoy the wine. Jane, if you fancy something that's not on the menu, the server can run it past me. If I can do it, I will. I can't wait to tell Jill about this." He was still shaking his head as he went back to the kitchen.

Their server, who had been standing at Brian's side, topped off Jane's glass and then poured one for Matt. As she drifted away, they lifted their glasses.

"To new possibilities," he murmured, and his husky voice made her feel like each syllable was crashing into her skin.

She clicked her glass to his and watched him take a sip of the wine. His eyes fluttered shut just like hers had. "Would it be really awkward if I groaned?" he asked.

Even though her belly tightened, she was able to laugh. "No. It's worth groaning over, but I have to ask. How did you find a bottle of this?"

"I asked Brian to get something special. He called in a favor with a restaurant in Denver that I happen to know has an excellent wine cellar."

"Matt, this really is too much. You were squeamish about sharing one of my expensive bottles with you, and now this?"

He covered her hand. "Don't give it a thought. Really, Jane. I wanted to do something...*more* than the usual."

Well, a thousand-dollar bottle of wine shipped from a city a couple hours away was pretty darn special. "Thank you."

"You're welcome. Now, let's see what Brian has for us to eat."

He picked up his menu, but Jane had trouble concentrating. Inside she felt a change brewing—just like when the grapes were macerated and transformed into something beautiful and different. Matt was the magician. She looked over his shoulder and caught her reflection in the wide mirror on the far wall, which had been designed to give the impression of more space. Jane saw a new swan—one that didn't need any props for vanity. It held its head up proudly, knowing it was something special, that it was beautiful just as it was.

Tears gathered in her eyes, and she yanked her gaze down to the menu to keep Matt from seeing her reaction.

When the server came for their order, she said she'd start with the selection of pates accompanied by French baguette—yes, please—and cornichons, her favorite. Who didn't like little pickles? For her entrée, she went with the whole fish, and when the server asked her if she wanted it deboned tableside, she said she could handle it. Matt's mouth tipped up at that, but she ignored him. He ordered the mussels and then the steak and *pommes frites* for an entrée.

The server took their menus. The candle on the table flickered as the other diners' conversations swirled around them.

"This is incredible. Truly, Matt."

"Glad you like it. So..."

He was studying her, rather like he was trying to figure her out.

"So?"

"Since we're out on an official date, this is where you tell me all about where you're from, what your family was like, etc."

Oh God. That was exactly what she didn't want to do. "Really?" Then she realized how Elizabeth would respond to that. "But that's so boring," she said.

"No, seriously. I want to know."

Damn. She liked being out with him, but all this stuff about her past was ruining the relaxation and ease she'd felt.

"Okay," he said with a sigh, "how about an easy one? Did you have any dogs growing up?"

"One," she responded, and the pain of the situation rose within her again. "We had a lab." Because it was a decent, all-American breed. Her father had been down in the polls, and his advisor had told him buying a puppy for his daughter and releasing the pictures would give him a bump. She'd been in kindergarten at the time. She'd been elated by the arrival of the puppy...right up until she discovered it couldn't come inside unless photos were needed.

"Where were you just now?" Matt asked, taking a slow sip of his wine.

Shaking off the old memories, she lifted her glass as well. "Nowhere important. My background is pretty dull. Why don't you tell me about growing up here? Did you know Brian when you were kids? He seems nice."

He studied her for a moment longer, and then started to tell her stories about growing up in Dare. Where his family had lived. What it had been like to share a bathroom with three sisters. How he'd gone to high school here and that his family had moved to Denver when he was a senior in college since his dad had been offered an amazing position as a surgeon at Denver's best hospital. And yes, how he'd teased Jill and Brian mercilessly when they were kids since he was older than they were.

When her appetizer arrived, the contrast of the pate and the warm crusty baguette blew her away. Her favorite was boar's meat and pistachio with a hint of brandy. She spread some on a piece of bread for Matt to enjoy.

"That's good," he declared, so she made him another. "Never would have imagined liking boar. Try some mussels."

The garlic, white wine, butter, and parsley blended into the perfect sauce for the mussel she tried. "Oh, that's delicious. Do you like escargot?" she asked Matt.

"Snails? I tried them once, but couldn't stop thinking of putting salt on the slugs that used to feed on the plants in my mother's garden."

That made Jane laugh again. The server poured both of them more of the delicious Grand Cru, and she found herself relaxing again. Matt regaled her with a story about an elderly woman coming into his office to set up an education trust for her grandchildren. How she'd baked him a dozen chocolate chip cookies to welcome him back home to Dare.

"It must be nice to have roots here," she said as the server cleared their first course and scraped the baguette crumbs off the tablecloth.

"It is. Coming back with my brother and nephew, not to mention my mom, is just about perfect. We're hoping to talk my sisters into coming too. Denver's great, but the work/life balance sucks. Not to mention the traffic. What about where you lived before Dare? Was there a lot of traffic?"

Gads, he just wasn't going to give up. "Ah, some," she commented and reached for her glass again.

"You're going to have to tell me something, Jane."

Right. Or this wouldn't go any further. She could almost hear the hidden message behind his words.

"We can only talk about dogs so much. Or stocks. Come on. You can trust me." The earnestness in his gaze confirmed what she already knew, but there were some secrets—not all her own—that she just couldn't share.

"I lived in Nevada," she said, feeling like she was navigating a minefield. Plus, he was a lawyer, so she could all but feel him circling the conversation back to what he truly wanted to know.

More about her.

On any other date, she would have been flattered.

"Are you going to make me guess?" he asked as the server set their entrées in front of them.

"Las Vegas," she said and was delighted to see how clear the color of her fish's eyes were. You could always tell how fresh a fish was by its eyes, and this Branzino looked like it had just been caught, packed in ice, and shipped to Brian's back door.

"Ah, so that's the poker connection," Matt said. "Did

you meet Mac there?"

How to answer? She'd known Mac for a long time. She concentrated on her dish, edging back the fish's skin and then slicing through the middle and lifting it off the bones in one fell swoop.

"You look like a pro," he commented, gesturing to her plate.

"I...ah, ate a lot of fish growing up," she commented.

"And where would that be?" he asked, cutting a piece of steak, perfectly served to order medium rare.

"Back east."

"Jane."

"Fine. Connecticut." She bit off, *happy now?* Then she realized she was being a bitch. "I'm sorry for being so querulous, Matt. They just aren't good memories—not like yours with your family."

"That's definitely a Harvard word," he mused. "Querulous."

"You're a lawyer. I bet you use those five-cent words pretty often yourself."

His mouth tipped up. "Only to intimidate witnesses."

"Nice." But she knew how it worked. Her father had wanted her to go to law school, but she'd managed to convince him an MBA would be better for the family manufacturing business. She'd feigned an interest in taking over, even though she'd had no intention of doing so. She apparently did have something from him inside her, but it wasn't a part of herself she liked.

"Jane," he said, giving her a few French fries. "I'm not trying to unsettle you. I'm only trying to get to know you better."

"I've told you all the important things. I love dogs and wine and stocks and..." Even to her it seemed lame.

"Can you tell me about what you did at The Grand Mountain Hotel? Before you started working with Rhett?"

She looked down in her lap. God, this whole date was falling apart. Without the dogs, she had no way of distracting him, and by withholding information about herself, she was making him think she wasn't interested.

"Matt," she said, "I'm glad you want to know more about me. I want that too, but honestly, there's a lot I don't want to talk about. The past is in the past, and I want it to stay there. Can you understand that?"

He set his fork aside. "Of course I can, but sometimes it's good to trust other people, Jane."

"I can't talk about the hotel and my work there." She lifted her glass and took another sip, not tasting the wine at this point. "I signed a non-disclosure agreement."

Something flickered in his eyes. "I see. I remember Mac made Jill sign one when she first started working for him."

Whew! Well, that helped her case. She wasn't about to correct him by saying she'd signed one for Rhett, not Mac, or that she and Elizabeth had been the ones to make him draw one up for them. They'd done it to protect him from any questions that might arise if it should become known they were more than his poker babes. Their disguises had allowed them front-row access to the tables at some of the bigger tournaments, which could potentially cause trouble for Rhett.

Of course, the main tourney for the World Series of Poker was now happening in two stages, beginning in the summer. Since the final table was now played in the fall, there was ample time for all the final contenders to study tape and scout their competition. But it hadn't always been that way. Some troublemaker could raise a fuss about how close Vixen and Raven had gotten to the other players while they were posing as Rhett's pretty companions.

Matt wiped his mouth with his napkin. "Okay, Jane. We'll do it your way. For now." His gaze was steady, but she saw steely determination there. "How's the fish?" he asked, and for the rest of the meal he didn't pepper her with any more personal questions.

Sated on a dessert of fresh strawberries, chocolate ganache, and Chantilly cream, she walked back to the car with her arm linked through Matt's. He'd grown quiet after paying the bill, and part of her feared she'd ruined everything with her silence.

When he arrived at her place, he came around and helped her up the stairs. As she unlocked the door, the dogs pranced out, nudging her ankles. She leaned down and petted them both, glad to be home.

"Hey, guys," Matt said, scratching them behind their ears when they headed over to him for a greeting.

When she turned toward the door, he grabbed her arm and steered her inside, closing the door behind him.

"It's too cold outside to give you a proper kiss," Matt mused.

"You're going to kiss me?" she baldly asked.

"That's what usually happens after a date," he commented, a wry smile appearing on his lips. "Why are you surprised?"

Her chest grew tight, and she realized she had to give him some sort of honesty, even if it was only about how she felt, not who she was or who she'd been.

"I was afraid...that you wouldn't want to...you know, since I didn't answer all your questions..."

He drew her to him and tipped up her chin. "Not want to kiss you? Did you not see what you were doing to me while you sampled that wine in the restaurant?"

"But that was before..." She gestured with her hands.

He captured one and brought it to his lips, the gesture totally disarming her. "I can be patient."

Her breath rushed out then. "I need you to be, Matt. I don't want to mess this up, but there's so much I don't want to say. Can't say. It doesn't mean I don't like you."

He dropped her hand and gently cupped her cheek. "And just because you can't answer my questions doesn't mean I don't like you too."

"Matt," she said, searching his eyes. "Trust is...hard for me." It was such a meager confession, but it was so hard to say the words.

"I know that, sweetheart," he said. "That's why I'm being patient. Because I meant what I said earlier... You can trust me, Jane. With whatever it is that you can't—or don't want to—talk about."

She had to bite her lip at that. "You really are a good man," she whispered.

"Hush," he said, leaning down, just a hairsbreadth from her mouth. "Now kiss me."

Her arms wrapped around him, and her fingers fitted into his thick hair as she rose onto her tiptoes and brushed her mouth to his.

This at least she could be honest about. His tongue traced the seam of her bottom lip, and she opened her mouth to him. That first heated, silken pass had her moaning, and he pressed her closer to him, his hands settling on her hips. Their clothes were bulky, but even so, she could feel the heat of him, the hard lines of muscle in his back as she ran her hands over them.

He broke their connection to kiss her cheekbones, her eyelids, and then moved lower to her jaw line.

"Your scarf is in my way," he said, tugging it off and tossing it aside.

When his first kiss settled on her neck with such gentleness, her head fell back. "Oh, Matt," she whispered.

His mouth came back to hers, continuing to arouse, tease, and tantalize her. When he finally pulled back, he ran a finger down her cheek.

"Now, I should probably go."

She rubbed her tingling lips together. "You're not even going to ask to stay?"

He tugged on his gloves, which made her realize she hadn't noticed him pull them off. "I'd like to, but I can sense that you need more trust between us first."

His insight was keen and a little alarming. She might have rushed things tonight, wanting to give him at least that much of herself, but she would have regretted it. Sex wasn't casual to her, and he already meant more to her than the couple of partners she'd had before. Moving too fast would be a mistake.

"Okay, then. Goodnight. And thanks for a lovely evening, Matt," she said, taking a few steps to walk him to the door.

He held his hands out. "Best stay where you are. I can be a gentleman, but that doesn't mean I'm a saint. I'll see you later, Jane."

And with that, he let himself out the door.

As his car pulled away, she realized she was in dangerous territory. She couldn't continue to withhold everything about herself, but she just wasn't at liberty to talk about certain matters. What if their relationship didn't work out? He'd know about the true nature of her work with Rhett. Hadn't she seen perfectly reasonable and nice people do insane things after a breakup? All she had to do was think about what Elizabeth had gone through at Harvard to remember that lesson...

Well, she'd have to come up with something.

Because so far, he was the best man who'd ever come into her life.

And for now, she was planning on keeping all the cards in this perfect hand she'd been dealt by the Universe.

CHAPTER 12

Henry was doing his darndest to drive Matt up the wall. The dog raced around the couch in circles until Matt was sure he would make himself sick or run into something. But he wouldn't quit. It was as though he were an alien dog, making invisible crop circles around Matt to alert the mother ship that it was time to take over Earth. When his doorbell rang, he was grateful for the interruption from Henry's insanity...and his own. Crop circles! He was definitely losing it.

He jumped up and followed a barking Henry to the door. God, the house was a wreck—Henry's squeezie toys were scattered everywhere. And was that dog slobber on his cherry hardwood floor? Cripes. Oh well, nothing could be done now.

When he opened the door, his friend, Robert Preston, stood on the other side, looking very much like Matt used to look, from the black wool coat to the brightly polished Johnston & Murphy Oxford shoes and shiny briefcase.

"Still a killer?" Rob asked, gesturing toward Henry, who was barking and leaping beside Matt.

"Yeah, he thinks so," Matt said, keeping hold of the dog's collar. "Come inside. I'm going to put him in his crate. Then we can talk in peace."

Rob edged over, clearly not wanting to have his nice coat pawed by a dog. "It's crazy, you keeping that dog."

"It might be, but you know why." When he got back from crating Henry, Matt took Rob's coat. "How was the drive up?"

"Traffic was a bitch. Everyone was heading out to the mountains for some rec time."

"Andy and I went running during the work day not too long ago. Just up and left the office to hit a pristine mountain trail."

His friend shot him a withering glance. "Don't be mean to those of us who still live in the big, bad city."

"Did I mention the new ski resort up here at The Grand Mountain hotel? No wait time to get on the lifts."

"I'm going to kill you, Hale, and blame it on your dog."

Matt laughed. "Want a beer?"

"Sure."

They headed into the kitchen, which he had yet to clean up. Dirty dishes filled the sink. Oh well. It wasn't like his friend cared.

"Great place. Amazing what you can afford outside of the city. Damn, makes me want to buy my own cabin in the mountains."

"But you work too much, traffic's a bitch, and you'd never get to it," Matt finished for him. They'd talked about it before.

"You're seriously not bored?" Rob finally asked as they both popped open a microbrew and then sat down on his couch in the den.

"Nope. It's a change of pace, I grant you, but I'm loving it. It's fun to make my sisters cry by telling them about all the downtime I have here."

"And now you're going to run for mayor," Rob said. "Isn't it handy we worked together at Lexington, Kirkland & Rice before I started to work as a political consultant?"

"You're my man. Of course, I insist on paying you."

"Of course, and I'll happily take your money for that cabin I'll never buy. I'll just have to get a Maserati or something when I hit forty."

Rob always had been a smart ass, and that's why they were still friends. "With a blond half your age."

"God, what a thought. I barely have time to sleep, let alone date someone steadily. What about you? Anyone filling up all the new downtime you have in Dare Valley?"

He thought of Jane. She certainly had become one of the highlights of his day. "Yes, there's someone."

His friend tipped his beer toward him. "Oh, ho. It's serious. I've always been able to tell when you really like someone. You go all quiet."

There were so many things about Jane he liked, but he worried about the roadblocks between them. Like trying to get her to tell him about her father, the politician, before he told her about his run for mayor. It didn't take a genius to figure out she and her parents weren't close, and until he knew why, he didn't want to risk running her off with news that might upset her.

"It's early days," he responded, "but I'm hopeful. Let's head into the den, and I can run you through some ideas. I talked with my cousin, Jill, the other day, and she gave me a lot of great advice about how to connect with the local community."

They talked about his platform, which Rob helped him refine with his sharp insights. His friend was a speechwriter too, so he knew how to weave political concepts into a compelling story.

"People vote for someone they can have a beer with. Or lunch. Someone approachable." Rob set his legal pad aside for a minute. "You are all that, Matt, but I agree with your cousin. You need to talk about your last case, and why it inspired you to run for political office. It humanizes you, and that's what we want."

Matt's gut still clenched at the thought even though Jill had advocated for the same thing. Feeling like a failure was bad enough, but talking about failing in front of everyone in town? It was his worst nightmare. "What happened with Patricia was personal."

Rob leaned forward. "There's one thing you need to realize if you're going to go through with this, Matt... Politics is as personal as you get. There are going to be questions. About what you eat for breakfast. About this new woman you're dating. Even in a small town like this one. People are going to talk about you, and they'll want to know the person they're entrusting their city to. If you can't take that, I think you need to end this right now. The higher the office, the more invasive it gets."

Matt studied the fire blazing in the hearth. His mind took him back to Patricia's bedside the night in hospice. Suddenly there had been a rattling breath, the kind that shredded the heart into a million pieces, and then silence. His mom and sister, Natalie, had been there too. He hadn't asked Andy to come. They'd all kept vigil around Kim as a family, and seeing his sister-in-law pass away had left an open wound.

Seeing Patricia pass with no one around her but him and some of his family had somehow felt worse. No one should die without family. But at least she hadn't been alone.

"I want to make things better," he finally admitted, "but the rest of it...I don't like it. Some things really should be private."

Rob kicked his feet out. "I know. That's why I like you. Matt, I work for a lot of powerful people. Most of them crave the attention we're talking about like a heroin junkie. They get off on people wanting to know their dog's name and what they eat for breakfast, what their thoughts are on every single issue you can imagine. Maybe some of them started out like you and got corrupted, but I know it wouldn't happen to you if you were to serve people as an elected official."

He thought about those last moments in the courtroom when the judge's gavel had come down, dismissing the case. The shock of failing Patricia, just when she was barely holding onto life, had sent a sharp, sudden pain through him.

"Fine. Then I'll do it."

"Great. Contact this Tanner McBride and set up the interview. Be nice to have it run the day you file the papers for your candidacy. We have a week."

Rob picked up the legal pad again, and they bandied around a rough draft of an introduction letter to all the members of the Chamber of Commerce.

When he told him about Jill's idea about Uncle Arthur's Bingo night, Rob didn't act in the least surprised. "My last client attended the Denver Scrabble club since one of his campaign promises was an increase in vocabulary and spelling scores in grade school kids."

And the fun continues... "I don't know if Dare has a Scrabble club."

Rob's chuckle soothed some of his nerves. "Well, you're in luck. That's what you're paying me to find out."

"Of course, I can always ask my family. Between Jill and Uncle Arthur, they probably know everything."

"But you said your uncle will want to remain neutral, so I wouldn't push that."

Uncle Arthur might bluster about a Hale running for mayor, but deep down, Matt knew he would help him any way he could. "I know how to walk that line. Plus, Uncle Arthur has no problem speaking up for himself."

"I've always wanted to meet him," Rob commented, setting aside his beer. "What he's done up here, starting a newspaper from scratch and building it into an empire. Well, it's a tremendous accomplishment."

"I know it," Matt said.

Colleagues and friends of his in Denver read *The Western Independent*. It had always made him proud to see the impact his uncle had on people's lives. His was the voice of the West.

Perhaps he and his uncle had that in common—Matt too was interested in informing the public. He just wanted to take it a step further. He wanted to inform them of the ways in which their city was off course *and* help them change those things.

"Okay, so I think I know everything there is to know about you," Rob commented, resting his beer against his cashmere V-neck sweater.

Matt's eyebrow lifted at that. "Oh, you do, do you?"

Then Rob pulled out a sheet of paper from his briefcase and started to ask him all sorts of personal questions—some Matt had been expecting, and others that were flat-out flabbergasting.

"Have I ever been with a hooker or call girl?" he sputtered. "Seriously, man?"

Rob shrugged. "Things I gotta know."

"Hell no. Not my thing."

His friend checked what must have been the "No" box and kept right on going. When he finished, he smiled and said, "Okay, you pass the all-American boy test. Now all you need to do is make sure not to be seen with a hooker between now and November."

"What?" Matt asked, shoving off the couch. "As if."

"After working on election campaigns for years, I think there's some imaginary hooker download that happens once a man decides to enter a race. It's insane."

"I somehow don't see that happening in Dare Valley."

"No wild trips then," Rob said. Based on the way his mouth was twitching, he was clearly enjoying this conversation. "Now, tell me about this girl you're seeing."

That put Matt's back up. "No. Absolutely not. She's a

nice girl, but she's not a part of this."

Rob stood up and walked to stand by the fire. "Do people in town know you're dating?"

His sigh was long-suffering. "Yes, but—"

"No buts, Hale. If she's part of your life, she's going to be talked about. Who you see reflects upon you. Even more so since you're a single man running for office. They might be wondering whether she's good marriage material."

Matt shot off the couch then. "Now wait just a minute. We're a hell of a long way from anything like that."

Rob gave him that steady gaze all lawyers perfected in law school. "Did you or did you not grow up in a small town?"

When he thought about it for a second, he could almost hear the talk at Kemstead's Bakery over coffee and donuts. "Shit."

"I'm sorry, was that an answer? Have you forgotten how things work?"

Apparently he'd opted to remain ignorant. "You're pissing me off."

The makings of a smile creased Rob's face. "I know. What do you think your opponent is going to do? I'm supposed to piss you off first so you don't make a mistake in public."

A reluctant chuckle escaped from Matt. "Is that why I'm paying you the big money?"

"Yes. And there's nothing in my contract saying I don't get to enjoy seeing you flustered."

"Asshole."

"Thank you. I think I added that to my resume recently. Now, this girl..."

He turned and gripped the mantle, staring at a picture of his family. Were they going to be discussed too? Andy had mentioned people in town were already talking about their mom and dad's separation. And his mom was from Dare. Jane wasn't. The questions about her would be even more invasive, and he had an idea about how well she would handle that... Not well.

"I'm going to need another beer for this conversation."

Rob followed him into the kitchen. Matt popped the top off another microbrew and took a deep gulp.

"Tantrum over?" Rob asked.

Matt shot him a sharp look, but then began to tell him what he knew about Jane. By the time he had finished, his friend's brow was knit together, just like when he'd heard news he didn't like about a client.

"Everything sounds good until she falls off the radar after Harvard," Rob commented. "I mean, up until then, she's the perfect...companion to a man running for office. The rest of it... Well, something's not right. How do you leave Harvard with honors as an MBA and then disappear, only to reappear in Dare Valley working for The Grand Mountain Hotel before becoming the dog walker to a champion poker player? If she weren't using her real name, she'd be a candidate for witness protection."

"Let's not get carried away here."

Still, he couldn't ignore the fact that his friend's concerns mirrored his own.

"I'm going to have to look into her, Matt, if you're really going to run for mayor," Rob said, resting against the kitchen counter. His stance might be casual, but his gaze was sharp.

"No. I don't want that," he said, shaking his head. "I'm working on getting her to trust me. That will completely mess things up."

"Do I need to remind you that you lost Patricia's case because you didn't look deep enough into the nurse's background? Because you thought she was a good person for being a whistleblower?"

The burn seared through him all over again. She had

been a nice woman, just not entirely forthcoming. Rob was right—he should have done a better job. "It was buried deep," he muttered.

Rob crossed his arms. "Not deep enough. Matt, we practiced law together for long enough for me to know your cardinal weakness."

His jaw clenched.

"You believe the best of people, and sometimes my friend, it's not warranted."

"Just because there are gaps in Jane's life doesn't mean she's a bad person."

"No it doesn't," Rob agreed. "But even a first-year law student could deduce that there's something wrong here."

Dammit. Didn't he know that?

"You're paying me to do a job, Matt. If you won't take my word for things like this, our arrangement isn't going to work."

"Give me a few days, Rob," he compromised. "This is my life, and while I trust you to do your job, I get the final say here."

His friend met his steady gaze. "Understood. But you also need to remember that I'm not the enemy here. I want you to succeed, and it's my job to do everything it takes to make that happen."

"Within reason," Matt added, which for him did not include running a background check on his girlfriend. Oh God, his *girlfriend*. He hadn't used that word for her before, not even in his head, but it felt right.

"We'll have to see how things go then," Rob commented and wandered back to the main living area. "And now that I've put you in a bad mood, I'm going to head back to the big, bad city."

Matt followed him. "Hey man, I'm not doubting your counsel here—"

"Hale," Rob interrupted. "Do I look upset? You're going to need to toughen up if you're going to be in politics. As far as I'm concerned, this is just our first serious client consultation. It only gets more intense from here on out."

Not what he wanted to hear. "Dare Valley is a nice town with good people. I don't think running for mayor here is going to be anything like what you're thinking."

Rob neatly arranged his papers in his briefcase and then buttoned his coat. "I hope you're right, but if you're not, we'll deal with it."

"Let me take Henry out while I walk you to your car."

They shook hands in front of the Mercedes SUV. Rob rolled his eyes when Henry tried to jump on him, only restrained by Matt's hand on his collar.

"And try to get your dog under control. Voters love seeing a candidate out with his dog but not one who's going to jump on little children."

"Funny," Matt said as Rob got into the car.

When his friend's car pulled away, Matt leaned down to rub under Henry's soft ears. "You're getting better, aren't you?"

When he let go of the dog's collar, he jumped on him, and between the combined force of the blow and the slippery snow beneath his feet, he plummeted to the ground. Snow and ice crunched under him, and his stupid dog gave his face a couple of licks before he pushed the numbskull away and sat up.

"Dammit, Henry," he said as the dog bounded away.

Rising, he brushed off the snow on his backside. Great, he was going to have to change now. After chasing Henry down and bringing him inside, he mulled over what Rob had said and realized his chest felt like a boulder was sitting on it. He was worried about the situation with Jane.

And then he thought about how vulnerable she'd looked when she'd asked him to be patient with her. He wanted to give her the time she needed, but since he was announcing his run for mayor so soon, time was the one thing he didn't have.

CHAPTER 13

Jane was buying another outfit for Annie online, a hand-knit turquoise sweater with sunflowers and a matching hat, when she heard Rhett knock on the door. Her stomach turned as though she'd swallowed spoiled milk. She wasn't looking forward to this discussion.

When she opened the door, he was all smiles—as he was all the time now. Love looked good on Rhett, and after all the years she'd known him, seeing him so happily settled made her want the same for herself.

"Hey, sugar," he drawled and kissed her cheek before plucking a delighted Annie up off the ground and nuzzling her face. Tucking the little dog in the crook of his arm, he sauntered into the house like only Rhett could and dropped down onto the couch, Rufus following him patiently for a nice rub down.

"Thanks for coming," she said and then clenched her fists together. "Can I get you some sweet tea or something?"

He glanced over and raised his brows. "You made sweet tea? Now I'm really getting nervous. You aren't planning to quit on me, are you?"

"No. I love working for you." She was horrified he'd

even think that.

"Okay, then," he said, rubbing Rufus and then shoving off the couch, "let's get this sweet tea and sit for a spell. You clearly have troubles, and Rhett is here to help."

It comforted her tremendously when his big hand pulled her in for a side hug. You could always count on Rhett. "Thanks, Rhett."

"Sure, honey." Then he joined her in the kitchen.

Her hands trembled as she poured him a glass. "Lemon?"

"Yes, but let me slice it. I'm afraid you might cut off a finger, your hands shaking like that. You really have me worried, Jane. Should I call Elizabeth and have her join us?"

The guilt she felt over excluding Elizabeth rose up. "I wanted to talk to you first since this has the biggest impact on you."

After garnishing his drink, he picked it up with one hand and wrapped the other around her shoulder. "Okay, then, best spit it out before you give me a heart attack."

They returned to the living room and settled on the couch, and for once she broke her cardinal rule and brought Annie onto her lap for comfort. The dog rolled into a little ball, and Jane stroked the white cowlick on top of her head.

"Well, you know how I've been seeing Matt Hale," she began.

"Did he do something?" Rhett asked sharply.

She immediately shook her head. "No, nothing bad. It's just...well..."

"Weeds in winter could grow faster than you right now, honey. Just lay it out."

Right. She was hemming and hawing as Rhett was fond of saying. "Well, he wants to know about me. Things like my background."

He cocked his head to the side. "Ah, I see. And there's a rather large gap in your background."

"Yes. It's just...I've never felt this way about anyone, and Rhett...I don't want to mess this up or lose him because I can't tell him about my life."

He scratched his jaw. "How much are you thinking?"

Unable to sleep after their date, she'd greeted the sunrise with some difficult answers about her best steps forward. "I'm going to tell him where I'm from. About my parents. And more about Harvard. But I'd also like to tell him I've been working for you for the last seven years as your poker scout, which I know is a huge thing to ask."

He remained silent, his poker face as unreadable now as ever.

"I won't tell him about being Raven because...well, because it's too much to share at this point. And it places you and Elizabeth in an uncomfortable situation. While we didn't do anything illegal, some people on the circuit might make a ruckus if they find out your scouts were so close to the table. I would never want to risk that. Or cause any problems with people in Dare... But I have to tell him something." She thought of how kind Matt had been last night, what he'd said about trust. "No, I *want* to tell him something."

The sigh he heaved out was long and deep, and his chest rose from the sheer force of it. "Times are changing all 'round, aren't they? We've never talked about disclosing the truth outside our tiny circle because none of us have ever had anyone that important in our lives. Abbie knew about y'all all the time, even if she didn't approve, and none of us questioned her confidence. Now this... What we have here is a new situation. How does Elizabeth feel about it?"

Guilt made her look down. "I haven't talked to her yet. I wanted to talk to you first since I...well, I work for you. And I know she won't like it. She'll tell me all the reasons not to trust a man with something like this, something he can turn around and use against me. Us."

He leaned over and tipped her chin up. "You girls ever going to tell me what happened to her at Harvard?"

The whole matter was closed off in a box, and both she and Elizabeth had agreed years ago never to open it. "It has to be her choice, not mine."

His hand opened, and Annie jumped off her lap and into his. "Fine. We'll leave it for now. As for your issue, are you sure you can trust him with this? I'm a little concerned about it getting out. You're right—scouts are pretty common now, but some players might try and make an issue of the proximity."

She crossed her hands over her chest. Poker players weren't exactly diplomatic. It wasn't hard to imagine how rough their comments would be on social media—or the whispers that would be passed between key people at the big tournaments or hotels. Would anyone ban Rhett? God, it didn't bear considering.

"The other big issue is the poker babe masquerade. If people discovered that, especially in this small town, it would upset Abbie, and we've finally gotten past all that."

Yeah, who could blame the love of Rhett's life for being embarrassed by two poker girls named Raven and Vixen, even if they were her man's secret scouts?

"We like living in Dare," Rhett said. "And Mac does too. We've all decided to put down permanent roots. Mac's going to let Cincinnati handle most of the hands-on work with any additional hotels he decides to build. I don't want to mess up our inroads with this community. They're finally taking a shine to me now that I've settled down."

His wink didn't settle her stomach any. Seeming to sense her distress, Annie returned to her lap.

She knew what even a whiff of scandal could do in a small town. And this? Well, people might think she and

Elizabeth were Rhett's high-priced call girls. People on the tour had suggested salacious things before, but the three of them had just laughed about it since they knew the truth and it wasn't hurting anyone. Now, it could, and her fingers tightened on Annie, who gave a little bark.

"Sorry, princess."

"I need to talk to Abbie and Mac about the situation. No one has a finer head for this sort of tangle than Mac Maven. It's important to think through the angles, and it wouldn't hurt to check out Matt Hale just a little more. Any idea how he might react to hearing you were Raven?"

She shrugged. God, if that question hadn't kept her awake last night too.

"Of course, I warned him to treat you right," Rhett continued, "or he'd have to deal with me."

Suddenly it was like someone had lit a hearth, inside her chest. "You did? When?"

"When I ran into him at the hotel gym. He's a member." His hand settled on her shoulder and gave a comforting squeeze. "You need to talk to Elizabeth about this too, you know."

The bile in her stomach skyrocketed. "She's going to be angry with me for even suggesting it."

"Well, now, I think you two have been friends for long enough to handle upsetting the apple cart every once in a while. It's going to be okay, Jane. We'll figure something out. Why don't you tell Matt about your family for the time being and buy me some time to talk to everyone?"

Even that thought made her throat feel raw. How was she supposed to talk about the very thing that hurt her the most? "Okay. That should be plenty of this couple sharing thing for the time being."

His mouth quirked up finally. "That couple sharing thing. I'll have to use that on Abbie. Now, how about we

145

play some poker online and see who wins?"

Rhett was always challenging her to play, and today, the distraction was welcome.

"Are you sure you can take it? I'll probably kick your butt."

They rose, and he followed her into her office where there were two computer stations against the wall. She and Elizabeth often challenged each other to what they all called Poker Duels.

"It wouldn't surprise me," Rhett said. "I've been telling you for years that you're good enough to reach the final table."

Of course she wanted to play in the big leagues. Just not all the time. And not necessarily as Jane Wilcox. She didn't want the drama her parents would rain down on her if she tried that. Since playing as Raven wasn't an option, either, she made do with her online matches with Rhett and any spontaneous poker games they played when spending time together, Elizabeth included.

"Not only is it easy to underestimate you because you're...well, a woman," he continued, "and cute as a button at that. But you look so sweet until you turn into Poker Medusa and destroy all the other players with your betting strategies."

His praise always made her happy. "I've been happy to stay where I am mostly. These years with you and Elizabeth...well, I don't know what I would have done without you two."

Her life would just have continued in the lackluster way it had started. She would probably still be taking the anti-depressants she'd started in early high school at her mother's insistence. Elizabeth had tossed them down the toilet and helped her live.

Rhett tugged her against his chest and rocked her. "Ah, now, don't you be going there, or I'll start tearing up. We all needed each other, and we made a family of ourselves. Now that family is expanding, and so are we. There will be some growing pains, but we'll stay together."

"You're getting pretty wise, Rhett," she murmured and squeezed him tight before letting go.

"And I'm glad you've found someone you care enough to entrust with the truth. Hell, wisdom seems to be pouring out of me today like oil from a used car, but I'll just say it. The only way we can love someone and be loved is to share who we really are, the good and the bad, the ugly and the pretty. Being with Abbie has taught me that."

To keep him from seeing her tears, she turned on the computers, wondering all the while what it would be like to have Matt love her and accept her like that. Even Raven. She wasn't ashamed of anything she'd done as Raven, but considering what a decent man Matt was, she wasn't sure he could accept her past. Or believe she wasn't some of the things people had called her.

Would he understand why her family had driven her to become Raven? The point was moot for now, anyway. She would never share information about her *new* family—the family she'd chosen—without their knowledge and consent.

Rhett settled into the chair beside hers and brought up their favorite online poker site. "You ready?"

"You betcha."

CHAPTER 14

Meeting up with Matt was usually the highlight of Jane's day, but the knowledge that she intended to tell him all about her family and upbringing tonight made her feel like the mountain snowcap from across the valley had crashed into her stomach.

The sunset was releasing its first rays of light when she and the dogs arrived at the park, reminding her of the colorful ribbons her nanny had put into her hair when she went to kindergarten before her mother had laid down the law. Only one ribbon color. No multi-colored ones with rainbows or bunnies printed on them. And certainly not an assortment of thick ribbons woven through her then long, curling hair.

The wind was turning cold with the temperature falling from its record-breaking fifty degrees today. But when she shivered, it was from the memories coursing through her mind, not the weather. Only Elizabeth knew these stories, and she'd sometimes cried while sharing them with her friend. Would she be able to keep control of her emotions when she poured out the painful memories to Matt?

As the sunset streaked its pink, orange, and blue ribbons across the mountain range, she reached out as if to bring them inside herself. This was her time. These were her dreams. And she wasn't going to let the past ruin anything. He could take a few tears if they came, and so could she.

There was nothing wrong with emotional honesty, a hard-fought lesson for her after a childhood of repression.

A car door slammed in the distance, and as she turned, she realized she'd been so caught up in her thoughts she hadn't heard Matt pull up. Annie pranced in place and Rufus gave a little ruff as Matt opened the back seat for Henry.

The dog lurched on the leash, but at least Matt had gotten it onto him this time. There were a few runners in the park since it was so nice outside, a staggering forty degrees. But after the weeks of twenty-degree highs, today was lovely, and she'd taken a run earlier with Rufus while Annie hung out in the car.

As Matt came toward them, Jane could only marvel at his handsomeness. His broad shoulders made her fingers itch to trace the muscles she knew were underneath his black polar fleece. And those eyes. Even from where she stood, she could see the twinkle in that sea of blue. Since it was relatively warm, he'd forgone a hat, so the wind was playing with his thick brown hair. His jaw was granite, and she couldn't wait to feel the rasp of his five o'clock shadow when he kissed her again.

Which she was hoping would happen shortly.

"Hi," she called out, staying where she was along the park's ridge.

"Hey," he returned, his long legs eating up the distance between them. "Nice day, huh? If I hadn't been busy, I would have gone skiing. Do you ski?"

"I've been taking lessons, and I graduated to the intermediate class a month ago."

"Good," he said as he stopped in front of her, Henry giving some ruffs for attention.

Matt leaned down and kissed her on the mouth as though it were the most natural thing in the world, as if it were okay to declare their connection in public.

His spontaneous act only confirmed her decision to tell him about her upbringing. She ran her hand down his chest because she could. It was nice to touch him this way.

"We should go skiing sometime," he said, smiling down at her. "How was your day?"

"Good. Got in a nice run." She didn't mention seeing Rhett or the fact that they'd played poker for a few hours. Sure enough, she'd beat her boss, which always made her day. "What about you? You mentioned being busy."

"Yeah. Had a friend up from Denver," he said, leaning down to pet her dogs.

She did the same with Henry, who sprawled down on his back and displayed his belly. "Oh. Is he still here?"

"Nah, he had to get back. Work tomorrow." Matt threw out one of his hands to the sky. "Man, it felt so good to tell him how little I'm working right now. That I actually have a life. I don't dread Monday mornings like I used to."

She couldn't help it. She laughed. "You didn't have a life before?"

He bumped her. "Smartass. I worked a ton. I went out a little. And I saw my family. There wasn't time for a sunset stroll with a beautiful woman."

He might not have had time for a stroll, but there certainly had been beautiful women. He was too handsome, nice, and successful for there not to have been.

"I'm not beautiful," she said instantly, even though she adored the compliment. Her inner swan was gaining confidence, but she had a ways to go.

"Of course, you are," he immediately said and put

his hand on her arm, stopping her in her tracks.

"I'm petite and cute, but I'm not beautiful." Swans could be cute. Maybe even a little mysterious.

He cupped her cheek and gazed at her with those banked fires in his eyes. "Well, you are to me."

Her throat closed and all she wanted to do was embrace him right then, with the ribbons of sunset swirling around them, strengthening this bond she felt growing between them. "That's nice of you to say."

He reached for her free hand and held it as though they were a young couple going steady. "You women don't ever see how truly beautiful you are. Trust me, I grew up with three sisters, and they all thought they were just *okay* or *all right*, never beautiful. My friends always thought differently. Of course, if they acted on it without my sisters liking the attention, Andy and I would punch them because that's what brothers do."

Even though they were both wearing gloves, the warmth of his hand seemed to spread through her. "They were lucky to have you two. I always wished I'd had an older brother to look out for me," she said bravely and cast a surreptitious glance to see how he reacted.

He gave her his full attention. "Go on."

"My parents couldn't have any children after me," she said, and her throat suddenly felt as hot and thick as when she had a fever.

"That's too bad," he said.

"They really wanted a boy," she continued, "to carry on the family name. Heck, to lead the family business."

"A woman can lead the family business. You do have an MBA from Harvard."

He was too insightful. It was like he already knew why she'd made certain decisions. "Yes, but I realized it wasn't what I wanted."

"And they didn't like that, I'm guessing," he commented, swinging her hand playfully while Henry barked at a flock of robins.

"No." That one word seemed so inconsequential in comparison to how they'd reacted.

They continued to walk in silence—Henry barked at a few squirrels, but Jane only had to rebuke him a few times to quiet any mad outbursts. Matt was getting better at using the voice commands, but it was as though Henry wore earmuffs when it came to his master.

"What are you up to tonight?" Matt asked as they rounded a stretch of pines. "I was going to see my brother and nephew, but I'd rather spend my Sunday evening with you, eating pizza and watching a movie, if you're up for it. I know we only went out last night, but—"

"Who cares?" she burst out, making him smile. "That sounds like fun."

Plus she could tell him more about her family tonight, and part of her wanted to let out a dramatic sigh of relief.

"Good," he said and squeezed her hand. "We can meet up a little later after finishing here. Give me some time to pick up the house. I swear I have more dog toys and accessories lying around than a new mommy."

"Sounds nice."

A few hundred yards down the path, a man running with a double baby jogger waved and called out, "Hey, guys."

Squinting in the distance, Jane realized it was Brian. He stopped when he reached them, huffing from his run. Jane tried to let go of Matt's hand, but he held firm and shot her a questioning look.

"Sunday's my day off," Brian said, "and since it's so nice out, I decided to take Mia and Violet on my run. We just got this baby contraption. Isn't it the coolest?"

When Jane peered through the clear plastic, the little girls gazed back at her unblinkingly. Then they smiled in tandem, drool running down their cherub mouths.

"Want a better look?" Brian asked, unzipping the cover.

They banged their fists in the air as the cold air hit them, but they still grinned at their dad.

"They're beautiful," Jane said.

Henry, of course, tried to nose in on them, and when Matt held him back, he barked, making one of the girls cry.

"No, Henry," Jane said in a firm voice. He immediately stopped.

"You really are good with him," Brian said. "And hey, man," he said punching Matt on the shoulder. "Jill tells me she's going to be helping you run for mayor. She mentioned it when we had our Sunday brunch today. It's always our opportunity for catching up on adult talk. With the girls and our crazy schedules, we have to set aside a time not to do baby stuff. It's nuts when they're this little. Like some kind of time vacuum."

The words didn't register at first since he continued to chat about life with twins. It was almost like Jane was hearing them through a tunnel. And then they hit her right in the solar plexus. Matt was running for mayor?

Oh dear God, no.

"I'm happy for you, man," Brian continued. "I can't say I've ever thought about going into politics, but it suits you. You'll be great for Dare, and Jill's over the moon about it. I was worried at first since she wants to run herself someday, but she's completely cool with it. Between these little ones and our jobs, we have our hands full at the moment, and she sees helping you as great training for when she does throw her name in the ring. Plus, she says you're bringing in some big-shot political consultant from Denver to help out, and she wants to absorb as much as she can from him."

Big-shot political consultant? Was that his friend

who'd visited from Denver?

Matt said nothing beside her, just glanced down at her with a tight mouth.

Jane didn't understand why he was acting like that, and it really didn't matter. She was dead inside now. She'd fallen for a man who wanted to be in the same profession she'd done everything to free herself from. As she scanned the sky, she realized the colorful ribbons of sunset were gone, replaced with grays and deepening shades of black.

It was as if the sky had smothered her dreams.

Jane's hand went limp in Matt's and fell from his grasp.

"Well, it's getting dark," Brian finally said, "and it takes forever to buckle the girls into the car."

"We'll help you," Jane assured him, taking off for the parking lot. "As you said, it's getting dark."

She had to get out of there. Now. The hurt was welling, and she wasn't sure she could hold it in.

They were over before they'd barely begun.

God, it was so unfair.

How could he not have mentioned his plans? As they walked back, Brian chatting easily about the babies and the restaurant with Matt responding in monosyllables, their conversation a buzz in her ears. Suddenly she realized a stark reality: they hadn't known each other that long. That's why he hadn't mentioned it. He didn't think he owed her any explanations.

She guessed it was a good thing she'd found this out now, before she'd spilled her own guts. What if Rhett had given her the go-ahead to tell him about her years as a poker scout?

Disaster averted. No one had been hurt.

Except for her.

Henry barked suddenly at a few people leaving the park, but she was too numb to stop him. She could feel Matt's eyes on her, but she kept her gaze down. So he definitely sensed something was off. Well, she couldn't let that affect her right now.

If she focused on taking one step at a time, she could get into the car and then just leave.

She knew what time he came to the park, so it would be easy to avoid him.

The first bubble of pain rose from her heart to her chest.

She wasn't much help to Brian, after all, standing there mute. But Matt unzipped one carrier and unhooked one of the babies, easily settling her against his chest. The scene cracked her heart like an anvil. He was a pro with babies.

Well, it would make kissing them for the media all the easier, she thought.

Her father hadn't held her much growing up, but he'd never turned down a chance to hold a stranger's child, beaming at the cameras with his perfect white teeth.

"I need to run," she finally said. "Matt, I just realized I can't break off my plans with Elizabeth tonight, so we'll have to get together another time."

When she gave Henry a goodbye pat, she realized she was breaking her promise to help Matt with this grieving dog. The bubble burst, and she fled to the car, tears burning in her eyes.

"Jane," Matt said, jogging after her, putting his hand on her arm when she opened the back door. "Wait a sec."

"I can't," she said, grinding her teeth to control her emotions. "I need to go. See you later."

She pushed the dogs inside, something she never did, and hurriedly opened her door.

Brian was staring at her, his mouth twisted into a frown. Henry started barking as she reversed, and Matt only kicked at some snow.

The tears started to fall before she cleared the

parking lot.

The one thing she'd sworn never to do was fall in love with a man like her father, a man who wanted to be in the spotlight, a man who wanted to be in politics.

And she'd done just that.

CHAPTER 15

Matt watched Jane race off and fought a curse word. Brian shut the door to the SUV to keep the twins warm and shoved his fingers through his curly brown hair.

"Sorry, man. I had no idea she didn't know. I thought you two were dating."

His plan to get her to share her background first hadn't worked, although in the park tonight, as she'd started to talk about being an only child and a disappointment, he'd been certain she was about to tell him the whole story. A thrill of hope had shot through his heart while he listened and watched the sunset crest over her creamy cheekbones.

He hadn't been completely sure how she'd react to his news. Well, now he knew.

Badly.

"I need to go after her," he said and headed to his SUV. "See ya, Brian."

As he took off to her house, he realized they were about ready to have it out, and perhaps that was a good thing. They wouldn't be able to make it as a couple if they continued to keep things from each other.

And he very much wanted to see where these

newfound feelings would take them.

Henry jumped into the front seat, whining, but Matt was too focused on reaching her house to bother disciplining him. It was as though the dog knew they were running after Jane. When he arrived, smoke was just starting to puff out of her chimney.

He leashed Henry, who for once didn't fight him, and jogged up the steps to her house and knocked on her door. As he waited, his chest constricted like it did when he was about to deliver a closing argument on a case he knew could go either way.

He knocked again. Henry barked this time and pawed at the door.

No answer.

So, she was going to ignore him, was she? Well, if there was one thing he wasn't going to accept, it was the silent treatment. Being ignored only pissed him off and made him more determined.

"Jane. Open the door. I know you're in there. I see the smoke from the chimney."

He heard a dog scratch the other side of the door and give a slight whine. Rufus.

But still she didn't come.

"I'm not leaving until you talk to me. I have winter camping gear at my house, and I will literally set up a tent on your front lawn."

Henry barked again.

Steps finally sounded on the other side, and he found himself wishing the door had windows in it so he could see her.

"Matt," she said in a voice that told him she'd been crying, "please, let's talk another time. I really do have plans."

"Bullshit," he said. "You're upset about me running for mayor because your dad is a career politician, and clearly something went really wrong between the two of you. So, let's talk about it."

The door swung open, and there she was, tear stains on her cheeks, eyes puffy with a hard gleam in them.

"How dare you do a background check on me! You're just like every other would-be politician, digging into people's lives to see if someone in their circle might be a liability."

Rufus and Annie both whined in response to her harsh tone. She reached for the door to slam it in his face, but he was quicker and streaked through the opening with Henry.

Dropping the dog's leash, he grabbed her shoulders. "My brother Googled you because that's what big brothers do. I didn't stop him, which is on me. I didn't tell you about running for mayor because I suspected something might have happened between you and your parents, and since you didn't know I knew about them, I was hoping you'd trust me with your past before I told you. I was afraid you might react badly, and it seems I was right. I care about you, Jane. Don't shut down like this without even talking to me."

Even though she was petite, she looked formidable, standing there with her hands fisted against her hips. "Fine. You know that my father is a career politician. Well, I will never, never become involved with one. So, while it's been fun and I really hope we can be civil to each other, this is it. I'm sorry I can't help you with Henry anymore."

The rage she was projecting clearly came from a place of hurt. Whatever had happened with her family had scarred her. Badly.

"You're going to throw away what's starting between us just because I'm running for mayor?"

Her eyes hardened. "I told you—"

"I may not even win," he added.

"But you want to run for higher offices, don't you?" She waved her hand at him. "Why didn't I see it? You're the ideal candidate! Handsome, easygoing, from a great family... Not to mention that you recently had a case proving exactly what's wrong with the system. I never should have broken my first rule about not dating lawyers. God, how could I have been so stupid?"

The dogs whined again, and he finally unclipped Henry's leash, which was trailing on the floor. The dog plopped down and cried again, clearly sensing the tension in the room. Matt leaned down to pick up Annie when she nudged his ankle and stroked the wild tuft of hair on top of her head. He did it to calm her down as much as to calm himself. While he suspected something terrible had made Jane drop off the face of the earth after Harvard, he'd never expected this much vehemence from her.

So he went for the truth.

"Do you care about me or not?" he asked and looked straight into her eyes.

The rage faded, and he saw the hurt and the vulnerability in those chocolate depths. "Please don't do this."

"I care about you," he declared and set Annie down. He walked over to her and placed his hands on her shoulders again, the clear, pure truth rising inside him. "I think I'm falling in love with you."

"Stop," she whispered and turned her back to him, her voice hoarse now.

"Are you really going to let your parents win this round?" he pressed, putting his hands back where they belonged. Touching her. "Am I really anything like your father?"

She didn't return his gaze. "I didn't know him when he first started out as a young politician, but people say he was nice, an upstanding man, a pillar in the community."

He should have known she would have thought through every angle. She was too smart not to have. Well, he was a lawyer and could match her point for point.

"How old were you when he first ran for office?" he said, feeling her tremble beneath his touch.

Her breath shattered out. "Three."

"Did he play with you when you were little?" he asked.

Silence.

"Did he love you?" he pushed.

She shoved his hands away and turned around. "No! Is that what you want to hear? He didn't do any of those things. Are you happy now?"

He wanted to pull her to him and hold her until all the pain went away, but he knew they weren't there yet. "No, I'm not happy. In fact, it hurts me to hear that the father of the woman I care about was a total dick to her. Do you really think I would be that callous to my own child just because I'm running for office?"

Her face crumpled, and she shook her head. "No, but please stop this. I don't want to talk about it."

Too bad. She needed to talk about it…. It had probably been festering inside for years.

"And where was your mom the whole time?" he asked. "Did she—"

"What? Play with me? Love me?" Her head lifted. Now there was fire in her eyes. "No. Is that what you want to hear? Oh please go."

"So, let's sum this up then. Your father was a deadbeat scumbag as a parent, and your mom wasn't any better." It was time to push again. "Did they use you as the perfect little daughter for his political campaigns?"

"Yes! And I hated every minute of it!"

The picture was becoming clearer by the minute. "Am I asking you to be involved in any way in my run for mayor?"

The glance she gave him was withering, and he could feel the chill from where he was standing.

"Please. Don't treat me like I'm a novice," she said. "This might be a small town, but we both know who you're seeing matters for your campaign. I expect your advisor will tell you that if he hasn't already." She slashed through the air with her hand to make the point.

Rob's comments echoed in his mind. "You're right, I have been told that. But I'm still standing here."

"Then maybe you're the stupid one. You know nothing about me. I could be a liability."

He reached over and tipped up her chin. Her eyes were wet, and defeat hovered over her like a gray cloud.

"Then tell me."

She spun away again. "Don't you already know? Didn't your brother find out everything on Google? Hell, how about your political advisor?"

Rather than running from her emotions, he walked right into them, just like he did when he was deposing an emotional witness. "I only know what's on Google. That you're from a wealthy manufacturing family from Connecticut. That your dad is a career state politician and has declared his intention to run for Congress in the next election. You already told me about Harvard, but yes, I know you graduated with a whole shitload of honors. I could fit what I know on one page. But I don't care about any of that. I want to know about you. The *real* you! I care about you, Jane. What is it going to take to drive that through your thick skull?"

So much for acting cool and collected like Matty Ice.

She still didn't look at him, but a tear plopped on the floor beneath her. He couldn't take it. He yanked her into his arms, holding her face against his chest.

"Oh, Matt," she said, her voice tortured.

"Don't shut me out, Jane. Not about the past. We're good together." He cupped her cheek and met her gaze. "Please."

Her lip trembled.

"Tell me you're falling for me too," he whispered. "I

don't want to be alone in this."

She squeezed her eyes shut.

Her inner struggle pushed him over the edge, and suddenly he was drifting with her in his own messy emotions.

"Baby, you're not the only one who's afraid here."

Her dark eyes popped open then, and as he looked into them, he could feel himself falling. And he knew there would be nothing to save him from a painful landing.

"I don't want it to be this way," she whispered.

He lowered his head and brushed his mouth over hers gently, trying to connect with her, to reestablish that fledgling bond between them.

"Then don't," he whispered back. "Trust me, Jane. You can trust me. Don't throw this away."

A tear fell then and another, and he kissed her again, unhurried and unrushed, seeking to comfort and soothe her. And himself. She was so small and strong, and yet filled with more hurt than he could ever have imagined.

A sound of agony and distress rose from deep inside her, and then her mouth pressed forcefully against his. He had reached her. He had actually reached her.

CHAPTER 16

With her entire body trembling, Jane poured herself into the kiss. The earlier anguish of talking about her family faded. He was still here, even after she'd tried to push him away. And he'd said that he was falling for her, that he was scared of this fragile thing between them too. Her heart expanded. How could she turn him away?

She loved this man.

As she rose onto her tiptoes and threaded her hands in his hair, she realized he was right. He was nothing like her father. She pressed closer, angling her mouth to reach his, wanting their connection to be deeper, hotter, wetter. Lust shivered through her spine and then fanned out in waves across the rest of her frame. Soon, she was trembling against him, wanting him, wanting to crawl inside his skin.

She couldn't get enough.

When she put her hands on his shoulders to leverage herself against him, he helped lift her. She wrapped her legs around his waist, feeling that hard line of desire between them. It elated her that he wanted her in such a primal way—just as much as she wanted him—and that made her decision for her.

"Be with me," she whispered against his mouth, tugging at his bottom lip with her teeth.

Holding her with one arm around her back, he cupped her cheek. "I'm right here."

Standing intertwined in her living room, they devoured each other's mouths. She traced his ears, and he ran his hand down to her bottom. Clenching her legs around him, he groaned into her mouth.

"Make love to me, Matt," she whispered as she edged her mouth away from him for a second.

His eyes were blazing now, as blue as the ribbons of sunset she'd seen earlier tonight. Her sunset, she thought. Her dreams.

He was all wrapped up in them.

"You're sure?" he asked, his voice hoarse.

She traced his jaw with a finger. "I've never been surer."

The light shone in his eyes a little brighter, and then he kissed her again. Soon they were both breathless, sipping at each other's lips. Her entire body was electrified, and she wanted more. She slid down him and placed her hands on his chest once she was standing.

"Come with me."

He grabbed her hand and let her lead him to the hallway behind the den down to the last room, her bedroom. She shut the door when the dogs tried to trail in behind them. There was no way she was going to share this moment with anyone else.

She crossed over to him and reached for the zipper of his fleece. He found her mouth again as he shrugged out of it, and then she pulled back, reaching for the hem of his white T-shirt. When it came off, her mouth went dry.

"You're beautiful," she whispered.

His chest was a work of art, the defined muscles and angled tendons flowing together in perfect masculine harmony. With a hesitant hand, she ran her fingers down his chest to the hard ridges of his abdomen. When she reached for his black pants, he cupped her face.

"I want to see you, Jane."

What would he think of her boyish body? "Ah...there's not a lot to see. I'd much rather see you."

He tipped up her face, his gaze steady now. "Do you have any idea how much I want you? How much I want your body? Right now?"

But would he still want her when he saw how small her breasts were, how angular her body? "I'm worried I'm going to disappoint you," she whispered, looking down at the floor.

His finger stroked her jaw, a silent request for her to meet his gaze again. When she did, he reached for her hand and pressed it against his arousal. "Does that feel like disappointment to you?"

It didn't. In fact, it felt wondrous, and her fingers traced his hard length. "No, but you haven't seen me yet."

"Didn't we talk about trust just a little while ago? How am I supposed to know you won't be disappointed in me?"

That caused an unladylike chuckle. "Please. You're gorgeous."

His hands framed her face then, and he leaned down until his eyes were only an inch from hers. "You're beautiful. Let me help you see what I see."

Slowly her inner swan journeyed out, stretching in the light. It was time to trust. It was time to be brave.

His fingers traced her neck, stroking the skin there with a feather-like caress. "Your neck makes me want to kiss it and lick it and bite it gently." And then he did all of those things.

Her hands fell away from him as desire rolled through her.

He lifted the hem of her pink T-shirt and threw it

aside. Before she could feel any embarrassment, his hands covered the cups of her padded bra, his thumbs tracing the skin above the lace. When he leaned down and kissed the delicate rise of her cleavage, she gave a strangled moan. Nothing had ever felt so shockingly sensual. He unhooked her bra deftly, slowly sliding it down her arms, his mouth still exploring her. Nerve endings flashed across her chest, and when he brought the tip of one breast into his mouth, she gave a gasp and threw back her head.

Thoughts of her small shape were vanished as he cherished her breasts with his mouth and tongue and teeth. Soon, the liquid pool between her thighs grew demanding, and she tugged at his pants again.

He placed gentle hands over her own. "No, not yet. I want to drive you out of your mind first."

Nudging her back against the bed, he slid down her pants. She kicked them off when she fell back on the bed, wanting to feel his weight on her.

But he didn't follow her. He just stood beside the bed, letting his eyes take a hot, leisurely stroll up and down her body.

"You're beautiful," he said again, and as the embarrassment started to creep back in, he joined her on the bed and pulled her to him.

The hot skin of his chest against her own made her want to purr. And then he kissed her, his tongue driving deeply into her mouth while his hands caressed her breasts, making her arch and moan and fear she was going to make a lot of noise with him. Before that embarrassing thought could take root, he traced a hand down her flat stomach—at least one good thing about being flat everywhere else—and cupped her wet heat.

The sensation was so intense, she moaned again against his mouth. His fingers edged under the delicate, lacy thong that matched her pink bra, and he caressed her core.

Jane had only been with two other guys. One in Harvard and another when she'd first moved to Vegas. Both had been so forgettable and embarrassing she'd thought she was just one of those people for whom sex wasn't a basic need. With Matt, she was learning a new truth. Being with the right man, one who took his time, one she cared for—who also cared for her—made all the difference in the world.

Desperately wanting to show him how much he pleased her and how grateful she was for the care he was taking, she tugged on the waistband of his pants, her intention clear. Take them off right now or else. His mouth quirked up on the side as he kissed her. This time, he didn't stop her. Together they helped him slide out of his pants, and she laughed when he threw them across the room.

And instead of rolling onto her, he leaned back. Let her see him. Helped her see how it would be with a real lover, one with whom there was no embarrassment.

Her hand reached out to touch him, and the heat in his fiery eyes scorched her skin. Her first caress had him clenching his jaw. Her second had his lips peeling back. Her third had him jerking against her.

"Okay," he rasped. "That's all I can take right now. It's time for you."

He leaned over and kissed her belly, and the shock of his warm mouth against her skin had her gasping. His chuckle raised the hair on her skin as he continued on a downward path. He kissed the delicate line of lace framing her pelvis and then looked up at her.

"I want these off."

His throaty request made her reach down with shaking hands to do just that. He slid them slowly down her legs, following the trail with kisses until she was free of them. Then he sat back and ran his hand up her inner thighs, looking at her.

Again, the flutter of embarrassment played on her

nerve endings, but the feeling vanished when he cupped her core. "How could you ever think I'd be disappointed?" he asked, a trace of awe in his voice.

Tears filled her eyes then, and she reached out a hand to him. "Make love to me, Matt."

He grasped it and brought it to his lips. "Oh, I plan to, sweetheart. I plan to."

Then he lowered his mouth to the V of her legs and taught her a whole new lesson about being with the perfect man. He loved her slowly and patiently, and the first tremors that coursed through her brought his name to her lips in a sigh.

He left the bed when she went limp under him, but since her eyes were now closed, the bliss overpowering even her basic ability to see, she didn't know what he was doing until she heard a foil wrapper tear. Opening her eyes slowly, she watched him roll the condom down his length and then lower himself onto her again, positioning himself at her entrance.

"Okay?" he asked.

"Are you serious?" she said, her throat dry now, making her long for a glass of water.

He chuckled and kissed that delicate line where shoulder and neck met. Who knew it could be so sensitive?

He trailed kisses along her jaw until she lightly pressed him back, wanting to give to him too. His blue eyes burned into her as she caressed his back and then slid her hand lower until she was stroking the hard muscles of his butt. His hips jutted forward, and he moaned as he crushed his mouth to hers again, taking her on a new ride, one filled with belly-clenching kisses, red-hot urges, and total sensual oblivion.

His hand caressed her breast, and soon she was once again a field of raging desire. Pressing against his arousal with her hips, she pulled her mouth away to utter, "Now," and that was all it took.

Matt pressed slowly inside. His size stretched her, and she moaned.

"Take a breath, Jane," he ordered in a silky voice.

She did, and he eased inside a little more. His jaw was clenched, and he spread her legs a little wider with his hands.

"Christ, you're so tight."

"I'm sorry," she cried out, full of desire, full of him.

"Don't you ever apologize for that," he rasped and then caressed her breast with a hand.

Her back arched, and that was all it took for him to be seated fully within her. He stretched out over her then and cupped her chin.

"All right?" he asked.

The fullness was quickly changing to urgent need, and she lifted both knees to squeeze his thighs. "Please."

"Okay, baby," he whispered, "I know what you need."

And then he pressed back and gently slid forward. She moaned, the fullness and heat of him overwhelming her. His answering groan had her tangling her fingers into his hair and pulling him in for a hot kiss. The rhythm he set was easy and slow at first, but soon her hands were gripping him as urgently as her knees were, so he took the pace faster, deeper.

All of the friction, the heat, was so intense Jane threw her head back.

"Oh, God," she called out.

Matt shifted to his knees and grabbed her hands, raising them above her head. "Come on, Jane," he urged, thrusting into her in a frenzy now.

She wrapped her legs around his waist, feeling everything inside her pulse. Crying out, she squeezed his hands and poured out her soul.

He answered with even deeper, faster thrusts, and then he was calling out, shaking above her, until he folded over her, his sweat-soaked chest pressing against her body. His rapid breaths tickled her ear, but she was so far off in another realm she didn't open her eyes.

When he finally rolled them onto their sides, she wrapped her arm around him, not wanting to lose this precious connection. *This is what it all comes down to*, she thought, *the connection*. And, for the first time, Jane finally realized what it meant to become one with another person.

He stroked her back as their breathing slowly returned to normal. Then he kissed her neck. Nuzzled her ear. "Be right back," he whispered before untangling himself.

She mumbled protests, but soon he was back, fitting her to the long hard line of his body once more.

Rising on an elbow, she looked down at his beloved face. His hair was sweaty at the temples and standing up in spots. Then his eyes opened, and she fell into their fathomless blue depths.

"Matt," she whispered.

He traced her cheek. "What?"

She could feel a slow smile spread across her mouth. "Just Matt."

Leaning down, she kissed him and then settled herself against his side and fell asleep.

CHAPTER 17

When Jane awoke, her breath caught in her throat when she saw Matt sleeping next to her. He'd rolled onto his side and slung an arm across her waist as though he couldn't bear to let her go. Her body felt liquid and sore in a few places. Her throat was parched, and she desperately wanted some water, but she couldn't bear to get up.

Being with him was more powerful than anything she'd ever experienced, and while she didn't feel like she was on steady ground, there wasn't a place she'd rather be.

She loved him.

And she loved making love with him too.

Just remembering how he'd called her beautiful made her heart burst with joy. Her body pleased him, excited him, aroused him. This body. The one she'd found lacking since her mother's first snide comment to her in high school.

Well, at least we never need to worry about you looking overweight on TV.

The hurt of that comment and many more that had followed had never left her. She'd always felt lacking, but tonight, with Matt, she'd found new ground. And the utter preciousness of what she felt for him and what they were building brought tears to her eyes.

And in that minute, she knew she had to tell him the truth.

The whole truth and nothing but.

She wasn't going to risk their relationship with lies. He said she could trust him, and after everything that had passed between them tonight, she knew it was true.

It would be awkward to explain her past as Raven, but she knew he'd listen. And she could finally be fully herself with the man she loved.

But first she needed to talk to Rhett and Elizabeth. With the decision to tell Matt anchored inside her as firmly as her family's old yacht in its boat slip, she also knew it couldn't wait. When he awoke, he'd want to talk more, and she did too.

With no impediments between them.

Easing away from his warmth, she eyed the clock. It was just shy of eight thirty. Now she understood how people snoozed after sex. It was delicious...and vigorous. She almost laughed at herself.

She'd leave a note for Matt and slip out to talk to Elizabeth and Rhett. She knew they wouldn't hesitate to meet her if she sent them an urgent text.

As she slid out of bed, tiptoeing across the room to pick up her clothes, she glanced back at Matt. His chest was rising and falling evenly.

She let herself out into the hallway, freezing when she saw Henry raise his muzzle with sharp interest in his eyes. But when she shook her head *no*, he settled back down with her dogs. Whew! After dressing in the spare bedroom, she walked into the kitchen. She grabbed a bottle of water from the refrigerator and downed it, but it wasn't enough. Who knew sex could make you so thirsty?

She was discovering all sorts of things tonight.

After downing another bottle and filling a water bowl for the dogs, she found a pen and notepad and wrote Matt a note.

Hey,

Might sound weird, but I had to run out and take care of something. Will be back shortly.

Should she sign it, *Love, Jane*? When she tapped her foot, she knew she was making it too complicated, so she just wrote a simple J and set it on the kitchen table where he would see it.

Now it was time to deal with Henry. She didn't want to leave him in the house unattended. He was being surprisingly good, but who knew what he'd do after she left. And she hated to think of him waking up Matt.

As she led all three dogs into the laundry room, where she kept Rufus and Annie's crates, their tails were wagging as though the dogs were thinking, *Oh, it's friend time*. She opened the door to Rufus' crate and gestured to Henry. Another surprise. He went in without a fight. Yeah, he was a good dog. Just hurting and a little lost. And now she was around to help with that. She gave him a treat and rubbed him under the ears. After washing her hands in the laundry room sink, she gave Annie and Rufus a treat and patted them both.

"No bark."

And Rufus dropped his head like he understood. Annie just pranced around, ever the princess. "Stay," she told them and pointed to Henry, who was still crunching on his milk bone.

They both trotted over to Henry and sat beside the crate. She didn't usually close the laundry room door, but this time she was going to. She didn't want to take any chances.

Satisfied that the dogs were well settled, she texted Elizabeth and Rhett, asking if they could talk with her about an urgent matter at Elizabeth's house. Nothing bad had happened; she just needed to talk ASAP.

Her phone immediately buzzed with their answers—both yeses—so she shoved her feet into her boots, tugged on her outer gear, threw her purse over her shoulder, and went into the garage to get going.

Five minutes later, she was at Elizabeth's door. Her friend threw it open immediately—she'd clearly been waiting by it—and scanned her face.

"Did he hurt you?" she immediately asked.

Her mouth parted. "No, of course not."

Her friend sagged against the door. "Thank God. You scared the shit out of me, Jane. Never, ever do that again!"

She wrapped her friend in a hug and pulled her inside, nudging the door shut behind them. They held each other, her eyes squeezing shut. She was so lucky to have Elizabeth in her life.

She was about to test their bond of friendship, and her belly grew tight with nerves like it did when Rhett lost his stack in poker.

"I made love with Matt tonight," she whispered.

Her friend jerked back. "I just thought you were having a really bad hair day."

Laughter bubbled out, and she strode over to the mirror hanging in her friend's foyer. She took in her appearance—swollen mouth, puffy eyes from her earlier tears, and yes, matted and spiky hair. "Good God."

"It a full-on emergency. Come on, we can get you a brush before Rhett arrives." Elizabeth took two steps before halting abruptly. "Wait. This isn't a post-coital chat, is it? Otherwise, you wouldn't have asked Rhett to come." Her friend's eyes narrowed. "What's going on, Jane?"

The pounding at the front door interrupted their conversation, and Jane went over to answer it, since she was closer.

Rhett took one look at her and said, "Whoa, what happened to you?"

Jane scrubbed her hands through her hair. "Ah…"

"She had sex for the first time in years," her best friend informed him.

"Jeez!" he cried, shutting the door. "I really don't need to know these kinds of things." Then his eyes narrowed, and he took her shoulders in his big hands. "Did he hurt you? Is that why you texted like that? I'll kill him if he did."

"No!" she cried. "He was more than wonderful. He *is* more than wonderful."

Everyone stilled at the emotion in her voice.

"I love him."

Elizabeth's face fell like it did when she was about ready to unfurl her mother hen routine. Rhett only took off his coat and hung it on the rack.

"We just made love for the first time, and I left him sleeping because I realized I could no longer hold back the truth about who I am."

Elizabeth looked like someone had slapped her. She shook her head slowly. "No."

Jane rushed over to her and grabbed her hands. "Yes. Liz, I can't do it anymore. I told him about my family tonight, but I want to tell him *everything*."

Rhett put his arms around them and led them to the sitting area. "Come on, now. Let's get comfy. This is going to take a while."

The warmth from the fire heated Jane's body, but inside, a deeper cold was taking root as she took in Elizabeth's rigid frame.

"When we last spoke," Rhett said, "you only wanted to tell him about being my poker scout."

Elizabeth's gasp shot guilt into Jane's body like an arrow. "What? You two have already talked about this? How could you have not told me?"

"Because I knew how you'd feel," Jane said quietly. "I knew all of the reasons you would give me for not telling him. That I barely know Matt. That no man, save

Rhett, can be trusted."

Her friend's mouth pursed, but Jane wasn't done. She had to say it all.

"And that I'm naïve when it comes to men."

Elizabeth didn't disagree.

"Look this isn't about your past," she told Elizabeth, "this is about my present and my future. I have a real chance to have something special and...well...lasting with Matt." After tonight, she knew she could be with him forever. Yes, they hadn't known each other long, but she knew how she felt. "He's a good man, and he deserves to know the truth. Especially since he's running for mayor."

"He's what?" Elizabeth said in a near shout, tucking one of her legs under her. "Have you lost your ever-freakin' mind? You want to entrust the truth about who you are—who we were and what we've done—with a man who's just like your father?"

Her blood boiled. "You know me well enough to guess how hard it was for me to find out he's running. Well, I've dealt with it, and he's nothing like my father. He's not like Vince either, Liz."

Her friend's face went chalk white at that, and her lip trembled. "Don't you dare bring up that man's name. How could you?"

Her eyes filled with tears. "Elizabeth, I love you like a sister, but I can't make the same choices as you. I'm done with living in the past...and hiding from it."

Rhett patted her leg, which was quivering. "I take it Vince is the person you were running away from when we first met," he finally said to Elizabeth. "We've been together a mighty number of years, and you've never told me the full story. I think now might be the time."

Elizabeth only shook her head, mute for once in her life.

"Vince was someone she started dating at Harvard when we were in the last semester of our M.B.A. He

177

stalked her when she broke things off."

"How dare you tell him!" Elizabeth raged and pushed off the couch, facing the fireplace.

"It's time, Liz. And God knows we can trust Rhett. Vince was from a very powerful family, and suffice it to say, he didn't take her rejection too graciously."

Rhett clenched his fists in his lap, his eyes flinty now. "Are you going to tell me more about this, Elizabeth, or are you going to let Jane? What more do I have to do to get you to you trust me?"

Elizabeth's profile was illuminated by the red-gold firelight, making her even more beautiful. "I hate talking about it, Rhett. I swore I wouldn't."

"Tell me, darlin'."

"Things were bad," she finally whispered. "He followed me everywhere. Got into fights with the men I dated. Slashed my tires. Broke the flower pots we had in front of our graduate housing."

The blood froze in Jane's veins as she let herself remember all of it. How it had gone from annoying to downright scary.

"I changed my number when he wouldn't stop calling. We went to campus police first, and then to the Cambridge police. We filed all their paperwork. Jane even paid for a lawyer to file a restraining order. It went to court, but Vince's lawyer was one of the best in the country. He made up lies about me, saying I was unbalanced, and dredged up my childhood of living in a trailer park, which he found out by doing a background check on me. He claimed I was trying to get a settlement out of Vince because he was rich."

Rhett rose and walked over to Elizabeth, who gripped his hand.

"The judge denied the restraining order, and as Jane and I were leaving, Vince told me he wasn't finished with me. That if he saw me with another man, he'd kill me *and* him. He said I was his or nobody's."

Their big champion enfolded her in his arms and rocked her, and the sight of it broke Jane's heart.

"Jane and I stayed up nights with baseball bats in our hands after that. My lawyer said he needed more evidence, but I knew it was futile. I was afraid Vince would ruin my chances at Harvard and beyond. Graduation was only one month away, so I didn't go out with anyone. Kept a low profile."

They had both felt like prisoners in their own home, and Jane had never been more afraid in her life. Each time she'd stepped outside, she would look over her shoulder. More often than not, Vince would be watching, and a cold chill would shoot down her spine.

"The week after we graduated, I was applying for jobs on my laptop in the library when he suddenly sat down next to me. He told me that I needed to be real nice to him or he and his family would make sure that I didn't get a job anywhere."

Rhett let her go when she pushed away from him.

"He ran his finger down my neck and told me not to cross him anymore, to come back to him. When I got home, I told Jane we needed to get out of town. I knew something bad was going to happen."

Elizabeth had come home, hysterical, telling Jane about Vince's threat. They both knew he could make good on it. His family had powerful connections at the big firms, and even Jane's parents couldn't match his connections. Not that they would have lifted a finger to help. Her parents had always considered her relationship with Elizabeth to be in poor taste because of her "trashy" upbringing.

"Jane's parents were breathing down her neck about joining her father's campaign and working for them full-time, so we went to Atlantic City to disappear for a while," she said. "Make some decisions. And that's where we met you, Rhett. When you offered us jobs, we both knew it was a chance to escape. Jane could make her family ashamed of her by becoming Raven. Very bad for the senator's image. And I could disappear off Vince's radar forever."

By the time silence descended on the room—save for the popping and crackling of wood in the fireplace—Jane felt years older. Elizabeth had made her agree they wouldn't speak of Vince again, and it was so dark and draining to return to thoughts of that time.

"I always knew it had to be something to do with a guy, something bad," Rhett said. Then he put his hand on Elizabeth's shoulder. "I wish you'd told me this years ago, Elizabeth. I would have beaten him within an inch of his life for threatening you."

Her mouth formed a smile that fell flat a second later, as though she didn't have the energy to hold it in place. "That's why I didn't tell you. He would have caused problems for you, Rhett. And I didn't want him to find out where I was. I changed my name, you see. Legally."

He cocked his head. "What's your real one?"

"Well, it's Liza Parenti," she told him. "It took some doing, but Jane's family helped because they didn't want anyone to find out about Raven and ruin the senator's political career. The Wilcox political machine knows how to bury damaging connections."

"The only benefit to being in my family," Jane tried to joke. "That's why I didn't change mine. I knew my parents would cover our tracks regardless, and since all my family trust funds and accounts were in my real name, it would have been more complicated."

"Well, that explains why you gals had those private companies created for our financial relationship with names that had nothing to do with your own."

Jane rose to join them, feeling they'd weathered the storm for the moment. "That's right. Plus, it was so much safer and smarter financially for you to run your earnings and our employment like a business."

"Safer for everyone involved," Elizabeth said. "Or at least it was until Jane decided to threaten it."

She gazed at her friend. "Vince can't hurt you anymore."

"It's not just that." Elizabeth's throat rippled, and she put her hand to it. "This situation involves all of us. What if Matt decides to tell people about Raven and Vixen if you two break up? Rhett could get into some deep trouble if someone wants to make a stink and pretend we were counting cards. Are you ready to risk that?"

"Let's take a step back," Rhett said, holding up his hands like a white flag.

"How do you even know Mr. All-American is going to be broad-minded enough to accept that his new girlfriend was Raven?" Elizabeth continued. "He's running for mayor, right? Something like that would hurt his chances."

Her words burned like a cigarette to the skin. "That's why I need to tell him. He needs to have the choice."

"It's too early in this relationship," Elizabeth said. "Six months or a year from now, I might reconsider if he's proven himself, but this...blind faith...is too much to ask of us. Of me."

Jane looked down at her boots. This is where the rubber met the road, she realized. "Sometimes, you don't need six months or a year to know a person. I love him, and I want to be honest with him. Rhett? What do you think?"

He gave a long-suffering sigh and sat down in front of the fire, his hands on his knees. "As I told you, Janey, it's not just about me anymore. Abbie and Dustin and I are making a life here."

Her face fell, and the bitter sense of defeat spread throughout her.

"But while I can't talk about what happened to Abbie, I also know what it is to love someone who has a secret. Matt's a smart man. He's going to know something's up. There's no way someone as smart as you are leaves behind a top-notch education to be a dog caretaker."

She waited with expectancy to hear what he said next.

"I talked it over with Abbie and Mac, just like I said I would. We all agree that it's common enough for poker players to have scouts now. I'm okay with you sharing that fact with Matt. But I agree with Elizabeth. It's too early to tell him about Raven, especially given what that news could do to all of our lives in this town."

Elizabeth gave Jane her back. "It's a mistake."

"I'm sorry you're upset, Elizabeth, but I'm willing to trust Jane. And I know it's not what you wanted to hear either, Jane, but it's the best I can do for everyone right now."

As a compromise, she could have done worse. Still, she was desperate for Matt to know everything.

"In time," Rhett continued, "we can see how things go between the two of you." Clearly sensing her reaction, he crossed over to her and pulled her in for a hug. "If he loves you, he'll still love you when he finds out about Raven. Real love can survive anything, I've learned, even when it's news like this."

She made herself put her arms around Rhett, who kissed her on the head.

"And Elizabeth, I swear to you on my mama's life that I will never let that lowlife get anywhere near you ever again, no matter what. You're safe, and you're just going to have to trust me on that. I don't want you to live in fear. Do ya hear me?"

Her friend shook her head, saying nothing.

"Well, I feel like I've been ridden hard and put up wet, so I'm going to mosey on home to my family. Jane, we'll keep talking about this. Matt seems like a good guy, but we don't know him well enough yet. If there's *any* chance he's untrustworthy and might tell someone you're my scout, I expect you to let me know pronto. Then he and I will handle things man-to-man."

"It won't happen," she said.

"Good to hear." He kissed Elizabeth on the forehead and then headed to the door to pull on his coat. "I'll talk to y'all tomorrow. Get some sleep."

The wind howled when he opened the door, and then everything went quiet again when it shut behind him. Now it was just Jane and Elizabeth, but the comfortable understanding between them had been shattered.

"I'm not doing this to hurt you," Jane whispered, her chest feeling like it had been crushed by a metal compactor.

"I know," Elizabeth said in a flat tone, but her eyes were still hard. "You talked to Rhett without checking with me first."

"He's the boss, and I knew what you'd say." Jane walked over to stand beside her friend. "I didn't know what Rhett would say. You know the two of you are the only family I have, right? I would never willingly put you at risk, but this is important to me."

"And yet you're jeopardizing everything."

"Why don't you want me to be happy?" Jane finally shouted, the hurt pouring out. "This is the first man I have ever cared about, and he cares about me deeply too. When I learned he was going to run for mayor, I ran away from him, but he came to *me* to tell me he was falling in love with me. That I needed to trust him. To not shut him out."

Elizabeth rubbed the bridge of her nose and walked back over to the fire.

"This is the kind of man I want to build a life with, Elizabeth. I know you don't know him, but I want that to change. I'd like your approval."

The fire crackled as her friend gazed away, still

quiet.

"Are you really going to let this come between us? After everything?" Her face crumpled and she sank onto the couch, her hands covering her face as the tears came.

Then she felt Elizabeth's arms wrap around her. "I'm sorry. I'm scared. Like I used to be when we'd see his car out the window."

Jane reached out and hugged her, pressing her face into her neck. Thank God, she'd softened. She couldn't stand the thought of being estranged from Elizabeth, not even for a day. "I'm sorry, but Rhett's right. Vince can never touch you."

"It's not just that. It's this new life we've built. I don't want it to come crashing down around us. It's the only thing I have, Jane." Her voice shook when she said it.

They clung to each other even tighter. Yes, she had felt the same way, but life seemed to be opening up in new ways now that she was with Matt.

They rocked each other until her friend pushed away. "You should probably get back to him. I don't think I've ever heard of anyone leaving their *own* house after having sex."

Her mouth quirked up. "Doesn't that show you how much you and Rhett mean to me? That I was willing to leave him sleeping in my bed to talk to you about this?"

Her friend's eyes darkened. "Yes, but it also tells me how important he is to you."

"Liz," she said. "I know we've talked about sex before, but this...I can see why people call it making love now."

"I'm glad for you, Jane. I really am." She squeezed her hand tight, but her face was drawn, her expression shuttered. "We'll see what comes next, okay? Now get going."

Jane knew deep down Elizabeth was pushing her

out so she could deal in private with the demons they'd
unleashed tonight.

"I love you," she said.

"I know. I love you too. Now go."

After she'd put on her coat and gloves, she kissed
Elizabeth on the cheek again. "I'll call you in the
morning."

"Just go enjoy yourself. You deserve it."

As Jane left, she decided Elizabeth deserved a good
man too. Once more, she prayed Vince hadn't left
enough of a mark on her friend to make that impossible.

CHAPTER 18

When Jane left, tremors overcame Elizabeth, and she sank to the floor. Cold swept through her insides as though she were outside without her coat on in below-zero temperatures. She forced herself to stagger to the fire, grabbing a purple throw as she passed the couch.

Oh God, oh God was all she could think.

The fear was back, and it was choking her.

They could lose everything over this…

Rationally, she knew it had been seven years since she'd seen Vince, but right now, she was the same terrified, quivering young woman she'd been in those horrible last days in Cambridge.

As she'd learned to do in her counseling sessions, she took several deep breaths, but it didn't help. She started to choke as the grief rose up in her chest and swamped her.

And there was no fighting the tears.

Fifteen minutes later, her head was buzzing, her nose was running, and she couldn't get warm—not even in front of the blazing fire.

Vince.

Just hearing his name again had driven a spike of

terror through her whole body. A fear deeper than any other threat could engender.

He can't hurt me, she chanted over and over again.

Vince had gotten married a year ago, she knew, and worked at the biggest investment bank in New York. But that knowledge didn't assuage her fear one bit.

When Elizabeth finally settled down, her body spent, she stared into the fire from her supine position on the floor. The long-time question arose within her. How could an innocent couple of dates turn into something that had destroyed a part of her life, a part of her?

As Vixen, she'd been able to forget all that... She'd felt in charge. In control. If a man wanted her, well, he didn't want the real her. And because she wasn't real, *he* couldn't find her.

Vince didn't know her new name.

Heck, no one did but Jane. Not even her parents. They would try and bleed her dry if they found her.

And now Rhett knew. Well, it was about time. It wasn't that she didn't trust Rhett. She did...with her life. But the last thing she wanted was for him to find Vince and exact revenge on him.

She'd never wanted to risk that.

And deep down, she had needed to lock the door to that horrible time and throw away the key.

Too bad Jane had a spare, and boy, had she opened that box tonight.

"Stupid, stupid, stupid," she said, her voice hoarse from crying. This whole thing was stupid.

Still, Elizabeth wanted to be happy for Jane. She loved her friend more than anything. But she'd just met this guy, and that was what hurt the most. That her best friend would put them in danger for something this fast. Plus Matt Hale wanted to be in the public eye, which could put Jane in the public eye...and her too. They'd discussed the potential impact of Jane using her real name when she came forward as Rhett's dog walker, but her surname had never been used in the media. No one would give Matt or Jane that promise if they stayed together and he continued in his run for office.

And who could really trust a politician anyway? Since that was what Matt Hale wanted to be, Elizabeth was suspicious in spite of what Jane had told her about him.

She pushed herself off the floor, and stood, weaving in place. Taking a few more deep breaths, she let herself settle.

"Dammit!" She hated being back in this place.

Deep down, she was stronger than this. Just not right now.

She went into the hall closet and pulled out the Louisville Slugger bat she'd bought for her first apartment in Las Vegas when she'd still been tortured by nightmares. Clutching the wood in her hand, she checked the alarm and every lock on every door, and because her paranoia was at an all-time high, she made sure all the windows were locked too.

When she'd bought this house on its gorgeous four acres, she hadn't thought for a second how isolated it was. She'd just been happy to have land—a heck of a lot more than she'd ever imagined calling hers while growing up in that run-down trailer park.

Now, she felt the isolation, the blackness outside, and the wind made her tremble.

Nights like this she wished for a loving, trusted man beside her, but since it was a man who had put her in this position in the first place, she knew all that happily ever stuff was a load of horseshit.

Walking back to her bedroom, she locked that door too and then, for good measure, wedged the vanity table chair under the door knob. Then she lay on her bed, fully clothed, clutching the bat, prepared to keep her vigil until the fear finally drained away and she could sleep.

CHAPTER 19

Matt's fingers clutched around the beer he was holding when he heard Jane's SUV crunching the snow on the driveway and the garage door open.

Staying where he was, dressed again—and hadn't that been weird?—he watched as Annie and Rufus ran off to greet her. He'd let them out of the laundry room as soon as he noticed they were in there. Henry was still in the crate where Jane had left him. He hadn't wanted to deal with the dog's antics when he was knee-deep in doubts, confusion, and...acute discomfort.

No one had ever left him like that after sex since he'd made a cardinal rule once he'd become a man. He wouldn't sleep with a woman if he didn't want to wake up with her. So far it had worked out.

But now that Jane had flitted away—from her own home, no less—after the hottest, most intense lovemaking he'd ever experienced, he was completely out of his element, like a novice lawyer in his first major trial case against a lawyer with thirty years of hard-won experience.

Why had she left?

He'd just told her he thought he was falling in love

with her, for Christ's sake!

The note he'd found hadn't put much of a dent in his chaotic emotions, and he'd crumpled it into a ball in his hand.

But he'd decided to stay, reach deep for patience, and muster all the trust he could to believe that she'd left for a damn good reason.

It had better be a damn good reason.

Her footsteps were slow and hesitant. Then they stopped. He set his beer on her side table and turned his head to look at her.

"Hi," she said, her voice hushed. "I was hoping you'd stay asleep."

He didn't move from where he was. This was her show. "No," he replied, taking in her stiff frame. "It was only a catnap. Why don't you grab a glass of wine and tell me where you had to go?" Even to his ears, his tone was reasonable, and he would have patted himself on the back if the stakes weren't so high.

"I'm sorry I left," Jane said. "There was something I needed to do. Something that involved us."

His gut burned at that. Her secrets wrapped around him like an errant cobweb discovered in an old basement. "Go get your wine. I'm not going anywhere."

The right side of her mouth tipped up. "I'm glad."

"I wasn't happy to wake up with you gone, but how could you possibly think I'd leave after what happened between us?"

She looked down. "I don't...this is new territory for me."

"Get your wine," he repeated.

Nodding, she took off to the kitchen, her dogs following her. Minutes later, she was back, the wine bottle in one hand and two glasses in the other.

When she sat down, she held out the bottle.

"Wow," he commented, eyeing the label. "A 2001 Margaux, Chateau Bordeaux Blend. What did that set you back?"

"Doesn't matter. We're celebrating." Her eyes tracked to the beer. "Ah...do you want some wine?"

Celebrating, huh? Well, this situation kept getting curiouser and curiouser.

"Sure thing," he responded, trying to keep it casual when his gut felt like he'd consumed saw dust for dinner. "What are we celebrating?"

She poured him a glass, which he took, and then one for herself.

"The truth," she whispered, her brown eyes glowing. "And trusting good men."

That did it. She couldn't have been more effective in claiming his heart for her own if she'd shot an arrow through it. Earlier, staring into the fire, he'd analyzed everything between them from their friendship to the intimacy of their lovemaking. These emotions of his were swinging like a pendulum, from the sweet joy he felt when he was with her to the raw fear of being left naked in the bed where they'd just made love.

He was completely, totally in love with this woman. Tonight had confirmed it.

"I can drink to that," he responded, sensing she was about to tell him more about herself.

She clinked her glass to his and then took a deep drink. Even though he could barely wait for her to speak, he made himself take a sip.

And he was immediately glad of it. The Bordeaux might have been the best wine he'd ever tasted. Full. Lush. Alluring.

Just like Jane.

"My God, you do know your wine." His casual remark went against everything he was feeling.

When she set her wine on the side table closest to her, he did the same, edging it next to his discarded beer.

He held out his hand to her as though it were the

most natural thing in the world. Her eyes gleamed bright and true then like the North Star, guiding them both to the safest course, and she took it. Her deep breath told him what he already knew.

Whatever she was about to entrust him with was one of the hardest things she'd ever done. Enough clients had told him deep, dark secrets for him to know when one was about to be unearthed.

"Matt," she began, breathing shallowly now. "When we went on our first official date, and you asked me about myself, I wanted to tell you...about my past, but there were reasons...that I couldn't."

His every nerve was on edge, and he wanted nothing more than to tap his foot in anticipation, but he forced his body to relax. He needed to give her time.

"When I realized how deeply I cared about you, I had to ask some people close to me if I could tell you about...well, about what I've been doing since Harvard."

His solar plexus tightened with fear of what was to come. What in the world could she have been doing?

"They...well, he's been thinking about it. I didn't have an answer when we...ah...made love tonight, but afterward, I felt the need to press for an answer." She looked down at their joined hands and then raised her wary gaze to him. "I don't want to lose you. And I don't want to keep things from you anymore either."

Since he could tell how tortured this whole thing was for her, he cupped her cheek. "Baby, I'm right here."

Her exhale was like a gust of wind. "Okay, so here goes. I'm Rhett's poker scout. I have been since graduating from Harvard."

He was sure his lawyer face had been blown to smithereens. His mouth parted. "His poker scout?" Of all the things he'd been expecting, it hadn't been this. He'd imagined she might have discovered something disturbing about her father's political dealings or her family's corporate interests. Maybe even lost a dear friend in a tragedy.

But this…well, he didn't know what to think of it.

She tried to force a smile. "I told you how difficult my life with my parents was. When it came time for me to graduate, all they wanted was for me to join my father's political team. He was running for another term, you see, and it was expected. They wouldn't listen to me, and it was all so…damned hard. So I did the one thing I knew they could never accept. I went to work for…well…a pretty flamboyant poker player in a capacity…well beneath what they thought was appropriate."

He blinked a few times, trying to take the information in. "*Okay.*" God, he just didn't know what to say. She was a poker scout? This soft, warm-hearted dog lover?

"It's not exactly…illegal. And it's certainly much more common and accepted now than it was seven years ago, but I signed a confidentiality agreement with Rhett long ago, and I didn't want to jeopardize his reputation or his status in the poker community or his newfound home here in Dare with Abbie and Dustin—"

"By sharing the information with someone you'd just met," he finished, starting to see her conundrum.

She eagerly nodded her head, as though she was delighted he understood. "Yes, and there was the whole matter of what you might do if things…well, didn't work out between us."

What kind of bastards must she have known in the past for her to think him capable of that? And yet as a lawyer, he'd seen that kind of betrayal over and over again. He ran his gaze over her face now, seeing the tense muscles there. "I swear to you, Jane, that I will never use this to hurt you. Never share it with anyone unless we talk about it first."

"What do you mean by that?" she asked, the pulse in her neck beating fast and strong now. "Who else?"

He pulled her closer, their thighs brushing each other. "I love you, Jane, but I come with a family. I want you to get to know them, and I want them to get to know you. When and if the time is right, we should tell them the truth. We don't keep secrets in my family."

"Wait," she said, shaking her head. "You really love me?"

"Yeah, I wasn't too convincing earlier when I said I think I do. I was...not quite myself." He closed the distance between them, needing to touch her, and pulled her onto his lap. "Yes, I love you. All the way."

She traced his face, a slow smile spreading. "I love you too. All the way even though I know we haven't known each other long. That's why I had to tell you as much as I could. I don't want secrets either. I want us to have a chance, but I'm scared of telling other people, Matt. Even your family. I'd have to talk to Rhett and..."

Her brow knitted, and he ran his finger along the line. "I'm not talking about right now, but I want to be as honest with you as you've been with me. Family means everything to me, Jane, and if things work out, I'd like for you to be a part of that."

"There are still some things I can't tell you yet," she whispered, clutching his shoulders, "but I'm hoping you'll be patient until I can. I didn't get...clearance to tell you...something else."

Well, he didn't like hearing there were more secrets.

"No top secret security clearance for me, huh?" he tried to joke.

She blew out a long breath. "I'm afraid not. This has happened awfully fast, and they don't know you yet."

Her use of "they" intrigued him.

"Don't you mean, Rhett?" he asked and watched as her eyes flashed to his.

"Elizabeth too."

Right, her friend from Harvard, who was now Rhett's publicist. She *would* be concerned with his image. And he suspected it was no accident that she and Jane worked together now. There was more to it, and perhaps it had to do with the secrets Jane was still hiding.

"I have to ask just this once. These other things you can't tell me yet..." Damn it, he didn't want to ask, but he had to be sure. "None of it was or is illegal, right?"

"Oh, God, no!" she said so forcibly that his muscles immediately relaxed.

"Good," he said. "Then we'll take our time, build our trust in each other and in the people in our lives who matter."

"Rhett and Elizabeth are my family," she told him.

"Well, that explains him pulling the big brother act on me at the gym over you."

"Yeah, that's Rhett. I don't know what would have happened if I hadn't met him. He changed my life."

No one could mistake the love and joy in her voice. "I'm glad. So, the whole story about you working for Mac is..."

She scrunched up her face. "Contrived. We didn't want people to know about our work for Rhett. In Vegas, we...ah...mixed it up, playing at different hotels, but The Grand Mountain Hotel is the only game in town..."

"It's harder to blend in," he added.

"Ah, yes, so we had to come up with a compelling reason for me to go to the hotel without being...ah, discovered."

"Are you going to tell me about how you scout?" he asked, not having a clear picture yet.

"Not really," she said. "Trade secrets. But beyond watching the real action, I can tell you that I watch a lot of tape and keep files on all the players. We never know how the cards will fall, but poker is as much mental preparation as anything else. Then you have to see how Lady Luck treats you and play your opponent."

My God, she shone like a star while talking about her work. "So you must be pretty good at it then. Poker."

"I don't play in public or anything, but Rhett and I play a lot of online poker, and I usually beat his butt."

Goodness, she was such a complex woman. Dog lover, wine connoisseur, stock market junkie, and now poker-playing fiend. "There's a lot more to you than I ever imagined when I first met you."

A shadow crossed her brow. "Is that a good thing or a bad thing?"

He could hear the fear in her voice, so he leaned in and gently kissed her on the mouth. She immediately twined her arms around his neck and kissed him back, falling into the embrace so sweetly that he felt his heart turn over in his chest.

"It's a good thing," he finally murmured against her mouth. "You can ask my mom. I get bored very easily."

Stroking his face, she smiled. "I'm glad." Then the happiness dimmed. "But Matt, I have to tell you up front how...scared I am about us being together while you run for mayor. I know how important this is to you, and I don't want to hurt your candidacy. If you feel we need to—"

He pressed his lips to hers, silencing her fears, and slid his hands down her back, caressing the skin at her waist as he raised her shirt.

She pushed back. "I'm serious."

And because he knew she was, he didn't reach for her. "I'm listening."

"This is a small town, and I'm from one of those. I'm also intimately familiar with the fact that something like my...profession...could sink your candidacy. We might not be...well, married...but people will still care who you're dating."

She sounded so much like Rob that he had to bite back a smile. "And?" he encouraged even though he knew where she was going.

"I could never forgive myself if the truth came out and hurt you. And I've told you that there's more..."

Yeah, that whole "more" thing did worry him. But she'd sworn it wasn't illegal...

"I don't want you to worry about it. I'm not."

"But maybe we should stop seeing each other until the election is over," she said, biting her lip.

Her willingness to sacrifice for him would have brought him to his knees if he hadn't already been sitting. No one outside his family had ever done anything like that for him.

"God, I love you." He kissed her hard on the mouth. "Jane, it's February. The primary isn't until May. That's three months away. I am not going to stop seeing you for three months or, if I win the primary, until freaking November. That's insane."

"But Matt—"

"No buts," he said, his voice sounding as sure as he did. "If something comes out, we'll deal with it. Together."

She grabbed his face and looked straight into his eyes. "You were right earlier. You're nothing like my father, and because of that, you *will* be a great politician."

They'd come so far in one night, rather like the distance spanned in an instant by one of the bottle rockets he and his siblings used to set off. "Do you know how I felt when I woke up and realized you were gone, Jane?"

Her eyes widened. "I'm so sorry."

"Hush," he said, kissing her again. "I didn't say it to make you feel bad. I only told you because I want you to understand the way I feel. Jane, this might be new to me too, but I can recognize something valuable when I come across it. I'm not letting you go."

This time she didn't pull back to argue when their mouths met. Instead, she surrendered to him in the sweetest, most trusting kiss he'd ever experienced. And as he lowered her to the couch to make love to her again, the fire between them—as fierce yet comforting as the one in the hearth—burned away the last scraps of doubt and fear between them.

CHAPTER 20

Bingo night had to be one of the craziest functions Matt had ever attended. Uncle Arthur led him through the large room at the old American Legion building, introducing him to The Old Guard of Dare Valley. According to his uncle, who'd winked at him as he said it, he had a good chance of becoming mayor if they approved of him.

The room had old wood paneling for walls, cracks in the plaster ceiling, and he could see dusty cobwebs on the ancient brass chandelier that swayed ominously overhead when the ancient heating system kicked on. The whole place reeked of an unfinished basement, the mustiness making him rub his nose, and liniment, the kind he used when his muscles burned after a game of basketball. There was another odor, but he wasn't even going to analyze *that*.

This was where his uncle swore he received all the important local gossip?

They'd come forty-five minutes early to get in what his uncle called "social time." Dozens of eyes set in wrinkled faces watched his every move. He was the youngest in the room by at least forty years, but he was okay with that. He respected his elders. And he trusted

Uncle Arthur. Though it might not seem like it, this was an important first step in his campaign.

Matt followed Uncle Arthur, smiling and nodding to men and women as he walked past what he called The Trail of Metal—walkers, canes, and wheel chairs. His uncle stopped at every chipped Formica table and made a particular point of introducing him to the group sitting in the metal chairs marked with AL on the back for American Legion. Almost everyone was retired, but they all volunteered in the community: the church, the Chamber of Commerce, the Dare Community Center, and a bunch of other places that boggled Matt's mind. These people were serious about Dare. They'd never left, and they loved this town. Supported it with their time and effort.

There was no mention of him running for mayor. That would be "just crass" according to his uncle. Matt had filed the paperwork on the day of the deadline, Friday, and now it was official. Letters had gone out to every business listed through the Chamber of Commerce, announcing his desire to meet with them. His calendar had blown up in the scope of two days, and he had thirty meetings to attend in the next month.

Besides, everyone knew his plans anyway, his uncle had told him. Sure enough, Betsy Davis, the former librarian of the Dare Valley library, dropped a hint when they shook hands by telling him she served as a poll worker at election time.

"Not the stripper kind," she said. "P-O-L-E," she spelled, which made everyone guffaw. Matt's brain practically imploded from the image of this sweet elderly lady using her cane for something other than walking. When the group's hilarity died down, everyone at the table nodded their heads and told him they were also poll workers, which resulted in Morie Leonard asking Patty Drivers to give him a lap dance.

Dear God, these people were crazy.

But fun. And he found himself lightening up.

Then Horace Smithens asked him how he felt about Dare's school system, and he saw a few people turning up their hearing aids to tune in to his answer. A few nodded as he explained how the system was doing its part, but he'd heard around town that there were some improvements that could be made. Then he asked what they thought.

And they told him, each person at the table outlining their points like a seasoned lawyer at a trial. His uncle nudged him in the ribs, as if to say, *and you thought we were just a bunch of old fuddy-duddies?*

Yeah, smart as a whip, this crowd. He'd have to stay on his toes tonight.

After moving on, he shook hands with some veterans at another table and thanked them for their service. A few of them pulled up their sleeves to show him sagging, faded tattoos, telling him tattoos were a terrible idea. Then Lanone Jenkins batted her faded blue eyes at him through coke-bottle glasses and boldly asked him if *he* had a tattoo anywhere. Even though most of them had bursitis and bad backs, he could have sworn all the old ladies at the table leaned forward, waiting for his answer. Dear God!

"No, ma'am, I don't."

Then his uncle slapped him on the back—a pretty good slap for a man in his late seventies—and laughed. "Does he look like an idiot? We don't have any of those in the Hale family."

Matt decided not to point out that Natalie had gotten a Celtic knot on the inside of her ankle on a sisters' night out after her divorce. The rest of his sisters had chickened out. So technically, Natalie was the only Hale with ink.

His mind swung suddenly to Jane, as it so often did these days. He knew *she* didn't have a tattoo because he now had kissed pretty much every inch of her body.

Being with her over the last two weeks had only reinforced his love for her. He couldn't wait to drop by her house tonight to tell her about his wild time with the old folks at Bingo. But he needed to focus. He was here to press the flesh like a politician, and at that thought, he almost laughed out loud.

His uncle was rubbing his hip by the time they found his usual table, and sure enough, there were two empty chairs waiting for them.

"I've been sitting at the same table with these miscreants for probably forty years," his uncle informed him.

"Forty-three," an old lady with curly snow-white hair and a yellow sweater said. "I still remember Harriet dragging you here one night to get you away from the office."

His uncle rubbed his chin. "You're right. That woman. She told me that since I surrounded myself with words all day at the newspaper, we might as well make a game out of it. One I could win some money at."

Even Matt could hear the gruffness in Uncle Arthur's voice. What would it be like to be married for nearly fifty years? And how hard would it be to lose your partner? He decided then and there to have his uncle over for dinner more.

"She was a good one," the lady in the yellow sweater said. "God needed her in heaven. Matt, I'm Joanie. Harriet and I were best friends, and Arthur and my husband, God rest him, were friends too. Oh, what fun we used to have."

His uncle patted her hand. "The dancing. The card games. The potlucks. Those were the days. Now, enough of that old talk. Let me introduce young Matthew here to everyone."

Matt's mind was already spinning with names, but he used the word association technique he'd learned in law school. Luckily, remembering names was one of his strengths.

Uncle Arthur managed to complete the introductions before a grizzled old man stepped onto the podium holding an ancient spinner filled with balls. "We're going to start," he shouted, "so make sure you turn up your hearing aids. I'm only going to yell the combination on the ball twice."

There were a few grumbles at that, and his uncle leaned in to whisper, "That's a new rule. Last time Pat Lentley shouted for Old Man Jenkins to repeat the combination at least five times. Made the rest of us batshit crazy. The game was going on for so long a few of the really old people fell asleep and started drooling and snoring, which made it hard as hell to hear."

"That Donald Sharton sure can snore," Joanie of the yellow sweater said. "My God, an explosion at the sewage plant couldn't wake that man up when he gets to sawing logs."

Matt had to bite his lip to prevent himself from laughing out loud.

Then his uncle ran him through the game, something he'd already looked up online. Until tonight, he'd never played Bingo in his life.

As the combinations were called out—B15, D28, C4, and on it went—the people at Matt's table ran the gamut of local gossip, from a single schoolteacher entertaining a male guest to Brasserie Dare becoming a more popular hangout than the formerly preeminent Chop House. Uncle Arthur puffed out his chest at that, saying Brian had a good head for business just like his granddaughter, which is why he'd invested in his grandson-in-law's business.

Matt sat back and took it all in. He had two chips on two squares, but he needed five across to win, and when he looked around the table, he noticed a few people already had four in a row.

The infernal squeaking of the spinner made him

wince. Finally Old Man Jenkins called a stop and grabbed a can of WD-40, which fortunately put a stop to the sound.

"We've had that spinner for at least thirty years," his uncle said. "No one wants to throw it away. It's an antique."

"Exactly," Farley Johnson agreed as another number was called. "When *Antiques Roadshow* comes to Denver, we should see if it's worth any money."

"Hurrah," a few of the players agreed.

When the next combination was called out—D40—Matt smiled and reached for another chip.

"Bingo," a woman yelled out and then pushed back from her chair, grabbing her cane. Old Man Jenkins handed her an envelope when she reached the front of the room.

"What's the prize?" Matt asked.

"Five dollars," his uncle said. "It used to buy you coffee and a donut at Kemstead's Bakery, but now it will barely buy you a cup of coffee. Certainly not at my granddaughter's establishment with all her fruit- and nut-flavored mumbo jumbo. Good heavens, I'll never understand why people want to put all that crap in a cup of Joe."

Matt had been around long enough to know how much bluster his uncle dished out about Don't Soy with Me. It was all part of the banter between him and Jill.

"Most of the people here are on fixed incomes, Matt," Joanie told him, "so at least it's something."

"And where does the money come from?" he followed up.

"A fundraiser we do through the Knights of Columbus. The tootsie roll drive is very popular, and most of us buy a ton for our grandchildren."

"And how many grandkids do you have?" He didn't feel comfortable calling her Joanie, but he didn't know her last name.

"Eight. All right here in Dare. It's an incredible blessing to have a big family, but you know that. Your mom is an angel. I'm glad to have her back in town. I was her third-grade teacher."

He turned to give her his full attention now, not caring about the next combination. "You were?"

Her smile was soft. "She was a good student. Even then she was a mother hen. I remember because she'd help me redo the ponytails of the girls who'd swing at recess. I should have guessed she'd have a big family. Matt, dear, Old Man Jenkins called F13. Put your chip down. You never know. You just might win." And then she winked at him.

He didn't win that round or the next, but he quickly fell under the spell of Joanie Perkins. He'd finally asked for her last name and more stories about his mom in school.

By the time the fourth round of Bingo came around, he was starting to think this whole running for mayor thing was going to be great. These people were fun to be around. Yeah, it wasn't his normal scene, but what in the heck was? His scene in Denver had been his office, an assortment of conference rooms, court, the gym, and home.

Time to be a bit more broad-minded, Hale.

"So, you're seeing a new girl?" Farley asked him from across the table in between spins. "Jane, is it?"

The chip he held bounced across the table as his fingers went suddenly lax. Joanie slid it to him and patted his hand.

"Yes, Jane Wilcox." And just like that, all eyes focused on him as though he were under cross-examination.

"Where is she from originally?" Farley continued. "Other than working at The Grand Mountain Hotel and for Rhett Butler Blaylock, we don't know much about her."

The urge to loosen his tie was suddenly overwhelming. But he was used to being in uncomfortable situations, so he did what came naturally: he danced around the question like he would if something he couldn't discuss came up in court.

"Well, I can tell you she's as pretty and sweet as Joanie here, and that she means a lot to me." And he put his arm around Joanie for good measure.

Uncle Arthur nudged him again in the ribs. "Now, none of that. We don't allow any PDA at Bingo night. Cripes, Farley, do you remember when Kurt Walters and Rosaline Yonker made out in the hallway by the bathroom last year? Those two needed to get a room. Shocking at that age. No one should have ever told Kurt about Viagra."

"Every woman in Dare had to watch him after that," Joanie said and clucked under her breath. "Just appalling."

It might have been amusing if Matt hadn't been holding his breath, hoping the inquisition about Jane was over. Fortunately, they moved on to the topic of the new stoplight at the edge of town.

But he caught his uncle's loaded stare before Uncle Arthur looked back at his sheet and shouted, "Bingo."

"I'll get your prize, Uncle," he told him and pushed his chair back, wanting a little space from the table.

When he went up to the stage, Old Man Jenkins smiled at him and shook his hand before giving him the envelope. He returned to the table, earning another sweet smile from Joanie. He decided then and there to adopt her as his second grandmother and leaned in to tell her so, earning himself a half hug.

"You're a sweet boy, Matt. If you mind your Ps and Qs, you've earned at least one voter tonight."

Her comment made him wonder how many others felt the same way. Well, time would tell. And as Rob told him, it started with one person, one room.

"Thank you. I'm honored."

When the game finished at eight o'clock, it took another forty minutes to say goodbye to everyone. Bingo, he realized, was probably one of the only ways some of these people connected with others. They didn't have offices to attend. Their children were grown and gone. Many had lost their spouses.

This was community personified, and he was glad his uncle had brought him.

When they were finally situated in his car, heading to Uncle Arthur's house, his uncle finally broke the silence. "I'm giving you my five dollars tonight."

"Why?" he asked.

"It's my contribution for you to hire a better political consultant. That one from Denver isn't worth spit."

"Why would you say that?" Matt looked over sharply. "What did I do?"

"Sonny, next time someone asks you, you'd better be able to give a better spiel about your girlfriend. And trust me, they're going to ask."

Shit. "I realize that. We haven't…talked about what I can share about her. I don't want her to be involved in the campaign." He thought of how scared she was about the whole thing, how it dredged up the past she'd been running from for years.

"Do you love her?" Uncle Arthur asked with his usual directness. "Your mother seems to think so."

He hadn't talked to his mom about it, but she always seemed to know how he was feeling. "Yes, I love her."

"Then she's involved. This is a small town, and people are going to want to know all about her. Where she comes from. Who her people are."

His iron grip on the steering wheel didn't help him simmer down. This wasn't what he wanted to hear.

But it was what Rob and Jane had tried to tell him. And now Uncle Arthur too. All people he trusted.

"You can keep your five dollars," he said. "My

political consultant told me exactly what you just said. Jane did too, by the way. She said I was naïve to think her story wouldn't matter."

"Smart girl," his uncle mused. "Didn't expect you to fall for a dumb one, but this new generation..."

They drove in silence the rest of the way. The moon was a crescent, making the snow look like a pile of white cotton candy. When they arrived, he put a hand on Uncle Arthur's.

"I'll see you to the door. My parents raised me to be a gentleman," he added to take the sting off his uncle's pride. Still, he wasn't about to risk that the older man would fall on the ice.

As he stepped out of the driver's seat and around the car, he heard his uncle fuming, and he was treated with a venomous glance when he opened the passenger-side door.

"If you try and lay one on me, I'm going to beat you with my cane."

"Sorry," he said, holding his hands up. "I don't kiss on the first date."

Finally, his uncle laughed and exited the car. Matt didn't take his arm, but he was poised to catch him if he slipped.

"That Joanie sure is sweet," he mused. "If I were your age, I'd totally go for her."

At the door, his uncle pushed up his glasses on his nose and leveled him a glance. "And what makes you think I haven't gone for her?"

Well, that pretty much made him tongue-tied.

"We've known each other all our lives and both of us were married to our great loves. But we're friends. And now that our spouses are gone, well, there's some comfort in being together."

Matt could only nod at that.

"Bring your girl by for dinner next week," his uncle said, unlocking the door.

Arthur one-on-one with Jane? Ever the reporter, his uncle would ask more questions than a nightly news anchor.

"I'm starting my meetings with all the community organizations. Every night is booked solid." It wasn't completely a fib.

"I'm not asking, Young Matthew. I hear Tanner is going to be running an article on you. He hasn't let me see it yet, blast him. Said he didn't want my blood pressure to rise since he knows how I feel about the neutrality of *The Western Independent*."

He and Tanner had sat down at his house for the interview. His cousin-in-law's questions had been insightful, particularly when they'd talked about Patricia's case. Matt knew he could trust Tanner to portray their conversation accurately.

"He's a good guy," he told his uncle. "Meredith's lucky to have him."

"Aiya," his uncle said.

"And you're lucky to have him at the paper too," he added.

"The next generation," his uncle mused, taking hold of his arm at last. "It's not all bad. Goodnight, Young Matthew. Other than the Jane incident tonight, you did very well. Heck, you might actually make a good mayor."

"Good night, Uncle Arthur," he said with a small smile as the door closed.

So, he *had* done well tonight.

Right up until the questions about Jane.

They were going to have to talk about that issue and soon.

He looked at his watch as he strode back to his SUV. She was on her way back from a big poker tournament in Cabo. Rhett had won, and it had been so fun to listen to Jane's play-by-play of the event when they'd talked last night. She'd trusted him to care for Rufus after insisting he could handle it, and he had to admit that her dog made him think he was an awesome pet owner. Henry remained the errant child in the family, making him pull out his hair, but he and Rufus had gotten along like old friends.

He texted her.

Are you home yet? I miss you.

She immediately texted back.

Almost. Miss you too. Can you come tonight? Can't wait.

A bolt of arousal shot through him at that.

Me either. Heading your way.

Bring Henry and Rufus with you.

His fingers punched in the message, *Yes, Mom.*

LOL. See you soon. Can't wait to hear about Bingo.

Yeah, she would say that. While she didn't want to be involved in his campaign, she always asked about it. And it wasn't just because she thought she should. She really listened, and sometimes made inventive suggestions.

But he remembered those questions he'd been asked at Bingo, and a cloud hung over him as he drove home to pick up the dogs.

CHAPTER 21

When Elizabeth pulled into Jane's driveway, Annie gave a bark from the backseat. Yeah, Jane was happy to be home, particularly since she knew Matt was coming over to give her a proper homecoming. She rubbed her arms, letting herself revel in the feeling.

She let Annie outside, and the dog hurried off to do her business.

"I'll help you with your stuff," Elizabeth said, putting the car in park.

"Why don't you come inside for a little while and have a glass of wine? We can celebrate our first major tourney in our new roles."

Even though part of her wanted Matt all to herself, she desperately wanted her best friend to get to know him too. Elizabeth had turned down every invitation to hang out with them so far, always citing a date. While she was popular with the single men in Dare Valley, she wasn't *that* popular.

"Okay, just for a sec," she agreed and grabbed Annie's crate in the back while Jane lugged out her suitcase.

"God, do you remember how much luggage we used

to have to haul to tourneys? This was the first trip I wasn't over the limit."

They both laughed as they headed inside, Annie following behind with a jaunty walk. The house was nice and toasty thanks to her remote temperature control. Whoever had invented that—a woman, she'd bet— should win a Nobel Prize or something. All they needed now was a fire and a good bottle of wine.

After stowing her luggage in her bedroom, she selected a 1997 Chateau Lafite Rothschild, taking out only two wine glasses for the moment. Elizabeth would be onto her ploy if she brought three.

"So," she said, pulling her feet underneath her on the couch as the fire she'd lit flickered to life. "How do you feel about the weekend?"

"Cheers, by the way," Elizabeth said.

"Cheers."

"To answer your question, I have to say things went swimmingly."

"Swimmingly," she said in her best British accent, causing Elizabeth to snort her wine.

"Cut it out. You know what I mean. We didn't need to waste hours getting dolled up. And it made a huge difference for Rhett's social media platform for me to be tweeting throughout the tourney. And asking Rye and Rhett to take selfies for me to post didn't hurt. The fans went crazy. It exceeded my expectations."

"And of course, Annie was a big hit. And everyone seemed to respond well to Rhett's new look."

It was hard not to miss the changes in their friend, from the toned-down clothes—he was buttoning up his shirts fully now—to his calmer demeanor at the table, and there had been any number of comments about it. Of course, he still hung out with the other guys and bought everyone a round of drinks after a day of hard play. But all of the poker babe action was gone, and he'd probably slept more at this tourney than any he'd ever played in before pursuing Abbie.

"Of course, he drove me nuts by talking about Abbie the whole time," Elizabeth said. "I never imagined seeing him like this."

Which is why Jane hadn't talked about missing Matt. She knew her friend was still adjusting to the way their circle was expanding and changing.

The sound of tires crunching snow announced Matt's arrival, and Elizabeth immediately narrowed her eyes at her. "You little trickster," she said, standing. "I should have known something was up when you invited me inside. I'm outta here."

Jane jumped up and grabbed her arm. "Please stay, I want you to get to know him. At least finish your wine."

"Another time," she said and reached for her coat.

"Please, Elizabeth. This is important to me."

"I know, but not tonight."

A dark thought suddenly filtered into her mind. "You don't think we're going to last, do you?"

Her friend shook her head. "No, I'm afraid you're going to discover that being with him long-term means returning to what you hate, being a politician's accoutrement. I think this whole thing will break you in pieces..."

Jane's breath sucked in as the punch landed in her stomach. "You're wrong. I'm not going to be involved with his campaign." But she was lying to herself to think it could be that simple.

Elizabeth hugged her then. "You will be. You know it. And so do I. Think of what will happen if you end up marrying him..."

I'll become my mother, she thought. "No, it *will* be different. Matt's different, and so am I."

Her friend tugged her gloves on and picked up her oversized Gucci bag. "I hope so because all I see is heartache for you, Jane, but I promise I'll be there for you no matter what."

There was a raucous bark from the other side of the front door and Annie trotted over, her tail wagging like a hummingbird in flight.

"I love you, Liz, but you're really pissing me off."

"Then I guess it's better for me not to pretend I want to get to know Matt. I'll talk to you later."

Elizabeth opened the door, and Matt's grin faded when he registered the look on her face. "Hi, Elizabeth. How was your trip?"

Henry gave a bark, and Jane immediately disciplined him. Rufus wagged his tail and then nuzzled Annie in greeting.

"It was great," her friend replied. "I was just helping Jane with her luggage. You two have fun." And she sailed out the door without another word.

Rufus headed straight for Jane, and she leaned down and let him nuzzle her face, her thoughts troubled.

"You're frowning," Matt said, keeping a hand on Henry's collar as he shut the door behind him.

"Yes, Elizabeth means well, but she's ticking me off." She stood, and Rufus and Annie leaned against each other in greeting again, a sight that instantly warmed her heart. Crossing over to Matt and putting her hands around his waist warmed it even more. "Hi."

"Hi," he said, his gaze falling to her mouth.

"Let Henry go," she said. "He's going to be a good dog, aren't you, boy?" And, sure enough, when Matt let him go, he just sat right there beside him.

"If I didn't want to kiss you so badly, I would be in awe of your ability to make him chill."

"What's stopping you?" she asked, rising on her tiptoes and pressing a kiss to that strong, freshly shaved chin.

"I was going to be a nice guy and ask you more about your trip."

Oh, how that intention set her heart aflame in her chest. "Please don't. We can talk later. Right now, I just want to be with you."

His blue eyes stared into hers, as endless and fathomless as the sky after sunset, and then he pressed her to him, the hard line of his body adding to the heat of their embrace.

"You asked for it."

He fitted his mouth to hers and gave her the sweetest, hottest kiss of her life. When she was gasping for breath, he moved his delectable mouth down her neck. She put her hands on his shoulders, and he hoisted her up so their mouths were level. Wrapping her legs around his waist, she tangled her hands in his thick hair and poured out how much she'd missed him.

It had been new, missing someone, but he'd never been far from her mind, not even while she was working. God, it was good to be back.

His tongue tangled with hers, and soon he was carrying her down the hallway to her bedroom. When he shut the door and then lowered her onto the bed, she rolled until she was on top of him. Her desire was out of control now, like a Ferrari testing the limits of its engine, and all she wanted was to feel his hot flesh against hers. She stripped off her navy cashmere wrap and then her white T-shirt.

Her self-consciousness seemed to have evaporated like the rare raindrops in Las Vegas on hot pavement. Before she'd left, Matt had held her naked in front of the mirror after a shower and told her all the things he loved about her body. She had decided to give herself the same gift. While she was in Cabo, she looked at herself alone in the mirror, and for the first time in her life, she saw more than a tiny body without any curves. She saw her luminous skin, her supple strength. Matt had told her she had a dancer's body. While ballerinas weren't big-breasted or curvaceous, they were beautiful and graceful. And so was she.

That revelation had brought about a profound shift inside of her.

So, when she and Elizabeth had chanced upon a lingerie boutique in Cabo, she'd fearlessly gone in and bought something perfectly suited for her body. Not needing any support due to her small breasts, she'd decided to embrace what she had and selected a sheer lace bra, which she was wearing tonight. Her nipples were visible through it, and it had been a little shocking to her when she'd tried it on, but she'd bought it anyway, imagining Matt's reaction.

"Oh, Christ," he wheezed out. "You're going to kill me if you keep wearing stuff like this."

And when his hands covered the lace and plucked at her nipples, her head fell back, his words music to her ears. Then he shocked her by levering himself up and fitting his mouth to her, lace and all. He was pulsing underneath her, and she ran her hands down his back until she could pull on his coat, which he hadn't even bothered to take off.

His laughter reverberated against her, and he leaned back. "It zips."

"Take it off then," she urged, frantic for him.

"You did miss me," he murmured as he shrugged out of it, his slumberous blue eyes twinkling with desire. It had been less than a week, but it had felt like an eternity.

"I told you," she whispered. "I want you naked. Now."

He rolled her onto her side and scooted until he was off the bed and began to strip, making her mouth water as more of those hard, defined muscles were exposed. Seeing him in a navy blazer with a red silk tie gave her a strange moment. Right. Bingo Night.

"Who am I to deny a lady?" he asked, throwing his clothes on the floor.

She tugged off her boots, leggings, and socks, but left on the bra and panties. His eyes immediately went to the lacy patch between her thighs.

"Feel free to wear that all the time. Just promise you won't tell me you're wearing it when we're out in public. I wouldn't want to embarrass myself."

"We'll see." God, this playfulness was sexy.

He tossed a condom on the bed and lowered himself beside her. "I missed you too, Jane," he whispered. "So much."

His arms fitted her to him, and their mouths met with hunger. Sweetness was there too, as fingers traced skin which had become so cherished, so beloved, so desired. He trailed kisses down her torso and then kissed her through the lace, causing her to cry out in delight. Setting his mouth to her in a tantalizing rhythm he helped her cross that first peak. Gasping, she felt the slow slide of the lace down her legs as his mouth kissed a path down the sensitive skin of her inner thighs and calves until he tossed aside her underwear and gently bit her heel. The flash of desire was a shock, and she leaned up on her elbows to look at him.

His smile was wicked as he slid up her body again, his kisses more urgent now.

"Matt," she whispered, wanting to feel him deep within her.

He slid his hands over her nipples and then put his mouth on her there too. She moaned at the sensation as he reached behind her back to unhook the bra. Then he was sliding that off too, and those perfect lips closed around her bare nipple, first one and then the other, until she was arching her back like the ballerina she now saw herself as.

When he rose from her and slid on the condom, she held out her arms. He returned to her embrace and settled against her frame, his weight on his elbows.

"Oh, Jane," he said when he pressed deep inside her.

Urging him with a hand to his back, she met his gentle rhythm, but soon it wasn't enough for either of them. She gripped his hips as he drove into her hard, groaning now. The heated slide of him inside her, the friction of them coming together, and that steady gaze of his on her face sent a tidal wave of energy slamming through her. She cried out as she pulsed over and over again, and he came hard inside her.

His breath rasped against her throat as she succumbed to the force between them. *Home*, she realized. She was home. Her heart beat radically in her chest at the thought, but she knew it was true.

"I love you," she whispered, kissing his cheek.

He nuzzled her neck, still wheezing. "Me...too."

Rolling them to their sides, he dispensed of the condom and then slid back against her. His skin was dotted with sweat, and she traced a bead that rolled down his chest.

"I wasn't sure I was going to make it these past five days," she admitted. Which had been insane after going so long without sex. But she knew why. It was because she wanted *this* man. No one else could make her feel this way.

"I know," he said. "I tried to run it out of my system every day, but when I got into bed at night, there it was again."

He traced her cheek, and they just stared at each other. It was a perfect moment.

Finally she smiled at him. "I need water. What about you?"

"Definitely," he said, sitting up. "And a shower. And then I want to hear more about your trip."

"Sounds like a plan."

They brought their water glasses into the shower, and after only a few minutes of soaping each other up under the steamy water, Matt raced out of the shower for another condom, which made her laugh like a giddy schoolgirl. Soon he was back and pressing her against the tiles. The steam from the shower, her already sensitized skin, and the deep, urgent strokes of his body into hers soon had her calling out his name again. God, she was so lucky, she realized as they finally toweled off. And she slapped his butt with her towel just for the fun of it.

His brow rose. "I like this side of you."

She did too, she realized. She could be playful. Have fun. Not have to worry about one single thing. The freedom of it was a potent elixir, like a good wine. Which reminded her.

"I opened a 1997 Chateau Lafite Rothschild to celebrate coming home."

He finger-combed his wet hair, which made him look so sexy. Tousled wasn't Matt Hale's normal style, but it suited him. She could look at him like this forever.

Elizabeth's earlier words echoed in her mind, but she shook them away to focus once more on the present.

"Woman, you're going to turn me into a wine snob," he said, pulling her against him.

"Do you mind?" she asked half-seriously, and from the way his eyes flickered, she knew he understood she wasn't only talking about the wine.

"Not one bit. So, tell me more about your week."

She ran a brush through her hair. It was already mostly dry, which was the nicest thing about short hair. "Okay, but then you have to tell me about everything I've missed, especially Bingo night."

"Deal."

He shrugged into the robe he'd started to leave at her place and then took her hand. Soon they were settled in front of the fire with the dogs at their feet and two glasses of a brilliant Bordeaux, and they caught each other up on what they hadn't been able to share in their phone calls and texts.

"It was great to see Rhett win," she finished,

"especially since it means I get a bonus."

A wry smile flashed across his face. "Ah, so there's an incentive program."

"Yep. Rhett said early on that..." She had to stop herself from saying "we." Elizabeth could not be included in her account—at least, not as anything other than Rhett's publicist. "Well, he insisted I have a share of his winnings. He figured it was only fair. I get five percent on top of my annual salary."

Matt whistled. "Well, well. What was the pot he won? Three million?"

"Uh-huh. There's more pricy wine in your future."

"Good to hear. This stuff is ridiculous. I'm serious. I may never be able to drink wine from a box again."

"Not that you should," she said, stroking his thigh. God, this was nice. The sex, the talking, seeing him in that green terrycloth robe with his hair uncombed, knowing he was going to sleep over tonight and wake her in an inventive way in the morning.

"Did anyone miss his old poker girls?" he asked.

Thank God she hadn't been drinking her wine, or she might have spewed it across the room. This was uneven ground, and the guilt she felt about everything he still didn't know strangled her.

"A few people asked, but they didn't miss them." Was her voice steady? "There are always tons of poker girls around."

All of which was true. No one had truly missed Raven and Vixen. They had part of the scenery—two poker babes out of the dozen or more who hung out at tourneys with players to make them seem more Alpha at the competition. It was like being in the chorus of a large Broadway ensemble. No one truly noticed anyone but the lead actors. For a few moments when she'd first stepped out with Rhett in her new role as Annie's keeper, her stomach had trembled. But no one recognized the new her. Or Elizabeth for that matter.

Their disguises had been remarkable, so it would be shocking if anyway *did* notice her, but still... These were faces they knew well, had known for years. For a moment, the anonymity had made her feel meaningless while Elizabeth had simply been relieved.

Still, it didn't take long for Jane to make peace with her new role. She liked who she was becoming. With Matt. And with...well, herself.

"Did you ever meet them while you were working at The Grand Mountain Hotel?"

Oh, crap. How was she supposed to answer that? "They kept to themselves."

"Well, I'm sure Annie held everyone in her thrall this weekend. She could outshine a poker babe any day. I'll bet you brought some crazy outfits for her to wear."

Sitting in front of the fire, Matt took her hand then and held it, the gesture so sweet it almost brought tears to her eyes. God, she couldn't handle continuing to lie to him, not when they'd admitted they loved each other.

"Yes, she was terrific," she told him, her voice hoarse suddenly. "We even had a couple fashion designers contact us to see if they could design clothes for her as Rhett's sponsors."

"You're freaking kidding me!"

Poker was a crazy scene sometimes, and fortunately, it seemed as though Matt's questions about Raven and Vixen were over. "No, totally serious."

"That's...I don't even know what to say..."

As if she knew what they were talking about, Annie stood beside the fire and wagged her tail.

"Yeah, you, girlfriend," Jane said, her voice back to normal now. "Now tell me more about what you've been up to."

He'd been busy while she was away, and he told her about the ten local organizations with which he'd already met, but it was his account of the Bingo game that made her laugh so hard she needed to set aside her wine.

"A pole worker," she sputtered. "That's awesome! I can't imagine anyone from my hometown ever making that joke."

"It was really fun, and I thought, hey, I'm going to enjoy this mayor thing," he said, his thumb making circles over the back of her hand. "And then someone asked me something that upset me."

Her laughter faded as quickly as it had come to life. "What happened?"

He met her gaze, his bold eyes never leaving her face. "They asked about you. Where you were from. Who your family is. Jane, I...you and Rob were right. I'm not going to be able to keep you out of it, so we need to figure out what I *can* say."

Her insides curled like the newspaper she'd used to make the fire. It was exactly what she'd feared. Dammit.

"I don't want you to get scared here," he said, tipping her chin up. "I love you, and I'm right here. Talk to me."

The fire drew her gaze, and suddenly the room shifted, and she was back in her father's office at campaign headquarters. She was sixteen, and a damaging report had just been issued about her uncle's recent investments with a corporation the FCC was investigating. The spin doctors were throwing out ideas on how to package the story to underplay any embarrassment or scandal to the campaign. She knew how to spin—she'd been trained in the art of it just as most children were taught nursery rhymes.

Oh, how she'd wished never to use those skills again... The very thought made her feel like she was dying inside.

She wet her lips. "You can tell them that I'm from a small town back east like Dare and that my father is a public servant in state politics like you." Her heart accelerated, and her breathing grew shallow. "That I graduated from Harvard with an MBA."

"Jane—"

"That I run The Women's Freedom Scholarship Foundation to support young women who want to go to college and make their own way in the world." A choice she'd never really been given.

Matt took her shoulders in his hands. "Stop."

She shook her head. "You can tell them that I lived in Nevada before coming here because I like the West— the wide open spaces, the independence of the people..." And she could hear her father's voice in the back of her head as he recited words she'd written in one of his speeches.

"Jane!" Matt shook her now.

"No! Let me finish." She pushed out of his hands and stood by the fire, the blaze burning her legs. "That I love dogs, so I was happy to become a dog walker, and that I helped Mac out at the hotel on some special projects because I'm good with investments."

Matt rose, his jaw clenched. "Enough."

"That I plan to vote for you in the primary not only because I love you, but because you are the embodiment of the best qualities of a public servant."

The room was silent when she finished save the falling of embers in the fireplace.

"I don't want this to hurt you," he finally said, his voice quiet. "But I can see that it does, and I don't know how to stop that."

The fire was burning her now, but she was rooted in place by all the old memories. "You can't. But it doesn't change how much I love you, and I know you wouldn't ask this if you had a choice. We expected people would ask questions, so this shouldn't be a surprise."

Running his hands through his hair, he stared into the fire. "There are times, like right now, when I wish I wanted something different. It's tearing me into pieces seeing what this is doing to you." Then he finally looked up, and the anguish in his eyes made her tear up. "And I'm afraid it's only going to get worse."

Swallowing suddenly seemed impossible. "Are you saying you want to call it quits?"

"No!" He crossed and pulled her into his arms, away from the burn. "I am not going to lose you over this."

She remembered Elizabeth's comments again and pressed her face into his chest. "I don't want to lose you either. Just please...be patient with me."

Hs cupped her cheek then. "Always. Just promise me something."

"What?" she said, letting his touch cast some of the dark shadows away.

"That you'll keep telling me how you feel as the campaign continues. The whole truth. Even if you know it's going to hurt me."

"All right. If you'll promise to do the same."

"I will. Are we okay?"

For now. God only knew what the future held. She had been a part of enough campaigns to know how nasty they could become.

She nodded.

"Then come to bed with me. I want to make those shadows under your eyes go away."

"I'm just tired," she said, scrubbing at her face.

His hands pulled hers down, and he held them gently in his. "No, you're not."

The smile she tried to give him was an effort. "You're right. I'm not."

"You can tell me how you feel, Jane. I can take it."

A pocket of air rose up in her chest, and she had to let it out. "I'm scared."

"I know. I am too sometimes. Like tonight. I don't want anyone to ask you questions while I'm running for mayor, but I know I can't do anything to prevent it. Besides, it's as chauvinistic as hell, and my sisters would read me the riot act."

"But it's sweet, and I know why you feel that way."
Didn't she want to shield him from her past as Raven?

*God, please don't let anyone find out about that
during the campaign.* It might destroy his chances
entirely.

"I want to protect you too," she said. "Running for
politics isn't for the faint of heart. Not that you're
weak... But you're still so nice, Matt."

He brought her hand to his mouth and kissed it.
"You just can't stop seeing me as the damsel in distress,
can you?"

She knew he was trying to ease some of the tension
between them.

"I'm glad you fell that day. Otherwise, we might not
be here right now."

They both stared at the fire, and he pulled her closer
to his chest. "Oh, I think we would have gotten here
eventually."

CHAPTER 22

Matt was wrapping up his notes for the next day's talk to the Dare Valley teachers association when his secretary stuck her head through the crack in the door.

"Matt, there are some people here to see you."

He glanced at the clock. It was nearing five o'clock.

"I'll be with them in a sec, Alice," he told her.

Running for mayor was eating up more of his time, and with sunset still biding winter's call, he often needed to rush out of the office to meet Jane at the park before dusk. Fortunately, she'd come up with a brilliant plan because she was a brilliant woman. She'd started to pick Henry up so he could just meet them there.

After their walk tonight, they were going to head to Jill's house for a larger than usual Hale family get-together. She would finally meet his immediate family. His sisters had left Denver early to beat the Friday rush hour and were spending some time with their mom before the party.

Pulling on his suit jacket to look more presentable, he rose from his chair. Seeing people was part of his job now, and he couldn't beg off when they came to his office. When he walked out, any minor irritation he'd felt instantly faded.

Joanie Perkins was standing there in what had to be her signature yellow with two other older ladies, one wearing a lavender coat and the other a pale pink. With their soft white hair curling around their smiling faces, the three of them looked like an advertisement for the Sweetest Grandmothers on Earth convention.

"Joanie," he said and crossed the room to give her a gentle hug. She was so short that he had to practically bend over.

"Matt," she said, hugging him back. "I hope you don't mind us dropping by. These are two of my dear friends, Hazel Walters and Margo Burgess. We've known each other since grade school, if you can imagine that."

He couldn't, and it only made him smile.

"I've told them what I think about your candidacy for mayor. All good things, by the way," she added with a wink. "And these girls have heard lots of great feedback from other people all around Dare. So we're here to volunteer for your campaign."

For a moment, he was speechless. For some reason, he hadn't really thought about people actually volunteering to help him. Rob had said it would take time to build support, and the actual primary election was still a ways off.

"Now, don't be thinking that we don't have what it takes just because we've seen a few years," she cautioned him, misunderstanding his silence.

"I do Zumba over at the community center," Hazel said.

"And I lift weights," Margo commented. "Wanna see my muscles?"

He laughed when she flexed her arm without waiting for his answer. "I wasn't doubting your stamina for a moment, ladies. I was stunned, if you want to know the truth. You're my first volunteers."

Joanie patted his arm. "Well, we won't be the last, dear, I can promise you that. Especially now that Florence Henkelmyer has pushed her son to run against you. I swear that woman is so uptight it's no wonder her curls look like corkscrew pasta."

The other women nodded.

This was news. So far he'd been running unopposed for the primary seat. "When did this happen?"

"Just this afternoon. Florence was on her soapbox at Kemstead's, talking about another outsider trying to change Dare. She thinks you have big ideas."

And that was considered a bad thing?

"Of course, I reminded her that you grew up here and were a Hale, nonetheless, but she only scoffed, which made her choke on her bear claw. After Tim Franks pounded her on the back, she gasped that the Hales have way too much influence in this town. And she went on and on about how Jill ruined the town by helping The Grand Mountain Hotel get launched. Florence is a strict teetotaler and firmly against gambling. She hates the new hotel."

"She hates everything," Hazel whispered, clenching her black purse against her lavender coat. "I'm not even sure she likes her own son."

"I don't seem to remember him," Matt said, his mind spinning out all the possible scenarios. He'd have to call Rob and have him come down so they could re-strategize about the campaign.

"He's older than you. Works as an accountant for one of the local firms. He's always been a mama's boy, so you can be sure it's not him who'll be running, but Florence through him. She darn well knows that no one likes her."

"She's a sour puss," Margo exclaimed.

All the ladies made tsking sounds.

"Well, this will certainly make things more interesting," he said neutrally, though it sounded like

Florence was going to be a real pain in the butt. "What's the son's name?"

"Horace Henkelmyer," Joanie told him. "But don't worry, dear. You're from some nice people. Everyone in Dare loves and respects the Hales. You just need to keep doing what you're doing. Meeting people. Talking about why you're running. That story about your last client just breaks my heart when I think about it."

It was becoming easier to share, and a more in-depth version of his campaign platform would be featured in Tanner's article about him in this Sunday's paper. The timing couldn't be better.

"Ladies, you have made my day," he said, calculating the time in his head. He'd made a deal with himself that he would never become too busy for Jane, and he didn't like the idea of missing their walk in the park. "This new development requires some thinking. Can I get back to you on what I might need you to do?"

"Sure thing, sweetheart," Joanie said, and he refrained from telling her that calling the mayoral candidate that endearment might not be good for his campaign. "We've all volunteered for elections in Dare before."

"We know where the bodies are buried," Hazel whispered conspiratorially.

"Don't scare the man," Margo said. "You'll be fine. Just watch out for Florence. She can be a viper."

And he hated snakes. "Good thing I have you lovely ladies to be my snake charmers."

They all laughed.

"We might even be willing to wear those outfits—you know, the ones with all the sheer veils?" Hazel said.

The image of those sweet, old ladies in such sensual get-ups made the muscle in his eye twitch.

"But it's as cold as a witch's tit right now, so there will be none of that," Margo added.

"They're just kidding, Matt," Joanie assured him.

"Now run off to the park with your girl and have fun with the Hales tonight. Tell your mom hello for me."

He wasn't even going to ask how she knew about his plans. There were obviously no secrets in Dare. Except for Jane's, of course...

"I told my mom about meeting you at Bingo. She said the two of you would have to have coffee some time and catch up. But she won't recite her multiplication tables for you," he said with a grin.

"I wouldn't want to hear those anyway. They bored the heck out of me when I was a teacher. Now, run along. No woman likes to be kept waiting."

All three of the ladies nodded their encouragement. It really was late. "You don't mind?"

"No, we're going ourselves. But button up. It's frigid outside."

His visitors pulled on hats and gloves that matched their individual coats and waved goodbye. As he watched them go, he decided to dub them the Easter Brigade, since they were dressed in pale pastel tones of yellow, pink, and lavender.

They might not look tough, but they were a heck of a lot more tuned into Dare's local gossip circuit than he ever could be. That alone would be an excellent contribution to his campaign. Plus they knew this Florence, and they'd already given him invaluable information about her son. He'd have to ask Uncle Arthur and his mom what they knew about them. He had a vague recollection of the older woman's name, but couldn't put a face to it.

Well, he had an opponent now.

And a potentially mean mother pulling the strings. What was this? *The Manchurian Candidate?*

CHAPTER 23

Jane was doing her best not to shiver when Matt finally pulled into the parking lot. Henry barked as his master ran toward them, wearing his wool coat rather than his normal black North Face jacket. Sunset was quickly disappearing behind the mountains, bleeding from the brilliant orange and blue into black.

"I'm sorry," he said, kissing her immediately as he shoved aside a jumping Henry. "I had my first volunteers show up, and it set me behind."

"Henry," Jane said to quiet him.

Matt gave all three dogs an absent pat down, those brilliant blue eyes never leaving her face.

"I figured something must have come up," she said. "I was going to give you another five minutes before texting you and heading home."

"You're freezing," he said, pulling her into his body to shield her from the wind.

"The temperature's dropping," she said, cuddling into his warmth. "We're supposed to get more snow tonight."

"Great," he said and then cupped her cheek with his gloved hand. "Then we won't have anywhere to go in the morning, and I can make love to you all I want."

Didn't he always? She had to admit she was beside herself with joy about having that new connection in her life. He was changing the way she saw everything, and even though it sometimes still scared her, she couldn't imagine wanting anything else.

"Sounds like a plan," she said and squeezed him around the waist.

"I need to go home and change for the party tonight. And call Rob. There was a new development today."

He ran her through what the Easter Brigade had told him about the new candidate. Fear crushed her lungs, making it hard to draw a full breath. This candidate's mother would go for the jugular. Her father had run against people like that before, the ones behind the scenes, and they were often the most vicious. For them, it wasn't about winning. It was about trying to sling enough mud at the other candidate to make him or her lose.

And that was bad news. God knew Jane had enough secrets in her background to weaponize an entire army of mudslingers.

"It's going to be okay," he said, tipping up her chin. "Whatever comes, we'll face it together."

He was smart not to promise he would make sure she didn't get hurt. They both knew he couldn't. And he didn't know how much her secret could hurt him...

"I know," she said and stood on her tiptoes to kiss him. "Let's get going. Looks like snow's on its way."

There was a mellow peach glow in the east, punching through the darkness, and she'd learned to respect that particular shade in the sky. It usually meant snow and lots of it.

"All right. I'll change quickly for the party and then meet you at your house in a jiffy. You good with keeping Henry with you?"

She arched her brow. "Aren't I always?"

"Yes," he said, finally giving the dogs the full attention they craved.

He was always doing that, attending to her first, and once they were...well, *connected*, then he would turn to the dogs. Some pet owners fawned over their dogs more than their guests. Whenever Jane visited people like that, she felt a bit slighted, like her company didn't matter to them. Matt never acted that way, not with anyone.

"I'll see you in a little while then," she said when they reached the parking lot.

He waved, and she noticed he was already talking to someone in the car as he pulled out. Rob, she expected, the political consultant she had yet to meet. Didn't *want* to meet, truth be told.

When she arrived home, she gave the dogs fresh water and then changed for the party. Her nerves were so tight she felt like she could jump out of her skin. Matt had a new opponent and tonight she would be meeting his family... What a day.

Matt had said dinner would be casual, but she'd called Elizabeth to run through what she should wear. Her friend was still acting a bit distant, but she'd helped anyway, just as she always did. She ran her hands down her green wool dress. It had a ballerina feel to it—the bodice was tight, and then it flared out at her hips and stopped a few inches above her knees. Her black tights created a nice contrast with her new high-heeled caramel boots from Italy. The metal studs on the back of them drew a person's gaze to her slim calves. They gave her a few more inches, which she desperately needed, and made her feel chic. His sisters were from a big city, and she suspected they were all pretty put together from what he'd said about them.

To finish off her look, she added a chunky amber jewelry set she'd bought in Moscow when Rhett had played in a tournament there. The golden tones glowed against the green wool, and the tear drop earrings enhanced the delicate line of her neck. Her eyes were smoky, and she added a pale rose lipstick to her mouth.

Satisfied, she poured herself a glass of Domaine Meo-Camuzet Richebourg Grand Cru, Cote de Nuits, a gem of a wine, because after today, she had freaking earned it. When Matt opened the door fifteen minutes later—she always left it unlocked when she was expecting him, and she loved that he just came in now— he stopped suddenly, ran his eyes down her body, and whistled.

"Are you sure we should go meet my family tonight? You looked like you're dressed for an evening on the town."

The whistle had given her goosebumps. "Trust me. Your sisters aren't going to be dressed as casually as you've been suggesting."

He'd only introduced one woman to his family, a girl in college, so she darn well knew they knew how important this was to him.

"You're probably right," he said, shedding his coat as the dogs pranced around him.

He gave them all a casual pat and then crossed over to her. His eyes took in the wine glass resting on the side table beside the couch. "And what are we drinking tonight?"

When she told him, he groaned. "Okay, give me a half a glass since I'm driving. But first..."

Then he kissed her, and she all but melted into him. His mouth was unhurried as it tugged on her bottom lip. For once, she didn't have to raise herself on tiptoes to tangle her hands in his hair, and soon they were both breathing hard.

"You're taller," he mused, tracing her cheek.

"Funny what a difference heels can make," she noted, smiling like a total idiot. Some days her face hurt from all the smiling she was doing, but she just couldn't seem to stop.

She was happy.

Everything in her life was almost perfect. If he hadn't been running for mayor, it would be.

"I like the earrings," he commented. "They make me want to..."

The gentle bite he gave her neck made her clutch him and groan. "Do we have time?"

His head turned to glance at the clock. "Yes, but it'll have to be quick."

Right. A quickie before meeting his family. "Maybe we'd better not," she said, pulling back, taking a deep breath.

"Worried my family will be able to tell?" he asked, an amused gleam in his eyes.

"Yes," she answered honestly. "I want to make a good impression."

He stepped back and ran his hands down her arms. "I know you do, and you will, so why don't you pour me some wine, tell me about your day, and then we can head out?"

The freedom she felt with him was beyond anything she'd known outside of Elizabeth and Rhett. He never pushed her to do anything she didn't want. "I really did want to make love to you, even if it was a quickie."

A grin flashed across his face. "I know that. You can't keep your hands off me. And who could blame you?"

She was still smiling when they arrived at Jill's house, Matt keeping her entertained with more of his usual banter. The driveway and street were packed with cars, signaling that they were likely the last to arrive. When he turned off the engine, he reached for her hand.

"At first they're going to love you because I do, and then they're going to love you because they've gotten to know you like I do. Just be yourself."

His words...well, they loosened every knot in her

belly.

"Have I told you how much I adore you?" she said softly.

Those blue eyes of his seemed to glow with pleasure. "Have I told you it back?"

"A few times."

"I'll make sure to mention it a lot later, but right now, my family's waiting. Just remember, how could you not love them? You love me, right?"

She knew it wasn't that simple. In her experience, there were rotten apples in every basket. But maybe his would be different. They *sounded* different.

"Okay, let's do this," she said.

He didn't knock here either, just stepped inside. She kind of loved that. The house was packed with people, conversation, and laughter intermingling into a loud but friendly chaos in the living room adjoining the small entryway. The smells of roasted meat and garlic had her mouth watering. Having a chef as your host wasn't a bad way to go. A little boy was running through the throng of adults making an airplane sound to accompany the red flyer he carried over his head. Matt's sisters drew her gaze.

She'd called it. They were chic. And beautiful. And tall.

All eyes turned toward her and Matt, and the sound level dropped significantly.

When Jill spotted them, she called out, "Matt! Jane! Come on in." One of the twins was nestled in her arms.

Matt took her coat and then shed his own. When he finished, he put a hand on the small of her back. As a show of support, it couldn't have been more welcome.

"Just throw the coats in the closet for now," Jill said. "Brian had to get more hangers. Welcome, Jane. What can I get you to drink while Matt introduces you to the Hales from Down Denver?"

Brian reappeared with hangers and handed them to

Matt, who hung up the coats. "It's a pun on Down Under. She thinks she's being funny, but I say it's sleep deprivation. This house could be a test site for a new clinical study on the effects of sleeplessness on normally functioning people."

"Quit complaining, babe," Jill said. "Now...oh yuck. Bri, Mia just barfed down my back. Can you grab a burp rag?"

He scuttled like a track athlete and was soon wiping up the white mess trailing down Jill's purple and red print tunic from his daughter's cherub mouth.

"Jane," Brian said, looking up at her. "I brought something from the restaurant especially for you. Will you do another blind test? I told one of my chef friends about your talent, and he insisted I make you do it again."

"It's all he's talked about," Jill said, patting a drooling Mia on the back.

With the open floor plan, much of the first floor was visible from the foyer, from the sunshine-yellow den to a large doorway showcasing the bold red dining room, where an enormous table was covered with dishes of food, everything from roasted meats, braised Brussels sprouts, mini-quiches, a basket of baguettes that made Jane's mouth water, a plate of cheeses, a tray of fruit, and a three-layer chocolate cake covered with raspberries. Oh yeah, this was going to be awesome. Her mouth was already watering.

"Matt," an older woman called, coming forward.

Jane immediately knew it was his mother. His blue eyes and deeply searching gaze had come from her. She was a few inches taller than Jane with chin-length brown hair shot with red highlights. "Aren't you going to introduce us to Jane?"

One of his sisters came forward too, approaching until she stood beside them.

He kissed his mother's cheek and then the other

woman's. His other two sisters came in next, followed by a man who had to be Matt's brother.

"Jane," Matt said, rubbing her back. "This is my mom, my sisters Natalie, Caroline, and Moira." Fortunately, each of them gave a playful wave when her name was called. "And this is my brother, Andy."

A young boy plowed into him. "Uncle Matt! What took you so long?"

"And this is my nephew, the erstwhile flier of the tenth brigade, Danny Hale."

On cue, the boy started to zoom around with his airplane again.

"Hi, Jane," they all chorused.

"It's wonderful to meet you," she said, making sure to meet everyone's eyes in turn. "Thank you for having me."

His family must have made an impression everywhere they went while he was growing up, not simply from the sheer number of them, but from their striking beauty. They shared the same thick brown hair with glimmering red highlights. Natalie could have been a shampoo model with her long and lustrous mane and body decked out in skinny jeans and a red silk tunic. Moria's hair was chin-length like her mother's. She was the shortest of the sisters, likely five eight if Jane had to guess, and dressed the most casually in a gray cashmere sweater and black pants. Caroline's hair was shoulder length, and her style held an air of elegance, from the black wool skirt and white silk blouse to the mauve velvet jacket Jane immediately identified as Vera Wang.

"Aren't you going to introduce her to me, Young Matthew?" an old man shouted. "What am I, chopped liver?"

Matt kissed his other sisters as they crossed to the man Jane knew to be his uncle.

"And this is Uncle Arthur. And Meredith, my cousin, and Tanner, her husband."

She nodded to the couple standing beside his chair and then turned her gaze to the older man. She'd seen him around town before, walking with his cane, and she knew the stories about all the Pulitzers he'd won and how he'd created a newspaper empire out of nothing.

"Young lady. It's good to finally meet you. Mac and Rhett can't stop talking about how nice you are, and since neither of them are pushovers, that counts for something."

"It's good to meet you too, Mr. Hale," she said, following her instinct and extending her hand, which he took in a firm shake.

"Please call me Arthur. If you call me Mr. Hale, at least two other people might answer, one of whom is your boyfriend, which would just be strange."

Jane agreed. "Arthur, then. I know we've never officially met, but I want to tell you how much I admire what you and your paper have done. I grew up with *The Western Independent* in my family's home, and I always found your articles compelling. It's admirable how much your newspaper broadens the debate on important issues facing the country, especially around election time."

His blue eyes might be a bit dimmed by age, but there was no mistaking the shrewdness in them. "I hope your father, being a politician himself, found the paper's stances on key issues particularly illuminating."

Matt stiffened beside her. "Dammit, Uncle Arthur."

Jane forced her smile to lift the corners of her mouth. "It's okay, Matt. Your uncle is an award-winning journalist, and from what Rhett and Mac have told me, he looks out for his family. It only makes sense that he would know something about my background."

"Just so, my dear."

Her belly filled with ice, but she'd been raised to smile even in the most hostile of rooms, and this was nowhere near that. "Find anything interesting?" she challenged. Best to find out right away if he knew her secret about Raven.

"Well, I knew you were a smarty pants, which you're only proving right now. And you're as rich as Midas from your family's manufacturing empire, so you don't take care of Rhett's dog because of the money."

She lifted her chin and stared him down. She'd been around enough powerful men to know when it was important to show strength, and Arthur Hale was just the kind of man to respect some backbone in a woman. "You're well informed on those fronts. I am as rich as Midas, which your grandson-in-law is about ready to confirm by having me blind test a very expensive French wine. But I've used that money and the money I've made from investing—another hobby—to create a foundation for women to go to college. And you're right. I work for Rhett and take care of his dog and my own because I love it. I also love Matt and this town. Anything else you want to know?"

Matt cleared his throat and ducked his head to hide a smile.

"Like any good journalist," he answered, "I always ask questions when something new comes up. For the moment, Jane Wilcox, I'm satisfied."

Meredith rolled her eyes, and Tanner's shoulders were shaking with silent laughter.

"Well," she responded. "That's all that matters then."

Brian appeared with a wine bottle wrapped in a black tea towel and a crystal glass in his hand. "You don't mind if I pull Jane away for a moment, do you?"

"She was just talking to us about her love of good wine," Arthur commented, stroking his chin. "Let's have her do the blind test here. I haven't seen one in years."

"Oh, put a sock in it," Meredith said, coming over to her. "I swear, Grandpa, it's her first Hale gathering, and you're treating her like she's a person of interest during the Cold War. For heaven's sake. Tanner, get him another scotch. Maybe that will help him simmer down."

"I'll show you simmer, young lady," he blustered, but gave her a wink before turning to Tanner. "You should talk to your wife about speaking to her grandfather that way."

"I don't even talk to my wife about speaking to *me* that way."

Another harrumph sounded in Jane's ears as Meredith, Matt, and Brian led her to the kitchen. Pots and pans pretty much occupied all the counters, discarded from earlier use. The Viking range drew her eye. Only serious cooking should take place on such a stove. They'd had one in her house when she was a kid, though her mother had never used it. This was a chef's kitchen, all right, with cooking utensils laid out like a surgeon's and copper pots hanging on a metal rack above a kitchen island covered in caramel-colored granite.

"Thank God, Violet sleeps like I do," Brian told her as he poured an ounce into her glass.

Her gaze went to the floor. She'd been so enraptured with his professional kitchen that she'd missed the other twin girl sleeping in her carrier, a bulldog by her side like a guardian. Man, she was cute, breathing out of her little mouth in small puffs of air.

"And that's Mutt, our dog. Now, then. Do your stuff." Brian extended the wine to her.

"I hope you don't mind me watching," Meredith said, sliding in beside her brother-in-law. "Brian couldn't stop talking about what you did at the restaurant on your first date with Matt."

"This I have to see," Natalie said, coming into the room and snaking a hand around Matt's waist.

Seeing him being so casual and loving with his sister shot pure sunshine through her. They were a unit.

"Just you wait," Brian commented. "She's incredible."

"She sure is," Matt said, his gaze bringing a smile to her face.

As Brian rubbed his hands together like a delighted little boy, Jane picked up the glass, eyeing the color. The deep ruby shade hinted at mineral-rich dark soil.

She let her eyes close as she drew the glass to her nose and inhaled deeply. The first whiff of dark fruit and smoke had her body floating to France's Burgundy region, to the vineyards nestled between Nuits St. Georges and Flagey-Echézeaux. In her mind, she could see the worn and crumbling stones of the Abbey of Saint Vivant where the wine had begun—the church of Vosne, the village from which the wine took its name. As she took that first sip, she knew exactly what she was going to taste: the perfect balance of weight, structure, elegance, and longevity. Her tongue soaked up the tart red fruits of cherries and raspberries like parched earth soaking up rainwater. And like the final rain turning to steam on a warm summer day, she picked up a few final echoes of licorice and smoke.

She was aware of the silence in the kitchen, but part of her was in the village she'd loved visiting when she was in France, and she wasn't ready to return.

"What are you—"

"Shhh," a chorus of people immediately told Brian.

It took effort to elude the lure of that place, the earthy scents of loamy soil and fragrant flowers dotting the fields, but she did. Opening her eyes, she met Matt's heated gaze and had to look away. She was already swept away enough as it was.

"Emmanuel Rouget Cros Parantoux, Vosne-Romanee Premier Cru," she told Brian and set down her glass.

He slapped his knee. "Holy crap! You're like a wine superhero. Care to venture a year?"

That was always the hardest, but she ran through what she knew of the harvests. "2001?"

"Close. 2000. Shit...I mean. Sorry, I'm not supposed to say that anymore in front of the girls. Holy crap! That's freaking incredible. Seriously." He hugged her. "You're my new wine diva."

"Just so long as you remember who warms your feet at night and feeds your kids," Jill said, entering the room to lay a sleeping Mia in the carrier next to her sister.

"I'd never want to forget that, babe," he said, snagging her as she walked by to give her a big smacker on the lips. "But seriously. Jane is ridiculous."

"That is pretty impressive," Natalie commented. "Brian, please tell me you're planning on sharing the love with the rest of us. After that little display, I will not be denied. Jane, if I were into women, I would have jumped you, watching you go through your little ritual. My brother here was on a tight leash."

"Hey," Matt said, bumping her.

She elbowed him. "Well, you were. Am I embarrassing you, Matty Ice?" Her voice crooned.

"Matty Ice?" Jane asked.

"It's our way of teasing him for the frosty lawyer he used to be. He's walking the saintly path now, but we still use the nickname because it irritates the crap out of him," Natalie informed her with a wink.

"I see," she said, wondering about that other man he'd been.

The look Matt gave his sister could have withered even the most stalwart vines in Burgundy. "Be nice, or I'll start in on you."

"Fine," his sister said. "We don't need Jane to head for the hills after meeting the Hales. My God, that was a lot of H's. Try and say that fast three times."

Jill did, and the way she boggled the final sentence made everyone laugh. Brian twirled her and then dipped her low. "I love you, even though you have a momentary speech impediment."

"Haha. Let me up. I need to go pump."

"And then she ruins it," he murmured and was rewarded with a jab to the gut.

The rest of the evening ran pretty much like the moments in the kitchen. Jane being watched. Matt's family cracking jokes while they playfully elbowed, kicked, or shoved each other—even their mother. Well, not the kicking or shoving part. But April Hale held her own, and it was clear to Jane that even though she was the shortest of her family and was drastically outnumbered by her five adult kids, she was still respected.

When she linked her arm through Jane's and pulled her away from Matt with a smile, Jane wasn't in the least bit surprised. For a few moments, it had looked like his sisters had wanted to do the same, but Matt had stayed by her side the whole evening, sending them a clear message.

"Matt tells me you're a wonder with Henry, and I wanted to thank you for that. We were concerned when he told us he was planning on keeping Patricia's dog, God bless her soul. When it was obvious Henry wouldn't listen to Matt, I hoped he would let someone else raise the poor dog, but Matt's conscience wouldn't allow that."

Not wanting Matt to be concerned, she steered his mom into the kitchen. She didn't need protecting, and it was important to send a message to everyone here tonight. She was her own woman, not a doll to be cosseted.

"And what's that trait, Mrs. Hale?"

"Please call me April," she said and patted Jane's hand. "He's loyal. It's mostly a laudable trait, but the flip side is that he has trouble letting go. Henry reminds him of Patricia and the guilty sentence he's leveled onto himself."

Was there a warning in April's story? Rather than saying anything, Jane nodded for her to continue.

"Matt always does the right thing, and he puts family and his sense of integrity above all else. I love that about him. I've raised all my children to behave that way, but Matt's profession of being a lawyer has sometimes...made it more difficult than, say, Andy's of being a doctor."

"He's a good man," she told April. "It's one of the first things I noticed about him. That and his sense of humor."

A string of raucous laughter from the other room seemed to make her point.

"Yes, he is, and he's not the type to just fall for a woman with a pretty face, which is why I know there's something very special about you. I hope you'll allow us to get to know you better now that you and Matt are together. Come over for dinner on Sunday afternoon. Maybe someday soon, just us girls can go to lunch together."

"How about we do lunch this Sunday and not dinner?" Natalie said, appearing by her side as if summoned by magic. "We can head back before traffic gets too crazy."

"And this would be my eldest daughter, who always got into trouble for eavesdropping growing up."

"Uncle Arthur told us it was the best way to find things out," she said. "So, how about it? Lunch with us girls at Brasserie Dare on Sunday?"

"I'd love to," she replied, and April patted her arm again. "Good. Now I need to find one of Jill's babies. I just can't get in enough time with them."

Natalie rolled her eyes. "The woman has five kids. You'd think she'd be over holding babies and burping them, but not my mom."

"What about you?" she asked. "Don't you like kids?"

"I love them. Danny especially. I'm divorced because my ex didn't want kids. He was too focused on football. Don't you love a man who puts sports over everything?"

This was new. Matt had given her short sketches of all his siblings, but not this much information. "I'm sorry. Was he a professional athlete?"

"Yes," Natalie said and went over to pull a beer from the fridge. "He's the quarterback for the Denver Raiders."

Jane blinked. "Your ex is Blake Cunningham? He's like—"

"A god? I know. *He* knows. No one could ever fault his looks. It's his heart that's still in question, but that's water under the bridge. What about you? Any exes to drive Matt crazy?"

Because her eyes were twinkling, and contained not a trace of judgment, Jane answered, "Actually, your brother is the first man I've ever loved."

"You're smart. He's a keeper. I keep wishing I'll meet a man like him who isn't a blood relation. Andy's the same way. Oak trees, both of them. Solid. Comforting. Awe inspiring."

"You're so lucky to have them," Jane said, watching the people in the other room weave around each other with ease and familiarity. "I always wished I had siblings growing up."

"Nat," Matt said, grabbing her around the waist from behind. "You better not be bothering my girlfriend." Natalie squealed when he lifted her off her feet, and her knee-high boots kicked at him. When he set her down, he immediately raised his hands in front of him, ready to bat down any attempts at retaliation.

"I'll get you later, Matty Ice. Watch your back." She waved to Jane as she walked backwards out of the room, her eyes flashing.

"Everything okay?" he asked, bringing Jane's hand to his lips.

"Everything is perfect."

And it was.

But she was still keeping an enormous secret from him, and she realized she couldn't wait any longer to tell him the truth about Raven.

CHAPTER 24

On Monday morning, Elizabeth was watching tape of Rhett's poker tourney in Cabo, looking for any signs of weakness in his play. Of course, they all knew it had been risky to go all in with a hand of three jacks against Calvin Bulrow, but it had worked. Calvin had folded, and Rhett had advanced to the semi-finals. Rhett was known for having some of the biggest balls on the poker circuit, and being with Abbie hadn't changed that even if it had changed everything else.

She rather missed Vixen, though certainly there were no avenues for a woman like that in Dare. Sometimes she'd gone out to a club with some of her girlfriends in Las Vegas dressed as her alter ego. Elizabeth laughed at the notion of dressing like that and heading to Hairy's Irish Bar, Dare's most popular meeting place. A few of the men might faint.

There just weren't any men in this town who could handle a woman like that.

And she wasn't sure there were too many who could handle Elizabeth Saunders either.

God, she might have to start online dating with men in Denver. But that would mean commuting for dates—

and sex—and where would that lead?

Jane and Rhett were happy here, but while the mountain vistas couldn't be more incredible, she was starting to develop itchy feet. Jane might have survived epic Man Fasts, but she wasn't interested in doing the same.

Not that Jane was on a Man Fast right now. No, she was late for their morning meeting for the first time *ever*, having texted that she was running late.

Yeah, late.

When her friend rushed inside, her cheeks flushed and her eyes glowing, Elizabeth crossed her arms and smirked. "And how was your morning?"

She plopped her red oversized Coach bag on the table in the foyer and dug out her files. "Fine. Sorry about that."

"Please! At least one of us is having sex," Elizabeth said.

"Is that why you're cranky?"

"Probably. You're practically beaming from the afterglow right now. I may need sunglasses just to look at you."

Jane dug hers out and waggled them. "Here, you can have mine," she said with a small smile.

They hunkered down and watched more tape. Elizabeth rewound to the parts she wanted Jane to see, and they conferred that Frank Pickers was bluffing when he stared at Rhett without blinking.

"He's trying to intimidate him," Jane said.

"Like anyone can do that with Rhett."

They ran through four more hours of tape. When they finally took a break, Elizabeth realized she had avoided asking Jane for details about meeting Matt's family. Friday night's party had turned into Saturday skiing at Mac's hotel, and then Sunday had been filled with lunch with his sisters before his sisters had returned to Denver. Other than a few texts, they hadn't really done their whole go-into-details conversation.

"Okay," she said, manning up. If her friend was serious about this guy—and she certainly seemed to be—she could set aside her doubts and fears for the moment. "Tell me about this weekend."

The smile that spread across Jane's face told her how much she'd been wanting to do exactly that. By the time she finished, though, Elizabeth was frowning.

"The old man could be a problem," she mused out loud.

"You sound like a moll in a mobster movie," Jane tried to joke. "I know what you mean. It made me realize he might dig deeper. He protects his family."

"Was Matt upset?" If not, he was a class-A jerk.

"Yes, and really surprised. He wants to protect me, Elizabeth, but there's no way he can." She scooted closer and put a hand on her arm.

Oh, no. She was going to ask her again, and her heart rate spiked. Her answer hadn't changed, not one bit.

"This new candidate who's challenging Matt...well, his mother is known for being a mean old lady who stirs up trouble. I'm afraid she might cause problems. And I'm tired of still holding back from him. This weekend confirmed how serious we are. I really want to tell him about Raven, Liz."

She made herself look away from Jane's entreating gaze. "If you tell him about Raven, it's not much of a leap to tell him about Vixen too. And what in the world happens when he tells the rest of his family? His extended family owns a newspaper, for God's sake. What if they decide that it's news fit to print? I mean, it's a juicy story about local persons of interest, especially since we worked out of Mac's hotel. You know the controversy caused by the opening of the hotel."

Jane looked down in her lap.

"And what about Rhett and Abbie? It would

embarrass them beyond words, Jane. And that's not even considering what it could do to Rhett on the circuit."

"I trust him, Elizabeth," her friend said softly. "He has more integrity than any man I have ever met. Rhett included."

Now that stopped Elizabeth in her tracks. "What do you mean?"

"Rhett has been a loose cannon at times without intending to be. All that's changing now with Abbie, of course, but I can assure you that Matt is solid. He would never say anything to his family if I asked him to keep quiet."

Elizabeth rose and paced by the fireplace. "You don't know that. From what you've said, they're incredibly close. We may not be used to that dynamic, but families like that don't keep things from each other... I need a drink."

This whole conversation was only causing her more anxiety. She wasn't sure how long this situation could go on this way.

"When will it be enough that *I* trust him, Liz?" Jane asked, following her. "What if he asks me to marry him? Can I tell him then? Will that be enough of a declaration of faith?"

Marry him? "Jeez, he hasn't mentioned that, has he?"

"No, not yet, but I'm hoping that's the way we're headed. His family is including me like I'm one of them, Liz. He's only introduced one other girl to them, and that was in college."

Well, that did sound serious.

Jane grabbed the glasses from the cabinet as Elizabeth reached for the sweet tea she'd made earlier. She blamed Rhett for introducing her to the Southern concoction. She didn't need the sugar, but it sure hit the spot. Especially with a slice of orange, her favorite.

The two of them arranged a tray and Elizabeth carried their drinks out with some grapes she'd washed earlier. They settled back on the couch and sat in silence. Jane barely touched the grapes or tea, instead staring straight ahead into the cracking flames.

There had to be a solution...one that would keep everyone safe while giving her friend what she so desperately wanted. And then it dawned on her. "I have it!" she cried, and Jane dropped a grape she'd been holding.

"What?" she asked.

"You can hire him to be your lawyer. It would be covered under attorney-client privilege."

Jane rose and put her hand to her heart. "You want me to pay my boyfriend money so I can tell him something vital about my past?"

When Elizabeth heard the quiver in Jane's voice, she set her glass aside. "It's also vital to my past, let's remember."

"You're hamstringing me, Elizabeth. If he finds out that I've kept something this big from him, it could ruin us."

"I would think you'd see this as a compromise."

Jane's hand slashed through the air. "Compromise? When have we ever needed to make one of those when it comes to the big stuff?"

Her heart squeezed. Jane was right. They'd never been at odds like this before. And it hurt. Made her want to cry, dammit, and she hated feeling that way.

"You know what we're facing here? You're losing sight of the big picture because you've fallen in love for the first time. Give it time."

"Right, and that's something you'll never allow yourself to feel. Not even when you were with Terrance that summer."

Right. Chef Terrance Waters of the Peacock Hotel in Atlantic City with his badass attitude, deep soulful eyes, and rock hard tattooed body had made her feel unhinged. The magnetic attraction between them, coupled with a warmth and intimacy she'd never before experienced, had made her feel weak...vulnerable. So she'd broken it off.

"What happened with Vince destroyed your faith in love," Jane continued, "and I'm sad for you because there is nothing more precious than knowing you are cherished by a good man. Matt *is* a good man, and dammit, I wish you'd open your eyes enough to see that."

The ground was cracking between them like an earthquake separating tectonic plates, putting them on opposite sides of the fissure. She rose and reached for Jane's hand, and for the first time, her friend ignored the peace-making gesture.

"This is the best I can do right now," she told her. "Have you talked to Rhett?" Perhaps it was time to deflect her views.

"No, I wanted to talk to you first since I knew you had the biggest concerns. Rhett understands what it means to be in love, to trust someone."

The accusation hung between them like the thick smoke that coiled from the fireplace when the flute was shut.

"I've told you what I can live with right now," she said.

"Fine. I'll talk to Rhett." Jane walked to the door and grabbed her coat and purse on her way. "But I've told you that you need to do better, and I know you can."

"You're a big talker." Jane was being unfair, and her anger spurted out. "But are *you* ready to leave the past behind? Everything with your parents?" Not that she had with her own.

She gave her a hard glance and left without putting on her coat first. Elizabeth dropped onto the floor by the fire. Drawing her knees up, she lowered her forehead to them.

Everything was changing, and she hated it. All of it.

CHAPTER 25

After attending to her dogs, Jane fumed the whole way over to Rhett's. She had texted him with the request to talk as soon as possible, and he'd told her to come on over. Elizabeth's idea that she should hire Matt as a lawyer rankled her completely. As she rolled down the window to cool her flushed cheeks, she took in a deep gulp of the mountain air. And realized suddenly that Liz was right. It wasn't only her secret. Dammit, though, the whole bloody business felt like one of her father's political Gordian knots. Elizabeth had suggested an out-of-the-box solution. It would undoubtedly upset Matt, but she hoped he would trust her.

And it was time for him to know the truth, however it needed to be delivered.

She'd loved him before meeting his family, but seeing the Hales together had made her fall for him even more.

When she arrived at Rhett's, he met her at the door. "From that look on your face, I'd say you and Elizabeth had a fight."

"We did." They'd had their squabbles, but never like this.

He took her coat and hung it on the brass coat rack by the door. The house where he lived with his new family was warm and welcoming, with its muted gold walls decorated with dark furniture, landscape paintings, and spring bouquets arranged in eye-catching vases of glass and crystal on the various surfaces.

"Come on in and tell ol' Rhett about it."

It took a while for her to get it all out, but when she finally finished, he swore. "This sure is getting complicated." Rising, he stalked to the window that framed a stunning view of the valley, including snow-capped peaks, a jagged tree line of pines, and a breathtaking expanse of blue sky.

"I know."

"Any way you look at it, someone's happiness is at stake," Rhett mused. After another moment he turned around. "That's what concerns me. I've talked to Mac. We're fairly certain that I'd be okay if this whole business were to come out. At the highest levels, we don't think anyone wants bad press. There could be media blitzes on cheating, and no sport—even one like poker—comes off looking good in those articles."

Jane thought of baseball and all the performance-enhancing drug scandals and nodded. Scouts weren't illegal per se, but... Gray areas didn't matter to the media.

"Mac is concerned about some of the rising players, though, the ones who've been trying to stick it to me. And I talked to Abbie too."

This time he turned back to the window, and her stomach dropped.

"She understands your conundrum, but she wants to raise Dustin here, and she's worried what might happen if the news were to come out. High school kids can be cruel."

None of this surprised her. In their shoes, she would have felt the same way. Which left Elizabeth's suggestion. "And what about Liz's solution?"

His sigh was long and deep. "It's worth considering. Of course, if I were in Matt's shoes, I wouldn't like it one bit."

"I know."

"But he's a lawyer, so perhaps we're underestimating him. God knows, we pay lawyers enough to deal with these moral gray areas. Maybe he'll surprise us."

He might understand why she needed to do things this way, but it still needed to be done, and the sooner the better. The fear that someone was going to find out and use the knowledge against him had become bone-crushing.

"I'm sorry about all this, Rhett," she finally said and put her face in her hands, suddenly overwhelmed by the situation and how it was threatening her relationships with the people she loved.

Elizabeth.

Matt.

Rhett.

"Hey, now," he called and drew her hands away from her face, kneeling in front of her. "I hate seeing you like this."

"Do you want me to quit, Rhett?" God, just saying it was like driving a stake through her own heart. "Would that make it better?"

He pulled her into his arms. "Cut that out. You know it wouldn't. Now you're really scaring me." Pushing her back a step, he stared into her eyes. "Okay, we'll go with Elizabeth's solution. Hire him. Tell him the truth. We'll play the hand, one card at a time. I'm not going to lose you over this. We'll figure it out."

God, she was such a baby because tears welled in her eyes. "Oh, Rhett."

"Now, now, it's going to be all right, Janey. If you need Matt to talk to me, you just let both of us know.

We've opened our circle to a few others before without any bruises, and I do believe you're right about him being trustworthy. Plus, a man in love always protects his woman. That alone will make him want to keep this to himself."

It all made sense, but when she imagined telling him like this—as his client—all she could see was his face falling, his disappointment in her painfully clear. Would he walk away from her for good?

"Okay, we'll see how he reacts. I honestly don't know."

"If he loves you, he'll find a way to accept the truth."

She hugged him again, and he squeezed her tight.

"None of us ever thought we would come this far when I hired you girls so long ago, but you know what?"

"What?"

He tapped her nose. "I wouldn't trade it for anything."

"I wouldn't either," she responded, and that gave her some peace.

"Now, off with you. Don't you have some dogs to walk?"

"Yes, boss."

"Right. Boss. Hah!" He put his arm around her shoulders as they walked to the door. "Like you girls ever treated me that way."

"You wouldn't have wanted us to," she said, tugging on her outerwear.

"You're right. In that way, I am totally unconventional."

"One of the reasons I love you. Thank you, Rhett. For everything."

"Hey now, you'd better stop that before I tear up. You girls mean the world to me."

As she drove home, the thoughts swirling madly through her head, something else Elizabeth had said drifted to the surface. Jane's parents *did* still have a hold over her.

Perhaps it was time to address that too.

She dialed the number she knew from memory and pulled off the road onto a mountain overlook. The sun cast a brilliant glow over the valley, making the snow sparkle like diamonds.

"Wilcox residence," a familiar voice answered.

"Betty?" she asked. "Is that you?" It was good to know her parents' long-time housekeeper still worked for them. Betty had to be getting on sixty by now, and while she'd always been stern, she'd sometimes given Jane a lollipop when no one was looking.

"Miss Jane? As I live and breathe. We lost all hope of ever hearing from you."

That had been the plan. "How are you?"

"Good. Busy as ever. Your parents are having twelve people over tonight, so I'm finishing up the final preparations."

Nothing had changed there. "Are they around? Is my...mother there?"

Betty clucked her tongue. "No, I'm sorry. She had some meetings in town, just like your father. But I'll tell them you called. Can you give me your number?"

She recited it. They chatted a little while longer. When she hung up, she exited the car. Let the wind blow across her face. What would she have said if they'd been there? Well, maybe they'd call her back. She wasn't the same scared girl she'd been at Harvard. Maybe they had changed a bit too, and she could come to a new understanding with them. It felt right, the idea of burying the hatchet.

One of her biggest questions had always been whether they missed her at all. She was their child, their *only* child, so surely they had. On holidays and her birthday, even she found herself missing them, wishing things could have been different.

Well, she'd taken the first step, and now she'd just

have to wait and see.

Now it was time to confront Matt—even if she didn't like the means by which she would share her deepest, darkest secret with him.

CHAPTER 26

When Jane cancelled meeting him at the dog park, asking if she could swing by his office instead, his gut told him something wasn't right. She'd never come by his office, and right now it was filled with his small crew of volunteers. They were calling Dare citizens from his two conference rooms, asking them to attend his first town hall meeting. Rob had organized the event a few weeks ago, and they'd thought it would be a cake walk. Now, Florence Henkelmyer was stirring up trouble around town, calling him an outsider who was out of touch with Dare Valley's needs. Her son had actually put up signs around town with an X over Matt's face and the bold letters of the word OUTSIDER at the bottom. If it had happened to anyone else, he might have laughed.

He gently herded everyone out of his office, including his secretary, by telling them they'd worked hard enough for one day. But his lovely Easter Brigade lingered by the door, and he was still talking to them when Jane arrived. Her face looked wan, and he knew deep down she was hurting over something. He introduced her to Joanie, Margo, and Hazel right away, and she managed a small smile for them. The stiff way she held herself made him long to take her into his arms and reassure her that whatever it was, it would be all right.

When the older ladies left, she swept her arm across his reception area. "Lots going on here. I'm sorry about the signs, Matt. I saw them when I came down Main Street."

He ran his hands through his hair. "Well, it was to be expected, I suppose. My mom told me she took some down. I told her they'd be back up tomorrow, but she said she'd just do the same. That they weren't right."

"Can we talk in your office?" she asked. "Is everyone gone?"

"Yes," he said, snaking a hand around her waist to pull her close. "I'll introduce you to Alice, my secretary, another time. I want you all to myself, since this is your first visit. It's not nearly as impressive as the law firm I worked at in Denver, but I like it. Has everything I need. Two spacious conference rooms, an office, a reception area, and a break room. I might have to rent a new space for the campaign though. Things are getting kinda cramped, and I don't want clients to have to wade through my extracurricular activities."

"That's probably wise."

She was stiff in his arms and looking at everything but him.

"Bad memories?" he decided to ask.

"Some. I called...my parents today."

Well, that was a shock. From what he knew, they'd been estranged for years. "Really."

"I decided that I didn't want the past to.... I ah...thought talking to them now might change things. I don't know what to expect or if they'll even call me back, but I don't want to be afraid of them anymore."

So that was why she'd come. The worry he'd been carrying instantly lightened. "I'm proud of you, Jane."

Then she gazed up at him, her chocolate eyes

troubled, and his gut tightened again. Whatever she needed to tell him had nothing to do with her parents, he realized. This was only a primer.

"Don't be proud yet. Can we go into your office?"

"Sure," he said, sensing she was finally about ready to tell him the other secret she'd been carrying. "But why don't you kiss me hello before we do? I didn't feel comfortable doing that in front of the Easter Brigade."

She traced his cheek. "I want to keep things separate while we're in your office. If you still want to kiss me after we talk, we can do it later."

Now that worry turned into outright fear. "Jane, you're scaring me here."

"Is that your office?" she asked and moved toward the door.

He followed her, and she gently shut it, enclosing them in silence.

She dropped her red purse onto the chair in front of his desk. "Do you remember how there was something I couldn't tell you? Something involving other people?"

He unbuttoned his suit jacket with shaking fingers. "Yes."

Drawing an envelope out of her purse, she handed it to him. When he opened it, surprise rippled through him. It was a cashier's check for a thousand dollars made out to his firm from her personal bank account. This was not good.

"What is this Jane?"

"It's a retainer. The only way I can tell you what I want to tell you is by having you agree to be my lawyer. It's the only way my colleagues would allow it. It's not what I want, but...this is the compromise."

His eyes flicked up from the check to her as he shoved it back into the envelope. Anger was flickering up inside him now. "You want our conversation to be privileged?"

He'd agreed to that one other time with someone he

loved, and it had been a disaster. He'd vowed never to do it again.

"It's the only way." She leaned back against his desk.

It couldn't be. He tossed the envelope to her, which she caught. "Okay, now I'm half scared and half pissed. What in the hell do you need to tell me that requires attorney-client privilege? You swore that it wasn't illegal."

She wrung her hands. "It's not."

"Then why this elaborate scene. Aren't we together? Didn't you just spend the entire weekend with my family? If you have something you need to tell me, why can't you trust me enough without putting money between us, without making me your lawyer?"

Striding forward, the envelope in her hand, she said, "Because it's the only way my partners will agree to let me tell you this. I don't want it to be this way, but it's something you need to know. It's something that could impact you."

The pieces finally came together. "It could hurt my campaign."

Her lip trembled. "Yes."

He shoved away from her. "Dammit, Jane." What the hell was he supposed to do now? "I don't date clients, and I don't work for people I care about."

Only silence greeted him.

"Ever."

"I'm sorry to hear that," she whispered, and from the hoarseness of her tone he finally understood what she was asking of him.

"Jane, please understand. It's been one of the most important rules I've set for myself. After I graduated from law school, I agreed to work with one of my best friends from college." Jason had three brothers, and he'd become close to all of them.

"Jason hired me to handle his part of the inheritance after his father passed away. You have to understand, I was close to everyone in his family. I felt like I was one of them... Well, the whole thing turned ugly between him and his brothers. It was a sizable estate, and they fought over how it had been split. Jason told his brothers that I was the one telling him to go for more, and when they asked me as a friend, I couldn't tell them the truth. He used our attorney-client privilege against me. It ruined my relationship with his whole family. They thought I was a Judas, and I had no way of defending myself."

Losing his friends that way had made him vow never to work as a lawyer for anyone he cared about. Of course, every law professor he knew had hammered that home, but the personal lesson was the one that had stuck.

When he looked back, she had already turned away from him. Her back was rigid, and she had her face in her hands.

"Can't you understand? I can't go there again. I promised myself. Talk to me, Jane," he said, going to her and putting his arms around her. She was shaking, which made him press his cheek against her hair. "Whatever this is, you can trust me with it."

She turned, and her eyes narrowed. "Don't you think I know that? Haven't you been listening? I love you, but my partners will only let me tell you if we do it this way...and you can't because of...this Jason."

His arms fell away from her. "So I'm supposed to break a cardinal rule because your partners can't trust me with something I need to know?"

"I'm sorry!" she cried out, shocking him. "Don't you know how hard this is for me? I'm risking all of my important relationships. And what about trusting me not to act like Jason?"

"Stop it! Don't talk like that," he said, his own heart breaking now as he took in how tortured she was. "You can tell me, and I swear, your partners will never know you didn't hire me as your lawyer. And you have my word I won't tell anyone else either."

It was the only way. He hated to see her in this kind of agony, but whether it happened now or later, he was certain that putting money between them would ruin their relationship.

"Trust me, Jane."

She stepped back. "But *I'll* know, and I can't break my promise."

He swallowed thickly then. "Where does that leave us?"

Her inhale was long and jagged, as though she didn't have enough air. "Maybe...it's better that we separate while you're running for mayor. If... Well, if we run into each other later on and want to..." She shook her head and clenched her eyes shut. "Please, Matt. I don't want to lose you. Can't you please do this for me? Just this once?"

The quiver in her voice almost broke him. "Ask me anything else, but no. I won't risk our relationship this way. I can't. Jason and his family were a huge part of my life, and everything changed as soon as I became his lawyer."

"But I'm not asking you to do anything bad," she shouted. "Or hurt anyone."

"What kind of future do we have if it takes a retainer for you to tell me something like this? Dammit, I love you! I'm with you every night. I wake up with you every morning. What more do I have to do to prove you can trust me?" Dear God, what dark secret could be behind this kind of ultimatum?

She reached for her purse and swung it over her shoulder. "I should have let you kiss me before we came in here."

As she swept in front of him, he almost grabbed her to stop her. But to what end?

"I figured out why Henry doesn't listen to you," she

said, turning at the doorway. "Since we won't be..." Her voice broke, and he loosened the knot in his tie, which was choking him. "He senses that you only took him in out of obligation, and that you don't love him. Once you...open your heart to him and start to consider him your dog, not Patricia's, he'll listen to you."

Her words hung between them as he realized she was right. His mind flashed back to how Patricia had sounded when she'd asked him to take Henry, her voice thready and weak. He hadn't wanted to do it, but he hadn't been able to refuse her, not when she was so sick. Poor Henry.

She stared at him in the lengthening silence. "Goodbye, Matt."

"Don't do this," he pleaded. "I love you. Trust me, goddammit!"

She shook her head, her eyes filled with tears now. "I told you how it has to be..."

When she hurried out, he sank into a chair and ran his hands through his hair. His chest hurt, and he had this horrible feeling of wanting to heave his desk over to shatter all the things on it.

How had everything gone so wrong so quickly? She'd just met his family, for Christ's sake.

For the first time in his life, he wished he were a lawyer who could play fast and loose with his principles.

The price of integrity was sometimes too steep.

CHAPTER 27

One upside to having family in town was the ability to see them immediately when things were rough, so Matt headed over to Andy's house after pulling himself together at the office and taking Henry out at home. He'd gone for a run alone at sunset—not in the park where he and Jane usually went—but in one that had no memories of her.

It didn't help.

All he could feel was the shock of their break-up, which hadn't worn off one bit. He needed to talk through what had happened or he'd go crazy, and because he could trust his brother not to say anything, he was going to lay it out and get his take.

As he drove to his brother's house on the bench, he realized he could smell her in his car. His throat closed, and he punched up the gas in anger. What was he supposed to do with that?

Danny opened the door when he arrived. His new scooter was lying on the floor next to a basketball, and the warm house decorated in neutral colors of brown and greens smelled like his brother had burned their dinner.

His nephew immediately launched himself into his arms. "Hi, Uncle Matt. Is Jane with you? I *really* like her. She's so cool!"

"She's not with me."

The lump in his throat grew. Yeah, everyone in his family loved her.

He picked Danny up and hugged him, gripping him tighter than usual.

"Uncle Matt, is everything okay?" he asked.

His brother appeared in the doorway, and the smile he had on his face instantly faded when he saw Matt. Just like that, he knew.

"Having a rough day, is all," he told Danny. The boy didn't ask to be let down—he simply wrapped his arms around Matt's neck.

"Dad burned my mac and cheese and was upset too, but we'll make it better," the little boy said. "Won't we, Dad?"

Matt's brother nodded. More than anyone, he had reason to know that some things just couldn't be made right.

"Come on, let's play video games. That's what Dad and I do when he has a bad day."

His brother brought him a beer and gripped his shoulder for a second, and then they launched into two hours of gaming. His nephew's skill, even at the towering age of five, kept him focused, and every now and then his brother stepped in to beat the pants off him.

"You two are way too good for me," he commented, sinking back into the sofa. God, he was tired. The day's events had drained the life out of him.

Danny snuggled next to him on the couch, and the feel of that trusting little body soothed him like always. There was something magical about being around kids.

"Are you feeling better, Uncle Matt?" he asked, his expression much too serious now.

"With you as my company," he answered, interjecting some pep into his voice, "how could I not?"

"Okay, it's bath time, and then one story," his brother said, storing the controls in the home television unit.

"Two," Danny chirped before running off, his feet pounding up the stairs.

"We can talk after he goes to bed," his brother said. "Why don't you grab another beer?"

Matt cruised to the kitchen and put the leftover dishes in the dishwasher to help his brother out. The burnt macaroni pan was already soaking. Even though he'd looked up to his older brother all his life, he admired him even more now that he was a single dad.

There were new crayon drawings on the refrigerator, and Matt studied them as he popped his beer open. One was of Danny skiing down a mountain, and the other was the scariest leprechaun he'd ever seen with a pot of gold, likely for St. Patrick's Day. Thank God he had family here to visit when he needed them.

He took the steps two at a time and found Andy toweling Danny down, the boy doubled over in giggles.

"What's so funny?" he asked.

Andy shrugged. "He's lost his mind."

"I'm just laughing," his nephew sputtered.

"Over tired, more like. Come on. Into your jammies and then off to bed. One story."

"Two."

Matt's lips pursed. The little negotiator.

"Fine. Uncle Matt can read to you while I clean up the kitchen."

"Already done," he told him, and his brother smiled. "Thanks, man."

"It's nothing."

They ended up reading the story together, both of them putting on funny voices for dramatic effect. Danny snuggled between them. Matt's eyes tracked to the framed picture on the bedside—Kim holding Danny when he was a baby. God, she'd been so full of light.

And now she was gone, missing her son's wild giggling during baths and story time.

Life just wasn't fair sometimes.

After kissing Danny goodnight and tucking him into bed, they headed downstairs. Andy grabbed a beer and joined him on the couch.

"Okay, tell me what happened with Jane."

He didn't spare any details, and at the end of the telling, his throat was raw.

His brother gripped his shoulder. "It sounds like she wants to do the right thing, but can't. Of course, you can't either, not after what happened with Jason. You didn't even act as my lawyer when Kim was dying."

Right. He'd recommended his brother have another lawyer draw up her DNR. Part of him couldn't have handled the task emotionally, but he also hadn't wanted to put the law between him and the brother he loved. End of life issues had torn some families apart. Fortunately, Andy had understood.

"So you don't have any idea what this could be?" his brother asked.

"It has to be poker-related. I can't imagine her doing anything else that would be so hush-hush." He rose and started to pace the floor in front of the couch. "I'm scared she's in trouble, Andy."

"She'd have to be to walk away from you."

That stopped him in his tracks.

"I saw the way she looked at you, Matt. She loves you. Already loves our family. And in her own way, she's trying to protect these partners of hers as well as you and your campaign."

"None of this sounds like Rhett. I haven't known him long, but he seems to be a pretty straight-shooting kind of guy." He fell back onto the couch. "I'm at a loss, Andy. I can't do what she wants, but I don't want to lose her."

His brother sipped his beer. "So find out what this big secret is yourself."

"What?"

"We happen to be related to some of the best investigative journalists in the country, or are you forgetting what Uncle Arthur pulled when he first met Jane? And you know they won't say a word. They're family."

Right. The idea took shape. "If I find out what it is, then she won't have to break their confidence."

"And she'll have to trust you then."

He rubbed his chest. "That's what hurt, Andy. That she couldn't trust me without money between us."

"I think you're being too hard on her. It sounds like this was her best option. And when it was clear that you wouldn't go for it for reasons I totally understand and support, she put you and your campaign first." He rubbed his now bare wedding ring finger. "That's the kind of woman you want in your life. That's the kind of woman Kim was."

The mantle clock ticked away the seconds as Matt considered his brother's words. "What if it's something bad, something I can't overlook, something that could destroy my campaign? She seemed to think it might..."

His brother turned to stare at him. "Do you love her?" The emotion was stark on his face, and Matt knew he had to be thinking about his wife.

"I do."

"Then who the hell cares? Kim could have robbed a bank or been a hooker before we met, and it wouldn't have stopped me from loving the woman she'd become. Hopefully it won't come down to that, but you have to decide what's more important to you. Saving the world as the mayor of a small town or being with the woman you love."

Matt didn't have to ask what his brother would

choose.

"I've never been in a relationship this hard before."

His brother scoffed. "You've never been in a relationship, period. What you had with what's-her-face in college pales in comparison to what you feel for Jane. Everybody in the family knows that after seeing you two together."

Memories of the weekend rolled over him. Jane laughing with his sisters. His mother's hand on her shoulder. It had felt like she was a missing puzzle piece.

"Is it too late to swing by Meredith and Tanner's house, do you think?" he asked, eyeing the clock.

"No one but a single dad who has surgery in the morning is going to be asleep by nine o'clock. Text Mere and ask."

He drew out his phone to send her a message. Her response was immediate and affirmative.

"She told me to come over," he said.

"Good. Now get moving. There's no need for you both to suffer any longer than necessary. Life is too short."

"Thanks, Andy," he said and pulled him in for a man hug.

His brother clapped him on the back. "Keep me posted."

"Don't tell the family about this development, okay?"

"What? Do I *look* stupid?"

"Only some days," he said, feeling lighter now as he tugged on his outer gear at the front door.

"She loves you, Matt. Whatever you discover, remember that."

With those words, he stepped outside into the bitter wind, a new flame of hope burning in his heart.

CHAPTER 28

To work off her ongoing fear and frustration over the Jane situation, Elizabeth decided to take an early morning Zumba class. She and the sunrise didn't much like each other after her years of staying up late with Rhett on the road, but Dare wasn't exactly Las Vegas. Everything pretty much died down by ten o'clock during the week, midnight on weekends if you were lucky.

The class was surprisingly full for seven o'clock in the morning, and it took her body longer to sync to the beat than usual. Her classmates shared her sluggishness. But by the time a peppy meringue number came on, her hips were swaying just fine, and her feet moved in perfect time with the teacher's.

She caught Carol after class and gave her the papers she'd completed to go through the teaching certification. They chatted for a while, and Carol set some dates for her to complete her training.

Elizabeth left the studio with a new spring in her step and, deciding that a special coffee and croissant was in order, walked to Don't Soy with Me. Things might be shitty in other parts of her life, but at least she was doing what she could to be happy. Growing up in a trailer park, she'd learned how to compartmentalize her life and create magical places for her free spirit to reign.

When she entered the coffee shop, she took a moment to appreciate one of her favorite haunts in town. The roasted coffee scent always made her salivate, and the bold colors of the yellow and red walls lifted her spirits. Patrons were scattered across the coffee shop with laptops and tablets set out next to their morning coffee. A pleasant jazz tune filled the air, and Elizabeth's hips swayed to the beat.

After ordering a bold French Roast with a shot of hazelnut cream, Elizabeth wandered to the side to wait for her coffee.

She felt someone's eyes on her then—she intuitively knew they were a man's—so she casually turned her head to the right.

Terrance freaking Waters was standing in the line, waiting to order. His mouth tipped up in acknowledgement of her gaze. God, was she gaping? She swiveled her head around as her heart started to pound like the frantic beat of the Latin music in Zumba class.

It couldn't be him. It wasn't uncommon to think you'd seen someone only to realize it wasn't that person.

She took a second look.

Those seductive lips that had kissed every inch of her body were tipped up at the corners, accentuating the small scar on the right side from a long-ago fight.

It *was* him.

Holy blooming hell.

What in the world was he doing in Dare Valley? Her mind raced through dozens of scenarios. He knew Mac and Rhett, so he could be here to see one of them, but why hadn't she heard anything?

She smelled him before she felt him come up beside her, that spicy, erotic cologne he wore playing havoc on her senses.

"Hi there," he said in a voice that was like sin

chewing on marbles.

Biting her lip—*keep it together, girl*—she gave the barista a hopeful glance.

"I've heard this is the best coffee in town," he observed, trying to draw her into his web. "I'm Terrance, by the way."

When he extended his hand to her, she had no choice but to turn toward him, which he'd totally planned. God, she didn't want to touch him, so she clenched her fingers together and shook as quickly as possible. It might have been the worst handshake on the planet, but it still sent a familiar burst of sensation shooting through her body.

"Hi," she replied hoarsely.

"The barista seems to be backed up," Terrance said again, probably mistaking her weirdness for that of a fan.

Chef T was, after all, a rising celebrity chef, one who had a popular TV show called *The Tattooed Chef*.

"Of course, that's fine by me. I like talking to beautiful women."

Right. He'd always been a smooth talker.

Face to face with him now, she couldn't stop herself from lapping up the sight of him. His black hair was cut military style, accenting his muscular neck. His signature tattoos were concealed by the casual attire of a thermal black shirt and fleece with faded designer jeans. The man she'd fallen for two years ago had worn white T-shirts to showcase the griffin tattoos flying down his arms. In private, she'd seen the entire canvas of ink on his body, and it had always filled her with lust.

She stared into those forest-green eyes, her knees weak.

And waited to see his reaction.

In a few moments, the truth was undeniably clear: he didn't know who she was without her poker babe get-up.

Oh, the wrench in her heart. She'd always wondered if he'd recognize her as Elizabeth and not Vixen. Well, now she knew.

He didn't.

Then he cocked his head to the side. "I know it sounds cliché, but have we met? There's something really familiar about you."

Okay, so that made her knees want to give out, and she leaned a hand on the nearby counter for support.

"I get that a lot," she replied, not answering him directly. "Must have one of those faces."

"I wish I was staying in town longer. We might have found a way to become more familiar with each other."

The relief was sweet. He was only passing through.

"Mmm," she merely hummed. There was no way in hell she was telling him who she really was, so the less they interacted, the better.

The shock of seeing him was too fresh, and what good would it do to tell him? Who in the hell knew how he'd react? Would he be pissed? Or would he just shrug those muscular shoulders she'd loved running her mouth over and say, "Good to see ya, babe?"

Her belly tightened with lust. God, he was still so hot, downright badass, and all she wanted to do was shove him into one of the bathroom stalls and devour him.

The barista called her name then, and she carefully reached for her coffee.

"Elizabeth," he murmured, handing her a napkin.

She automatically reached for it, but instead of letting go, he tugged on it, creating resistance between them. The spark of arousal inside her was fresh and dark.

"I like that name."

"It was good to meet you," she ground out, making herself step away from him.

"Perhaps we'll run into each other again sometime,"

he said mysteriously, his voice husky now.
She didn't answer.
She fled.

CHAPTER 29

Crying had become her new normal in the hours after the scene in Matt's office. Jane even broke her own rule and let Annie and Rufus sleep with her that night. The hurt was like a brand, the pain throbbing and insistent. She realized she'd never hurt this much.

Even as she tried to tell herself it was for the best, nothing could make the pain go away.

She didn't get dressed the next morning. Stayed huddled under the covers. The white light from the sun touching the snow glowed through her closed blinds.

Today, she decided, was a day to shut out the world. She was no good to anyone like this. Yeah, she could use some groceries, but she could picture how that would go. She'd bawl her way through the produce aisle, picking up bananas and oranges while the other patrons stared at her in confusion.

Why bother?

This had to get better, right?

But deep down, the thought of losing Matt forever haunted her. She missed him. The warmth of his skin, the spicy scent of his cologne, the feel of his lips and body moving over hers.

How was she supposed to survive a broken heart? Now she understood why people had such a hard time getting over the loss of someone they loved.

It hurt, dammit.

When Rhett texted her around noon to ask how it had gone with Matt, she simply replied, *Not good.* Then she turned her phone off and threw it on the floor.

When someone pounded on her door a few hours later, she burrowed under the covers. No way she was taking company in her condition. Rufus whined and cocked his head at her.

"Stay," she told him, her voice hoarse from crying.

When the pounding increased, sounding like a lumberjack chopping down a mighty tree, she knew it could only be one person.

Rhett.

A man determined to get his way.

Well, if he was going to be like that, he was just going to have to deal with the outcome. She stepped over the balled-up tissues she'd tossed on the floor and pulled on a white terrycloth robe.

"Go away," she croaked out as she padded to the door in her bare feet. Cripes, she needed to turn up the heater, which she'd lowered before going to bed.

"Open the door, Jane," her friend commanded. "I'll tear it down otherwise. You know I can do it..."

She did. Rhett and his meaty hands.

When she unlocked the door, he was standing there on the stoop in his sheepskin coat with a red scarf Abbie had given him for Christmas wrapped around his thick neck.

"Oh, honey," he said gently. He walked inside, slammed the door, and pulled her to him.

His body was cold from being outside, but the comfort he provided warmed up the barren space inside her. She started to cry.

"I'm a mess," she whispered. "You don't want to see

me like this."

"Wasn't I a mess over Abbie when I thought I'd lost her?"

Hence the tearing-down-the-door incident in Monaco.

He led her to the couch, released her to shed his coat, and then made a quick fire. As it was starting to spark and crackle, he grabbed a box of Kleenex and carried it to the sofa, pulling her against him.

"Okay, you tell ol' Rhett everything that happened."

It couldn't have been a pretty sight—she took her time in the telling, stopping every so often to wipe away tears or blow her nose. He was patient, but as she continued the story, a line appeared between his eyebrows.

"It's over," she finally said. "I know it's probably better this way. I would always have been a liability for him."

"Honey," he scolded gently.

"Who would know better than me? My father has destroyed political opponents on less, and Matt wants to run for higher offices. Being the mayor of Dare is just the first run in what could be a long career. My father used to seek out and mentor young men who had great political promise, and Matt would have met his every requirement."

Rufus whined at her tone, so she leaned down to stroke him under the ears.

"But he loves you, and you love him."

"The Raven and Vixen secret is dangerous to everyone we love. You and your family, Liz, even Mac for being our front. We're going to have to keep it quiet. Since he's refused to accept a retainer from me, I just don't see another way."

Rhett took her hand. "There has to be. I've never seen you like this, Jane, and as someone who had the shit kicked out of his own heart, I know a bit about what you're going through."

From his thunderous frown, she knew he was remembering that horrible year after Abbie had broken things off with him. She, Rhett, and Elizabeth had pretty much been like sailors, playing poker overseas in every possible venue from Monte Carlo to Macau.

"It hurts, Rhett," she whispered, pressing a hand to her heart.

"I know it does, baby," he said and then just held her close and rocked her.

More tears fell as the finality of it all washed over her. It was done. Matt was gone. She'd never walk the dogs with him again. Never kiss him. Never talk to him. Never make love to him.

"I might need to leave Dare for a while," she said, trying to pull herself together. "Move back to Vegas. I...don't think I can take running into him here."

"No, I won't stand for any of this. You and Elizabeth are fighting. Your heart is broken. There has to be a way to fix everything."

"There isn't. He won't accept the retainer because he had a horrible fallout with a friend the last time he mixed his personal life with his profession. Part of me understands that. I've seen what happens when lawyers take on friends as clients. They stop being friends. We're at an impasse."

"Bullshit."

The resolve in his voice was just as strong as when he declared he was going to win a tourney. "Just let it go. I have to resign myself to the way things are."

"What are you? The queen of bloody England? Resign yourself? Screw that! We need to find a way to make it work. And I don't like all these assumptions you're making about you being a liability to Matt's career. You're taking away his choice. Didn't I make changes to my career to suit Abbie?"

She rubbed her heated cheeks. "It's different. You

didn't have to give up poker. Rhett, even if I could tell him, Matt couldn't win an election if he's seeing the woman who used to be Raven. His refusal has forced me to see the naked truth."

"You don't know that."

A spurt of anger broke through the fog of grief. "Don't tell me what I do and don't know! Rhett, I used to dress like a slut for work. Trust me, voters, especially the conservative kind, would crucify a good man for being involved with me even if I went on record saying that I'd found God and all that political bull. Men have 'reformed' successfully in politics, but not women, and it wouldn't matter that Raven was all an act."

"I don't care about that crap," he said, rising and towering over her. "You deserve to be happy, and it kills me to know I'm partially to blame here."

Ah, so that's what it was. She stood and put a hand on his arm. "Rhett, you are not to blame. We all made the decision. No one forced me to be Raven."

"I don't regret that. It helped you escape your parents, and now that I know about Elizabeth... Anyway, I know you wanted to tell Matt about Raven early on, and Elizabeth and I stopped you. Well, it's going to end now."

"Rhett—"

"No, I'll talk to Elizabeth. And Abbie and Mac. This isn't going to stand!" His decision made, he tugged on his coat and strode to the door. "I'll take care of it, Jane."

"No, Rhett—" Part of her couldn't bear to dredge up all the hurt again.

And where would it leave her and Liz? Would their friendship be over for good? She wasn't sure she could take that.

"It's time to come clean, Jane. I'll be in touch once I've taken care of things."

CHAPTER 30

The day was interminable to Matt. There was no news from the Hale journalist clan after he'd told them what he needed. Of course, even though he didn't have to say how important it was for them to keep their research confidential, he had. Meredith had gently caressed his back and said, "Matt. We're family." Tanner had nodded in agreement. They'd promised to tell Uncle Arthur first thing in the morning at the newspaper, and Meredith had texted him at around noon to say they'd made Jane's past a priority and were digging into it.

But he didn't stop there. Jane was too important.

He also called his forensic accountant friend—someone he'd been friends with since college and could trust with his life. As he was about to leave the office, his friend called with an update. He'd already hit a wall. Jane's companies—she had five of them, it seemed—were receiving money from three companies, also registered in the Cayman Islands. No information was available on the owners. Only a Post-office box was listed as the companies' address in the States. There was nothing illegal about them, his friend assured Matt. They paid taxes. It was just going to take him more time to track the source of the payments, since they were routed through Swiss bank accounts.

Swiss bank accounts? The obscurity boggled his mind. *Jane, Jane, what are you into?*

His friend ended their conversation with something Matt already knew: whoever had set up the companies knew how to hide things.

Well, she did have an MBA from Harvard.

After he ended their call, Matt stood at his office window for a few minutes, his gaze unfocused, a new chill running down his spine.

When he finally cruised home, he looked at Henry, whose tail was wagging in delight. His dog thought it was time for them to go to the park.

The park. Sunset. Jane.

He sank into a chair and put his face in his hands. God, he missed her. He was so desperate to hear her voice, to see that sweet smile reserved only for him.

Well, giving into despair wasn't productive. He needed another run. A lung-burning, heart-pounding run. He went to the park where he and Andy had gone running, and he didn't stop moving until his legs were burning. Maybe he'd actually be able to sleep if he exhausted himself.

After showering, he dressed and then texted Meredith to say he was coming over, asking for a time. She told him to come for dinner.

Like he could eat.

When he arrived, Uncle Arthur's car was already parked in their driveway. He pulled in behind it and strode to the house. Meredith greeted him at the door with a warm hug.

"Matt," Meredith said, taking his hands after he chucked off his coat. "Let's get you settled. I think we found something."

Meredith led him into their navy dining room, where Tanner and Uncle Arthur were already sitting.

Papers, a few files, and two laptops were scattered over the white tablecloth shot through with gold thread along with the dishes for the meal he wouldn't be able to eat.

"You look like shit," his uncle said from his chair without any preamble. "Did you sleep at all last night?"

"No," he said, shaking Tanner's hand when the man rose to greet him. "Meredith said you found something."

Uncle Arthur rose too and gently tapped his foot with his cane. "First, let me say how insulting it was to hear from Meredith that you actually had to ask us not to say anything to anyone."

"I'm sorry." It was hard to meet the older man's eyes when he said it.

"Well, that's settled, so let's take a seat," his uncle said as he settled back into his chair.

Meredith gestured to the chair next to Tanner while she sat beside Uncle Arthur across from them.

"Now onto the findings," his uncle said. "It's...unusual to say the least. We wanted to show you in person."

"Tell me."

His uncle swept out a hand. "We hit one wall after another today when we searched for information on Jane's whereabouts for these last seven years. We couldn't even find a copy of her driver's license."

Now that surprised him. "How is that even possible?"

His uncle pushed his glasses up further on his nose. "Someone paid for it to be removed from the system, I expect. Highly unusual. It's like no one wanted her to be found. And if my theory's correct, I have a pretty good idea of why. Tanner, show him the video."

Tanner slid his laptop to him and hit play. "I want you to watch this footage of one of Rhett's poker tournaments. Tell us if you see Jane anywhere."

The footage was seventeen minutes long, and he kept scanning the crowd when the cameraman panned to it. He even paused the feed a couple of times, his foot tapping with increasing frustration. At the end, he pushed the laptop back to Tanner.

"I don't see her."

"Neither did I. And I didn't see her in any of the other footage clips I watched either," Tanner said. "Arthur said it wasn't possible for her not to be there. Poker scouts have to be onsite, right? We have further proof of that too. Jane wouldn't have traveled with Rhett to his tournament in Cabo otherwise, which we know she did. You told us she did."

They were onto something. "Exactly."

"So Grandpa started musing about how he'd handle the situation if he didn't want other people to know about his scouts," Meredith said. "We came across some poker blogs that have written about that, saying scouts have only recently become a more accepted facet of the game."

"There's nothing saying they're illegal," his uncle said. "But when Rhett first started out, things were different. The World Series of Poker tournament didn't allow a long break before the players met at the final table. Now the final table is actually months after the first part of the tournament begins. Everyone knows the players have scouts. Hell, it's expected."

He was following their logic. "But it wasn't then."

"So what if Jane was hiding in plain sight?" his uncle said. "In a way that suited Rhett's...ahem...flamboyant style? Hand him the photos, Tanner."

The man opened a folder beside him and drew out a blown-up color photo of Rhett and his poker babes. "Look at the blond first," Tanner instructed, handing it to him.

Matt scanned her features. She was definitely playing up the Marilyn Monroe look with the blond hairdo, pouty red lips, and beauty mark, but that smile... It looked familiar.

"Show me the footage again." It took another ten minutes, but it finally clicked. "Holy shit! That's Elizabeth."

"Yes," Meredith finally said, her brows knitting.

"But she's his—"

"Publicist?" his uncle said. "It was genius of Rhett to put on his whole bad-boy redneck act from the start of his career. No one would have suspected he'd pull something like this."

Could that be part of the secret? Was Jane afraid to tell him about her career with Rhett because it risked exposing Elizabeth, her best friend? But that still didn't explain the question of why she wasn't in the footage...

"Elizabeth also seems to be missing a history," Tanner told him. "It's like she doesn't exist."

"This is crazy."

"Yes," Uncle Arthur said as he rose from his chair with the help of his cane. He walked over to Matt's side and put a warm hand on his shoulder. "Look again at the photo, Young Matthew. The brunette this time. Tell me what you see."

She was stunning. Curvaceous in all the right places. A man's fantasy come to life if his tastes veered toward porn stars. Matt's didn't. "Long hair. Big boobs. Curves." He squinted, trying to see more. He was missing something—he just didn't know what.

"What about the shape of the eyes?" his cousin murmured.

The big bangs she wore concealed them a little, but he could tell her eyes were a stunning blue, a shade so unusual he suspected color contacts. "I'm sorry, I just don't see what you're hinting at."

Meredith met his gaze when he finally looked away. "Don't worry. Tanner and I couldn't see it. Grandpa has the eyes of a cat, it seems."

"I've studied more mug shots and police drawings than all of you combined. I've become a master at separating out facial details. Okay, Tanner, show him the mark-up."

Tanner pushed his chair back until it angled away from the table so he could sit sideways. He handed Matt a photo with two pieces of paper obscuring everything but the person's eyes. They were chocolate brown with a twinkle in them.

"We pulled this picture from some media reports on Rhett's tournament in Cabo," Tanner said. "Now look at the brunette's eyes again."

"The shape is the same," he said, and he felt something ping in his gut—a confirmation, a warning.

"Take the paper away, Tanner." His uncle gripped his shoulder now.

The trap door was about to open. Matt could feel it.

"Take a breath, Young Matthew."

Matt fell back against the chair when Tanner took away the overlay, revealing a picture of Jane holding Annie in a casino. Rhett was in the background.

"No," he said, his ears buzzing with shock.

"What better way to hide poker scouts than to make them part of your bad-boy show in a way no one would expect?" his uncle asked. "I've played enough poker with Rhett to know how diabolical his mind is."

"It can't be her," he hissed out, gripping the two photos in his hands now, scanning them. They had to be missing something. "That woman doesn't look anything like her. Her body." Her breasts, he almost sputtered out. "Shit."

His head was spinning, and he lowered it into his hands, elbows digging into the table.

"Meredith, get him some water," Uncle Arthur commanded.

"I'll grab you a bourbon while we're at it," Tanner said.

Before he knew it, Matt had a tumbler of bourbon in his hand. He downed it before Meredith returned. "I can't... It can't...be true."

"But I know I'm right. Jane's eye color...and, well, a whole heck of a lot else may be different, but you can't hide the shape of those eyes even with all that gunk on her face. We have more photos, if you'd like to see them."

His mind had gone blank, like a sledgehammer had shattered his skull. "Not right now. I...can't seem to wrap my head around it."

"It makes sense in some twisted way," Uncle Arthur said, patting Matt's arm before wandering back to his seat. "What else would Jane want to tell you under privilege? This could hurt Rhett professionally."

"Jane and Elizabeth were pretty close to the final table, which technically gave them an advantage as scouts," Meredith added.

"Are you saying they cheated?"

He ran this hand through his hair. Shit, if that were true...

"No, Rhett doesn't strike me as that kind of man," Tanner said, "and I've known him over a year now. I know a cheat when I meet one. Jane and Elizabeth's roles as Raven and Vixen were carefully designed to be both part of his bad-boy act, putting them closer to the action so they could scout the other players. It's genius, if you ask me, though incredibly unorthodox."

Raven. Vixen. Hell, even their names made them sound like porn stars.

"But it doesn't even look like her!" he said again, thrusting a hand out at the photos lying on the table.

"That, I expect, was the idea," Meredith said, setting a glass of water beside him and giving him a half hug. "Jane went to Harvard. She's an heiress from old money. The daughter of a politician. It would be an important secret to keep."

"But she hates her family."

"Then what better way to hurt them," Uncle Arthur

said, "than by dressing as a poker babe? My God, the enmity between her and her parents must be fierce. How sad."

He studied the photo again, which seemed burned into his brain.

Meredith rubbed his shoulder in comfortable circles. "I have to admit to being pretty shocked myself when I saw the photos of her in...those outfits. It's...ah...quite the transformation."

"Her father would have the resources, financially and politically, to make her records disappear," Tanner said. "And Elizabeth's. And as for the private companies..."

He tried to focus. "She set them up in the Caymans. Swiss bank accounts are involved too," he told them. "My forensic accountant friend already hit a wall."

"A lot of people's reputations are at stake here," his uncle said. "Including your own, Young Matthew. This is what Jane wanted to protect you from. If this were to become public, it could ruin your political career, here and in any other office you choose to run for in the future."

His throat grew tight, and his finger traced the photo of her with Annie. When his eyes tracked to the other photo, the one of Raven, he wanted to punch his fist through a wall.

"I'll have her confirm it," he told Tanner, finally pushing back from the table. He couldn't sit a moment longer.

She was going to say this to his face.

"Not tonight," Meredith said, resting her hand on his sleeve, her eyes imploring him. "Don't do anything rash. Remember that she loves you."

Loved him? At the moment, even that one certainty had been burned to ash.

"I have to go," he said, absently kissing her cheek before glancing at Tanner and his uncle. "There's no way I can eat now. I'm sorry."

He wanted to run as fast and far as he could.

As he strode out of the dining room, he heard his uncle's cane tapping the floor in pursuit. He grabbed for his coat—still anxious to get out as soon as possible—but stopped in his tracks when he realized that his family had gathered a short distance away from him. They were all frowning.

"Matthew," his uncle said, leaning on his cane, looking tired now. "You might have forgotten that your Aunt Harriet came to Dare Valley under an assumed name."

Suddenly it came back to Matt—the story of how Aunt Harriet had come to Dare to find evidence to disprove a career-destroying article about her father that had been written by his uncle. Aunt Harriet had been devastated to discover her father's guilt, but she'd stayed in Dare and fallen in love with Arthur.

"When I found out the truth, I was downright pissed."

Shock rippled over him, hearing his uncle talk like that.

"I had fallen for a woman who wasn't who she said she was. She'd been working as my secretary, lying to me every day, and then... Well. It was a hard thing to forgive at first. And it was a big secret to keep in this town until she chose to tell everyone. Thank God, my family stood behind her, so it made the road less bumpy."

Though he'd heard the story before, of course—it was part of the Hale family canon—it was still hard to conceive that sweet Aunt Harriet could have done something like that. Hell, he knew her as the great aunt who could always be relied on to sneak them chocolate chip cookies.

"What I'm trying to tell you is that Jane has a step up on Harriet in this situation, and yet I still managed to forgive her."

He thought of the photos of Jane as Raven. "How's that?"

"She wasn't trying to hurt you by keeping this information from you. From where I'm standing, she was between a rock and a hard place. She wanted to protect *all* the people she loved. Think hard about that before you confront her. Trust an old man: it's hard to erase words said in anger, and right now, you're more pissed off than I've ever seen you. Go talk to your brother or head to your fancy gym to use the punching bag."

His fists clenched at the very thought. Yeah, that sounded good right about now.

"Just don't, *for the love of God,* talk to Jane right now."

Meredith and Tanner reached for each other's hands, but stayed silent.

"Thanks for finding this," he forced himself to say. Thanks? God, he wasn't sure if knowing the truth was better or not.

"That's what family is for, Young Matthew," his uncle said. "We'll be here for you too, no matter how things play out. Don't forget that."

Well, that tore his heart in two.

"Jesus," he finally said, thinking of his family. "What if we manage to stay together and this somehow comes out?"

"Take it one step at a time," his uncle said.

"And what?" Matt nearly shouted, the anger rushing out. "How can I keep this from the rest of my family?"

"As I said, you need to think it through," Uncle Arthur said, limping toward him now and patting him on the back. "When I told my parents about Harriet, even though I felt yellow with fear on the inside, I knew they'd support me. No matter what. And that's what we'll all do for you. Whatever you decide."

His uncle hugged him then, and Matt wanted to bury his face in his shoulder, just for a moment, but he didn't. It would only embarrass them both.

"I'll think it through," he whispered. It was as much a promise to his uncle as it was one to himself.

"Well, God knows you have the mind for it. Just don't forget to listen to your heart. Another lesson from your old uncle."

"Thank you," he said, his voice hoarse. "Thank you all." His gaze flicked to Tanner and Meredith, who nodded their acknowledgment.

When he left, he decided not to head over to Andy's. He was too raw, and his uncle was right. He needed to take a moment for reflection.

The woman he loved had led a double life.

As a poker babe.

Dressed like a slut.

His mind flashed back to that picture of her, the way she'd been leaning into Rhett, her cleavage pressing into his side. God, had there been anything between them? Rhett called Jane his "girl" and acted much too possessive for a boss. Had she—

Dammit, he couldn't go there.

He knew Jane hadn't slept around. There'd been too much hesitation and innocence with him in the beginning.

When he arrived at his house, he shed his coat and made a fire. Henry jumped onto the couch with him, but Matt didn't rebuke him, especially when he laid his head on Matt's thigh and looked up at him with troubled eyes. Suddenly he realized Henry hadn't barked once since he'd come home yesterday, upset over Jane. In fact, the dog had been a real comfort.

"You *are* a good dog, aren't you? Just like Jane said."

His throat clenched, and inside all the rawness came to the surface, as though his skin was being turned inside out. His wounds were on display, throbbing, painful, enormous.

"I'm sorry I didn't want you before. That I only took you because Patricia asked me." Henry whined and pressed his wet nose into Matt's hand. "You're my dog now, okay?"

The sorrow he'd been trying to hold back was suddenly impossible to ignore.

He buried his face against Henry's coat and let go.

CHAPTER 31

When a knock came on his door, Matt's laptop was resting on his knees, and a glass of thirty-year-old single malt from Islay was cradled in his hand. Henry lifted his head from his place beside Matt on the couch. With a final glance at the current picture of Raven on the screen, he snapped the computer shut.

The simmer in his blood had shot to a boil after researching "Raven" online.

Poker fan websites were covered in pictures of her and Vixen. The shockingly sexual comments about them had made him want to hurl his laptop into the fire, but he'd fought for control, grinding his teeth. People thought she was a slut, apparently, and they talked about her like she was one too.

Dammit!

And God, she looked the part, dressed like that.

What the hell had she been thinking?

This woman, *this Raven,* was nothing like the woman he loved.

It scared him shitless. And pissed him off.

When the knock came again, Henry nudged him and then leaped off the couch, tail wagging, as if waiting to walk with him.

His earlier meltdown had shifted things between them, and he rubbed Henry's head before pulling himself off the couch to answer the door. God, he hoped Uncle Arthur hadn't called his mom. He couldn't face her now.

When he opened it and saw Rhett, the man for whom Jane had dressed in that slutty getup, his anger shot out like lightning piercing the sky.

"We need to talk," Rhett said.

"You son of a bitch!" Matt growled, clenching his fist and letting it fly.

He hit Rhett with an upper cut under the chin. The big man staggered a few steps backwards in surprise. Henry started to bark wildly, and Matt grabbed him by the collar to keep him from charging their unwanted guest.

When Rhett straightened, he rubbed his chin. "Well, now—"

"I fucking know what you made her do!" he yelled. "How could you make her dress like that? Let men talk about her and look at her like that?"

"Whoa!" Rhett held up his hands in mock surrender. "Seems as though you already found out what I was going to tell you, even if the conclusions you drew were wrong. Can I come in, or are you planning to beat the shit out of me on your doorstep?"

Even Matt was shocked at his violence, his throbbing knuckles. He'd only gotten into scuffs when he was a kid with his brother and a couple of bullies from school. "I want to tear you apart for making her the subject of some of the dirtiest comments I've ever seen on the Internet."

Rhett sighed. "I didn't like that either, Matt. Trust me, if I could have prevented it, I would have. I love those girls."

Matt threw out a hand. "Girls! Stop calling them

that."

Rhett eyed a still barking and growling Henry. "I told you once that they hate it when I call them that, but it's part of the way I speak. I don't mean it like you clearly think I do. I love them like sisters, and I respect them more than I do almost anyone."

The cold air was pouring into the house through the open door, but Matt wasn't ready to let Rhett inside. Not yet. "If you cared for them, you would have found another way to have them scout for you on the down-low."

"Can I come in? Seems you and I need to come to an understanding. You're making me out to be some sort of pimp, and that's something I just won't abide. Are you going to check Fido there?"

Matt stared him down. "You have a hell of a nerve, coming here."

Rhett rubbed his chin. "I came here to tell you the truth, some of which you seem to have figured out on your own. The rest is total bull puckey. So, why don't you put your dog somewhere while we sort this out? I'm here because I love Jane and want to make her happy. Since you seem essential to that, I've done some serious high-stepping with the two other women I love, Abbie and Elizabeth."

Even though Matt was nearly shaking in anger, he stepped back. Best hear it all. "I'll put Henry in his crate."

"Are you going to take another punch at me if I take my coat off?" Rhett asked.

Matt didn't answer him. He rubbed down a trembling Henry and gave him a treat before closing him inside his crate.

When he returned to the den, Rhett had his hands on his waist. God, the guy really was massive. Likely had four inches on Matt. He couldn't believe he'd hit him, but he sure as hell wasn't about to apologize.

"Well, spill it," he demanded. "Normally I'd pour you a drink and tell you to sit, but I'm not feeling particularly welcoming."

"Understood. All right then. Tell me what you know."

Matt almost laughed. "No way. You're on my turf, and I'm not a rookie lawyer. You tell me the truth, the whole truth and nothing but, from the beginning."

Rhett's mouth quirked up. "Got a *Bible?*"

When his only response was silence, Rhett shoved his hands into his jeans. "All right then. From start to finish. Might take some telling."

"I'm not going anywhere."

And so Rhett began, telling him about meeting Jane and Elizabeth that first time, both of them desperate to escape something. Jane, her family. Elizabeth, he wouldn't say. He told Matt how smart they were, how being Raven and Vixen was the perfect ruse that answered all their various needs. Jane's parents had covered up their tracks for political reasons, confirming what Matt had heard from his family tonight. When he told Matt about falling for Abbie and her outright disgust of the poker babes, Matt wanted to growl again. Even Rhett's wife had thought they were slutty. Rhett insisted more than once that there had never been the slightest bit of "impropriety" between him and his scouts. An old-fashioned term to Matt's way of thinking, but as Rhett continued with his tale, he decided that the colloquialism seemed to suit the man.

"When I saw her today," Rhett said, wrapping up the whole sorry story, "still dressed in her nightgown at noon—a first, mind you—her eyes swollen, her nose red from crying, I said I'd fix it. I told Abbie I wanted to entrust you with the truth without all this lawyer privilege mumbo jumbo. After some smooth talking, she agreed. Elizabeth...well, she was a tougher nut to crack for reasons I can't share. But she loves Jane, so she

THE PARK OF SUNSET DREAMS

finally agreed too."

Matt's jaw ticked, and he forced his heart to stop beating as he listened to Rhett.

"Jane still thinks this news will hurt you politically if you two stay together, and for that reason she's willing to walk away from you forever even though you're the only man she's ever loved."

God, it hurt. Hearing that.

She was the only woman he'd ever loved too.

But this...

"When she told me she wanted to move back to Vegas because she couldn't handle being here—"

"She what?" he asked, swinging around.

"Well, that got your attention. I was wondering what was going through your mind."

"I think my mind exploded when I learned the truth," he admitted.

"One thing I learned with Abbie is that the mind means nothing when it comes to how you feel. It's like weighing a feather against an anvil."

Matt liked the analogy, but the situation wasn't that clear to him. "Just answer me one thing. Is Jane truly the woman I know or does she have a twin sister called Raven living inside her?" Part of him feared that the woman he loved didn't really exist.

"I expect that's something you need to talk about with Jane. What I can tell you is that she's everything you know her to be and more. Jane, Elizabeth, and I used to laugh ourselves silly over the way we were fooling everybody. Jane even used to say they were like The Mirage in Vegas."

A mirage. Yes, that sounded about right.

"And the bitching they did about the makeup, the outfits, and the...err, enhancements, well...they didn't like the outfits or the way they were treated in them. But we all knew the truth, and that softened it. They're wicked smart, smarter than me, and I owe them everything I've become."

His revelation shocked Matt. Rhett was the champion, and yet here he was, crediting it all to Jane and Elizabeth.

"I only had my mama growing up, and I ran pretty wild at times. But Jane and Elizabeth and me...well, I guess we all helped each other grow up." Then he frowned. "I sure as hell wouldn't be standing here, talking about my feelings to you, if this wasn't important to her. I wouldn't have taken a punch without knocking you on your ass if she didn't mean the world to me."

Yeah, and he knew Rhett could knock him on his ass and then some.

"Anything else you want to know?" he sneered. "If not, I'm going to head home to my family."

Matt met his challenging gaze. "I won't tell anyone."

"I'll pass that along," Rhett said.

"You didn't know that when you came here?"

"No," Rhett said. "Not for certain, but I was willing to do it for Jane."

He shrugged into his coat then and walked to the door. Matt stayed where he was, still reeling from the man's story.

"Think carefully about what you want, Hale, because I can promise you this. If you hurt Jane in any way about her past as Raven, I *will* beat the living shit out of you. 'Night, now."

Cold air washed over him again as Rhett left. He ran his hand through his hair, his mind examining all the different angles of what he'd heard, rather like a mental Rubik's cube.

Jane had wanted to tell him the truth without knowing how he'd feel about it. And how *did* he feel about it?

Sick, he had to admit to himself.

But sad too, particularly when he thought about how

desperate she must have been to escape her parents.

And what of taking on this secret with her? It would likely ruin him politically and hurt everyone involved.

After staring into the fire, absently stroking Henry's shiny coat, he came to the inescapable truth.

His heart burned for her. He loved her.

His uncle was right. What else mattered?

CHAPTER 32

Wallowing was not a Wilcox trait, but since Jane really didn't want to be a Wilcox, she decided to give herself more time for her pity party. She poured herself another glass of wine and resumed her fourth Bond movie of the day. Some girls watched chick flicks when they were feeling down. She watched Bond. But not the ones with poker because they were horribly inaccurate.

Right now, Sean Connery's voice was like a lullaby in *Dr. No*. Rufus and Annie perked up on the couch beside her—another rule blown—when they heard a car crunching down the snowy driveway. It was Elizabeth or Rhett, she decided, untangling herself from her red throw. Her money was on Rhett. She downed the rest of the wine in her glass, bracing herself for his news.

Patting down her short hair probably didn't help. She hadn't showered and was still in her robe and P.J.s. Oh well.

When the knock came on the door, she retied her bathrobe—a small mercy—and went to answer it. She opened it to find Matt, Henry by his side, and shock rippled through her.

"Matt!"

Annie and Rufus nudged his legs, tails wagging

wildly, and greeted a surprisingly calm Henry. *"Jane. Can we come in?"*

God, that dear, dear face. He looked more handsome than ever to her despite the grooves around his mouth from stress. She just wanted to kiss him senseless. But that wasn't wise.

"I don't think that's a good idea."

He pushed inside anyway, Henry following and still not jumping. Matt shut the door slowly, intentionally. Then he turned around, blue eyes blazing. "I know, Jane," he said, his voice razor-sharp.

Had Rhett told him without telling her?

Her whole frame went ramrod straight. Oh God, he couldn't... Her bravado was forced, but she managed to keep a steady voice and say, "What do you know?"

"That you're Raven."

The gasp she uttered was punctuated by a bark from Rufus, who clearly sensed her distress. "How did you—"

"Shut up," he whispered and yanked her to him.

His mouth crushed hers, his arms wrapping around her like a vise. He fed on her, and she on him, the agony of their horrible parting cleansed away by that one, fierce kiss. It went on and on and on until Jane wrenched her head back.

"And?"

"I'm here," he whispered hoarsely and dove back in.

She tunneled her fingers into his hair, standing on the balls of her feet now. His clothes were cold, but soon she was hot all over. He swept her into his arms and carried her into the bedroom, kicking the door shut behind them. He laid her on the bed and shucked off his coat.

"I'm sorry I couldn't tell you," she said softly, the connection between them delicate now that they weren't touching.

"I know, and I'm sorry I couldn't do it your way," he murmured, stripping off his clothes and then tugging on her bathrobe. "You've been crying."

"I didn't want to lose you. Not over this."

He covered her with his now-naked body and pressed his forehead to hers.

"Not ever!" The words were a harsh cry from her lips.

"Oh baby," he said, kissing her again. "I'm here. We'll figure it all out."

She slipped out of her robe awkwardly and swept aside her pajama top. "Thank God! I was sure I'd lost you."

He slid her cotton pants down her legs and then pressed himself fully to her, his skin warm now, igniting fires, soothing her broken heart. "Never. I love you, and I mean that. You can tell me your side later."

"But how—"

"Later," he said again and then took her mouth in another drugging kiss, his hands running over her, making her feel cherished again. Making her feel loved.

"I love you," she whispered when he sought her breasts, and then she simply surrendered to everything between them.

The heat. The urgency.

It was all too much after the wild swings of emotion, and she came hard against him when his fingers sought her wet warmth. A foil packet tore as she panted for more. Then his hands found hers, and he pressed his full length against her, stretching her hands over her head. When he entered her, she gripped him with her knees, never wanting to be without him, without that slow slide of him inside her.

"Give it to me, Jane," he whispered, teeth clenching as he thrust into her. "I need you."

His desire fueled hers, and soon she was caught in the throes of pleasure again, only this time he was right there with her. Their breaths were in time with their bodies, and the union they entered was new and scary and fragile, which made her heart tear open wide when she came again.

His groans punctuated the silence, and then he froze above her. She squeezed his hands tight and nuzzled his head when he pressed his forehead to her neck. They stayed that way for a moment. She did not know how long.

Time ceased to have meaning. Sensation was everything.

The power of her love for him returned with joy.

"Oh, Matt," she whispered, tears leaking from her eyes again, but for an entirely different reason now.

"Shh, I'm here. I'm right here."

He rolled them to their sides, dispensed with the condom, and then pulled her onto his chest, running his hands over her back, his caresses soothing now.

When she quieted, they laid there in silence, fingers caressing each other's cooling skin.

Soon she couldn't ignore the reality. The new knowledge he had of her was lying between them like an old lover.

"How did you find out?" she finally asked.

His hands froze on her damp flesh for a moment before resuming. "First let me say that I wasn't ready to let you walk away, and since you wouldn't tell me what it was without putting money between us, I was determined to find out. Lucky for me, as Andy pointed out, we have investigative journalists in the family."

Oh God, she thought as confusion fogged her mind.

"Don't freeze up on me. I recruited Uncle Arthur, Tanner, and Meredith to help me because I knew I could trust them. I know we have different families but when it comes to mine, they are rock solid. Do you trust me on that?"

How in the world had they discovered her secret? Shoving onto her elbow, the fear over her. "They know? But how? I thought Rhett had—"

"Yeah." A half smile cruised over his face. "He visited me right before I came here, but I had already found out from my family. They had a hard time unraveling the knots, trust me, but Uncle Arthur boasts he's been studying mug shots for decades. He figured it out after comparing some photos."

His words didn't soothe the tightness in her chest. She knew they wouldn't say anything if Matt had asked them to, but if they could figure it out, couldn't someone else?

"I should also probably tell you that I took a shot at Rhett," he continued, giving her arm a gentle caress.

Her mouth parted when he waggled his bruised knuckles in front of her face. "You did what?" That so wasn't the Matt she knew. "Why?"

He lifted a shoulder. "Because I thought he'd forced you to wear those outfits and look..."

When he trailed off, she pulled away, but he yanked her back.

"Oh, no. I'm not letting you shut me out." His blue eyes were stormy now. "I'm here, and I love you."

"You were going to say 'like a slut,'" she finished for him. "That's what you were thinking."

He sighed. "Yes, but I know you're not."

"And yet I dressed as Raven for seven years."

He propped the pillows up against the headboard and drew her to him, covering them both with the bedspread. "Okay. Tell me why."

She fumbled at first, but as his gaze remained steady, his hand holding hers tightly, she found her voice. When she finished, he cupped her cheek.

"It's hard for me to imagine a family ever being as...pushy seems like an inadequate word. They were destroying you with their own plans and ambitions. I'm glad you found a way out—even if it was rather unconventional."

"Raven makes you uncomfortable."

"Jane, I've gotten used to seeing you...well, like this. All cute and petite. Smart and sexy. I know you. I love you. But I don't know that other woman."

"And you're not sure you ever want to." Wasn't that the crux? "It doesn't matter now, I guess. She doesn't exist anymore."

"I think you're underestimating her...and yourself. Aren't fantasies our way of tapping into places inside of us we'd like to explore?"

Crap. He was right, and her vulnerability grew with that knowledge. "I wanted to be beautiful, okay? I wanted to be a woman men fantasized about, but one who was in control. And with Rhett..."

His face softened. "He was your protector, so it was safe."

She nodded. "I didn't want to act on any...well, sexual fantasies when I was dressed as her. Not that it would have worked out well. Once I started taking my clothes off, it would have become clear I wasn't all that...ah, endowed."

God, her face was heating just from talking about it.

"You are beautiful, Jane," Matt said.

This time she caressed his face. "With you, I'm starting to believe that for the first time in my life, and I can't tell you how much I appreciate it. My childhood was hard. My mother always found me wanting, and being a smart girl didn't help."

He kissed her fingers. "I happen to like smart and beautiful."

"Lucky me." But a new pocket of fear rose up now as she thought ahead. "I'm still a threat to you politically, though. If your family could figure it out..."

"Hey," he said quietly. "They knew they were looking for something. I don't want you to worry about any of that."

She flopped back against the headboard. "Matt, I meant what I said before. You are such a good man, and you'll make an incredible politician. I don't want to do anything to hurt your chances."

It would drive a wedge between them if she did.

"And what if I said I'm willing to 'roll the dice,' to use your terminology?"

"That's a particularly stupid game of chance with little likelihood of winning."

"Now you're sounding like an expert. Did you know that you glow when you talk about poker? You're going to have to give me some lessons. I expect you're incredible at it."

He wasn't going to listen, and because she didn't want to lose him, she let it go. For now. "I am. I even kick Rhett's butt most of the time."

He drew back, his brow raised. "Ever think of competing yourself?"

She punched the pillow behind her. "Sometimes. But I owe Rhett and want to support him."

"Somehow I think you underestimate Rhett. I bet he'd go bananas over you competing by yourself. When he first warned me about being good to you, I didn't realize you'd been working for him for so long. But after our talk tonight...well, I think he'd do just about anything for you."

Yeah, that was Rhett. And the fact that he'd gone to Matt to tell him the news himself... Her heart was aglow. She'd have to text him later and thank him.

"You were right about Henry, by the way. We've come to a new understanding, and it's changed everything. It's only been a day, but he's actually listening to me. I told him he's my dog now."

And didn't that make her tear up again. "I'm...really happy to hear that. So what next?" she asked, clutching the bedspread.

He unpried her fingers and pulled her to him, caging her hips in his hands. "Didn't I make that clear? We move forward. We take our daily dog-walking trips at our park."

Our park. God, she loved those words.

"We see each other as often as we can." Then he kissed her so sweetly and softly, she felt her bones dissolve. "And we make love."

"That sounds nice."

As his hands trailed across her skin, she gave herself up to him.

CHAPTER 33

Matt's sisters were what Elizabeth would call a trip. Jane had never heard that phrase until Liz used it in their first few weeks at Harvard, but she loved it now.

This was their second lunch together. Matt's campaign was moving forward, and with the primaries just over a month and a half away, he was busier than ever. His Easter Brigade, as he called them, had recruited more volunteers, and Jane had met them all at his office.

Still, the campaign felt like an albatross around her neck. And most days, she felt like a possum waiting to be discovered behind the woodpile.

"So, what is everyone having today?" Natalie asked, the biggest foodie of the group. "Brian's recitation of the specials made me hungry."

Her red cashmere wrap gave her a powerful look, almost as if she'd been wrapped up by a Spanish bullfighter.

Jane set aside Brasserie Dare's elegant menu. "I'm going for the ham and brie quiche. Nothing more traditionally French than that."

"I'm having the Provencal salad," Moira said from

across the table. She was decked out in a lovely emerald-green shirt that suited her name and Irish coloring.

"On a diet again, Mo?" Caroline asked, fingering her wine stem, the most elegant of the group in a white suit jacket with large gray buttons that looked like ancient Roman coins.

"Pacing myself. All we ever do when we get together is eat."

Natalie leaned in to Jane and whispered, "Mom's been cooking for three days. We had fresh cinnamon rolls this morning. God!"

"You know how much I love to feed my kids," April said. The Hale matriarch was sitting at the head of the table, her beauty understated in a simple navy cable-knit sweater. "You could always elect not to eat them."

"Like that's going to happen," Caroline said. "Good thing Andy suggested we take a long run this afternoon."

"Exactly why I'm eating a salad," Moira said. "Otherwise, I'll be upchucking later."

"Stop," Caroline pleaded. "That's so gross."

"Whatever," Moira snapped back.

"So, Jane, tell us a little more about your week," their mom interjected.

"I see how it is. Don't ask us, Mom. Not that there's much to share," Natalie said. "It's pretty much work, work, work."

"Feel free to move to Dare Valley, dear," her mom said, not missing a beat. "Otherwise stop complaining."

Natalie rolled her eyes.

Editing her week for family consumption sat in her stomach about as well as week-old wine and even less so when their food arrived. She told them about the dogs' antics, which delighted them, and an evening out with Matt.

But she couldn't talk about watching poker tapes for

The Grand Mountain Hotel's upcoming tournament, and it sucked to lie to them, if only by omission.

Matt didn't seem too bothered that his...well, nuclear family didn't know about her yet except for Andy, whom Matt had told after talking to her. His extended family had mostly reassured her. Arthur Hale's mouth had tipped up at the corners when they'd bumped into each other last week at one of the weekly Hale get-togethers. Meredith had hugged her longer than usual, communicating her acceptance, while Tanner had pulled her aside to tell her that he thought her job was cool.

"What do you like most about living in Dare?" April asked when she finished telling them the abbreviated version of her week.

"Ah...other than your son?" she asked, making them laugh. She almost did a dance in her chair. "Well, it's a beautiful place to live. I like being so close to the outdoors."

Matt had taken her snowboarding last weekend. Crashing into the snow hadn't been great, but being with him, laughing as the wind off the mountain cooled their cheeks, had been downright perfect.

"And downtown is lovely. Lots of great new shops keep opening up."

"You should open a gourmet grocery store here, Natalie," April said. "Leave your deputy to manage the catering in Denver."

"Mom," Natalie said, toying with her Croque Monsieur sandwich, which was loaded with juicy ham topped with mouthwatering broiled Gruyère.

"And Caroline could open an art gallery here," she continued.

"Oh heavens," Caroline moaned. "She's been *planning*."

"And what about me, mom?" Moira said with a frown.

"I'm still thinking about you," she answered and patted her daughter's hand. "But you don't like your human resources job."

"Nice. You get the pass." Natalie took another bite of her sandwich.

"Or she didn't think about me as much as she did you two. Like usual," Moira said.

"Oh, Lord," Caroline said, holding her hands up to the ceiling. "I hear a pity party coming on."

"Enough. You know I think about you all equally and pray for you every night and morning. Sometimes more when you're pulling something I don't like."

"Hmmm..." Natalie murmured.

"Not like that's ever happened," Caroline said, batting her eyelashes.

"Right," April said dryly. "What about your family, Jane? It must be interesting to have a career politician as a father."

This at least she could be honest about. "Not really. Actually, it was pretty stifling. We're not very close."

They hadn't called her back after her weak moment of wanting a Hallmark reunion. Why had she even bothered? How could she have forgotten what they were like?

"I'm sorry to hear that, Jane," April said, reaching for her hand.

The sweetness of her gesture, so unlike her own mother, made Jane's throat squeeze shut. "Thank you."

"But hey, you have us all now," Natalie said, putting her arm around Jane's shoulders.

Their support was so welcome and humbling she almost told them she was Raven on the spot.

But that was hardly suitable conversation for lunch. And in a public place, no less.

Maybe it was time to talk to Matt about that. Her trust in the rest of the Hales was growing.

And then she saw Elizabeth walk into the restaurant

with a lunch date and she remembered Rhett and Elizabeth had only agreed to tell Matt. Of course, they both knew Arthur Hale, and Tanner and Meredith had discovered the truth too. Rhett trusted them, since he knew them through Mac and Peggy, Tanner's sister. But Elizabeth didn't, and she'd put up quite a stink. Their relationship was on a bumpy road right now—a fact that was underscored by the look her friend gave her when their eyes finally met. Jane feared they would soon come to a cliff if they didn't veer off this path.

"I see a friend of mine," she said, pressing back from the table. "I'll be right back."

Natalie snagged her arm. "Bring her over. We'd love to meet her."

Jane nodded, thinking a hurricane was more likely to hit landlocked Dare than for that to happen. As she crossed the restaurant, moving past stunning pictures of the French countryside and Paris, she fisted her hands at her sides. Elizabeth's mouth tightened a fraction, but she forced a smile.

Jane's quiche turned into scrambled eggs in her stomach.

"Hi Elizabeth," she said. "It's good to see you. I'm Jane Wilcox. I work with Elizabeth," she said as she turned to her friend's ruggedly handsome companion.

"Paul Franklin," the man said. "I'm her new ski instructor."

"Oh, how lovely," she replied.

She and Elizabeth had taken a few ski lessons together, but their practice had fallen by the wayside since she'd started dating Matt.

The hostess was heading toward them, so Jane stepped out of the way. "Well, it was good to meet you. Elizabeth, if you have time, come over and meet Matt's family. They...said they'd like that." God, even to her ears it sounded awkward.

"Sure. We'll see."

They were seated on the other side of the restaurant, and Elizabeth didn't come over.

Not that Jane had expected any different.

The only time they'd come close to being normal with each other was when Elizabeth had come over to tell her about her impromptu meeting with Terrance in Don't Soy with Me. Her friend's freak-out had turned to calm over a glass of wine. Other than that, Elizabeth had her head up her butt and was letting all her fears get in the way of their long friendship. Her heart hurt from it.

When she left, she and Elizabeth shared a final glance as she pulled on her coat, and then her friend turned back to her date.

The cut was sharp and deep.

CHAPTER 34

Elizabeth gunned her SUV up Jane's driveway. Her date had sucked because she couldn't stop thinking about the look Jane had given her before leaving the restaurant. Like one of those sad rescue dogs at the pound.

When she parked, she firmed her shoulders and walked up the stairs. She and her friend had their crazy moments with each other, sure, arguing over anything from poker tells to the best shade of eyeliner to match a sequined gown.

But never this.

After knocking, she stood there in the cold, already shaking with nerves. How was she going to explain how she felt, and what was Jane going to say?

Her friend opened the door, dogs panting and wagging their tails by her side, and just stared at her.

No smile.

Nothing.

Zip.

"Can we talk?" she asked.

Jane stepped out of the way, still unresponsive. Well, Elizabeth couldn't blame her. She'd been a bitch earlier. Now it was time for her to explain why.

"I'm sorry for how I acted earlier. I..." Crap, this was the hard part. "I saw you with all those other women, laughing and smiling when I walked in, and...well, I know it's stupid, but I got scared, okay?"

Her friend crossed her arms. "Of what? Them finding out about Raven and Vixen?"

To do something with her hands, she leaned down and picked up Annie. "I won't lie, I'm still upset that Matt's journalist family found out the truth, but that's not it... I'm worried that they're going to replace...well, me."

"Replace you?"

"Yes." Elizabeth stroked Annie's fur, and the little dog tunneled against her coat. "We've always been a unit, but that's slipping away. Rhett isn't who he used to be, and now..."

"Me," Jane finished. "Dammit, Elizabeth. If we're slipping away from each other, it's because you haven't been trusting me."

She set Annie down. "I do trust you. I just don't trust them, and the more people who know..."

"What?" Jane cried. "What happens if it comes out? Vince isn't going to come back here for you. It was seven years ago. It's time to let it go."

God, how she wanted to. "I haven't been able to sleep in my wonderful big house, which I used to love. Now I prop a chair under the door while I spend the night listening to the branches scrape the windows."

Jane's brow knitted together. "Liz, I don't know how to help you feel safe. But Rhett and I are here for you. We'll always love you. Adding new people into our lives isn't going to change that."

They were quiet for a long moment. "Jane," Elizabeth finally said. "I don't want to lose you over this. We've been friends for too long."

Her friend's face fell. "It's hurt me the way you've

treated Matt."

Rare tears burned in her eyes, and her feet dashed across the short distance separating them. She wrapped her arms around Jane, crying softly.

"I know, and I'm so sorry."

"Oh, Elizabeth," Jane said, crying now too.

"How about I cook dinner for you and Matt?" she said, hiccupping between tears.

"We'd love that. And I want you to try and stop being so afraid. It hurts me to hear that you're scared to be in your beautiful house all alone now."

"Me too," she said, her stomach knotting at the very thought of it. "I'm working on it. Talking to someone."

Jane finally pushed back, her cheeks wet like Elizabeth's. "I'm glad. I'm here for you, and Rhett is too. You can come and stay with me until it gets better."

She shook her head. "No, we did that last time. I need to get through this on my own. If I can't beat it now, I'm afraid I never will."

Jane walked over to the side table on the couch and shook the box of Kleenex. "We're a mess."

Elizabeth took a couple of Kleenexes and dabbed her damp skin. "Is my mascara running?"

"Yes. Mine isn't since I'm not wearing any. Never liked that stuff to begin with."

"Are we okay?"

"Yes. Now when are you planning on cooking for Matt and me?"

Her nerves spiked. She'd make something over-the-top as an apology. Beef Wellington. But that might not be enough to convince Matt she wasn't a bitch. He had to be upset with her. "Will Matt like me, Jane? I mean, I haven't been the nicest..."

"Of course, he will. You're my oldest and best friend. You're my sister, and he gets that. He has three."

More tears burned behind her eyes, but she blinked them back. God, she hated being a girl sometimes.

"I called my parents, Liz," Jane blurted out. "I didn't tell you."

"You what?"

Jane headed toward the kitchen. "Come on. I need some water."

She followed, passing the doggie bowls tucked in the corner. The kitchen was neat as always, like the rest of the house, and an empty bottle of French wine sat on the counter.

"You called them because of what I said. Jane, I was a total bitch that day."

She poured them both water in crystal glasses and extended one to Liz. "No, you were right. They were still controlling me. I decided to see if things could be different. They didn't call me back."

Well, that didn't surprise her. Their Harvard preppie daughter was long gone, and she was the only facet of Jane that had interested them.

"I'm sorry."

"It's for the best, probably. I can't be who they want, and they aren't interested in seeing who I really am."

"Who you are is perfect. Don't let them hurt you again."

She sipped her water and tilted back her head as though she were studying the ceiling. "This time it was only a pinch, really."

"I'm glad." God, she wished her fear of Vince was just a pinch. "I'm proud of you, Jane. Maybe I should call Vince and tell him off."

The joke fell flat. They both knew what a horrible idea that was. She took a sip of her water and almost coughed on it as the sound of his hateful voice echoed in her head again.

Jane grabbed her hand. "Hey! Don't go there. You're here, and you're safe."

"Right," she said, her voice shaky.

"I know it's freezing outside, but how about we have

a bowl of salted caramel gelato?"

"That sounds really nice. Do you have any caramel sauce to smother it with?"

Ice cream always helped.

"Of course. It's your favorite."

And that's what friends did. They kept their best friends' favorite things around for tough moments like this one.

"I love you, Jane. I've missed you, and I'm really sorry."

Jane shut the freezer door and dropped the pint of ice cream onto her granite countertop. "I love you and missed you, and you're forgiven. Now, when are you cooking for Matt and me?"

She grinned. "Any time it suits the mayoral candidate's schedule."

Then they snuggled next to each other, their ice cream bowls in their laps, the dogs at their feet, and watched a Bond movie.

Girlfriends rocked.

CHAPTER 35

The rented room at the Chamber of Commerce had a picture of Dare Valley's small business leader award recipients. Matt's cousin, Jill, was the youngest of the group by far. Jane studied it while she waited for Matt to ascend the small stage they'd set up on a wooden platform with a microphone.

Tonight was his first town hall meeting, and just being here for him was one of the hardest things she'd ever done. So far, he'd done all of his events by himself. Realizing how she felt about politics, he hadn't asked her to come out tonight. He didn't even know she was here.

But she knew that it was important to him, and she wanted to show her support.

Even if it made her want to hurl.

It was also his biggest event to date. About two hundred people were present, and people kept glancing at her. *Yes*, she wanted to say, *that's my boyfriend, the guy running in the mayoral primary next month*.

Speculation about her was rampant, and all of the hushed voices circulating in the room made her feel as though she were back in high school with her mother sitting beside her, smiling fakely as they waited for her father to step onstage and deliver his speech.

Jill was going to introduce Matt tonight, and Jane knew that meant a lot to him. The rest of his family was here as well, including his Uncle Arthur, who had given her a brief wave as he walked by.

Jane was sitting in the back row in the corner, out of the way. Not with his family. Could she leave without anyone noticing?

She'd sworn she'd never attend another political event in her life, and yet here she was.

When he stepped on stage after Jill's funny, yet warm introduction, she knew why.

This man made her heart pound in her chest like no other.

His opener was a funny story about Jill from their childhood. She'd demanded an allowance from her parents after hearing that other kids at school had them. When her parents refused, she gave Matt a quarter and asked him to represent her since even though he was just in high school, everyone already knew he wanted to be a lawyer. The crowd laughed, and Jane could see the charisma in him.

He had the magic, intangible "thing" the political machines looked for.

If he won this primary—and at the moment, he was leading—he was going to make a competitive candidate. So far Horace Henklemeyer hadn't inspired much confidence, although his mother was still spouting off nonsense about Matt around town.

Hearing Matt tell the story about how he'd come back to Dare brought tears to her eyes. She knew he'd probably told it a hundred times to different groups, but it didn't sound rehearsed. There was a part of Matt that was still visibly haunted by losing Patricia's case, and she expected it would never go away.

She hadn't heard him spell out his platform in

public before, and she admired the way he weaved it into stories he'd heard from others in town. Matt even mentioned them by name and nodded to them in the audience.

Impressed, Jane glanced at Rob in the corner of the room. She hadn't met him, but she knew what a political consultant looked like, even if he wasn't the only person in the room wearing a three-thousand-dollar tailored suit. The man clearly knew what he was doing, she had to admit. That speech-writing style was classic. It personalized candidates in a way no facts or figures ever could.

Her heart swelled with pride.

God, Matt was so good at this.

Then her mind flashed to an image of her up there with him at the end of the speech, smiling for the cameras, and she fisted her hands in her lap.

An older woman came in late and sat across the aisle from her. The speech was nearing completion, and Jane wondered why a newcomer had even bothered to come. But she was elderly. Perhaps she had gotten the time wrong. Then Jane recognized the pinched mouth and angry gaze as belonging to Florence Henklemeyer.

Her stomach turned over.

People wildly applauded when Matt finished his remarks, and then they moved on to questions. One after another, members of the audience asked him about everything from his views on Dare's schools and what could be done to improve them to the ongoing potholes on Route 9 heading out of town. When he had an answer, he gave one. When he didn't, he told the questioner he'd look into it, asking the person to provide his or her name and phone number at the end of the town hall meeting. More often than not, he had an answer, but she liked that he was honest.

When he called for any last questions, the older woman sitting across from her rose. Since Jane was good at reading people—especially Matt—she noticed the facial muscles of his smile tense for a moment.

"Florence, do you have a question? I would have thought you'd be with Horace, helping him put up signs next to mine around town."

Some people laughed. Everyone craned their necks and glanced at the back of the room, where she stood all stiff and haughty.

"That's why I came in late," she threw back.

Nervous laughter spread throughout the crowd.

"I'm glad to hear it," Matt responded, not missing a beat. "Now, do you have a question? If you're interested in tonight's presentation, we'll be sending out the minutes to everyone on my mailing list. I'd be happy to take your information."

The banter caused more laughter, but even Jane could feel the change in the room. She'd seen it happen many times before. There was an edge now, one of political opposition.

Things were about to get ugly.

"Yes, I do, and it so happens the focus of my question is sitting right across from me."

It took Jane a moment to realize she was speaking about her. And then Florence actually pointed at her to underscore her point.

"I wanted to ask if you could tell us a little more about your girlfriend's work at The Grand Mountain Hotel. As you may not know, *since you didn't live here* at the time, I opposed the hotel before the town council approved it, fearing it would bring the evils of gambling, sex, and drink to our town."

If Jane hadn't felt like a specimen under a microscope, she might have laughed out loud. Sex and alcohol had been in Dare Valley long before the establishment of the hotel.

But this was her worst nightmare coming to light. Keeping a poker face was essential. Matt's had slipped.

He was frowning now, and Jane prayed he would keep his cool.

"I had heard about your opposition to the hotel," he responded, "and you're well entitled to your opinions. As for my girlfriend, she's not the one running in the mayoral primary. I am. And that's where the buck stops."

Florence looked over at her, and like a villain in a Disney movie, her smile was now an eerie sneer. "But no one at the hotel remembers seeing her working there in a...professional capacity. It's almost like she went to work every day and disappeared. It makes this old lady wonder..."

The audience stared at Jane, most of them sitting almost sideways in their seats now.

Her gaze met Matt's, and she had to fight to keep her lips from trembling.

"I'm not sure what you're implying, but this isn't a topic I plan on engaging in with you. My campaign is about the Dare Valley citizens and the issues we all care about. I don't plan on running a negative campaign, and I hope you and your son will choose the same policy. Thank you for coming, everyone. If you were too shy to ask a question earlier, I plan on staying around to talk to people. Please come up and introduce yourself. And have some of the wonderful baked goods made by my lovely volunteers. Good night."

He walked into the crowd, shaking people's hands. Jane instantly rose and picked up her purse. Coming here had been a bad idea.

Florence appeared at her side. "I know you were up to something. You're a bad seed, working for that hotel, working for poker players. I've heard you used to live in Sin City."

"Mrs. Henklemeyer. We haven't officially met," she said, extending her hand. "I'm Jane Wilcox."

Her old political acumen came back to her. She'd

long ago become accustomed to shaking hands with people who hated her because of her father. Who made mean comments about her flat chest. Or called her a smarty pants. The negative comments had run the gamut.

The woman hadn't expected friendliness from her, and she faltered a moment before taking Jane's hand in her limp grasp.

"I'm also from a small town like Dare Valley," she continued. "My father is a state senator who has served his community faithfully for almost thirty years. I graduated from Harvard with an MBA, and I also respect and admire Mac Maven and Rhett Butler for being men of integrity as well as incredible professional poker players. Thanks again for coming tonight."

And she walked to the front, praying her cheeks weren't flushed. Inside she was burning. The campaign had changed.

She'd been dragged in as the dirt.

Nothing was going to be easy or civil between the candidates from now on.

People wandered past her in the opposite direction, staring, and she smiled and nodded as they passed.

Matt was talking to an older man when he spotted her, and he shook the man's hand suddenly, pointed to her, and strode off. When he reached her, he grabbed her to him.

"I'm so sorry," he whispered into her ear.

She clutched him before pulling back. "You did great! I'm so proud of you."

His eyes narrowed a fraction, and then he pasted a smile on his face. "Thanks. It hit a rocky patch at the end, but I think we came out okay. Don't you, Uncle Arthur?"

When Jane looked over her shoulder, she noticed Matt's family was now behind her. Andy held a serious-faced Danny in his arms. April circled Matt to pull Jane into a hug, clucking under her tongue.

"That woman!"

"Mom," Matt whispered.

"She's a total bitch," Jill huffed out. "Right, Mere?"

"Little ears," Andy chided as Meredith nodded.

"Sorry, Andy," Jill said. "I'm only—"

"Not here, ladies. Please," Jane told them, but with a smile.

"Let's go ahead and thank the volunteers, Matt, and help everyone clean up," Jane said, and with those words, it was as though she had fallen back into the old life, the one she'd run from.

He took her arm. "Why don't you head on home? I'll swing by in a bit."

Everything inside her felt wooden. "No, I'm happy to stay." She spotted the Easter Brigade talking to some people by the baked goods they'd made. "I'll have to ask Mabel what I should try. I'm sure she makes good cookies."

God, she was about ready to choke.

Matt's face tensed, but she pulled her arm away and headed off without another word.

The wooden feeling didn't go away. Not after thirty minutes of sunny small talk with Matt's volunteers.

Finally, after what seemed like an eternity, someone came up to her and put an arm around her shoulders. She turned to look at Matt's Uncle Arthur.

"Come on, little missy," he said. "You can take me home."

They made their goodbyes, Matt fighting to keep a smile on his face now.

"I'll be by in a bit," he said and kissed her cheek.

It was hard to mistake the narrowed gaze Matt's political advisor sent her way. Yeah, he knew they were in for a world of hurt going forward. Well, she would see his uncle home and strategize later. Matt would need a new plan.

"Meredith and Tanner brought me," Arthur said as they walked to her SUV, "but I figured it might be nice for us to talk on the short ride to my house." He gave her directions, which would fortunately be easy enough to follow.

He didn't mince words once they were buckled in. "Florence is a nuisance, but she's sharp as a tack. Mean too. You might want to talk to Rhett and Elizabeth about this situation. Mac too. Florence will be looking for information on what you did at the hotel. What will she find?"

Jane studied the road. "I can't say. We were obviously careful. Mac runs a tight ship."

"Might be good to check on that. I don't play favorites when it comes to elections in Dare Valley, but Matt's my great-nephew and I respect Mac and Rhett and their families. I think you should prepare for the worst. Florence isn't above making things up if she doesn't find anything."

Her mind was already spinning scenarios, running through the campaign's options. "We need to pre-empt it." That was the only other way she knew to avert disaster.

But the risk...

"Go on the offensive," Arthur said and whistled. "Not sure how this town will feel about it."

"Perhaps it's not a question of them believing I was Raven, a poker babe."

"What do you mean?" his uncle asked.

"If we tell them I'm Raven, they'll think I'm a slut, right? Or worse?"

The earthquake in her stomach registered at 7.0 on the Richter scale.

Arthur sighed. "I'm afraid so. You'll look like the fallen daughter of a politician. Or a party girl."

Her mind conjured up other politician's daughters who'd disgraced their fathers and their families that way.

"What if we told them I'm Rhett's poker scout?" It would be explosive to his rep, but Rhett could handle the heat. Could Elizabeth?

"No one will believe you were just a poker scout wearing those outfits."

She slammed her hand against the steering wheel, feeling the trap she'd built closing in on her. He was right. No one would believe that. Not even with her Harvard MBA and the foundation she ran for women's education.

"What if I showed that I was a true poker player?" she asked, turning onto his street. "As good as Rhett and Mac? Would that convince them?"

He made a humming voice. "It would help. People would see there was more to you than those outfits."

"We could say it was like training, and that my ambition was always to play poker with the big boys."

"Is that true? Can you really play at that level?" his uncle asked as they drove down his lane.

She turned in her seat when they stopped in his driveway. "I don't know for sure. We're about to find out."

CHAPTER 36

Matt checked his watch for the second time. Since it was late, Rob was going to stay over at his house. But after that stunt Florence Henklemeyer had pulled, he wasn't about to leave Jane alone tonight.

"Look," he said to his friend, "I know you're concerned. As I've told you a million times, I can't talk about what Jane did at the hotel or before that without her permission."

"Great! I feel so reassured," Rob said, loosening his tie even further so that it hung loosely now around his neck like a noose.

"I love her. I'm sticking with her. Trust me. We'll weather this."

They had to. He couldn't bear to see her become the perfectly wooden politician's daughter again.

"It's going to get ugly, Matt," Rob said. "I've seen plenty of opponents like Florence Henklemeyer in the past, and she's going to go for the jugular. If you're not open about Jane's past, people are going to start asking questions, and if your answers don't satisfy, they'll start to doubt you."

"Then let them. I don't want her dragged into this,

and I won't answer questions about my girlfriend."

He realized he'd totally lost his cool and was speaking louder than usual. Hell. Good thing he'd crated Henry as soon as he got home. Otherwise, his outburst would have garnered a reaction from him.

A knock sounded on the door, and he rose to answer it. He wondered if it was his brother. His cell phone had been ringing nonstop since he got home with Rob, but he figured he could talk to his family later. Right now, it was more important for him to focus on this powwow with his friend and political consultant.

When he opened the door, he was surprised to see Jane.

"Hey," he said, pulling her to him and holding her tight. "I'm sorry for taking so long. Did you call me? I was going to come over after wrapping things up with Rob."

When she pulled back, she patted his chest. "I expect Rob might have quite a bit to say. Rob, I think it's time we officially met. I'm Jane Wilcox, and as you saw tonight, I've just become a liability to Matt's campaign."

"Dammit!" Matt said, watching them shake hands. "Stop that talk right now."

"I like her already, Matt," Rob said, finally tugging off his red- and white-striped silk tie and stuffing it into the pocket of his navy jacket. "She's a politician's daughter. Of course she knows the score."

"Exactly," Jane said, crossing her arms. "Do you have any wine?"

Matt did a double-take. "Ah...yes."

"Why don't you boys grab a beer? We need to talk."

This take-charge version of Jane was new to him. She was in her element. Matt could almost see her in a conservative blue suit jacket and skirt, smiling woodenly for the cameras.

"There's nothing to talk about," Matt said. "We move forward. That's it."

Jane extended a hand to Rob. "Let's get those drinks, shall we?"

What was she? The First Lady now? "Dammit, Jane! I said there's nothing to discuss."

They ignored him and disappeared into the kitchen. He shrugged out of his own navy suit jacket. He'd discarded the tie Rob had selected as soon as he got home. When they emerged, Jane was carrying a glass of red wine and a beer for him. Rob was smiling in that shark-lawyer way he had when he thought he'd finally turned a hostile witness.

He believed Jane was on his side.

Well, they were both going to find out otherwise.

"You're not breaking things off with me," Matt growled when she handed him his beer.

"No, I'm not."

"God, I'm tired," Rob said, falling onto the couch. "Here I thought this campaign was going to be so easy. A small town. A squeaky-clean candidate."

"Rob, would you give me your assessment of tonight?" she asked, sitting next to him. "From start to finish."

Matt finally flopped onto the couch too, giving into the inevitable. "He already gave it to me."

"I'd like to hear it," she smoothly responded. "If that's all right."

Rob took a swig of his microbrew and then did as she'd asked.

"I don't have to tell you how troublesome Florence Henklemeyer is going to be. It's one thing to take down another candidate's signs but quite another to go after a candidate's girlfriend at his own town hall meeting. She can do it because she's not running."

"Yes," Jane agreed, sipping her wine. "And I don't think she's going to stop, despite what I told her after you finished speaking."

Rob's eyes narrowed. "You told her about being a

politician's daughter?"

"And about going to Harvard," she said. "I hate to name drop. It won't stop her, though. She thinks The Grand Mountain Hotel is Sodom and Gomorrah."

"Maybe we can turn her into a pillar of salt," Matt joked, but the humor fell flat.

"Matt's in trouble because of me. And that's the last thing I want." Jane ran her finger over the edge of her wine glass, making it sing.

"I'd love to hear your ideas, but first you need to tell me what you've been up to since you left Harvard and arrived here. Besides running the women's scholarship. Great organization, by the way."

"Couldn't find out?" she asked him, her chocolate eyes bold now.

Rob laughed. "I *did* try."

"I told you not to do that," Matt said. "Jane, I—"

"I believe you," she answered. "Just a quick question, Rob. Have you signed a confidentiality agreement to work with Matt?"

"Yeah. He didn't want one, but I did. I know he's a choir boy, but I learned a long time ago that confidentiality agreements are as much for my protection as for my clients. Then they're not tempted to kill me when I learn all their dirty secrets."

"Cripes, you're acting like this is an episode of *Scandal.*"

"I hope not," Jane said. "That show's even more over-the-top than real politics, and that's saying a lot."

"Amen," Rob agreed. "Okay, so what were you? Some secret spy?"

"Jane," Matt said, kneeling in front of her. "You don't have to do this."

Her eyes darkened, and she smoothed the hair off his brow. "I won't hurt your campaign if I can help it. Besides, it's time to come clean...to everyone. We both know it. We'll have to talk to Rhett and Liz tomorrow.

Then your family."

His chest felt like a crushed-up soda can all of a sudden. "Do you have any idea how much I love you right now?"

The soft smile she gave him was the one reserved for the moments after they'd made love, and he would have swept her into his arms right then and there if Rob hadn't been present.

"I love you too. That's why I'm doing this. Okay, Rob, prepared to be shocked."

His friend leaned into the sofa's cushions and set the beer against his chest. "Trust me, Jane. There's no way you can shock me."

She raised a brow and then began to describe the events that had led to her transformation into Raven, going so far as to pull her smart phone out and show him a picture from the Internet. Rob's mouth dropped open, and then his gaze slid down Jane's body in a way that made Matt want to punch him in the face. But he didn't.

When she finished, she gulped the rest of her wine.

"Okay, I'm shocked," Rob said.

Jane's laughter sounded like it had been squeezed out of her. "I'm trying to feel emboldened by that."

"My God, you *are* a woman of mystery, and I can't say that too often. I would never in a million years have imagined you being...well, a woman like Raven."

"And having an MBA from Harvard," Matt added, just to keep his friend on track. "Jane's smart *and* sexy. It's a killer combination."

Jane just smiled at him.

"So how does telling the world that you're Raven not ruin Matt's campaign?" Rob asked.

"I was just getting to that," she said and held out her hand to Matt. "Come sit down again."

He put his arm around her shoulders, seeing the tension that had crept into her muscles. "It will be hard to spin the story about me being Raven, and frankly I don't want to be ashamed of it. But I know people will see those pictures of me dressed like that and think...well, that I'm a slut."

Matt winced, hearing that word come out of her mouth. "They're morons if they think that. No one has more integrity than you."

"But you know as well as I do that people tend to judge a book by its cover," she said. "They'll say I'm a candidate for a new reality TV show. *Politicians' Daughters Gone Wild*."

Matt didn't like that one bit.

"Right, Rob?"

His friend nodded.

"So, we need to give them a new story. One that shows that I'm smart and savvy, that I'm using the skills I learned as Rhett's secret poker scout. Of course, I need to run all this by Rhett and our other colleague tomorrow."

Matt wondered what they'd say. Elizabeth had gone out of her way to be nice to him lately and had made them an incredible gourmet meal a week ago. She'd even gone so far as to volunteer for his campaign, which had shocked Jane and brought tears to her eyes.

"What's the plan?" Rob asked.

"I'm going to play in The Grand Mountain Hotel's upcoming poker tournament," she announced, so smoothly it took a moment for it to sink in.

He rose off the couch. "You what?" he almost shouted.

"I'm going to do my best to win it," she continued, smoothing her hands down her thighs, a gesture that seemed to indicate nerves.

"But you hate the limelight," Matt said.

"I haven't liked it in the past, but this time I'm stepping into it as myself. With Raven, I was hiding behind a character. Everyone's going to know it's me now. And when I sit down and play with the same men who used to ogle me and treat me like a dumb bimbo—because that's what I was playing—I'm going to have the satisfaction of beating the pants off them. Not literally, of course. This is professional poker, not strip."

"A professional poker player as a girlfriend," Rob considered, stroking his chin.

"I know there will be voters who will have serious concerns, but there's nothing I can do about that. I was Raven. I was happy to be Raven while working for Rhett. I'll never regret the freedom it gave me from my parents, but now it's time to be Jane Wilcox. To bring everything I am, everything I've become out into the light."

"Be tough at first, but it could work," Rob mused, taking another swig of his beer. "Are you that good?"

Her brow knit, and this was the first time Matt could see her doubts. "Well, I don't know. I beat Rhett almost every time when we play online, but that's different. I've never done it in a live tournament."

"And just how different is it?" Rob asked before Matt could.

She let out a slow breath. "Pretty different. Some men crumble under the pressure. Matt, you haven't said anything. If you're worried about how this will affect your campaign..."

He pulled her off the couch and into his arms. "You know I'll stand beside you, whatever you do."

"Even if it means losing the primary?" she whispered.

"Even then," he said. "But I want to ask you again... Are you sure you want to do this? It's a huge step."

She rubbed her neck. "Part of me has always wondered if I was good enough to play with the big boys. I've dreamed about it. Fantasized about it. Now I want to go all in, as my real self with my real skills. It's time to see what I'm made of."

"I'm so proud of you, Jane." He kissed her to punctuate his pronouncement. "And if we do things this way, it takes the power away from Florence Henklemeyer. What kind of a name is that anyway?"

"She'll still make waves," Rob said, looking away to give them some privacy, "but this just might be crazy enough to work. People might react positively to this kind of honesty."

Matt released Jane, and they both sat down again.

"At least we'll be calling the shots," she said. "We know what's true. That's half the battle in politics anyway."

Rob nodded.

"What will Rhett and Elizabeth say?" he asked.

"I don't know, but this will be a big step for all of us. We've operated in the dark for a long time."

"I'm coming with you to talk to them," he said, taking her hand. "We'll do this together."

Rob stood and set his beer aside. "I have to say, Jane. You're not the woman I would have envisioned for Matt. But I think you're the best choice he could possibly have made. I'm going to head to the spare room and let you two... Just take the dog with you if you're leaving. I'm not good with animals. Matt, call me tomorrow when things are more definite."

"Will do," he said, watching his friend head out of the room.

Rob stopped at the doorway. "Jane, it *was* great to finally meet you. I'll look forward to more chats. Tonight has been illuminating to say the least."

"Thank you," she said primly, and then tucked her legs under her and turned to Matt. "Is this plan crazy? It came to me while I was taking your uncle home."

"How'd that go?" he asked.

"About like you'd expect. He loves you and laid it out as cleanly as Rob did."

"That's not much of a surprise. Uncle Arthur doesn't

mince words."

She fingered the fold of his white dress shirt. "How will your family react?"

He pulled her onto his lap then and tucked her close. "They will be surprised. You are a woman of mystery, after all. But I have a feeling they'll come to the same conclusion I finally did."

Leaning in, she wrapped her hands around his neck. "And what's that?"

"That you're pretty awesome." He pressed his forehead to hers. "God, I love you. You know you don't have to do this, right? I'll take the punches and plead the fifth about your background. I don't want you to get hurt over this."

"No, it's fine. I need to own who I am. When I was with my family, I wasn't my own person, and when I was Raven, well...I was someone else. I need to be...myself, and poker has helped me realize that in a weird way. I know that sounds dumb, but it's how I feel."

"I can't say it enough. I'm so proud of you," he whispered. "And I pretty much adore you right now. I also wish we were alone."

"My house is only five minutes away."

"Three if I speed."

She clucked her tongue. "Mayoral candidates should not speed. What happens if you get a ticket?"

He was laughing as he scooped her up in his arms. They'd get Henry and take him to her house. And then he was going to make love to Jane Wilcox all night long. The politician's daughter, the Harvard MBA, the poker scout, Raven, and the dog walker.

And the bed wouldn't feel crowded at all.

CHAPTER 37

The next morning Jane and Matt prepared for their guests. Elizabeth arrived first and hugged them both right away. Yeah, her friend was making some serious strides when it came to accepting the man in Jane's life. The biggest surprise came when Abbie arrived with Rhett.

Rhett barrel-hugged Jane and lifted her a foot off the floor, and when he put her down to shake hands with Matt, Abbie gave her a gentle hug. Elizabeth gaped like a codfish, but Rhett just winked at them. It took a second, but Jane managed to wrap her arms around Abbie and return the embrace. She had obviously decided to be more accepting of the women Rhett considered sisters.

"Thanks for coming," she said to everyone. "Matt, will you take everyone's coats? We're just waiting for Mac to arrive. I figured he should be here too."

Rhett tossed his sheepskin coat to Matt and headed straight for the fire. "It's all over town about what Florence Henmaker pulled at your meeting last night."

"Henklemeyer," Abbie corrected softly, handing her navy wool coat to Matt.

"Whatever," Rhett said. "How is it that some women get away with actions that would get most men punched?"

"Are you all right, Jane?" Abbie asked, standing there in her winter white pantsuit, pearls at her neck.

"Yes," she responded, "but it was my worst fear come to life. I made tea and coffee for everyone. Let me serve it while we wait for Mac."

"Don't make this into a damn tea party," Rhett fumed, punching the air. "That Henkle woman is going after you and Matt, which means she's coming after us too."

"Calm down, dear," Abbie said softly, taking his hand. "I expect that's why we were invited over this morning."

"I'll help you get the drinks," Elizabeth said, threading her arm through Jane's. "How bad was it?" she whispered as they walked into the kitchen.

"Bad. I felt like a newly turned Jell-O mold on the inside, but my old training kicked in. I smiled until my teeth hurt."

"I expect that didn't feel great."

"Rather like having a root canal without meds." She smoothed out the small beverage napkins, straightening the folds as her friend pulled the milk and creamer from the fridge. "I wanted to punch her for going after Matt like that and then for attacking me directly."

"She approached you?"

Jane filled her in, and by the time she was finished, Elizabeth's face had lost all color. "She isn't going to stop, is she?"

"No," Jane said, picking up the coffee tray. "But I have an idea on how to have the upper hand."

Elizabeth hefted up the tea tray. "By giving her cement shoes and tossing her in the lake near Pohawatan Valley?"

"Cement shoes?" That made Jane laugh, and it felt

good even though her throat was tight. "What have you been watching?"

"Another mob show. I'm addicted. You'll have to come over and watch. We'll make buttered popcorn and drink good wine."

"I'd like that," Jane said with a smile. A noise filtered in from the other room. "Oh, that must be Mac. We need to join the others."

"I'll support you, Jane. Whatever you need."

God, she hoped so. "Don't make that promise until you hear what I'm going to propose."

When they returned to the sitting room, Mac was already talking with everyone in front of the fire.

She and Matt had agreed to put the dogs in her guest bedroom so they wouldn't be interrupted. Since Rhett hadn't asked about Annie, she knew his mind was on other matters.

Heck, so was hers.

Things were about to become very interesting.

Matt took the tray from her and placed it on the coffee table so she could greet Mac, who hugged her tight. She'd known him as long as she'd known Rhett, and he was one of the good guys.

"How are you doing after last night?" he asked. "I've already heard an earful from Jill. She was hot to trot at work this morning, let me tell you. I was afraid I might need to sequester her in her office to keep her from heading into town to give that woman a piece of her mind. Apparently, Florence walked into Don't Soy with Me this morning and asked the barista if she could tape one of her son's signs on the wall. Fortunately the barista declined and said she'd have to check with Jill first."

"That Henkle woman has balls," Rhett said.

This time Abbie didn't correct him. "How about we call her Flo? It will make it easier. Jane, I'd love some tea. Is that jasmine green tea I smell?"

"Yes," she said, pouring her a cup.

She was using her fine china today. Rhett was right. She was trying to make this into a tea party. And it was time for that to stop.

"Rhett's right."

"I usually am. What about this time?"

Abbie rolled her eyes.

"You can't put lipstick on a pig," she said.

"Or a feather boa on an armadillo," he added, pouring himself a cup of tea. "Jane, do you really expect me to use this itty-bitty cup with *my* hands?"

He held up a palm that could scoop up a small child. She laughed. "I'll get you a mug."

"Make that three," Matt added.

Once they were finally settled into their respective seats, Matt opting to stand beside Jane's arm chair while Mac settled in across from her on a matching chair, and Abbie, Rhett, and Liz sat on the couch, she let out a deep sigh.

"As I was saying, I won't try and put lipstick on a pig. This woman...Flo is going to make trouble. If she doesn't find out what I was really doing at Mac's hotel, she's going to make something up. She said last night the hotel was Sodom and Gomorrah, and since I'm from Sin City—"

"Jesus," Rhett breathed out before Abbie elbowed him.

"Well, there's no need to go further into her nonsense. I don't want Matt to have to constantly be on the offensive, pleading the fifth or saying I was working on special projects."

Elizabeth was holding her breath. Yeah, she knew what was coming now.

"I want to tell people that I was Raven, but I want to go one step further too."

Rhett's eyes narrowed, and Abbie took his hand. Elizabeth looked down in her lap. Mac just stared at her, waiting for her to continue.

"If I come out as Raven, people aren't going to believe I was Rhett's poker scout. Some might, but not without proof. They'll cast me onto the fire as a slut and burn me."

"Nice analogy," Mac said. "Can we shoot for something less violent?"

"You know how this would go," she told him. "You've had to handle the media each time you open a new hotel. You know that the smallest minds tend to be paired with the loudest mouths."

He took a sip of his coffee. "Unfortunately."

"I don't want this to hurt your hotel either. That's why I invited you this morning." She set her tea cup aside, her hands trembling too much to hold it. "I want to show everyone how smart I really am. I want to play in your upcoming tournament, Mac. And I hope to make the final table."

Elizabeth blinked at her. "But we've never—"

"No," she said. "We've never tried, but it's the only way I can see this working. We need to show this is above-board. People will knock Rhett around for using scouts, but it's becoming more and more common now, and I think we can weather it. What I don't think we can weather is the lascivious comments that they're going to make about me as Raven, and all of you because of your association to me. I know it's a big step for everyone, but we need to talk this through."

"There's another reason we should go public," Matt finally said, putting his hand on her shoulder. "I'm not letting that woman make us cower or create further shenanigans by her unsubstantiated bullshit. I'm willing to lose the primary to be with Jane, but I don't want this to be the skeleton that's hidden in all of our closets."

"Liz," Jane said, rising from her chair and sitting on the arm of the couch. "I won't mention Vixen at all if you'd prefer. I can't promise they won't figure it out, but

I'm not asking you to go public too. I know how hard that would be for you."

Elizabeth reached for her hand and squeezed it tight. "I know you do, but I've realized I need to break free of the past too... You're right, it's better for us to do it on our own terms. And Rhett promised to teach me how to shoot a gun."

Rhett coughed at that, his throat clearly clogged with emotion.

Abbie reached across Rhett and took Elizabeth's other hand. "I don't tell many people," she said in a quiet voice, "but I was date raped when I was in college. You can always talk to me. I know what it's like to be scared."

"And I can promise to keep tabs on this guy if it will make you feel safer, Elizabeth," Rhett said.

Rare tears sparkled in Elizabeth's eyes. "Thank you, everyone," she said with a sniff. "I think we all need to say boo to the ghosts. Isn't that what you always say, Rhett?"

"I remember him saying the same to me," Abbie said, and they shared a special smile.

"Peggy prefers to say boo with a shotgun and a police vest, but that's her," Mac joked, making everyone laugh.

The room slowly quieted. Jane stroked Elizabeth's hair before walking over to Matt again. This time she didn't sit.

It was time to make a stand.

"Rhett, I hope you don't think it's a conflict of interest for me to play in the tourney."

"Please. You've supported me behind the scenes for years. It's time for me to support you. Jane, I'm going to sit this one out. I'll be your poker babe, but I draw the line at the heels and sequins."

Her laughter was nervous and giddy. "I think you'd look wonderful in the stage makeup though."

"Does this mean I'm losing you for good, Jane?" Rhett asked.

She lifted her shoulder. "I don't know...I haven't thought that far ahead. I'm scared and excited about playing poker in a real tournament, but I'm not sure I'll like the spotlight."

"Then we'll take it one step at a time," Rhett said with a smile. "You're going to do great."

Her hand rubbed her tight diaphragm. She turned to the other man she respected, one whom she would be challenging in the tournament. "Mac, is it okay with you?"

"I have no problem with playing against you, Jane. I've always known that you and Elizabeth have a rare talent. I think you're going to surprise the other players."

"And I want them to know it's *me*," she added. "Or a new version of me. Elizabeth, will you help me dress the part?"

"I have just the dress in mind. And I'll be happy to act as your publicist for the day."

"Thank you."

"With everyone's blessing, I'm going to give an interview to Matt's uncle," Jane said. "You all know Arthur. I think he'll surprise people with what he writes."

"Your family is going to have a coronary," Rhett murmured.

"I tried to call them a few weeks ago to...I don't know. See if things were different. They never called back. That was their decision, so this is mine."

They probably *would* reach out to her once the article was published, and it wouldn't be a Hallmark moment. Her father's run for the U.S. Senate would be hurt by this revelation, no two bones about it, but that wasn't her business.

"They're assholes," Rhett said. "We're your family,

347

and we're the ones who are going to be in your cheering section at the tourney."

"Even I'll come to see this one," Abbie said.

Rhett kissed her right then and there. "Oh, darlin', how did I ever get so lucky?"

"Of course, you'll have to have a serious conversation with Dustin," Abbie said. "I caught him ogling both Raven and Vixen more times than I can count. He'll be more than a little surprised to find out the truth about you two."

"He's a teenage boy, Abbie," Rhett said. "Don't worry. He'll be a little embarrassed, but we'll throw a big party after the tournament and let him mingle with the girls as they really are. We'll all get over any awkwardness. You did."

"Thank you. I try."

"Yes, thank you, Abbie," Jane said, and Elizabeth seconded it.

"Well, I guess it's on," Matt said. "And I promise to be one of your poker babes too, if you think you can handle two men."

She circled her arms around her waist. "Nah, I'm a one-man kind of girl."

"Cut me to the quick, why don't you," Rhett said, stabbing himself with his hand as though it were a sword.

"You can be my poker babe," Abbie said and then giggled. "You *have* become a bad influence on me."

"I always was, and you love it," he whispered, earning him another elbowing.

"I guess that's that," Jane concluded. "I'm going to play in a major poker tournament."

"Don't worry one minute, darlin'. You're going to kick ass and take names."

She sure hoped Rhett was right. If she lost in the early rounds, she'd be labeled a stupid poker babe for the rest of her life.

CHAPTER 38

Elizabeth rushed up the stairs of The Grand Mountain Hotel, cursing the heels she'd worn. She was late, and she hated that. Rhett had kept her for longer than expected to go over the press release she'd drafted.

Today she was coordinating with Mac and his public relations director, Darla Adams, over the upcoming announcement about Raven and Vixen. Mac and Rhett were planning to go public at the same time. It would be interesting to see how Darla, with whom she'd worked in her capacity as Rhett's publicist, treated her now that she knew she was Vixen. Mac had told Darla everything so they could create a detailed media plan. Elizabeth was here to help. The goal was to make things as smooth as possible.

Not that she thought there was much hope of that.

But she loved Jane, and if her best friend was willing to go all in, then she was going to support her.

When she hit the landing, she collided into a man. On the verge of falling, she reached out and grabbed a handful of his shirt. His arms closed around her and pulled her away from the top of the stairs.

"Whoa now! Never wise to rush like that on the

stairs," the man said in her ear, and the gravel and spice in his voice made her hands clench on his shoulders.

Terrance? Not again.

When they eased apart, her breathing choppy from the fear, she felt as though she were falling down the stairs after all.

Terrance Waters stood before her in a gunmetal gray Fendi suit that perfectly suited his lean, rock-hard frame.

"Are you all right?" he asked her, releasing his hold, but keeping a hand to her back for support. The heat of it burned her.

"I'm...fine."

"Are you sure?" he asked, narrowing his eyes at her. "You look like you've had a few decades shaved off your life."

Say something, Elizabeth, she told herself. "I'll be fine." Right. Being held again by this man she had loved. This man she'd run from. The only one whom she'd been tempted to tell... well, everything.

Compose yourself. She held out a quivering hand. "We didn't officially meet before. I'm Elizabeth Saunders. Rhett Butler Blaylock's publicist. I was just going to meet Mac." He would find out the truth of who she was soon enough, but she had no desire to be present for his reaction.

"Seems we're going to be seeing a lot more of each other. I've just accepted the job as Mac's new head chef here at the hotel."

Her mouth parted. Oh God. This could not be happening.

"That's great," she managed, trying not to hyperventilate.

"I doubt that's what you're thinking," he said with shuttered eyes. "I'm Terrance Waters, by the way. But you already know that..." He trailed off, as if he had more left to say.

For a moment, she felt like a trap door was about to open.

"Vixen."

She fell through the hole. "You must have me confused with someone else," she replied with her best poker face. "I need to go. Mac's waiting on me."

Fortunately, he didn't stop her.

CHAPTER 39

The week leading up to the poker tournament was chaotic, messy, and surprisingly blissful. Once the story broke about Jane and Elizabeth being poker scouts, there wasn't a quiet moment, which was good because Elizabeth was still freaking out about running away from Terrance when he'd called her Vixen. Rhett fielded calls from top poker officials in the World Series of Poker and other big tournaments and satisfied any concerns. He talked to other professionals too, and Mac added his support by making over ten calls a day on his friends' behalf. The fans were shocked, and there were some interesting tweets and posts on various poker blogs with pictures of Jane and Elizabeth as poker babes with captions like *Smart Girls in Trashy Costumes* and *Rhett Butler Blaylock Creates the Ultimate Bluff.*

Dare Valley's reaction was equally messy. Florence Henkelmeyer had a field day, as expected. Within a day, signs were posted with pictures of Jane as Raven with the caption: *Do you want your mayor dating that?* Some people stared at her and Matt when they went to Don't Soy with Me or Brasserie Dare. Others thought it hilarious, thanks to Jill, who had posted a new sign in the window of her coffee shop. *Women. Don't Judge a Book By Her Cover.*

Matt added over fifty meetings that week to his schedule to talk with different groups about the news. Sometimes Jane attended; other times, she let him handle it, which he did with aplomb.

His campaign wasn't totally on the ropes by day three, and Rob was upbeat about Matt's ability to sway voters to his side.

The most important reaction came from his family, all of whom were standing behind them. Just as Matt had said they would. His sisters thought her alter ego as the mysterious Raven—a gorgeous poker scout—was awesome. His mom had actually laughed over the whole thing. And when Natalie had asked Jane where she'd bought her enhancements because she might want to try some, *everyone* had laughed. She'd felt accepted and loved, and the ice in her stomach had melted away.

Her parent's reaction had been just as expected. Her father finally returned her call, his voice booming with outrageous indignation as he accused her of ruining his chances for U.S. Senate. He ordered her to retract her comments and say it was a lie, that she'd made it up to hurt him. After trying to get in a word edgewise for fifteen minutes, she hung up. She cried for a moment over this final fissure in their relationship, and then she took the dogs for a walk.

She watched endless hours of tape. Studied the files of the players coming to the tournament. And played poker every night with Elizabeth, Rhett, Cincinnati Kilkelly—Mac's long-time deputy and a professional player himself—and Tanner, who was surprisingly good.

Her dreams danced with cards and sequined dresses. The pressure was enough to make her feel like she was wearing one of Lady Gaga's corsets.

Her alone time with Matt dwindled to the few hours they managed to spend talking and making love before falling asleep for the five hours their schedule allowed.

By the time the three-day tournament rolled around, Jane was edgy from too much caffeine, and her stomach was fluttering with nerves. But thanks to her best friend, she looked gorgeous.

"The dress rocks," Elizabeth said, studying her in Jane's bathroom mirror.

The silver sequins on the 1920s-style flapper dress sparkled under the floodlights. It required no jewelry, and they'd gone with soft eye makeup but bold red lips. She looked like a woman who would have graced The Grand Mountain Hotel when it had first opened before the Depression.

And damn if the sequined ballet slippers didn't feel like butter.

"I look like a million bucks," she breathed out. Even she could see it. Who needed butt and breast pads? She just needed to wear clothes that suited her natural body.

"I'm ready," she announced, knowing Rhett and Matt were waiting for them to leave. "You still don't have to go. I don't want you to run into Terrance and getting upset."

Her friend dropped the lipstick she'd been holding and reached down to pick it up. "Don't worry. I'm overreacting and have decided to take a chill pill. What we had was a fling. And it was two years ago. He's been with tons of women since. I'm sure he'll leave me alone."

Jane knew Terrance's reputation, but she'd seen him with Elizabeth. She was certain Terrance's feelings for her friend had run deep. "Okay, if you say so. Let's go then."

When they emerged, Rhett whistled, and Matt ran his gaze over her body.

"Holy moly," Rhett cried out. "Just look at you, Jane. The shitty players won't be able to take their eyes off you, and they'll bust out faster than buttons popping off a fat man after Thanksgiving dinner."

Matt took her hands and smiled. "You look beautiful. Powerful. Like a woman who knows what she wants."

"Thank you. That's how I feel...you know, beyond the whole I-might-puke-before-the-tourney-begins thing."

"I used to puke all the time when I was a rookie," Rhett announced, patting her on the back and then picking up Annie for a kiss. "You'll do fine. And I'll be holding this sweet thang like a good poker babe the whole time."

She petted the adorable dog, who was dressed in a matching silver sequined cape. They even had sequins for dogs, she'd discovered.

"Let's get this show on the road," Elizabeth said.

The tournament ran two days, starting at ten a.m. on this cold Saturday morning. She'd likely be playing until eight or nine tonight, depending on how long the last hand took. And the tourney would go on tomorrow until they had a winner, and she'd seen these things go on for as long as eighteen hours sometimes. She hoped to make it that far.

"My family's meeting us there, FYI," Matt said. "They can't wait."

His family was coming? "Are you sure?"

"They want to support you."

"Heck, even Dustin's doing his part. He's taking care of Keith so Peggy can come, and when he heard about Matt's nephew, Danny, he offered to watch him too. They're going to have a blast." Rhett slapped on the signature white cowboy hat he'd worn to many tournaments. "For old times. Abbie gave me the thumbs-up this morning."

"Let's go then. I want to take in the crowd." See people's reactions. Measure how much respect they were going to give her. She was a newbie to the circuit. And a woman.

Until she proved herself, she might as well be Tiger Woods' golf caddy.

When they walked in, there was quite a crowd milling in the sleek lobby of the hotel. The wall sconces and unique gas lighting made it feel like another world. Add in the old cherry wood, perfectly restored, the stunning staircase shot with a red runner, and a crystal chandelier from an old Rockefeller house, and Mac had created another winning venue.

Matt took her clammy hand as she moved forward, her head held high. Rhett shook hands as they walked the line, Annie tucked against his chest. He introduced her *properly,* he said, to some of the other players. No one was rude in front of Rhett. They all knew he'd punch them in the nose if they made one wrong step.

But the men in the crowd scanned her frame. One even shouted out that he missed her old getup, and Elizabeth, who stood on the other side of Rhett, had to restrain him from going over and making a ruckus.

"Rhett, I can take care of myself," Jane said when they entered the main poker room, which was arranged with acres of the finest poker tables, islands of green stretching as far as the eye could see.

It was time to stand on her own two feet.

"Of course you can," Mac said, appearing by their side. He gave her a warm embrace. "But I don't tolerate any crap in my hotel, so if someone is unprofessional to you, they'll receive a warning or be thrown out. I've told my crew to keep an eye out. You're going to be the subject of a lot of talk, especially among the players. But hopefully everyone will keep it clean."

"I can handle it," she said again.

"Oh, and Elizabeth, my new head chef—Terrance Waters, you remember?—said he's created something special to celebrate if Jane wins. He thought you might want to come see it in the kitchen and tweet about it."

Her friend gulped. "Wonderful."

She and Jane shared a look. It didn't look like Terrance was willing to let bygones be bygones. But she needed to focus on herself. Elizabeth was a big girl.

"Good," Mac continued, "then I'll tell you what Rhett always tells me when we play. For the next few hours, we're no longer friends. Good luck, Jane."

"Back at ya, Mac. I need to find my first table." She turned to Matt. "If you have to step out to meet with a local group—"

"I told you. I'm here for the duration. No campaign business this weekend. I'm just here as your poker babe."

"Then you're overdressed," Elizabeth joked, leaning forward to kiss Jane's cheek. "You've got this."

She pulled her friend in for a hug. "I'm playing for you too, you know."

"I know. Now go show the world what Rhett and I have always known. That you're a woman to be reckoned with."

Matt caressed Jane's arm and leaned in to give her a light kiss on the mouth. "I'm in awe of you."

"Thanks."

Then Rhett stepped forward and drew a silver jewelry box out of his leather jacket with one hand. It was wrapped up in a pink bow. "I thought this might be a fitting gift to commemorate your first tournament."

When she opened it, she had to battle to keep her poker face. The most beautiful Roman coin she'd ever seen lay against the white pillow.

"Every professional needs a chip protector," he said. "And I thought this would do. It's of Artemis, the Roman goddess of the hunt. The image is a bit faded, but she's depicted with her bow and arrows and her faithful hound. It seems like it was made for you."

God, she couldn't cry, but the sweetness of the gesture flashed through her like a shooting star. "Thank you, Rhett. That's just—"

"Enough of this blather, or I'm going to start bawling, and that won't do. Now you go play your heart out. Jane, you love this game. Play from that place, and no one can stop you."

Her heart expanded with that reminder.

"I'll see you all later," she said. And after giving Annie a final pat and Matt a parting glance, she took off.

The first day she held her own. Rhett was right. A number of unseasoned players busted out in the early games, staring more at her than their cards. With ten thousand as the entry fee, it was an expensive mistake. Mac was also right. A few players who'd started drinking way too early and too much—not serious ones at all—made some off-color comments about her being a woman or a slut. Some received warnings, and when a man grabbed her ass as she reached her fifth table, he was immediately thrown out.

Word spread.

She was not to be messed with. And she decided to be grateful for Mac's intervention rather than looking a gift horse in the mouth.

The skills she'd learned while working for Rhett came through beautifully. She bluffed a few hands and won, dragged in a few small pots, even went heads up against another player on a hand that fizzled out on the River card.

After the first day, she was still alive. Had a good percentage of chips. And was starting to find her own.

Rhett congratulated her grandly, holding Annie above his head as he gave that shrill whistle of his. She told him to save his congratulations for tomorrow.

Then she went home and slept like a baby.

When Sunday morning rolled around, she cracked her knuckles and shimmied into her red flapper dress. This one was decorated with fringe instead of sequins, which gave the dress movement. She loved it.

Poker babes from behind the crowd line shot her

dirty looks when she arrived, flanked by her own entourage. Funny how she hadn't noticed them yesterday. Some of the women she'd stood next to for years, cheering on their respective players, clearly felt betrayed.

Well, that was too bad. She wouldn't let herself be held back by what anyone thought of her.

Tuning out Matt and his family was easier on the second day. She fell into the moment, tracing the corners of her cards, fingering her Roman coin, rubbing the green felt of the table, studying the faces of her fellow players.

Inside she was as cool as a meat locker, and it felt good to discover that inner sanctum all serious players talked about. She played one hand at a time, gathering more chips as she went. The number of players around her continued to dwindle as the day progressed. The remaining players were the usual suspects. She had a file on each of them.

They were poker royalty.

She took the chip lead by winning a monster hand with two other players. All three of them had gone all in, and she'd won by playing a hand most people wouldn't have raised on, demonstrating her boldness even further.

When Cincinnati Kilkelly, the Master of Ceremonies, announced the final table, she was one of the nine players whose name was called. And for the first time all day, a smile crested over her face.

Rhett had taught her to savor every victory, and making the final table was a heck of a victory. She punched the air and did a happy dance in the bathroom stall during the break.

Of course, Mac was at the final table, along with seven other long-time players, including Lance Jenkins, who had won the World Series of Poker two years ago. But she was going to play to win, even if she was in the big leagues now.

Before the final table started, she walked over to the viewing area where the crowd was cordoned off. Rhett swung her up and spun them around in a circle. "I am so proud of you. Jane, you're playing like you always do when you whip my ass in online poker."

When he set her down, Elizabeth rushed her next. "My God, you look fierce. I think Rhett has you pegged. You are Artemis personified, just like on that coin."

"I rather like that idea. A goddess."

"I'm pretty fond of Jane Wilcox," Matt said, stepping forward. "Is she still around?"

Her mouth quirked. "I think she's still in here somewhere."

"God, babe, you are incredible," Matt said, giving her a giant smacker. "I can't believe you've never played professionally. You're a natural."

She took a deep breath. "Thank you. I'm playing one hand at a time."

"Can my family congratulate you or will that break your concentration?" Matt asked.

"Let's save it for later," she said. "I...well, I'm in the zone now."

Rhett snorted out a laugh. "You sure are, darlin'. Now go kick Mac Maven's butt. I love that boy, but if I can't beat him today, I want you to do it for me."

She shook her head. Mac was as cool as they came at the table and one of the hardest to read, which was saying something when it came to professional poker players.

"I need to get back. I want to be already sitting at the table when the other players return."

"Good strategy. Stare them all down like you're going to spit in their eye," Rhett said.

With that colloquialism, she took off.

After smoothing down her red fringe dress, she settled into her prescribed seat at the table and asked for another sparkling water with lime. The final table was magical, with sleek lines of mahogany, custom drink holders, and cushioned armrests to offset hours of grueling play. The time was nearing four p.m., and the sun was already descending in the sky toward the mountains through the hotel's windows. The crowd was humming, eager for the finals to begin. She tuned it out and smiled when Lance Jenkins swaggered toward the table.

He was a known womanizer and had made overtures to Raven more times than she could count.

"Good to see you in the finals, Jane," he said smoothly, taking his seat. "Can't say I'm not surprised by your transformation. I hope you'll forgive a good ol' boy for ever treating you a tad improper."

"No hard feelings, Lance," she said.

Mac joined them, unbuttoning his suit jacket. Of the nine players who were left, she and Mac were the only ones who were dressed for an elegant dinner party. Everyone else looked like they were attending a NASCAR race, clad in jeans and T-shirts—some with their sponsors' names slathered over them. A few were even wearing ball caps. But the one who gave her most pause was Kentucky Prattling, a short and stocky player who topped off his casual ensemble with yellow-tinted skeet shooting goggles. He was known for being one of the most aggressive players out there, and she made sure to meet his gaze when he sat down.

When they resumed play, she dug deep. Played her heart out.

After five grueling hours of play and one hundred and forty-four hands of poker, five players had busted out. She was part of the Final Four, along with Mac, Lance, and Kentucky. When Elizabeth approached her during the fifteen-minute bathroom break, she waved her off, not wanting to talk to anyone. She needed to stay in her zone.

When they began again, she was in second place with twenty-five percent of the chips needed to win it all. Mac was in first, with thirty-five, and Lance and Kentucky were tied with twenty.

She won the first hand with an ace-king, a terrific starting hand. But she had the worst position at the table, which meant she had to make her move before knowing how the others would bet. They tripled the blinds again, and she became the aggressor, using Kentucky's playbook against him, and went all in. She forced him to fold, proving she could stand up to him. His goggles fogged up then, forcing him to wipe them off with a handkerchief.

In the next hand, she played queen-jack. Mac was sitting to her left and had the best position at the table this time, since he could see everyone act first. There was a lot of raising as they went around the table. At one point, Mac called immediately, alerting her to him having a pretty good hand. When the cards came around again, the Flop card was queen-jack-five. Lance and Kentucky checked. With the two pair, she decided to go aggressive and bet half the pot. Mac called, but he didn't re-raise.

Did he have a queen or middle pair? she asked herself, studying him. But Mac didn't look at her. Just kept gazing off in the distance, tuning everyone out. Lance and Kentucky folded.

Then Mac met her eyes, his gaze unblinking. Was she up for a head-to-head with him?

Yeah, she thought. You bet I am.

The Turn card was a seven—a card that helped no one. She eyed the cards, certain she had the best hand. She bet half the pot again. When Mac put on a Hollywood spectacle, spending nearly five minutes thinking before making his move, she started to lose her cool. The wait was killing her. She was in this pot deep, having put a significant portion of her chips on the line.

362

Then Mac called.

She let her breath out slowly, careful not to show that she'd been holding it.

The River card was a two and wouldn't help Mac if she was right about what he had.

The hand she was staring at was about the best she could hope for, so she bet half the pot again. Mac's mouth turned up then. He re-raised her and went all in.

In that moment, she started to suspect it was a trap. Was he just bluffing, or did he have a better hand? If so, she was going to lose most of her chips if she kept going.

She thought about it forever and took her time while running through the hand. Had she missed something?

Kentucky called the clock on her, startling her. Had she taken that long?

The floor manager came over then and told her she had one minute to act or her hand would be folded.

What to do?

"You have ten seconds," the floor manager finally announced. "Nine. Eight. Seven."

"I fold," she announced, showing her cards, her gut cramping as though she had a bad case of flu.

"Oh my God," Kentucky cried out. "How could you have folded with that hand?"

Then Mac turned his cards over, showing a set of fives. "That was a good fold."

Sure enough, he'd trapped her. He had the better hand.

When she felt the anger rise at her own naiveté, she forced it back. No, folding was a strategic retreat. She'd saved herself.

And when she looked up, Mac's gaze was on her. In his eyes, she saw a new speculation, one she'd seen the best poker players give Rhett.

They played another thirteen hands, Jane ignoring the piercing pain in her belly from nerves. Kentucky and Lance grew low on chips, confirming her earlier fold, which had kept her from being in the same position. She hit a big score on two consecutive hands, her chip pile growing again. Jane forced Lance and Kentucky to go all in, and in one hand, she busted them out, taking the chip lead with seventy percent to Mac's thirty.

It was just the two of them now, and a sliver of ice went down her spine when they received a new deck of cards for the table.

This was it.

With the next hand, she was dealt another ten-nine, and since it was the hand that had put her at the final table, she took it as a lucky sign. The pain in her belly receded, and she imagined herself walking in the park at sunset, dreaming about winning a big game like this. She could almost feel the cold winter wind on her cheeks. Imagine Matt's warm hand in her own.

This was her time.

So she turned Mac's strategy on him and trapped *him* this time.

He didn't see it coming until it was too late.

She made him think she didn't have a strong hand, biting her lip just once for an Oscar-winning effect, letting him think the pressure had become too much for her. She even shifted a fraction of an inch in her chair, being careful not to overplay it. God knew, she'd been sitting for enough hours today for her butt to truly hurt.

When Mac went all in immediately after the River card, she knew the game was hers. She instantly called and was elated to watch his eyes narrow a fraction. If she hadn't studied his face for hours, known it for years, she might not have noticed. Certainly no one else would have.

Then he sat back, his mouth quirking up. Yeah, he knew she had him.

"I have the nuts," she said in honor of Rhett, who delighted in using that catch phrase to describe the best hand possible.

The crowd went wild.

"A nut straight," Mac murmured as the cheers buffeted them, showing his lesser hand.

She'd won.

She'd actually won!

Mac stood and extended his hand, which she shook. "Well played, Jane. I expect big things of you." Then he walked off, head high as always.

She sat there for a minute, her ears buzzing, and then she put her hands to her face. Every ounce of strength she'd exerted to keep her poker face intact evaporated. The trembling started. The fatigue kicked in. And the euphoria.

She'd done it. By God, she'd actually done it!

Big arms plucked her out of the chair and tossed her up in the air. She knew it was Rhett, so she turned and grabbed for his shoulders.

"Holy hell, girl. You trapped the Maverick. I'm so proud of you!" And Rhett being Rhett, he squeezed the life out of her before thrusting her at Matt. "Sorry, man. I just had to grab my girl."

"I get it," Matt said, his eyes shining. "I don't even know what to say right now. Jane, you won!"

Her head started to work again, and the reality slowly sunk in. "I did, didn't I? I just won three million dollars by beating Mac *freaking* Maven."

"You sure did!" Elizabeth shouted, pulling her into a hug next. "You were incredible! I can't wait to watch it on tape. I chewed my fingernails off."

Her friend never did that.

"I almost threw up," Jane admitted.

"But you didn't," Rhett said. "You held your own. Girl, you are going to be a player to contend with."

Her eyes sought his. "I can't be your scout anymore," she admitted.

The truth had come to her earlier that day, but she'd forced it back, not wanting to acknowledge it yet.

"I know it. It's time for you to be your own player. I'm so proud of you, Jane."

Tears burned in her eyes. "I'll never forget what you've done for me."

He grabbed her shoulders. "Now, stop that. I'm going to bawl like a girl. You're my sister and my friend. Nothing changes that. Even when we play against each other. Heck, even when you beat me, which I expect you will." He tipped his hat to her. "Of course, I'm still going to do my best to beat you. Mac and I've managed it for years. You and I will too."

She sniffed and gave Annie a good rub under her ears. The dog wiggled in Elizabeth's arms.

"Now it's time to party," Jane announced. "I have some pretty special Dom Perignon waiting at the house."

Abbie had been hanging back, letting them have their moment, but now she stepped forward. "No need to wait."

"What?" she asked as Abbie handed Rhett a full bottle.

He grinned, taking off the wrapping and the wire. "Don't you remember what we did when I won my first big tourney?"

As he shook the bottle, she edged back, running into the solid wall of muscle behind her. Matt was smiling when she tipped her head up to look at him. "But Mac's hotel," she sputtered, trying to get out of the way. Rhett was going to soak her.

Matt held her in place, laughing now.

"I told him I'd pay for it."

Then he popped the cork, the sound exploding like a shot, and showered her with champagne.

Abbie and Elizabeth cried out and ran away when he tried to get them next. He was laughing like the demented man he was, and Matt was no better. He held her in place as champagne covered her short hair and dripped down her face and her dress. By the time they were finished, she was soaked.

But laughing.

God, there was something about Rhett.

She turned in the arms of the man who was holding her. "You think this is funny?"

"I think this is awesome! Jane, I love you. I'm so proud of you." Then he pulled her against him. "How about a kiss for your favorite poker babe?"

"We need more champagne," Rhett mused. "I'm outta ammunition."

Still sailing on her euphoria, she climbed on top of the chair she'd been playing in for hours and wrapped her arms around Matt's neck. "This is better. Now I don't have to lean up on my tiptoes to reach you."

He grabbed her wet dress in his hands. "Did I mention how much I love a woman on top?"

Leaning close to his face, she caressed his wet nape. "You might have mentioned it once or twice." And she put her lips to his and gave him a long, drugging kiss, not caring that his family was probably still watching and a whole heck of a lot of other spectators with camera phones.

"I love you," she finally whispered. "So how does it feel to be involved with a professional poker player?"

"I think we're going to make a formidable match. Now, let's go celebrate with my family. They're all so proud of you. Even Uncle Arthur cheered when you beat Mac."

"God, I love that old man."

"Me too. And I think you've proven to anyone who cares a flying flip that there's more to Raven than meets the eye."

Still standing on the chair, she surveyed the room. She waved at Matt's family, who waved back wildly and finally headed toward them.

"And do you know what?" she told Matt. "I finally

feel like I know the full Jane Wilcox. There might be a lot of facets to her, but that's what I like about her. She's unique."

"You can say that again and more," he murmured, tracing the drops of champagne on her face.

And as his family arrived, and Rhett rushed back with more champagne—which Tanner immediately wrestled away from him—she felt like she finally knew who she truly was and what she was made of.

CHAPTER 40

The sun was setting in brilliant hues of copper, gold, and turquoise when Matt parked the SUV. For once, he and Jane had driven together to the park, and it was the way he planned for it to be from now on.

"Are you sure you have time for this?" Jane asked, unbuckling her seatbelt. "I know the tide seems to be turning in the primary race now that I've won the poker tournament and showed my genius, but still."

He'd been teasing her about her victory for days now, and she'd finally started owning it.

"I'm not concerned about that right now," he said. "In fact, let's leave the dogs in here for a little while and just walk. You and me."

"Henry might not like that," Jane mused, arching her brow. "What are you up to?"

If only she knew.

"Henry, sit," Matt commanded, turning in his seat. "Now, stay. We'll be right back."

When the dog lay right down without complaint, Matt puffed out his chest. "I seem to have regained the full strength of my Inner Alpha."

Jane laughed, petting her dogs and telling them to

stay before exiting the car. "I never doubted your Inner Alpha."

"Bull," he said, coming around and taking her hand.

She was wearing a red fleece cap and a white North Face jacket with black fleece pants and boots. Jane was finding a new style all her own in the week since she'd won the poker tournament. It was elegant with a little edge. And he liked it a lot.

"What are you up to?" she asked. "You know that I'm a master at reading faces, right?"

Oh, she was blossoming. "I love seeing this newfound confidence in you."

"Well, there's still a lot to work out. We're two weeks away from the primary, and though things are looking better for you, we still don't know what will happen."

"Honestly, that's the last thing on my mind right now."

"I came to a decision today," she told him. "I don't want to play on the circuit all the time, but I do like the idea of playing at The Grand Mountain Hotel and in major tournaments every once in a while. You know I'm really a homebody at heart. I mostly want to sit by the fire with you and the dogs at the end of the day. It was nice of Rhett to give me Annie as a present for winning the tournament. I imagine he's right. He can attract enough buzz on his own. But unlike him, I don't need to be center stage."

"Neither do I." That had never been his reason for wanting to become mayor.

The snow was sparkling like one of her sequined gowns as they walked to the edge of the park. Dare Valley stretched out below them, the town of his birth. The town he was so glad he'd returned to.

Otherwise he would never have met Jane, and he couldn't imagine his life without her.

"You know, this is my favorite place in the park, right?" she asked. "I'd come here and gaze out at the sunset and whisper all of my dreams. In my imagination, the wind took them off into some magical place to be crafted and packaged up for me. You topped the list."

He cupped her cheek. "I'm glad to hear it. That's why I wanted to be alone with you here for a little while."

"You're not dropping out of the primary, are you?"

It was a fear she'd voiced more than once.

"No," he said firmly.

She was concerned about how her desire to be a professional poker player might affect him if he wanted to keep running for office. He'd assured her that he wasn't worried, and today he planned to prove it to her.

"We'll see how the cards fall, right? Being mayor means nothing without you." He released her hand and dug into his pocket for the ring he'd bought for her in Denver. He'd gone there the previous day to shop for one with his sisters. They'd gone bonkers with excitement, and after fielding their ring ideas, he thought he'd found the perfect one.

He knelt in the snow and had the delight of seeing her face transform, her mouth dropping open and then tipping into a radiant smile. "Jane Wilcox, when I came home to Dare Valley, I hoped I would make a life here. Find the right woman to be my partner and wife. Then I found you, and every dream I'd ever had about that paled in comparison to how things really are between us. You inspire me. You encourage me. You make me want to be a better man. I want to live every day with you by my side. Will you marry me?"

Falling to her knees in front of him, she said, "Oh, Matt."

He took off his gloves and opened the tiny box, drawing out the ring. "I didn't think you'd want something traditional, so I hope you like this."

The sapphire winked at them in the waning

afternoon light. There were two smaller diamonds set around the large square stone. "I thought a woman like Artemis might like this ring. Plus it reminded me how the sky looks after sunset when we leave the park together."

She pressed her hand to her chest, her chocolate eyes on fire. "I love it. Yes, I'll marry you. I started to dream about this day after we first made love. I fell in love with you so fast, Matt, and I never want to be without you either."

He finally released the pocket of air that had felt locked under his ribs. "Thank God. I thought you'd say yes, but I had nightmares about you arguing that you wouldn't be good for my career in political office." Tugging her gloves off, he slid the ring on the correct finger. It fit perfectly.

"Actually," Jane said, "one thing I realized after winning the tournament was that we're unstoppable together. I had to dig deep inside myself because of my love for you, and I can't ever imagine that being a bad thing. What we have together makes us *both* better, Matt."

He was glad she'd finally realized that. "You're right. And if I don't win the primary or whatever comes after that, it won't change who I am or what I want to do. I want to be with you and our family and help this community. Nothing matters besides that."

"That's what I want too," Jane told him, the sunset making her face glow. "That's why I don't want to make poker my whole life. I want this more. You and me and the dogs walking in the park after work."

"And someday, we'll bring our kids here," Matt said, imagining it.

They would play with the dogs while he and Jane strolled along the mountain's edge.

"I'm going to teach them how to wish on the sunset," she said, "and to believe with all their hearts that their dreams can come true."

As he pulled her into his arms, he realized all his dreams had come true too. "You know what? If I'm elected mayor—"

"*When* you're elected mayor," she corrected.

"Right," he said. "I think I'm going to name this park. It doesn't have one. I looked it up on the local map. It just lists it as a recreation area."

"I like that. I think we should call it The Park of Sunset Dreams."

He pulled her up with him and cupped her cold face. "That's a pretty romantic name for a park."

"People need a little more romance in their life. Plus, it will be a nice legacy for our kids someday."

"Then I'll make it happen, even if it raises a few eyebrows on the town council." He'd met the current town council, and he'd wager romance wasn't something they'd experienced much of lately.

"If we can deal with Florence Henkelmeyer, we can deal with that."

"She seems to be running out of steam at the moment. You and Rob were right. When you came out as Raven and won the tournament, it took the wind out of her sails. More people are standing up for us around town. They're even taking those ugly signs down."

"Good," Jane said. "I've grown fond of this place and don't like seeing it polluted by small minds. Now, let's go tell the dogs we're engaged."

He laughed at that. "You think they're going to understand?"

The look she gave him clearly told him her thoughts.

"Fine. Then we can drive over to my mom's house and start spreading the word. There's going to be another family celebration tonight. My sisters drove down earlier today as a surprise. They helped me pick out the ring."

"Can Elizabeth and Rhett and Abbie come over too?"

she asked.

"Of course, and Mac and Peggy," he added. "Mom already counted them when she bought all the food for tonight. They're part of the family now."

"I like that word. Family."

Yeah. She hadn't had much of that, but she would from now on.

"Well, there's another aspect of family you'll have to get used to with my wild crew." As they headed toward his SUV, Matt led her to the rear. "Natalie added her sick humor to my ride yesterday when I wasn't looking."

There were two bumper stickers, one yellow, the other in blue. *I'm a Sensitive Guy,* one said. *I Sleep With My Dog,* claimed the other.

Jane started laughing uncontrollably.

The dogs peered out the back at them, nosing the glass.

"Of course, there won't be any dogs in our bed," she finally said when her hilarity stopped. "I want you all to myself."

He gave her a long and lingering kiss in the parking lot. "Fancy that. I feel the exact same way."

"Let's walk the dogs and then head to Don't Soy with Me before going to your mom's house."

"Jill's going to be at the party," he told her as they opened the back door of the SUV and leashed the dogs.

"That's not why I want to go. I saw the perfect bumper sticker for Natalie's Audi."

"I like where you're going with this. You're already thinking like a Hale."

She beamed. "It says *I Kiss Bald Men. No Exceptions.*"

If that didn't sound like Jill's sense of humor, what did?

He grabbed her free hand. "We'll swipe it on her car right before she leaves so she won't see it until morning. Under the cover of darkness and everything."

They retraced their steps down the path to the edge of the mountain, the dogs walking with them now. The fiery orb was nearly halfway gone, the sky a maze of red and violet.

"This is my favorite time of day now," he said.

"Me too."

And with her hand in his, they walked down the path in the park he vowed one day would be called The Park of Sunset Dreams.

Dear Reader,

Gosh, I was really sad to see Jane and Matt's story end, but in many ways, it's only the beginning. Don't you just love happily ever afters? And weren't their dogs the cutest things ever?

If you enjoyed this book, I would really appreciate it if you would post a review. Your thoughts on this book help more readers decide to check out my story. If you do post a review, let me know at ava@avamiles.com so I can personally thank you. Please also consider recommending it to your book clubs and discussions boards. Thanks!

To keep up with all of my awesome giveaways like Dare Valley swag and other fun prizes, my new releases, and any sales I have, please sign up for my newsletter and connect with me on Facebook if you haven't already done so.

Elizabeth and Terrance's story is really pulling at me. Who doesn't like second chances at love? I can already feel the sizzling chemistry between them, and since you know I'm a former chef, you can bet food will be a big part of the novel. I can't wait to dive into the story and then share it with you.

Thanks again for reading. You're making my dreams come true.

Much light and love,
Ava

ABOUT THE AUTHOR

USA Today Bestselling Author Ava Miles burst onto the contemporary romance scene after receiving Nora Roberts' blessing for her use of Ms. Roberts' name in her debut novel, the #1 National Bestseller NORA ROBERTS LAND, which kicked off her small town series, Dare Valley, and brought praise from reviewers and readers alike. Ava has also released a connected series called Dare River, set outside the country music capital of Nashville.

Far from the first in her family to embrace writing, Ava comes from a long line of journalists. Ever since her great-great-grandfather won ownership of a newspaper in a poker game in 1892, her family has had something to do with telling stories, whether to share news or, in her case, fiction. Her clan is still reporting on local events more than one hundred years later at their family newspaper.

Ava is fast becoming a favorite author in light contemporary romance (Tome Tender) and is known for funny, emotional stories about family and empowerment. Ava's background is as diverse as her characters. She's a former chef, worked as a long-time conflict expert rebuilding warzones, and now writes full-time from her own small-town community.

If you'd like more information about Ava Miles and her upcoming books, visit www.avamiles.com and connect to Ava on Facebook, Twitter, and Pinterest.

35980723R00218

Made in the USA
Lexington, KY
04 October 2014